PRAISE FOR MU[...]

"With the setting in a ch[...] shop, allusions to du Mau[...] endearing canine companions, this cozy will appeal on many levels."

—*Booklist*

"*Murder Always Barks Twice* is delightful cozy mystery reading. Highly recommended. . . . especially to fans of pet-themed mysteries." —Open Book Society

"I liked Emma and rooted for her and I loved the Cornwall setting as well. . . . This was a stellar read."

—*Mystery Scene*

PRAISE FOR *TO FETCH A FELON*

"Two paws up! First in a wonderful new series. . . . Take one smart—albeit somewhat reluctant—amateur sleuth, Emma Reed, add an idyllic English village setting, colorful characters, a puzzling mystery, and a talking corgi . . . and you get the perfect mix of all things cozy."

—*New York Times* bestselling author Sofie Kelly

"Effortlessly blends a woman's drastic midlife career and environment change with a solid murder mystery and a dash of paranormal pet communication. . . . Unique and intriguing and full of heart." —Criminal Element

"A promising debut for dog lovers, who'll delight in the clever talking corgi and his charming owner."

—*Kirkus Reviews*

"Absolutely delightful. I cannot wait for the next installment. Highly recommended!" —Open Book Society

"The perfect cozy launch—I loved Emma and the other characters in Trevena. The setting is lovely, and Oliver is a delight. . . . A not-to-be-missed book for those who love cozy mysteries as well as for dog lovers."

—The Neverending TBR

Titles by Jennifer Hawkins

TO FETCH A FELON
MURDER ALWAYS BARKS TWICE
A COLD NOSE FOR MURDER

A Cold Nose for Murder

JENNIFER HAWKINS

BERKLEY PRIME CRIME
New York

BERKLEY PRIME CRIME
Published by Berkley
An imprint of Penguin Random House LLC
penguinrandomhouse.com

ISBN: 9780593197127

First Edition: July 2022

Printed in the United States of America
1 3 5 7 9 10 8 6 4 2

Book design by George Towne

AUTHOR'S NOTE

The Vincent Black Lightning motorcycle that belonged to Jack Ehret and was used to set the Australian speed record in 1953 was sold at auction in 2018 for $929,000 USD. For story purposes, I moved that auction about eight years into the past. I trust motorcycle enthusiasts will excuse the liberty. In this, I'm following the advice of Mark Twain, who said, "I would move a state if the exigencies of literature required it."

All other mistakes in this book are accidental, and entirely my own.

1

"EMMA!" LIZA GREENLAW CALLED FROM BEHIND THE BAR. "There you are!"

"Sorry we're late." Emma Reed had to use her shoulder to open the pub door, because she was carrying a cake stand in each hand. Brian Prowse followed close behind with a stack of loaded cupcake carriers.

Oliver, Emma's Welsh Pembroke corgi, wasn't about to wait for the humans. As soon as Emma got the door open, he zoomed past them both, ready to give every ankle in the noisy, crowded pub a good snuffle.

"I had a last-minute call about an order," Emma explained to Liza as they reached the bar. "I needed to go over some lists."

Liza laughed. "I should have known!" Emma's lists were just about as well-known around the village of Trevena as her baked goods and energetic corgi. "Just as long as your lists included my cupcakes."

"Well, you know Emma." Brian hefted the two cake carriers he was holding. "Should be plenty and to spare."

"Well, I also know this lot, and I wouldn't count on it." Liza's tone was dramatically despairing, but a cheerful glint shone in her blue eyes. Liza was a strong, stout, gray-haired woman who ruled her pub with a firm hand. She and her husband, Sam, had taken over the Roundhead when Sam's father, Walter, retired. Now they ran the pub and its brewery with help from their two grown children. The Greenlaws were planning an unusual expansion of the business, and they'd decided to turn it into a celebration. Villagers—mostly other shop owners and local farmers—filled the old whitewashed common room with cheerful, bantering conversation.

"You can just put that lot on the table, if you please," Liza instructed.

"Right away, ma'am." Brian bowed his head humbly.

Emma grinned and threaded her way through the crowd to the loaded buffet table. Brian followed, but Oliver was busy running from guest to guest, barking and wagging his hindquarters in greeting, not to mention shoving his nose into every available corner.

"Grass, sheep, petrol, coffee, seawater, more petrol," Oliver yipped. "Sam, ginger, cats, more cats. Ooo, Biddy and Farley were here, and . . ."

Emma struggled to avoid rolling her eyes. To everyone else in the room, Oliver sounded like a normal, noisy, happy dog. Only Emma heard him "talk." Being able to communicate with a beloved dog was a trait that popped up here and there in Emma's family. Not that anyone would ever admit they actually believed in it. Not out loud, anyway.

It was admittedly very odd, and sometimes it got awkward, but Emma loved her bubbly, bouncy corgi. So, most days, she just rolled with it. However, while Oliver might talk, he was still a dog, and he saw the world from a dog's perspective. That meant he spent a lot of time talking about what he smelled, like it was the daily news report. Which, to be fair, it kind of was.

"Beer, and there's more beer, and that one's just mud and . . ."

"So, this old tunnel Sam and Liza are opening in the cellar," said Emma to Brian as she set her cake stands down on the end of the buffet table. "It is really there, isn't it? It'd be a shame if it turned out to be some kind of legend. I mean, I heard about the tunnels when my family used to come here on holiday. I must have spent hours looking for hidden entrances. Drove my brother Henry mad."

"Not that that ever stopped you," said Brian solemnly.

Emma grinned. "Not even a little bit."

Brian ran the village garage and taxi service and was a specialist in vintage cars. He was also cheerful, handsome and the tiniest bit cheeky. The combination filled Emma with the sort of warm and fluffy feelings she hadn't known in a very long time. "As far as I know, the tunnel is real," he told her. "My dad remembers it from when he was a boy. He says that Sam's dad said it had been used by smuggling gangs since before the Battle of Trevena. Only Sam's mum made them brick it up, because it wasn't stable, and she was afraid for the kids."

"Can't wait to see what it's like," said Emma. She might have gone from being a banker to being a baker, but she had never shed her childhood love for mysteries and the dramatic.

"Going to take a chance with the betting pool, then?" Brian nodded toward the slate hanging on the wall beside the bar. Once, it had been used to keep track of the patrons' bar tabs. Today, though, it had been commandeered for taking bets on what would be found once the Greenlaws broke through the tunnel entrance.

Emma surveyed the list of current guesses with a critical eye. People were clearly treating the question with all the seriousness it deserved. The most popular choices seemed to be: nothing, black market whiskey (of course), a dead body (ditto), Father Christmas, the crown jewels, and a Cask of Amontillado.

"Put me down for the crown jewels." Emma fished a couple of pounds out of her shoulder bag. The money was going into a big jar beside the register. A notice said fifteen percent would be donated to the Royal Society for the Prevention of Cruelty to Animals.

"Will do. Get you a cider too?" suggested Brian.

"A small one, thanks." The Roundhead's cider was positively lethal.

Brian gave Emma a wink and headed over to the bar. Oliver left off investigating the shoes of the other guests and trotted after Brian. As soon as they both reached the bar, the corgi sat up on his haunches expectantly. Brian laughed and obligingly fed him a biscuit from the jar Liza kept for her four-legged patrons.

Oliver crunched and woofed and scampered back to Emma where she was setting up her cake stands.

"Brian is an excellent and thoughtful human."

"As it happens, I agree with you." Emma snapped open the lids on her cupcake carriers. She wasn't worried about being overheard talking with her dog just now. The room was filled with plenty of chatter.

"He's very understanding about snacks." Oliver wagged his entire bottom. "Those smell like good snacks. Are they, Emma?" He bounced eagerly, trying to get his forepaws up on the edge of the table.

"Down, you," ordered Emma. "We don't want to get barred because you're pinching food off the table."

Oliver ducked his head, chagrined. At the same time, he gave her an extra optimistic wag. Emma shook her head. Realizing he wasn't getting anywhere (this time), Oliver ducked under the table in case anyone had carelessly dropped anything important, like crumbs or a splash of coleslaw.

Emma laughed again and turned her attention to the important business of arranging her cupcakes on the tiered stand. She'd moved to Trevena to realize the dream of running her own tea shop. So, when Liza had asked for some baked treats for the party, Emma had been happy to oblige. In fact, she'd obliged with three different kinds.

The first was based on her apple cake. It used the Roundhead's cider in its mixture, along with a blend of Bromley and Granny Smith apples. The second was a ginger malt sponge with a lemon curd center. Finally, there was a rich chocolate sponge with raspberry icing.

"Hullo, Emma!" Genny Knowles, who had been Emma's first friend in Trevena, came up and gave her a one-armed hug.

"Hullo, Genny! I wasn't sure we'd see you tonight."

"Martin and Josh threatened to go on strike if I didn't get out for the evening." Genny smiled sheepishly and took a swallow of her pale ale. Like Emma, Genny was a short, round woman of a certain age. But where Emma was best described as a "faded ginger," Genny had blond hair and blue eyes and plenty of laugh lines around her broad mouth. Her summer tan had just begun to fade, returning her skin to what Genny referred to as "its usual combination of pink and pale."

Genny ran Trevena's chip shop, The Towne Fryer. Like a lot of Trevena's shops, it was a small family operation, and Genny tended to get caught up in the work. There was also the added responsibility of being a mother of three boys, ranging from ten-year-old Adam to sixteen-year-old Josh. With all that going on, it occasionally took firm insistence from her husband to get Genny out the door for some self-time.

"These look fabulous!" Genny gestured toward the cupcakes.

"Try one of the malt and lemon ones." Emma handed her a cupcake.

Never one to be shy, Genny took a big bite. "Oooo . . . that's amazing!"

"Thanks. It's a new recipe for fall."

"Well, it's a winner." Genny raised the partially eaten cupcake in salute. Then she paused. "I'm not seeing Angelique and Daniel," she added. "Didn't they come with you?"

"They should be here soon." Emma's cake shop operated out of the King's Rest Bed & Breakfast, which was owned by Angelique and Daniel Delgado. "There were a few things to clear up back at the B and B. Speaking of missing persons, I thought David and Charles would be here."

"Liza said they might stop by later. They were on a buying trip out to Edinburgh and they weren't sure they'd be back in time."

"Oh, that's right. I remember David saying something about that." David Kemp and his husband ran the boutique shop Vintage Style and were some of Emma's best friends—and best customers.

"Emma?" Oliver crept out from under the table and bonked her calf with his hard nose. "Emma, you did promise we would be having snacks. There are many snacks on the table, Emma."

Emma laughed and ruffled the corgi's ears. "Somebody's getting restless," she said to Genny. "And I haven't had dinner yet."

"Make sure you try the ham," said Genny. "It's from Matt Trenwith's farm, and it is absolutely scrummy."

Emma didn't need any more urging. She promptly fixed up a plate, helping herself (and Oliver) to several thick slices of the ham, along with rolls, mustard and apple and cabbage slaw, as well as some of Liza's fiery piccalilli. She caught Brian's eye across the room and gestured toward one of the empty tables that had been pushed up against the window. Brian nodded back to her.

Genny sat down across from Emma. Oliver took up his favorite position, sprawled full length under her chair. Wincing at what the vet was going to say about his dietary habits, Emma slipped him half a ham slice and some apple slaw. Like Emma, Oliver was quite full-bodied as it was. Fortunately, the hills around Trevena provided plenty of opportunity for long walks to help keep their rich country diet from catching up with them—too much, anyway.

Around them, the party was in full swing. Liza circulated among the guests. The blueprints for the planned improvements hung on one wall, and Sam was showing them off for his intrigued audience. The cellar where the tunnel opened would become a private dining and event area, with the tunnel itself as a small historical attraction.

Brian was delayed at the bar, saying hello to friends and neighbors, but Emma wasn't neglected. Her own bundle of friends and customers stopped by the table to chat with her and Genny. They talked easily about their lives, gossiped about the village, and praised the food, including Emma's cupcakes. Most of them took a minute to pet Oliver and ask how he was doing, how her cottage was doing, how had her new garden turned out? It was astonishing how fast Trevena had come to feel like home.

Brian made his way through the crowd and handed Emma her cider.

"For the loveliest woman in the room."

"Whew!" Genny whistled. "He does lay it on thick."

"Five minutes in and he's already tipsy." Emma pulled an exaggerated face at him.

Brian laughed. "Not so much I don't know what I'm seeing."

The fact that Brian could make her blush like a teenager might have been annoying if he didn't have such an amazing smile.

He was smiling at her now, and Emma's insides responded by melting into an entirely undignified puddle.

"Better go get myself something before this lot eats it all," he said to them. "Be right back."

Oliver crawled out from under Emma's chair and shook himself. "Brian shouldn't be alone," he grumbled. He trotted after him and plunked down at the end of the buffet table.

Emma sighed. "Oh, fickle corgi!"

"Not jealous, are you?" asked Genny.

"Nah." She sipped the sharp, warm cider. "Oliver knows who's got the key to the kibble bin."

Genny arched her brows. "You actually lock your kibble bin?"

Emma nodded seriously. "You would be amazed at what a determined corgi can get into."

Before Genny could add anything else, a young, blond

woman with a heavy camera around her neck made her way up to their table.

"Hullo, Emma! Hullo, Genny!"

"Pippa!" exclaimed Emma. "I didn't know you'd be here."

"Wouldn't miss it. My editor wants pictures of the 'grand opening.'" Pippa made the air quotes with one hand.

Pippa Marsh was a willowy woman whose personal style leaned toward men's fedoras and brightly embroidered jackets. Today's hat was a pearl-gray, snap-brim number with a black grosgrain band. She insisted that it made her feel like a real reporter. Pippa worked for the *Cornwall Coast News*, mostly writing up the social events—town council meetings and the like. Her real passion, though, was photography.

Pippa had done a very nice piece on Reed's Tea & Cakes when Emma had opened, and was a particular fan of Oliver. Oliver returned the admiration. He shamelessly abandoned Brian and came over to sit up on his hindquarters in front of Pippa. He let his mouth hang open in that way that made him look like he was laughing.

There's more than one shameless flirt here tonight.

"Oh, so cute!" Pippa crouched down to snap a shot, which Oliver promptly spoiled by charging the photographer so he could lick her face.

"Off, you idiot!" Pippa laughed. Oliver backed away, but mostly because Emma happened to drop another bit of ham just then.

Pippa straightened up and switched over to full reporter mode. "So, any thoughts on what we'll find downstairs? I mean real ones." She jerked her chin toward the chalkboard.

"Could be just about anything." Brian edged past her, carrying his loaded plate. "If what everybody says is true, the smugglers' tunnels have been there hundreds of years."

"Ten to one, it's nothing at all," said Pippa.

Genny arched her brows. "So you're just here for the food?"

"Is that a problem?" She popped a pickle into her mouth and crunched loudly.

Their laughter was still going around when the man in the tweed jacket walked through the door.

"Well, well." He clapped his beefy hands together. "Clearly the place to be!"

Heads turned to look, and all the cheerful conversation died clean away.

2

IF THE MAN NOTICED THE SUDDEN SILENCE THAT FOLLOWED his entrance, he gave no sign.

"Hullo, Sam! Hullo, Liza!" He strode straight to the bar. The people clustered there made room—a little reluctantly, Emma thought. "Quite the turnout. Well done, you." He held out his hand to Sam.

Sam Greenlaw was a match for his wife—a big-bodied, Cornish native with a squarish, cheerful face, blue eyes and pale skin that had been roughened by the salty sea air. He had a quick laugh and a generous nature, but he eyed the newcomer like the man hadn't paid his tab in over a year.

"Reggie." Sam's voice was flat, but he did reach over the bar to shake the man's hand. "I hadn't heard you were coming."

"Who is that?" Emma murmured to Brian and Genny.

"Reginald Tapp," answered Brian.

"He owns that touristy gastropub, the Donkey's Win," added Genny.

"Just wanted to stop in and wish you luck on your new enterprise," Reggie was saying. His gaze swept the room, and his affable smile didn't falter once. "I only wish I'd thought of it first." He laughed heartily. Sam didn't laugh.

He rubbed the back of his neck and glanced at Liza. Liza shrugged.

"Yeah, well, thanks." And then, remembering his professional manners, Sam added, "You'll have a drink?"

"Well, now, I don't mind if I do. Pint of your pale ale for me."

"Right."

It was a cool welcome, but a welcome all the same, and it seemed to take some of the tension out of the room. Most everybody returned to their food and their conversations.

"Mr. Tapp there doesn't seem very . . . popular," remarked Emma.

"He's not," said Genny. "Fancies himself the king of Cornish entrepreneurs. Likes to spread his hard-won wisdom around for the rest of us to benefit from."

"I imagine that would get on people's nerves."

"You're about to find out," said Brian.

Brian was right. Having collected his pint, Reggie Tapp was bearing down on them.

"Right, I'm gone." Pippa touched her hat brim and slipped sideways into the crowd.

"Clever girl," remarked Genny.

Between a long career in London finance and serving the public from her cake shop, Emma had considerable experience sizing up people. Reggie Tapp radiated that particular sort of self-confidence that crossed over into self-importance. He was a tall, heavily built man. His face was younger than his age-spotted hands. His thick head of hair had definitely seen some intensive styling, and probably more than a touch of dye. Emma had the feeling he might have had one or two things lifted and smoothed. He certainly looked like he could afford it. His tweed jacket fit him like a glove. His scarlet turtleneck shirt was silk and his shoes were imported. So was the heavy gold watch on his wrist.

"Emma Reed!" Reggie boomed. "So glad to meet you at last!" He shoved out his hand and shook Emma's, too hard.

Oliver barked and then ducked his head. "Sorry, Emma."

"Good boy," Emma murmured. Privately, she understood how Oliver felt. She smiled weakly at Reggie and extricated herself as quickly as she could.

"Hello, Genny. Hello, Brian." Reggie beamed at the entire table.

"Hello, Reg," said Brian easily. "Marianne not with you tonight?"

"No, no, she's minding the shop, isn't she? Just can't pull herself away. If it was a man, I'd be jealous." He laughed again.

"You'll tell her we said hello," put in Genny.

"A' course, a' course. Now." He turned the full force of his attention onto Emma. "You know, you are making quite the splash, darling."

Emma felt her smile harden, even as she tried to be polite. "You've been in for tea, then?" Oliver, of course, picked up on her tension, and stood beside her chair, ears up and alert.

Reggie puffed out his chest. "I check out all the new businesses. You don't get to be in my position without keeping an eye on the competition. And my spies tell me you, darling, could be serious competition."

"I didn't know you served teas at the Donkey's Win."

"Not yet, not yet, but we're always expanding. Got to keep moving or you get stuck in the same rut your father dug, am I right, Prowse?"

Brian, who ran the garage and taxi service his grandfather had started after retiring as a chauffeur, made a noncommittal noise.

Reggie laughed. "Oh, now, no offense, no offense!" Emma wondered if he had another volume setting below "Loud and Hearty." "It's all right for some, just not for me! Nor for this darling here either, yeah?" His wink was probably supposed to be genially conspiratorial. Emma felt a sudden urge to growl. Down by her knee, Oliver's hackles rippled. "You saw an underserved niche in the market and you stepped right in to fill it," Reggie went on. "Very clever, very clever indeed, and very delicious as well. Skill and brains. I admire that! We need to get together and talk, soon now!" He touched her shoulder and then wagged his finger at her. "And I don't take no for an answer!" He laughed loudly and turned to bustle away, making straight for where Pippa was trying to talk to Sam and Liza.

Emma took a swallow of cider. "And that, ladies and gentlemen, is exactly why I quit finance."

"He smells fake," grumbled Oliver. "He puts all that fake flower and dead otter smell stuff on him and I can't tell what's really there."

That, thought Emma, might be one of the best descriptions of Reggie Tapp's kind of person she'd ever heard.

"Is he always that bad?" she asked Brian.

"Depends on the crowd size."

"Wow."

"Yeah," Brian agreed.

Emma was about to ask why someone with that level of ego had decided to stay in a small village like Trevena, but she was interrupted by Sam raising his voice over the crowd.

"All right, everybody! It's time for the Great British Break In! Make sure you pick up a party bag on your way down the stairs. Careful as you go, please!"

Conversation switched to an excited buzz of speculation and side bets as the guests started to follow Sam down the stairs, including Reggie. But Liza stepped into his path.

"I'm sorry, Reggie," she said. "It's special invitees only. Health and safety and all that, you understand."

"Ah, come on now, who's to tell?" Reggie grinned. Liza didn't. She also didn't budge. Emma felt the back of her neck prickle.

Finally, Reggie shrugged. "All right, all right, no hard feelings. I know when I'm not wanted. Still wishing you the best of luck, yeah? Can't wait to read all about it."

Reggie strolled out the pub's side door. Emma noticed

that Liza didn't move until he was really gone. Her curiosity was wide awake and sitting up on its haunches now. Reggie was obnoxious, and strained a person's patience, but there was clearly something else going on between him and the Greenlaws.

Or maybe just Liza—no. Stop it, Emma, Emma ordered herself firmly. Once it got going, her curiosity was almost as bad as Oliver's. This fact had gotten them both in trouble more than once.

The party bags proved to have earplugs, dust masks and safety glasses in them. Emma waited until everybody else had gone down, because Oliver's stubby legs made navigating steep stairs a time-consuming process.

"Are you sure Oliver's going to be all right?" asked Genny. "It could get pretty noisy."

"What do you think, Oliver?" said Emma. "Should we stay up here?"

"A noble warrior corgi isn't afraid of noise!" barked Oliver. At some point, Oliver had found out that corgis were supposed to have sailed with the Vikings, and he remained unshakably proud of the fact.

"He's game," Emma told Genny. Genny laughed in that way people did when she told them what Oliver was "saying." "But we'll stay near the door in case we need to make a quick exit."

Emma had never been in the pub's basement. Her imagination had sketched out a vaguely shadowy place with the low ceilings and black, exposed beams of the same vintage as the rooms upstairs, only with more cobwebs.

What she found was a brightly lit, sparkling clean, thoroughly modern space. The only thing that betrayed the cellar's age was the uneven flagstone floor. Metal shelving held bins, boxes and aluminum barrels. At the far end of the cellar, a second set of stairs led up to a pair of double doors used for the pub's loading and unloading.

Emma, Brian and Oliver joined the other guests as Liza directed them to the far corner. Everyone started fumbling with their protective gear. Brian unfolded the safety glasses and set them gently on Emma's nose. Emma returned the favor and they grinned at each other. Oliver barked again.

"I know just how you feel." Genny rolled her eyes.

Right across from where they stood was a broad alcove with an arched entrance. To Emma, it looked like the space had once been a side room, but the door had clearly been taken down ages ago. Sam was pulling on a pair of work gloves and a rather more serious pair of safety goggles than had been provided to the guests. Then he took up the sledgehammer his burly son, Ned, handed him, turned to face the guests, and cleared his throat.

Pippa snapped a picture, and another. She moved away from the rest of the gathering, angling for a better shot.

"Now," said Sam, "when I was a boy, this spot was a storeroom, and the back of the storeroom had a small pantry, and that pantry had a wooden back."

"And in the back was a hole, there's a hole, there's a hole in the bottom of the sea!" someone sang. The gathering laughed.

Sam chuckled. "My da told us that panel hid a smuggler's tunnel that had been there since Domesday. They'd nailed it shut when I was born, but when Ma caught my brother and me going in with a couple of pry bars, she insisted he brick it up properly.

"Now, for the first time in forty years, the Trevena smugglers' tunnel will be opened again. Are we ready?"

"Let's get on with it," called somebody. "I've got a fiver says you're going to find a case of Irish whiskey in there!" There was some genial laughter.

Emma scooped Oliver up and slung him over one shoulder, a move she'd started when he was a tiny puppy. She sometimes regretted it now that he was a full stone-and-a-half worth of solid corgi muscle with some pretty serious doggy breath.

"Ready?" she murmured.

"Ready, Emma," he growled in her ear. Emma snuggled him close. She also made a note that some corgi tooth care needed to get on the schedule. Soon.

Sam hefted the hammer in both hands. Emma backed towards the stairs, just a little.

"Careful, Dad," laughed Ned, lifting his own hammer. "You have a heart attack and Ma'll kill us both."

"You just stand back, young Ned. Let the old man show you how it's done."

Ned and Sam took up their positions, backs to the walls, as far apart from each other as the space allowed. Sam touched the hammer to the wall. "Ready, steady . . . Go!"

Liza pushed a button on a portable CD player, and The Anvil Chorus blared out. The guests laughed and applauded.

Both men swung.

The hammers slammed against brick and tore open holes to the sound of crumbling stone and splintering wood. Dust flew everywhere. Oliver whined, squirmed and scrabbled against her.

Brian, noticing their agitation, moved a little closer. Emma leaned toward him, just a little, because of course a mature, independent woman did not cringe toward her boyfriend because of a little noise. Oliver whimpered a bit and tried to climb up higher up her shoulder.

Might have to get us both out of here.

Emma took another half step toward the stairs, but just then Ned held up his hand. Sam lowered his hammer and Liza snapped off the music.

The crackling dust settled, revealing a dark, ragged hole a bit wider and higher than a normal doorway. Sam rested his hammer against the wall and switched on a torch to shine it inside.

Ned pulled his dust mask down. "What the . . . what is that?"

Of course, hearing that, the whole gathering crowded forward, including Emma, Genny and Brian. Liza got in front and waved them all back. They retreated in a tight bunch, reluctantly. Only Pippa refused to back away. She slid right past Liza, camera high, flash on, finger holding down the button for the shutter.

Now Emma could see that Sam's torch lit up a strange conglomeration of curves.

"Well. That didn't make the pool," murmured Sam.

"What on earth—?" Ned held his torch up higher.

At first Emma thought it must be a bicycle. She could see a spoked wheel, but it looked too big for a bike. Slowly, more details came into focus. Now she saw dusty black metal and chrome draped with cobwebs gleaming in the torchlight.

"It's . . . not possible," breathed Brian.

"What is it?" asked Emma.

But Brian didn't seem to hear her. He worked his way to the front of the crowd, moving steadily as if pulled by a magnetic attraction.

Emma set Oliver down. "Stay close." She ruffled his ears.

By now, Emma's eyes had adjusted, and her startled brain began to make sense of what she saw. That was an old-fashioned motorcycle, complete with sidecar—the sort of thing that would have been at home in a James Dean movie.

"Brian?" said Ned. "Is that what it looks like?"

"I think so." Brian answered in hushed tones. He took another step forward. "It's the Vincent. The Black Lightning."

A murmur of surprise rippled through the guests.

"But—that was stolen, wasn't it?" asked Ned. "David always said—"

"Uh, Brian, mate?" interrupted Sam. He was still shining his torch into the dark behind the motorcycle. "I think you maybe want to stay back."

"What?" Brian tore his eyes from the vintage machine and saw what Sam was pointing at. They all did.

On the floor beside the Vincent was an uneven cluster of dirty gray bits and blobs. Oliver barked, and Emma slapped her hand over her mouth. Pippa swore and unceremoniously elbowed Ned out of the way, snapping the shutter as if her life, or at least her byline, depended on it.

It was rude and not entirely responsible, but Emma could understand why she did it.

Those gray blobs beside the motorcycle were bones—a hand and a skull and maybe more. And even from where she stood, Emma could see they were most definitely human.

3

WHEN PC RAJ PATEL FINALLY EMERGED FROM THE ROUND-head's cellar, Emma saw him being greeted by a barrage of questions from the gathered villagers.

"So who is it?"

"How'd he get in there?"

"How long's that thing been down there?"

Pippa's camera flashed, and flashed again.

Liza had called the police as soon as they realized that it was an actual human skeleton in the tunnel, rather than some kind of prank. All the guests were so stunned that no one had put up any resistance when Sam said they should all go back upstairs.

In the pub's main room, Emma had huddled in a corner with Genny and Brian. Like the rest of the guests, they'd all immediately pulled out their mobiles—Brian and Genny to call their families, and Emma to message the Delgados. A few people had taken Sam up on his offer of a drink, but most of the guests were too busy calling and messaging. Emma reckoned that by now all of Trevena knew a skeleton and a stolen motorcycle had been discovered in the Round-head's freshly opened tunnel.

Through it all, Oliver had alternated between sitting protectively beside Emma and patrolling the room.

"All right! All right!" Raj raised his voice above the babble. PC Raj was a tall, slender young man with thick black hair, warm tan skin and dark eyes. His family ran a popular Trevena restaurant, and his grandfather had been the first police officer of Southeast Asian descent in Cornwall. Now Raj was Trevena's lone full-time police constable.

"Now, we don't know anything yet—" Raj was saying.

"Aw, come on, you can do better than that, Raj," cut in Pippa. "How long has the body been in there? Did you see anything to say how they died?"

"You mean aside from the fact that someone shut them up in a bloody great hole?" quipped a balding man Emma didn't know. There was a round of nervous laughter. Pippa grimaced, but otherwise stayed focused on Raj.

"Like I said, we don't know anything yet, so, you'll *all* just have to wait. Now, I've got a clipboard here." He brandished the board and a pen. "If everybody could please leave their names and contact numbers, just in case we need to talk to you later."

"Come on, Raj, you know us!" called somebody.

"I do," Raj shot back. "But my boss doesn't, so have a heart, Mickey."

"It's not like anybody here had anything to do with that poor b—person being bricked up in there," called out somebody else.

"Well, we don't know that, do we?" answered Raj. "Give us a break, mate, yeah? They'll be all over me if I don't come back with a full report. Just write your numbers down and you can go home." He looked toward Pippa when he said this. Pippa rolled her eyes.

There was some additional grumbling and a bit of trash talk, but in the end everybody queued up to write out their contact information. They then started filing out the door, until Emma, Genny and Brian were the last ones left.

Emma was just adding her name and her mobile and

landline numbers to the list when Oliver barked sharply and scampered towards the door. She looked up in time to see Charles and David Kemp shouldering their way against the tide to get inside.

"Hullo!" called David to Sam and Liza. "We saw the police car. Is everything all right?"

Charles and David had come to Trevena in the early seventies as refugees from swinging London. Since then, they, and their shop, Vintage Style, had become a popular part of village life. David was the shorter of the two. He had a snow-white mane of hair and was one of the most stylish men Emma had ever met. Even tonight, just back from what must have been a tiring trip, he wore a vintage mohair jacket, crisp white shirt and pleated gray slacks with a colorful scarf tied at the waist instead of a belt. He was the floor manager and chief salesman for the couple's shop. Around Trevena, it was widely believed he could sell a salmon to a Scotsman.

Charles, on the other hand, mostly took care of the paperwork and the back-of-the-house operations. He was a big, broad man with a long, horsey face. He always held himself a little bit on guard. Nowhere near as interested in fashion as his husband, Charles habitually wore plain button-down shirts and jeans and a brown leather macintosh he'd had for so long, David called it the third member of the family.

"Oh, lord, boys." Liza came forward to meet both of them. "There's been . . . well, there's no easy way to put this. We've found the Vincent."

"The Vincent?!" exclaimed Charles. "*Our* Vincent?"

Everyone in Trevena, including Emma, had heard David tell the story at least once. How the scene in London had been getting old, how Charles had swept David off his feet, quite literally, and into the sidecar, and together they'd taken off, driving until they got to the end of the world, or at least to the seaside. They even had their store's sign painted with a Black Lightning motorcycle that had a fedora dangling off one of the handlebars.

"It must be yours," said Brian. "Black Lightnings don't exactly grow on trees. I've never even heard of another in Trevena."

"But where? How?" demanded Charles. "It was stolen!"

Emma looked from one man to the other. Charles was stunned, disbelieving. So was David, but there was something more to it. For a minute, Emma actually thought he might faint.

"Stolen?" said Raj, which proved he had a cop's sense of hearing. He came over to them, pulling his notebook out on the way. "When was this?"

"Right after we came to Trevena," Charles told him. "All the way back in, what, seventy-two? Seventy-three?" He looked at his husband.

"Seventy-three," supplied David. "You've heard about it, surely," he added to Raj.

"Probably," admitted Raj. "But I'm afraid I'm going to need to hear it again."

"Yes, right," said Charles. "It was seventy-three. We got here in seventy-two. Some b—Somebody broke into the garage—well, the shed we used as a garage—and made off with it. I never thought we'd see it again."

Raj scribbled a note. "Did you report it at the time?"

Charles glanced at the notebook and Raj's busy pencil, then at David. David shrugged. Irritably, Emma thought.

"Didn't seem much point," said Charles. "It was stolen during the night sometime and we didn't realize until almost noon, I remember. We reckoned that if someone took it for a joyride, it would turn up again in a couple of days, and if they'd taken it to sell, it would already be long gone, wouldn't it?"

"We did ask around," said David. "No one could tell us anything."

"Sorry to have to ask," said Raj. "But . . . can you come down and have a look at what we found? Just to see if it really is your bike?"

"Yeah, yeah, lead the way," said Charles. "I can't believe

it. All these years," he breathed. "It'd be—well, it'd just be something to have it back again."

"Well, I'm afraid that'll be a bit," said Raj. "You see, the bike's not all we found."

"What do you mean?" David frowned.

"There's a skeleton as well," said Raj.

"A . . . ? You mean a human skeleton?" Slowly, all the color drained out of Charles's ruddy cheeks. "Oh, my God."

David put his hand on his husband's shoulder. "It's all right," he breathed. "Whatever happened, it was years ago. Years," he repeated.

Oliver, sensing Charles's distress, trotted over to his side, wagging and whining.

"We've no way of knowing if the skeleton is actually connected to the theft of the bike," said Raj quickly, but Emma wasn't even sure Charles heard him.

"Yes, yes," murmured Charles. He reached up to take David's hand and squeezed it. "I'm all right. I am. I suppose we'd better see it, then."

"You sure?" said Raj. "There's no rush."

Charles's face went rock-hard, and for a minute, Emma could clearly see the young tough he'd been. "No, best get it done."

"All right, then." Raj led the two men down into the basement.

"Should we go back downstairs too, Emma?" Oliver bonked her ankle with his hard nose. "We can help! That place smelled very strange. Raj won't be able to tell, but I will."

When they had first come to Trevena, Emma and Oliver had gotten mixed up in the investigation of a local woman's murder. Since then, Oliver had fallen in love with the idea that he was a furry, low-riding, amateur sleuth with Emma as his loyal sidekick.

Emma found herself feeling rather more ambivalent about this role.

"I know you know," Emma murmured as she bent down

to give him a quick pat. "But we need to give Raj some space right now."

"He's got space," said Oliver. "That was a very big space back there. You didn't even go inside, and there are all kinds of smells."

"I believe you," Emma murmured as she straightened up. "But we need to stay up here for now."

"Oh, all right." Oliver put his nose down and started sniffing around the near-empty room. Emma had the feeling her strange human attitudes were being patiently tolerated. For now.

"Whew," breathed Brian. "Not how I'd want to find my lost bike." Just then, his phone buzzed in his pocket. He pulled it out and looked at the screen. "Sorry, I need to take this. It's Geordie." Geordie was Brian's brother.

"Go ahead," said Emma. Brian gave her hand a quick squeeze before he went out into the pub's little courtyard.

Emma turned back toward the bar. Genny was making her way over to Sam. He sat on one of the barstools, his big hands dangling between his knees. He looked almost as pale as Charles.

"Do you need any help cleaning up, or anything?" Genny asked Sam.

"I . . . oh . . . no, thank you." Sam rubbed his face hard. "We'll handle it. But, I'm sorry, maybe if Emma can take the cakes—?"

"Right, of course," said Emma. She and Genny headed for the buffet table. Emma opened up her bins and started loading the leftover cupcakes back inside.

Liza came out of the back. Husband and wife moved instantly and instinctively into a warm embrace.

"I left your sister a message," said Liza.

Sam kissed the back of Liza's hand. "It'll be okay, Lizzie. I promise it will."

Emma dropped her gaze, paying very close attention to her hands and her bakes.

By the time Emma had the lid on the last bin, Brian came back in. "I'll help with those," he said.

"Ta." Emma handed him the first bin. As she did, Raj came back up the stairs with David and Charles. Both men looked gobsmacked.

"Come sit down, all of you." Genny pushed a chair towards them.

"Maybe a drink?" suggested Emma to Sam.

"Not for me," said Raj. "On duty and all."

"I'll take one," said David. Charles just nodded.

Sam pulled a bottle down and got out two glasses, deftly pouring a couple of fingers' worth of whiskey into each. Genny grabbed them and set them in front of the Kemps.

Charles drank his shot in one go. David sipped and set the glass back down. Emma couldn't help but notice his hands were shaking.

"So, is it your Vincent?" asked Brian.

"Oh, yes," croaked Charles. "It is that."

"And the body?" said Liza to Raj. "Do you know who that is?"

Raj blew out a sigh. "Not yet. About all I can say right now is that whoever it was, they've been down there a good long time."

"Was it . . ." began Sam. "Were they murdered?"

"We don't know," said Raj, but it sounded reflexive. "We'll have to treat it as a suspicious death, but as yet, there's nothing positively indicating foul play. I mean, aside from them being in the tunnel and all . . ."

Which was, Emma thought, a pretty big "aside."

"But *who* is it?" Liza demanded. "There must be some kind of, well, clue. A wallet, an ID card. *Something*."

"I'm really sorry, Liza, but there's nothing," said Raj. "The boots, the jacket and the belt buckle say it's probably a man, but we're not finding the remains of a wallet or anything of that kind. But we may have more luck with dental records."

"What makes you say so?" asked Sam. "I mean, my dad nailed that door shut when we were born, and it was bricked at least forty years ago. No disrespect, Raj, mate, but it's not going to be easy to find records going back that far."

"Well, Sam, I don't know if you saw it, but the skull's got gold teeth, four of them—two on the left side, and two on the right. That's unusual, and somebody . . ."

Liza covered her mouth with one broad hand. Sam had gone white. So had Charles. So white, in fact, that David shoved his whiskey glass over to his husband. Charles drank the second shot down as quickly as he had the first.

"Good lord," breathed Sam. "Sonny."

"Sonny?" repeated Raj. "Who's Sonny?"

Liza put a hand on Sam's shoulder. Some color was returning to his face; unfortunately, that color was a sickly gray. David and Charles didn't look much better. Charles had reached across the table and gripped David's wrist. Hard. David was watching Sam and Liza.

No, Emma realized. David was watching Raj, as warily and intently as Oliver might watch a strange cat.

"Wilson Greenlaw," Sam said. "A cousin of mine. Everybody called him Sonny. He got in an accident—well, he said it was an accident—when he was seventeen, knocked out a bunch of his teeth. I haven't thought about him in . . . donkey's years." He shook his head, bewildered.

"Why not?"

"He vanished," said Liza softly. "All the way back in the seventies."

Raj was staring at them both in sheer disbelief. "Don't tell me," he said. "Nobody reported that either."

"Yeah. Well, no." Sam scrubbed at his face. "He'd been planning on leaving town. Said he was going to London, get a fresh start. So when we didn't see him around, everybody just assumed he'd gone and done what he said."

"And when you didn't hear from him?"

"You have to understand, Raj," said Sam. "Sonny wasn't exactly the reliable sort. He was in and out of trouble, and on the outs with his parents and all. I don't think anybody really *expected* to hear from him."

Liza was staring out the window. Emma wondered what she was seeing. It certainly wasn't the little courtyard.

"Poor Sonny," she whispered and shook her head, slowly

coming back to the present. "I know he was a hooligan, but he didn't deserve . . . this." Liza looked at Charles, like she was going to say something more, but thought the better of it.

"Did you know Sonny Greenlaw?" Raj asked Charles and David.

Charles let go of David's wrist. His face had gone hard again. "A bit, yeah."

"He was one of those people who was always around," added David quickly. "You couldn't help knowing who he was."

"Do you remember when he went missing?" asked Raj. "Could it have been around the same time the Vincent got nicked?"

"It was forty years ago, Raj, or good as," grumbled Charles. "How could we remember that?"

"Well, maybe give it some thought, yeah?" Raj tucked his notebook away. "Losing that bike would have been an important event. It might jog loose another memory or two."

"Oh yes," said David, his tone studiously bland. "You can be sure we will be giving this entire situation a great deal of thought."

"Is there . . . is there any sign of what killed him? Sonny, I mean?" Liza asked.

"We can't say yet," Raj told her. "I've called the coroner's office. They're sending somebody around to pick up the remains. I'm afraid we might have to close you down for a bit."

"Nah, nah, it's all right. Sonny," Sam breathed softly. "I can't believe it. How in heaven's name did Sonny end up down in that old tunnel?"

"Here's another question," said Genny. "Emma? Where's Oliver got to?"

4

....

HUMANS COULD BE VERY DIFFICULT TO UNDERSTAND. OLIver kept trying, but some days he had to admit he was stumped, even when it came to Emma. Emma was, of course, his best human, and unusually intelligent, but she was still human. That meant there were times she behaved very oddly.

Tonight, for instance. All the humans wanted to know about the tunnel-place. They were all talking about it, and talking was making them scared, and sad. But none of them were actually going into the tunnel, which was where all the answers were.

Oliver wanted to say all this to Emma and point out it didn't make any sense. But he knew she wouldn't answer when there were so many other humans around. Emma insisted she had to be careful about talking with him too much when their friends could hear. She'd tried to explain why, but he didn't really understand it. It had a lot to do with words like "eccentric" and "completely bonkers," which were things he'd never smelled or seen in the real world.

Restless, Oliver started sniffing around the pub. Lots of people had come and gone tonight, which meant there were many scents all piled up together. It was difficult to separate one from the other, but Oliver put his nose down and tried. Hard. Maybe he could find something useful, or at least interesting.

Grass, mud, gravel, trash, petrol, dog, dog, cat . . . ooo, what's that?

A fresh draft brushed the tips of his ears and brought a fresh scent. A human. The lady with the camera and the hat. She smelled like soap and tobacco. What was her name? Pippa! Oliver followed her track into the pub's side room.

There was no one there, but the draft grew stronger. He felt it on his muzzle and paws. Nose down, Oliver traced the draft to the side door, and hesitated.

He heard voices behind him. Emma was still talking with the other humans in the big room.

Oliver gave the door to the outside a tiny little nudge.

The door opened, just a bit. Whoever had gone through it last hadn't closed it all the way. Oliver sniffed. It was definitely the Pippa lady. He could smell her clearly, even with all the other scents swirling around. She was close by.

That might be important. All the other humans were supposed to have gone home already. Pippa shouldn't still be here.

I should tell Emma.

But Oliver hesitated. Maybe the Pippa lady was about to go home. Maybe she'd stopped to talk to somebody, the way humans pretty much always did. Before he got Emma worried, he should see whether Pippa Lady was really still here. If he found anything, he could bark for her. Emma always heard him.

He pushed at the door with his muzzle. It swung open, just about far enough. Instinct urged Oliver to bark, but he didn't. He just shoved his nose through, and then his head and ears, and shoulders, and there he was, outside.

Hurray! He almost barked, and zoomed, again.

Nope, nope, he told himself. *A noble warrior corgi keeps his mind on the job.*

Oliver cast around on the gravel. He needed to hurry. If Emma got worried, or if he met another human who decided he needed to be taken back inside, he wouldn't find out anything.

Fortunately, the Pippa lady had left a very clear trail on the damp gravel. Oliver followed her scent around the first corner of the pub, and then around the second.

There she was. The Pippa lady stood beside the back door, with her fingers on the handle. She was looking back over her shoulder. Oliver didn't know what she saw, but she pushed on the door, and it opened.

There was no more time to think. Oliver darted forward and shoved his muzzle into the door's opening.

"What the . . . ? Oliver!" Pippa hissed. She caught hold of his collar and pulled him back. Oliver whimpered and shook. Pippa let go.

They faced each other on the gravel. It was dark, except for the light coming from the pub windows. Oliver looked up at her. She might change her mind if he looked long enough and wagged. Humans did sometimes.

"Oh, sugar," she muttered. "Go on back. Shoo!" She flapped her hand.

Oliver cocked his head at her. Where was he supposed to go? The only open door was this one. Besides, he was supposed to be here. She wasn't.

But then Pippa straightened up, like Emma sometimes did when she'd had a new idea. She looked back over her shoulder again.

"On the other hand—" She pushed the door open a little further. "Go on, boy. Quick."

Oliver didn't try to understand. He just ducked through the door and started hopping down the stairs as quickly as he could. Fortunately, the steps here were a lot shallower than the ones at the front of the pub, and there were fewer of them. Behind him, he heard Pippa shut the door and run down the stairs.

"Oh. Oh, no. Oliver. Don't. Come back," said Pippa, which was very strange, because she was ahead of him now.

Pippa was clearly a very complicated human, but Oliver didn't have time to think about that. He needed to hurry. He shouldn't leave Emma alone for too long. He told himself she would be fine. She knew better than to leave the pub without him.

He hopped off the last stair and zoomed toward the tunnel, ducking low under the big zigzag of yellow tape.

"Oh, no, Oliver," said Pippa. "Don't do that."

She couldn't have been that worried, though, because she climbed through right behind him. This was clearly some human puzzle. Oliver decided he would wonder about her later, and maybe ask Emma. For now, he had work to do.

Oliver put his nose down to the packed earth floor. All kinds of people had been through here already, laying their scents over top of each other. It was hard to work out which smell was which. There were plenty of older smells too, mice and even rats, and all the scents of dust and time and damp. Despite what he'd told Emma, nothing really stood out as bad, or even unusual.

But there is something. There is . . . Oliver nosed the prickly dirt, and sneezed, and nosed about some more.

"You're right." Pippa pulled out her mobile. "We need to be quick. Raj might be back any second."

Oliver wagged at her. She might be a little strange, but she was also clearly a very intelligent human. While all the others were talking, she was looking and doing.

"Right, okay, what've we got?" She held her mobile up high, using the light as a torch. "Is there a wallet?" She crouched down close enough to the skeleton that Oliver couldn't help but come look as well. "Probably not, although maybe Raj took it, yeah?"

Pippa was talking to herself. Oliver had observed that humans did that a lot. Emma certainly did, especially when she was working on a new recipe. She could taste and talk for hours.

It was strange that Pippa wasn't at all worried about the bones. Humans did not like bones. Especially if they'd been chewed on. These did not seem to have been chewed, but they'd been here so long, they'd lost their own particular scent, and just smelled like the dirt and dust around them. It was the same with the motorcycle. There were scents of cold metal and rubber, but nothing else to distinguish it from the rest of the tunnel.

Pippa had flipped her phone around and was snapping pictures with it. She lowered it, and turned around in a tight circle.

"What else?" she muttered. Oliver wagged, and barked. "Shh-shh!" She rubbed him quickly under the chin, and also dropped her voice. "Come on, what do you think, eh?"

Probably she was not really asking him. After all, she wasn't Emma, so she couldn't understand him. But Oliver decided to try anyway. He couldn't open human things, but she could. And if she did, he would see what she found, and tell Emma all about it.

Oliver rushed to a pair of old lumps on the floor that smelled strongly of leather and dust. They were handbags, or something like it, which meant there might be something inside. Emma kept all kinds of things in her bag.

Pippa came right over. "What've you got there, boy?"

Really, a very intelligent human, even if she's not very well trained.

"Saddlebags," Pippa murmured. "Makes sense, what with our rare vintage motorcycle and all." With the end of one finger she lifted up the flap on the first bag and shone her phone inside. "Clothes," she announced. "And a toothbrush and a safety razor. So, definitely a guy we've got here. Packed for a night away, did we? And this one . . ." She lifted the flap on the second bag. "Is empty. Now, that's odd, isn't it?" She peered closer. "Oh, no, wait, we got something . . . and it's a very old pound note. Interesting."

While Pippa thought about that, Oliver nosed around the space. There were little air currents everywhere, stirring up the old smells. He followed the ripples of air and scent into the darkness. The tunnel went on further than he thought it would. Oliver wasn't bothered by the fading light. As long as he had his nose, he knew exactly where he was and where he was going.

There was more dirt now, and stones, and broken sticks. In fact, there were lumps and heaps all over back here. In fact, there were piles. Well, one pile.

One very big pile.

It was made of dirt and stones. In places, sharp boards and timbers stuck up out of it. Oliver put his nose down and snuffled. The pile went from wall to wall, and up over his head. Maybe all the way to the ceiling. Maybe the dirt pile filled the whole tunnel.

Except not quite. He lifted his muzzle and snuffled the air.

Back by the tunnel entrance, Pippa was still talking to herself. "What's this? Another pound note. What are you doing way over here, little guy? Probably nothing much. Bit chewed on, aren't you? And what the heck is that . . . ?"

Oliver put his front paws on the dirt pile. It held. He scrabbled to get his hindquarters up as well. Using nose, whiskers, muzzle and paws, he picked a careful path up the side of the uneven slope.

"Hullo, what have we here?" Pippa was saying. "Hullo," she repeated. Oliver couldn't help but glance at her. That was the problem with humans talking all the time. It could be very distracting. But a corgi knew how to concentrate. Mostly. He did stop for just a minute to give her a side-eye, but Pippa wasn't paying any attention to him. She had bent over something on the floor. "And here. Okay, that's odd . . ." She picked something up off the floor.

Focus! Oliver reminded himself. There was a breeze up there, a strong, steady one. He could feel it on the tips of his ears. Oliver stretched up and planted his paws on one of the broken stones sticking out of the dirt.

This is important. He felt it with all his instincts. If there was a breeze, it was coming from somewhere, and that meant there was more space back behind this pile, and maybe more things to find.

He should tell Pippa. And Emma.

Oliver barked, loud and sharp. The noise bounced off the tunnel walls.

"Gah!" Pippa dropped her phone, and said a word Emma had told him was very rude.

Then she shouted, "Oh my lord! Oliver!"

Before Oliver knew what was happening, Pippa had scooped him up and yanked him back away from the dirt pile.

There were sounds overhead—people were running down the stairs. Pippa said another rude word, and Oliver squirmed, but she held on tight. She also hustled them both back to the tunnel mouth and climbed out through the yellow zigzag just as Emma and several other humans ran down the stairs.

"Emma! Emma!" barked Oliver. "There's a hole, Emma!"

5

AS SOON AS GENNY SAID OLIVER WAS GONE, EMMA cursed under her breath and jumped to her feet. *I cannot believe this!*

Everyone scattered around the room, even Raj, looking under tables and in corners. Charles and David joined the search, albeit a little more slowly than the rest of them. Liza headed into the kitchen, and Sam checked behind the bar.

"Oliver! Here, boy!" they called.

Emma had whistled, and whistled again. She opened the door to the little courtyard where the Greenlaws had set up a half dozen picnic tables.

"Oliver!" *Why didn't I notice he was gone?*

But she knew why. She'd been so involved in the conversation between the Kemps, the Greenlaws and Raj, she hadn't been paying attention to anything else.

Guilt circled her thoughts as Emma strained her eyes trying to see the familiar flash of white and tan in the shadows underneath the tables. Ever since last summer, Oliver had developed a habit of wandering off on his own. Emma hated to admit that she maybe sometimes had encouraged this—but that was only when it was really important.

He ought to know better. I *ought to know better.*

"Emma?" called Brian from the pub's TV room. "He might have got out this way."

Brian was right. The side door stood open, just a little. Emma leaned out and whistled as loud as she could.

Then she heard it—a faint, familiar bark. She turned on her heel.

"He's in the cellar!"

Emma hurried down the stairs, with Genny, Brian and Raj right behind her. David and Charles stayed behind with the Greenlaws.

Now all four of them clustered together at the bottom of the stairs and gaped in various stages of disbelief.

Pippa was crouched outside the tunnel alcove with its bright yellow zigzag of caution tape. She had Oliver by the collar, and he did not look happy about it.

"Emma!" Oliver barked and lunged forwards. "Emma, there's a hole! It's important!"

"You need to keep this little guy on a lead," Pippa said cheerfully. "You're lucky I was out there calling the boss"—she jerked her chin towards the loading doors—"or who knows where he'd be by now. I caught up with him right when he was about to get into the tunnel."

She let go of his collar, and Oliver zipped straight over to Emma.

"She did not!" he grumbled. "I found her! And she only told me to stop, but she didn't mean it. Not the way you do."

"Never mind." Emma crouched down and hugged him. "But you know you shouldn't run off like that! I was worried!" She gave him a gentle shake.

"But Pippa was in the tunnel too!" Oliver barked. "She was looking around and everything. She took something!"

"Naughty boy." Emma kissed his head. "You sure?" she whispered in his ear.

"Of course I am!" yipped Oliver indignantly. "It was paper! She picked it up and put it in her pocket!"

"Right." She rubbed his chin. "Thanks so much, Pippa."

"No worries," said Pippa easily.

Brian reached out a totally unnecessary hand to help Emma stand up. Genny watched them all with raised eyebrows. Then she nodded toward the tunnel. Emma looked and saw Raj leaning across the caution tape.

"Pippa?" Raj climbed through the tape. "You said you found Oliver before he got into the tunnel, yeah?"

"Right." Pippa straightened up and brushed off her knees. "He's really fast on those stubby little legs. I almost . . ."

Raj bent down. When he straightened up, he was holding a mobile. From behind Emma, Genny gave a soft snort.

Pippa blushed. "Oops. Ha-ha. Funny thing about that . . ."

Raj did not seem amused, or charmed. "Look, Pippa, this might not be an official crime scene yet, but you can't be mucking about down here!"

"I was just—" began Pippa, but Raj cut her off.

"You can tell us all about it upstairs."

"All right, all right! Just give me my phone back, yeah?" Pippa held out her hand.

"Maybe." Raj tucked the mobile into his chest pocket.

Pippa made a strangled noise. "Look, Raj, we're on the same side here. I can help you figure out who that is down there."

"We've got a lead on that . . ."

"Really? Fast work! Who is it?"

Raj groaned and rolled his eyes toward heaven, looking for patience.

"Aw, come on, Raj," said Pippa. "You've got to give us something. It'll cut down on the gossip if you do. And my boss won't be complaining to your boss about stonewalling the press, will he?"

Raj remained unmoved. "You know I can arrest you for interfering with a crime scene?"

"But you just said it's not a crime scene!"

"Everything all right down there?" called Liza from upstairs. "Did you find Oliver?"

"Erm. Yes, Liza," Emma called back. "We're all fine."

Oliver barked helpfully.

"All right, then," said Liza. "Only we'd like to close up if we can."

"Right!" Raj called back. "We'll be right up."

Pippa gave him an innocent grin. "May I *please* have my phone back?"

"No," snapped Raj. "Upstairs. Now." He pointed, just in case she'd gotten confused about the correct direction.

Pippa narrowed her eyes. If looks could kill, Raj would have been in serious danger.

What did Pippa take? Emma glanced over her shoulder at the tunnel mouth. *What could be that important?*

Aside from the skeleton, and the motorcycle . . .

"All right, Em?" asked Brian.

"Yeah, fine." Brian did not look convinced, but Emma decided to ignore that. "Erm. I'll just take Oliver around the outside. It'll be faster."

"Good idea," said Brian immediately. "I'll come with you."

"Me too," said Genny.

Emma smiled, but her heart wasn't in it. She'd hoped for a minute alone with Oliver to ask about what he'd seen Pippa doing. Unfortunately, her friend and her boyfriend seemed determined to frustrate her plan.

It was getting chilly outside. Emma shivered. Brian wrapped one arm around her and rubbed her shoulder.

Genny just folded her arms. "So, what was that back there?"

"What?" Emma tried very hard to sound innocently confused.

It didn't work. Brian and Genny just looked at each other. "You made that face," said Brian.

"What do you mean 'that face'?" Emma ducked out from under his arm. "I do not have a 'that face.'"

"You really do," said Genny. "You were thinking something. Or you saw something."

"Probably to do with whatever Pippa was up to," said Brian to Genny.

"Probably," said Genny to Brian. "Although she might

have noticed something funny about Oliver too. She does that."

"I'll say," Brian agreed. "It's a little spooky."

"It's only because Emma is very smart and listens to me," Oliver grumbled.

"That's enough, all of you." Emma stalked past them.

"Even me?" Oliver looked up at her with his most mournful eyes.

Emma sighed. "All right, not you." Oliver yipped, and trotted ahead proudly.

"But you did see something." Genny lengthened her stride to catch up with Emma.

"Not really," said Emma. "It's just . . . Pippa must have had herself a good look around while she was down there. I mean, why else was her mobile in the tunnel?"

"You think she found something?" asked Brian.

"Maybe. I mean, it probably wasn't anything Raj doesn't know about, but . . ." She shrugged. "She's a reporter, right? It's her job to find things. I was just wondering what it could be, that's all."

Brian opened the pub's door. "Well, if you're right, tonight just got even more interesting."

The three of them, plus Oliver, walked back into the pub's main room. Oliver instantly trotted over to Charles, wagging and whining, just in case he needed an extra friend, which he might. He and David were both slumped at their table, looking exhausted.

"Yes, yes, old chap, I understand. Been a long day." Charles lifted his eyes and caught David's gaze. "For all of us."

Something deep and long-standing passed silently between the two men in that shared look. Emma didn't know the specifics, but she felt it all the same.

Brian went over to David and put a hand on his shoulders. "All right, mate?"

"Oh, yes, yes," David said. "Or, at least, we will be." He breathed something else that Emma couldn't hear clearly, but she thought it sounded like "I hope."

Emma squashed her ballooning curiosity down, hard. Now was not the time to start asking awkward questions. Clearly Charles and David were about at the ends of their ropes for the day. Pippa was probably already plotting how to get back downstairs. Raj looked ready to arrest the lot of them. Liza and Sam stood together behind the bar, like they needed to put something between them and whatever was coming.

In true British fashion, Emma decided there was only one thing to do in a room filled with this much emotion.

"Well, we should get going," she said, too brightly. "I'm so sorry about your cousin," she added to the Greenlaws.

"Cousin?" said Pippa. "All right, I missed something here."

"That's what you get for wandering off," muttered Raj.

"Thank you," said Liza to Emma. "It's . . . it's a shame. Sonny, well, he had his troubles, didn't he? I reckon he just didn't move fast enough on the last one."

"Who was Sonny?" demanded Pippa.

Genny opened the door, and held it. "Later, Pippa, yeah? Everybody's knackered. Besides, I'm sure your granddad is wondering where you are. How's he doing anyway?"

Pippa now turned her glower on Genny. "He's fine, thanks. Colin Roskilly is over and they're having a drink and a good natter. Probably hasn't even noticed I'm gone."

"Well, that's nice," said Genny in her best customer service voice. "Maybe we'll see you tomorrow, yeah? Right now everybody needs some sleep. I know I do," she added pointedly.

Pippa gazed around the room and evidently saw the united, if tired, opposition to more questions just then.

"Yeah. Right. Well. Night, then." Clearly unhappy, Pippa stalked out the door.

Emma sympathized with her dissatisfaction. Pippa probably had a whole stack of questions she wanted answered. Emma certainly did. What kind of troubles had Sonny had? Did David and Charles, and Raj, for that matter, think Sonny stole the Vincent? That seemed likely. But if Sonny stole the Vincent, how did he and the bike get into the tunnel without anybody knowing they were there? Could he have stolen the Vincent and hidden it in there, planning to come back for it later? Was he alive when he went into that tunnel?

One thing was clear: forty years ago, something had gone very wrong indeed.

6

EMMA GRITTED HER TEETH TO HOLD BACK ALL THE QUEStions forming in her mind. She walked over to the abandoned buffet table. Brian, of course, came to help. He picked up the cupcake carriers while Emma took the stands. Emma mouthed *"Thank you"* before she raised her voice.

"David? Charles? Walk you back? If you're done here?" she added to Raj.

"Yeah, we're done," said Raj.

"Oh, good." Charles shook himself. "And thank you, Emma, but we'll be fine."

"Well, if you're sure . . ." began Emma.

David ran a hand over his disheveled hair and drew his shoulders back. "We're sure," he said. "We've been taking care of ourselves for a long time now. You young people can all just run along home."

It was a rebuke, and it stung, but Emma let it go. It was no surprise the men would want to be alone. After all, they'd both just had a huge shock.

Brian, Genny and Emma said good night to the Greenlaws and the Kemps and filed out through the courtyard gate and onto the high street.

"Poor David and Charles," said Emma. "What an awful way to find their Vincent."

Reflexively, they all glanced back toward the pub.

"Worse for Liza and Sam, don't you think?" said Genny. "They were counting on this to help bring in new business, and now they're not going to even be allowed to be open."

"It's a shocker, that's for sure," agreed Brian. But before he could get any further, Oliver started barking.

"It's her!"

He was right. Pippa was right across the street, standing beside a sky-blue Vespa scooter. Raj must have given her her phone back at some point because she was madly thumbing the screen.

"For heaven's sake," muttered Genny as she caught sight of what Oliver was barking at. "Need anything, Pippa?" she called sunnily.

Pippa tucked her phone away. "You could tell me who they think that skeleton used to be. Who's Sonny?"

They all looked at each other—which was apparently the last straw for Pippa.

"And you can stop with the meaningful glances and the side comments," she snapped. "I'm a reporter, and we just found a real, live skeleton in an old smugglers' tunnel. What am I supposed to do? Say 'Oh, wow, sorry the big event didn't go as planned, guess I'll be going now'?"

"Nobody's saying—" began Genny.

"Oh, no," agreed Pippa. "I'm just about deaf from how loud it was in there from all of you not saying anything."

"No, you're right," said Emma. "You've got to do your job, just like Raj has to do his. But you have to admit, this is pretty hard for everybody, yeah?" At the same time, she found herself staring at the reporter, like she thought she could see through her jacket to her pockets and find out what she'd taken with her.

Pippa sagged a little. "Yeah, yeah, I know. I do. Well, look, I've got to get going. We can talk later, yeah?" she said to Emma.

"You know where to find me," said Emma, aware that she sounded more cheerful about the prospect than she felt.

Pippa stowed her camera lovingly away in the Vespa's little boot, strapped on her helmet and rode off.

"You think you're going to regret being all willing to talk like that?" asked Brian.

"Maybe," Emma sighed. "But at the same time, everybody wants to know what happened, don't they? Pippa's got as good a chance as anybody to find out, and maybe she'd be willing to share."

Brian's eyebrows arched. "Devious. I like it."

"Of course, what I really want is to get answers for David and Charles," Emma pointed out.

"Of course." Brian patted her hand.

"You don't think either of them . . ." began Genny speculatively.

"Genny!" exclaimed Emma, so loudly that Brian jumped and Oliver yelped.

"What?" shot back Genny. Then she saw the expression on Emma's face. "No, no, I'm not saying they had anything to do with Sonny . . . being down there, but I'm wondering if maybe something happened, you know, back when the bike was stolen. You saw how upset David was."

Emma bit her lip. She had seen it, and she was worried about it. She wasn't a big believer in intuition, but it certainly felt like there was something more bothering the Kemps than they had let on.

And it wasn't just David and Charles who were holding back. It was Sam and Liza too.

Emma sighed. "I'd say there was a perfectly simple explanation, but what can be simple about finding both a skeleton and a motorcycle in an old smugglers' tunnel?"

"Well, I can tell you this, they're lucky they did find it," said Brian.

"You think so?" asked Genny

Brian nodded. "The Vincent Black Lightning is one of the rarest motorcycles in the world. There were only around thirty ever made, and most of them are lost or past repair. There was one in drivable condition sold at auction recently for close to a million dollars US."

"A million dollars!" exclaimed Genny. "For a motorcycle!"

Brian nodded. "Now, admittedly, that one was extra famous. See, it belonged to . . ." He must have noticed their eyes beginning to glaze over, because he stopped and blushed just a little. Emma thought it was sort of adorable.

"Do you think the Kemps know?" asked Emma. "About how much the bike is worth?"

Brian arched both brows. "They're professional antiques dealers. If they don't know now, they will soon."

"Gosh," breathed Genny. "It's like they won the lottery. I wonder what they'll do with it?"

Brian looked wistful. Emma laughed and patted his shoulder. "I'm sure they'll let you help with the overhaul."

"Nah, not me. Not this one. You want a specialist to give it a good going-over. Not that I wouldn't like a better look at her. She's a sweet machine." He got the kind of faraway look in his eyes Emma normally associated with high-quality chocolate.

"Well, not exactly the night out I had planned." Genny sighed. "You need a ride home?" she asked Emma.

"I brought her," Brian said.

"But thanks," added Emma.

"Right, well, I suppose I'll be talking to you tomorrow, then. Late tomorrow." There was a gleam in Genny's eye that spoke volumes. Emma frowned at her, which achieved exactly nothing.

Brian opened the boot of his vintage Volvo. Emma helped put in the cake carriers and stands, but she couldn't help looking over her shoulder at the closed-up pub one more time.

"They'll be okay, Emma," said Oliver. "You'll make sure of it."

Emma smiled, and gave his ears a good rub to let him

know she appreciated the vote of confidence. At the same time, she kept remembering the way Charles's face had lost all its color when he heard about the bones found in the tunnel. She also remembered how David's hands had shaken, and she wondered.

And she shivered.

7

CORNWALL COAST NEWS

SKELETONS IN THE ~~CLOSET~~ TUNNEL!

What was meant to be a minor expansion for a popular local business turned into something out of Agatha Christie when a human skeleton and a rare vintage motorcycle were found in the basement of the Roundhead pub in Trevena, Cornwall, Monday night.
The bones are believed to be the remains of former Trevena resident Wilson "Sonny" Greenlaw. Greenlaw was a cousin of the pub's current owners, Samuel and Elizabeth Greenlaw. The skeleton was found curled around the wheels of a 1952 Vincent Black Lightning motorcycle.

Emma crunched her toast and marmalade. On the floor beside her, Oliver was working his way through his breakfast kibble.

. . . Local police have yet to share any theory about the death or confirm that foul play was committed. It had been rumored however, that Sonny was involved with a local crime syndicate . . .

"What!" exclaimed Emma.

Oliver's head shot up. "What! What!" he barked.

"Crime syndicate!" Emma waved her toast at the screen. "In *Trevena*? Where'd she get that from?"

"Is it bad?" asked Oliver. "Did she drag it in from the garden?"

"Just about," Emma muttered and went back to reading.

> . . . when asked, both Greenlaws denied any knowledge of the body and the bike that had apparently been walled up in their cellar for the past forty years. Sam Greenlaw maintained that his father, Walter Greenlaw, had sealed the tunnel because of safety concerns. Questions remain, however, as to the exact timing of that closure . . .

Emma read that last sentence again. No. Pippa could not possibly be insinuating that Sam's family had something to do with the skeleton being in the tunnel.

At least, that's what she told herself until she got to the next paragraph.

> . . . with a local reputation for violence and wild behavior as a young man, Charles Kemp expressed delight at the return of his precious motorcycle. However, when asked, he also firmly denied knowledge of Sonny Greenlaw or what brought him to his bizarre and gothic ending, a denial that could be called into question as new facts are brought to light soon . . .

Oh, honestly! Emma slapped her laptop lid shut and glowered. She tried to remind herself it wasn't actual malice that motivated Pippa. She was a reporter. Of course she'd want to put the most dramatic spin possible on what happened last night. *As if a forty-year-old skeleton isn't dramatic enough.* At the same time, Pippa had come very close to accusing both the Kemps and the Greenlaws of at least knowing about a very strange murder.

Before there's even any reason to believe it even was a murder.

Except for the fact that people in general did not get accidentally stuck in tunnels along with rare vintage motorcycles.

Emma's jaw tightened.

There was no hint in the article as to what Pippa might have taken out of the tunnel, however. Unless it came under the heading of those "new facts" that might be brought to light soon.

Or this reference to a "criminal syndicate."

What has she found? Or what does she think she's found? Emma felt her brow furrow.

"Are we done, Emma?" Oliver barked and wagged. "You look done."

"Yes. We're done." She gave the laptop one final glower. *For now.*

THE ONE PART OF EMMA'S LIFE AS BAKER AND TEA SHOP owner that she did not actually love was that her days tended to start at five in the morning. It was all made a little easier by the fact that her cottage hot water heater was a deluxe model capable of providing her with a boiling hot shower, and that Angelique Delgado, her friend and partner, always had a pot of her famously strong tea ready by the time Emma and Oliver arrived at the King's Rest.

When Emma had first come to Trevena, she had thought she'd be setting up an independent shop, but when Angelique and her daughter, Pearl, had invited her to share space in their popular bed-and-breakfast, the possibility had been too good to pass up.

"Emma!" exclaimed Angelique as Emma pushed through the door into the B and B's kitchen. Oliver, of course, shot past Emma, barking and dancing on his hind legs in an enthusiastic early-morning greeting. "How are you? All right?" Angelique paused and patted Oliver's head. "No need to ask how you are, Prince Charming."

"Prince Corgi," barked Oliver.

Angelique was a broad, tall woman with dark brown skin. Her family had emigrated from Jamaica when she was a girl and she still retained a hint of her original accent. This morning, she wore her black braids tied back in a bright green and gold scarf. She had a strong face with high cheekbones and brown eyes that could look straight through you. This skill probably came from raising four children all while running a successful business.

"I heard we missed some excitement last night." Angelique set her bin of peppers and onions on the counter. Now that the summer season had ended, the B and B was mostly empty of guests. However, there was still an older couple from Liverpool visiting family, as well as a couple of young women finishing up their walking tour of the coast. So this morning Angelique was busy creating a somewhat abridged version of her famous breakfast buffet.

"Too right you did." Emma poured herself a mug of tea, took a swallow and sighed in satisfaction. The day suddenly felt much easier to face.

"And it really was a skeleton they found with the Vincent? It wasn't some kind of joke?"Angelique went back to the fridge for some sausage. Oliver trotted hopefully at her heels. "Nothing for you, you greedy thing," she told him.

"No, it was a real skeleton, all right." Emma took another swallow of tea. "Did you see the news this morning?"

"Not me," said Angelique. "Too much to do. Daniel looked at the *Coast News*, but says there wasn't much beyond what you texted us last night." Daniel was Angelique's husband. In the season he ran a fishing and tour boat. During the winter, he was mostly dry-docked, as he put it, and helped out with the B and B while their daughter Pearl was away at university finishing up her hospitality degree. "Is it right the body might have been one of the Greenlaws' cousins?"

"Well, Sam thinks it might be. Apparently there was a cousin named Sonny who disappeared back in the seventies."

"That's awful!"

Emma had to agree. "Sam said Sonny was planning to leave town, so when nobody saw him around, they didn't really wonder too much." She took another long swallow of tea. Slowly, reluctantly, her brain sputtered into motion.

"That article in the news mentioned a criminal syndicate? Any idea what that might be?"

"A bit before my time," said Angelique. "Although I understand there was still quite a lot of smuggling going on up and down the coast back in the seventies."

"Yeah, Brian said something about that." Emma looked down at her tea and felt the brew curdling in her stomach. Oliver, who was always sharply attuned to her mood, came quickly over and bumped his nose against her calf. Despite everything, Emma smiled. She also gave his ears a good rub.

"Well, Charles and David always did say the Vincent was stolen." Angelique pulled her chef's knife from the drawer and set to work on the peppers. "Now I reckon they know by who."

Which was, of course, the most reasonable conclusion. But even as Angelique said it, Emma felt herself frown. Again.

"What's wrong?" asked Angelique.

Emma shook her head. "I was just thinking maybe I should go check on the Kemps later." This was true. She had. She just hadn't been thinking it at that moment. "They were pretty shaken up last night, and things won't get any better this morning. That article also hinted that Charles should be considered a murder suspect." Even without the article, however, people would still be linking the Kemps to . . . whatever happened to Sonny. Emma pulled her reservations book out of the drawer. "First sitting for tea is at one today, so there should be some time for me to scoot over to Vintage Style around eleven."

"Good idea," agreed Angelique. "I was thinking I should check up on Liza and Sam myself. This has got to be hitting them hard."

"I'll say. You can take them some of the apple cake—oh, and some of Genny's fish stew."

"Good idea. I doubt Liza's going to feel much like cooking. We should have all the gossip to take to them by then as well."

"Oh, yeah," said Emma. "I don't imagine people will be talking about much of anything else."

EMMA WAS GLAD TO PLUNGE HER HANDS, AND HER ATTENtion, into finishing the baked goods for the morning. Nothing focused the mind like the realities of enriched dough, red currants, lemon sponge, candied ginger and, of course, the delicate magic that was the perfectly puffed fruit scone.

Once they opened for the day, though, her sense of peace and personal focus evaporated. As predicted, the news that a skeleton had been found in the Roundhead's cellar along with the famous Vincent Black Lightning was the major topic of conversation at Reed's Tea & Cakes. Almost everybody who stopped by the takeaway counter for a bun or a cuppa had an opinion about the grim discovery. If they didn't, they were eager to hear the details Emma had.

"Really, I couldn't see all that much," she said. In fact, she said it so many times she started to feel like a recording.

A disturbing number of customers, however, seemed to have read Pippa's article and were chewing over its contents along with their pastry. The speculation about what the Greenlaws and the Kemps could have known, or could have done, gave her goose bumps. Emma tried to take comfort in the number of people who declared they didn't believe a word of it. But still . . .

But still. Emma felt a fresh chill crawling up her spine.

At eleven, Emma handed responsibility for the counter over to her part-time servers and kitchen assistants: Becca Portman and her sister, Bella. She wrapped up two slices of her walnut cake with coffee icing, then a third, and then a fourth for good measure. In Emma's experience, personal crises called for extra cake, and given the swirling gossip, she had no doubt that David and Charles were going to need every crumb.

8

USUALLY, CHARLES AND DAVID OPENED VINTAGE STYLE BY ten, but today a sign hung on the door:

CLOSED WHILE WE REFRESH OUR INVENTORY.

PLEASE VISIT OUR WEBSITE FOR UPDATES.

Emma peered through the window. This building had originally housed a dry goods shop. Its main showroom was still dominated by the long wooden counter where fabrics and ribbons used to be measured and cut. Now, however, instead of dress models and bolts of cloth, the shop was filled with lovely vintage furniture, arranged by era and room. Drawers and cubby holes lined the wall behind the counter. Each cubby held a selected antique, which could be anything from a Royal Doulton teapot to a vintage teddy bear. She could just see the new rack of used records that they'd added along the far wall. Vinyl was apparently making a comeback with collectors, and the Kemps were more than ready to take advantage of the trend.

What she did not see was either David or Charles.

Always trying to help, Oliver barked and scrabbled at the door.

"Nobody home, Oliver," said Emma. "Nothing for it—we're going to have to climb."

The Kemps lived above the shop. Literally. A steep staircase with stout railings ran up the side of the building. David and Charles themselves seldom used it. "My knees can't take it these days," David had sighed more than once. They both preferred the easier climb from inside the shop.

"Emma, they should live on the ground floor," Oliver panted as he scrambled up the stairs. "It's not sensible for humans to live high up. You said you would talk to them about it."

Emma laughed, and puffed. "I will, as soon as I get a chance. Promise."

Despite Oliver's grumbles, they did both make it to the door, only slightly winded. Well, Emma was slightly winded. Oliver collapsed on the doorstep in full corgi-drama mode.

Emma turned the antique bellpull. There was no answer. *I should have called first.* She shifted the cake bag to the crook of her arm and dug in her pocket for her mobile. Just then, the door flew open, letting the strains of the Zombies and "She's Not There" flow out into the quiet morning.

"We told you—" began David. Then he saw who it was and pulled up short. "Oh! Emma! I'm so sorry. I thought you were a reporter. We've had a few hanging about."

"I just wanted to stop by and see how you were doing." Emma lifted her bag. "I brought walnut cake."

"Oh, well, in that case—" David attempted a laugh, but the sound was forced. "Come along in." He stepped back to give her and Oliver room to come inside. "Charles? We have a visitor."

"I did notice, thank you." Charles tossed down the paper he was reading and stood up to greet Emma. "Always glad to see you, Emma. You too, Oliver." Oliver hurried over to sniff both of Charles's palms and get his sides patted.

Since they'd settled in Trevena, Oliver and Emma had

become regular visitors at the Kemps's. The flat was open and airy. Its windows provided lovely views of Trevena's village-scape—ending at the sea on one side and the looming, dark green hills on the other. The white walls and hardwood floors were accented with colorful original artwork and a gorgeous vintage carpet. Well-filled bookshelves made it homey. An even larger set of shelves held the couple's jaw-droppingly extensive collection of vinyl records, each carefully encased in its plastic envelope. The elaborate stereo, complete with twin turntables, took up most of one wall.

Another corner was taken up by a floor-to-ceiling cat tree. This item was for the exclusive use of the other member of the Kemp clan—a truly massive marmalade cat called the Cream Tangerine—and she currently occupied the tree's top shelf.

Oliver, of course, trotted over to the tree. The Tangerine looked down and swished her tail. She also yawned.

"Do you think they're finally making friends?" Charles came over to the kitchen to join Emma and David.

"I'm afraid not," said Emma. "Unfortunately, Oliver thinks Tangerine is rude."

David chuckled. "I'm sure he's right. You should hear her when I try to make her shift on the bed. Tea?" He was already plugging in the kettle and reaching in the cupboard for cups. "Or do you have to get right back?"

"I've got time for a cup, thanks."

In the background, the Zombies finished complaining that she wasn't there and launched into a gothic-accented cover of Gershwin's "Summertime."

"Can you get out the tea, Charles?" David nodded to the silver caddy on the counter. Charles obliged, measuring four heaping spoonfuls into the pot—one for each cup and one for the pot, as Emma's Nana Phyllis would have said.

David brought out three Royal Kent cake plates with big pink roses on them, as well as some sterling silver forks and a matching cake server. His collecting urges had never been limited to the shop, somewhat to Charles's dismay.

"So." Emma unwrapped the cake slices. "How are you both?"

"Oh, bearing up, bearing up." David used the cake server to set the slices onto the plates.

"You're lying," said Emma.

David sighed and Charles chuckled, just a little.

"You used to be better at it, Davey."

"Yes, well. I learned from you, didn't I?" David filled the teapot and carried it over to the table they'd set up on the sea-view side of the flat. The Tangerine seemed to take this as an infringement on her territorial rights. With a deep meow, she leapt from the top shelf of her cat tree down to the back of the sofa and disappeared into one of the bedrooms.

"Hey!" barked Oliver. "You shouldn't say things like that!" He scampered after the cat.

David paused, kettle in hand. "Should we be worried?" he asked Emma.

"Tangerine can handle herself," said Charles.

"And Oliver's really just a big softie," added Emma as she handed the cake around. "I imagine you two didn't get a lot of sleep last night."

"A couple winks, if that much." Charles took a bite of cake. "This is marvelous, as always."

"Thanks." She spread her napkin on her lap. "Sorry if I'm being nosy, but you seemed pretty shaken up yesterday."

David quirked an eyebrow at her. "Is that one of those famous leading questions? I trust you're not working in concert with young Miss Marsh now?"

"Promise I'm not." Emma crossed her heart for good measure. "But you were pretty shaken up all the same."

"I told you she'd notice." Charles looked at David, his brows drawn tight over his nose.

"We all noticed," Emma said. "I'm just the one who got here first."

"Well, you can't blame a man for trying." David shrugged, and Charles shrugged right back.

"We did know Sonny," David said. "Rather better, I'm afraid, than we let on to Raj last night."

"I think Raj may have picked up on that," said Emma drily. "I'm surprised he hasn't been here already."

The men eyed each other.

"Oh," said Emma.

"That's part of the reason we decided not to open this morning," said David.

"So you were up-front with him, right?" Emma said in her best stern-auntie tone.

"We were, and we apologized," David told her. "One may *say* one has skeletons in the closet, but when confronted with the real thing—" He shuddered. So did Charles. "One's common sense doesn't always rise to the occasion."

"And can one's friend ask how one actually came to know Sonny?"

The men were watching each other again, and Emma felt a current of tension flowing between them. She got the idea that some argument or agreement was being silently replayed. She'd seen something similar happen with her parents.

And then it was over, but Emma knew she hadn't imagined it.

"I believe this is my cue to say you can *ask*," quipped David.

"But you won't," said Charles.

"Probably not," David agreed. "But one never knows." He smiled brightly.

He's trying too hard, thought Emma suddenly. But before she could think of what to say about it, David was talking again.

"I think we told you that when we first got to Trevena, we had planned to open a record shop?" he said.

"Right. I remember."

Charles's mouth twisted up into a tight grin. "I think we also told you we were pretty much skint?"

Emma nodded.

"Well, one of the things we did for cash then was sell

records out of our flat," David said. "Probably not strictly allowed, but—" He waved his fork dismissively. "Anyway, Sonny was hanging about all the time. Loved rock 'n' roll, got into the punk scene early . . . one of our best customers, when he had the cash."

"What about when he didn't?"

"Well, that was when you had to watch out," said Charles. "He had this bad habit of trying to help himself when your back was turned, didn't he? Oh, he'd say he was just looking at it if you caught him, but . . ." Charles shook his head.

Emma looked from David to Charles and back again. Both men seemed relaxed, but there was something going on underneath. She felt sure they were telling the truth, but not all of it.

"Is it possible that Sonny was into something serious?" asked Emma. "I don't mean Pippa's crime syndicate," she added. "But Liza said he had his troubles, and Angelique said there was some smuggling going on back in the day . . ."

Charles laughed sharply. "You might say." He stabbed his fork into his cake. "All the punters love a picturesque seaside town, don't they?" Charles stabbed his fork into his cake. "But they forget that there's always been more coming into harbor than boats and tourists."

"Like what?"

David was looking out the window, but Emma had the feeling whatever he was seeing was much farther away than Trevena's rooftops. "Booze and cigarettes, mostly."

"Could Sonny have been involved?"

Charles snorted. "Him and half Trevena, one way and another. Dodging the Inland Revenue is practically the British national pastime, even now."

In the distance, a bell jingled. Charles's head jerked around. David glared at his husband. "I thought you locked the shop door."

"I thought I had," Charles answered.

Oliver had evidently heard the bell too. He came scampering out from the back room and ran straight up to the inside door, snuffling along the bottom edge.

Charles wiped his hands and tossed down his napkin. "I'll go see. It might be Rory. He heard about what happened and said he was going to stop by this morning," he added for Emma's sake. Rory was Charles's nephew. He helped out at the shop part-time, and frequently accompanied the two men on their buying trips.

Charles headed for the door, brushing a hand across David's shoulder as he passed. David twisted in his chair, and for a minute Emma thought he was going to say something. But if he had, he changed his mind, and just watched as Charles closed the door to the inside stairs behind him.

David turned back to his cake. He stared at it long enough that Emma could almost believe he'd forgotten what he was meant to do with it.

"What's really wrong, David?" she asked.

"Nothing new," he answered. He drank the last of his tea. "As you say, not enough sleep. We're not as young as we once were, you know." He tugged meaningfully on a lock of snow-white hair.

"And Sonny really was involved in the smuggling back in the day, wasn't he?" she said, gently. Well, as gently as a person could say something like that.

"Oh, yes. Without question." David picked up the pot and refilled his cup. "But it was all so long ago, wasn't it? Maybe it'd be best to just let sleeping dogs lie. After all, Sam and Liza don't really need to hear any nasty old rumors about their family, do they? This has been enough of a shock."

You're trying to talk yourself into something, thought Emma. *Or out of it. What's going on, David?*

She was still trying to work out how to ask that when Tangerine stalked back out from the bedroom. The cat jumped onto the sofa arm, then the sofa's back. From there, she walked across the nearest cat tree shelf to get to the windowsill. Finally, she settled down with all four legs tucked under herself. David stroked her back. The cat meowed and headbutted David's hand so he would scratch her ears.

Emma was not surprised when Oliver came to her side, his entire attitude registering deep disapproval.

"That is a very rude cat," grumbled Oliver as he flopped down on his side. "Is there cake, Emma?"

Emma sighed and took up a bit of cake. "One day, I promise, I will stop letting him beg at the table."

"I'm sure you will, dear," murmured David with exaggerated kindness.

"You sound skeptical."

"Certainly not. I have absolute faith in you." He said it with such a straight face, Emma couldn't help but laugh. David joined in. Emma was glad to see David cheer up, even just a little. Then, very faintly, Emma heard the shop bell jingle again. David jumped, sloshing his tea.

"Are you all right?" asked Emma.

"Yes. Sorry." David batted hastily at his jumper. Cream Tangerine, obviously deeply affronted by the sudden motion, gave a contemptuous *merow* and flowed down to the floor. Oliver, of course, had to jump to his feet. The cat slid quickly out from under the table, and Oliver immediately followed along, just to see where the cat might be going.

The cat jumped up onto the barstool, and then onto the kitchen pass.

"Oh, get down, Tangerine, you naughty thing." David went to scoop the cat off the counter. "You know you're not allowed up there. As for you, sir," he said imperiously to Oliver, "you need to be a better guest. What are you playing at, upsetting your host like that?"

David in his showy self-righteousness was always a magnificent sight, and Emma couldn't help laughing again.

"It's not my fault!" yipped Oliver indignantly. "The cat started it!"

Emma smothered a snort. "Do you want to go see what's going on downstairs?" she asked David.

"No, no. I'm going to finish my cake. Whatever it is,

Charles can handle it." He smiled ruefully. "Charles thinks I hover."

"Charles is right," said Emma.

"Maybe a little," David agreed with a small smile. "Old habits die hard."

He carried Tangerine over to the table and set her on the windowsill. Of course she was not going to stay there. Instead, she jumped back up onto her cat tree. Oliver plumped himself down at the base, very much on watch.

Emma could have sworn the cat rolled her eyes. David, in the meantime, dug his fork determinedly into the last of his cake.

That was when they heard the shout.

9

....

IT WAS DAVID WHO GOT TO HIS FEET, AND TO THE FLAT'S inner door, first. He threw it open and hobbled rapidly down the stairs. Emma followed close behind. Oliver followed Emma, which she only knew because of the unmistakable scrabble of dog toenails against hardwood. Her attention was on David. She was afraid of what might be happening in the shop, but equally afraid that in his hurry to get down there, David might slip and fall.

Charles stood in the middle of the shop floor, flexing both his hands. His nephew, Rory Thorndike, was at the door, turning the key in the lock and pulling the shade down.

"Charles!" exclaimed David. "What happened?"

Charles stared at them, his face and hands both knotted tight with anger. Then he turned on his heel, marched into the office and slammed the door shut.

The sound faded, leaving the shop eerily quiet.

"Bollocks," muttered David. With a bit of effort, he straightened his back and strode to the office. The door slammed shut behind him as well.

Rory and Emma stared at each other. Oliver went to snuffle around Rory's shoes.

"Petrol, rubber, tarmac . . . he spends too much time driving, Emma. It's not healthy."

Emma ignored this. "Hi," she said to Rory.

"Hi," said Rory. "Good to see you."

"You too. Erm. What just happened?"

Rory sighed and dug both hands into his jeans pockets. It was easy to see the family relationship between Rory and Charles. They had the same long face, the same dark eyes and the same broad build. Rory had a head of black, waving hair and a summer tan that had only just begun to fade. He wore a red T-shirt and faded jeans, with a button-down brown corduroy shirt thrown on over top as a concession to the cooling weather.

Emma had liked the young man almost as soon as she met him. He was consistently cheerful. He might spend a lot of time teasing his uncles, but the affection between them all obviously ran deep. She'd yet to meet his mother, Charles's (much) younger sister, but she knew they talked frequently.

"Reggie Tapp is what happened," Rory told her. "I'd just pulled up, hadn't I? And I saw Tapp and Uncle Charles through the window, and it was pretty clear they were arguing. I let myself in and next thing I know, Uncle Charles is chasing Tapp out and threatening to kick him in the . . . privates."

They looked at each other, and then at the office door. Raised voices filtered through, but neither of them could understand the words. Oliver put his nose down to the crack under the door, as if he could sniff out the conversation.

Absurdly, Emma wished she could do the same.

Leave it, she ordered herself. *Give them their privacy.* At the same time, curiosity raged. What had Reggie said to Charles? What was so important that he had to come round in person, rather than call?

Emma could see clearly that Rory was experiencing a similar emotional tussle. Then the voices in the office fell silent.

Both of them moved to the office door as if they'd agreed

on it. Rory knocked, and then pushed the door open before anyone could tell him to stay out.

Oliver dodged inside immediately.

Charles leaned straight-armed over the desk, his head bowed. David stood behind him, his hands open, like he was pleading. Both men turned to see Emma, Rory and Oliver.

"I'm all right," snarled Charles. "You can just close that door on your way out, yeah?"

The Cream Tangerine appeared from somewhere, jumped up on the desk and rubbed against Charles's arm. He gave the cat a shove, hard enough to push her sideways, sending a pile of papers sliding to the floor at the same time. Oliver yipped, startled. Tangerine returned a deeply affronted look and jumped down from the desk.

"Charles," breathed David.

"I told you. I'm all right!"

"And I'm Margaret Thatcher," David shot back. "What did Tapp say to you?"

Charles turned. Emma knew both the Kemps were approaching seventy, but they were so sharp and vital, she seldom thought of them as really old. Right now, though, Charles looked like every single one of his years had settled on his shoulders.

"First, he said he wanted to talk about buying the Vincent."

David laughed, high and sharp. "Oh, he would. If I didn't think there'd be irreversible property damage, I'd ask him to prove he could ride it first. Can you imagine?"

But Charles wasn't laughing. Charles wasn't even smiling.

"I turned him down. The Black Lightning is mine, I said." He stopped. "Well, ours. It's come back, and we're keeping it."

"Of course," said David.

"Besides, there's no way that tosser could afford it," put in Rory.

"Then—" Charles swallowed. "Then he said I was going to need all the friends I could get, now that they'd found Sonny. He stood there, and he looked me right in the face and he—" Charles choked. "He said it was already in the papers, he said the whole town was saying it. He said everybody knew . . . everybody knew . . ." He stopped, and swallowed. His expression shifted and he seemed to reach a decision. "He said everybody knew I'd killed Sonny."

David moved forward, wrapping his husband in a strong embrace. Charles held himself rigid at first. Then, slowly, his shoulders sagged, and he pressed his cheek against David's. The two of them just stood there like that, each holding the other up.

Emma nudged Oliver backwards so Rory could close the door and let Charles and David have their privacy.

"I'm going to kill him," said Rory flatly. He meant Reggie, of course. Emma very much understood the impulse.

"I'm sure it was . . . just a nasty attempt at leverage," she said. "Reggie probably didn't know how hard it would hit him. Them."

"Well, he should have," growled Rory. "My mum told me Uncle Charles and Uncle David went through a lot back in the day. She said they were headed for some real trouble after they got out here and it took everything they had to turn it around. Tapp shouldn't be digging all that back up."

"I don't think he's the one who did," said Emma, remembering Pippa's article.

"Yeah, well, maybe, but he's making it worse."

"Yeah, he is that."

Inside, questions were piling up. *David and Charles were headed for trouble? What kind of trouble? Was their trouble related to Sonny's trouble? How does the Vincent play into it?*

But how on earth could anybody believe that two people as intelligent as David and Charles could do something as daft as hide a body in what's essentially a basement? Even one that had been boarded up?

Emma looked at the clock over the counter and breathed a curse. It was 12:35. She'd stayed longer than she had planned. She didn't want to leave, but she couldn't ask Becca and Bella to handle the tea service on their own. "Listen, Rory, you are going to stick around for a while, yeah? I'm not sure David and Charles should be alone right now."

Rory shoved his hands deep into his pockets. "I'll have to call my other job, but yeah, I'm staying. I was thinking about it anyway. This is really bad," he said. "I've never seen Uncle Charles this upset. Better call Mum too." He pulled out his mobile.

Rory retreated to a corner by the record shelves to make his call. As he did, the office door opened, and Charles came out, carrying Tangerine up against his shoulder. The cat appeared to be trying to wind herself around his neck like a football scarf. Clearly, all had been forgiven.

"I just wanted to say sorry about all that in there," he told Emma.

"No worries. With everything that's happened, it's no surprise you're on edge."

"Too right. I know it'll all sort itself out, eventually anyway, but right now—" He stopped. "You heard anything from Raj? Like if they're going to call in that detective friend of yours? He wouldn't tell us anything."

"That detective friend" was DCI Constance Brent of the Devon and Cornwall police. She and Emma had been thrown together a few times since Emma moved to Trevena, and it just happened to have been over a couple of dead bodies. Emma—and Oliver—had helped uncover the killers. This fact still surprised Emma and, she was sure, disconcerted the detective.

"Haven't heard a thing," said Emma. "I imagine they're still sorting out how they want to handle this. I mean, there have got to be different protocols for a forty-year-old body, yeah?"

"Yeah. Have to be." Charles stroked the cat's back, but Emma wasn't sure if he was trying to reassure his pet or himself.

The cat looked smugly down at Oliver. Oliver wagged,

in an attempt at friendliness, probably. Tangerine closed her eyes and snuggled her face against Charles's neck.

Rory finished his call and came back over.

"All right?" he asked his uncle.

"Yeah, no worries." Charles smiled, and Rory looked relieved.

Emma waited to feel her own bit of relief, but she couldn't. Instead, she remembered what Rory had said about David and Charles heading for trouble when they first came to Trevena. She tried to tell herself it would be surprising if there hadn't been some kind of friction. After all, they were Londoners moving to a small village, and their being an openly gay couple in the nineteen seventies couldn't have made things any easier.

But she couldn't quite believe that was all Rory had meant. She also remembered what Charles said when they'd been talking about the smuggling. Sonny had been involved, he said. *Him and half Trevena, one way and another.*

Emma, reluctantly, found herself wondering if Charles himself had been part of that half of Trevena.

She bit her lip and glanced at the clock again. She needed more time, and she just didn't have it.

"I'm sorry, I've got to get back and set up for tea," she told Rory and Charles. "Will you tell David I said goodbye and I'll stop back later, if it's all right?"

"Right. Will do," said Charles. Then, he paused. "And, hey, Emma? Nobody needs to hear about what happened here, yeah?"

Emma suppressed a wince. Nobody liked to think they were getting a reputation as a local gossip or a snoop, even if, maybe, there might be a reason for it. Genny had even coined a term for Emma's public curiosity. She accused Emma of "Marpleing."

"All right, I won't say anything, but I'm not sure what good it'll do," she told Charles. "Reggie Tapp doesn't strike me as the kind to keep his feelings to himself."

"Don't worry," said Rory. "I'll take care of Tapp."

"Erm," said Emma. Rory took a look at her expression, and laughed.

"Wow! No fear, Emma! I'm not going to start a fight or anything. I leave that kind of thing to Uncle C." He punched Charles lightly on the arm. Tangerine narrowed her yellow eyes at him.

"Mind you," Rory went on, "Tapp's got it coming. But I am going to talk to him."

"No, you're not," said Charles. "This has nothing to do with you."

Rory ignored him. "See you later, then," he said to Emma. "Maybe I'll stop by for a cuppa?"

Emma agreed this would be a great idea.

She'd left her bag back at the B and B, so there was nothing for her to collect upstairs. Outside, the clouds were gathering. The wind that blew down the street smelled of rain as well as the sea. The combination encouraged a brisk pace, as did the fact that the village hall clock was chiming the quarter hour in the distance. At the same time, Emma couldn't completely ignore the worry nibbling at the back of her brain.

Of course David and Charles were upset that a skeleton had been found in the tunnel beside their Vincent. It was like something out of Edgar Allan Poe. And being accused of murder, even a forty-year-old one, would upset anybody. But the Charles Emma knew would have passed something like that off with a shrug and some creative profanity.

What was it about Reggie's accusation that had hit him so hard? She was sure there was something he had not said.

And he wasn't the only one.

"Oliver," said Emma. "Yesterday, when you were down in the tunnel, you said Pippa took something."

"She did!" Oliver barked. "It was a bit of paper, on the floor by the wall."

"But you didn't see what it was?"

"It was a bit of paper, Emma. I just told you."

Emma suppressed a sigh. It was not Oliver's fault. He might talk to her, but he was still very much a dog, and he saw the world the way a dog did. Which sometimes made for confusion, and some very odd gaps in their ability to understand each other.

How do I find out what it was? Emma frowned at herself.

Because if Pippa had taken a piece of evidence that could help sort this mess out for her friends, Emma wasn't about to let it slide.

10

"THANK GOODNESS!" SAID BECCA AS EMMA AND OLIVER slid back into the kitchen at the King's Rest. "I was getting worried."

"Sorry!" Emma grabbed her apron and cap off the hook and then went to wash her hands. "Stayed a little longer than I meant to."

Emma and Angelique shared the kitchen in the mornings, but by afternoon, Angelique had moved on to the housekeeping and paperwork portion of running the B and B, and Emma had the kitchen to herself.

Before she left, Emma had laid her clipboards all out on the counter. Now she started looking through her lists. They had four tables for the first seating—a total of ten guests. Three tables wanted the *prix fixe* "Tea of the Day," which had a set list of offerings. The last table would be ordering from the (limited for the sake of everybody's sanity) menu.

Bella was working the takeaway counter, while Becca took on the prep work for the formal teas. Becca was the older, pinker, rounder, more freckled of the pair and wore wire-framed glasses that she kept pushing up on her snub nose. Her hair was dark gold, as opposed to Becca's pale blond.

Bella had laid out the bread and sandwich fillings Emma had made yesterday, setting up what they all called the "cream tea assembly line."

"So, is it true what they're saying?" asked Becca as she started methodically cutting crusts off slices of white bread. "That old Charles maybe had something to do with the body they found?"

Emma's head snapped up. "Where did you hear that?"

Becca did not seem at all bothered by her sharp tone. "Well, it was all on the news, wasn't it? Plus, Mrs. Grant said something about it, and Luke Roskilly, and old Mr.—"

"Forget I asked." Emma sighed. "And no, it is not true. And it wasn't a body, it was a skeleton. A very old one."

Becca rolled her eyes. Emma glowered at her, and Becca had the good sense to get back to work.

While Emma was always refining the menu, her teas followed a classic pattern. The sandwich stands had three tiers, one for each course. On the very bottom were the finger sandwiches. Today's selections were smoked mackerel salad with chive butter, egg mayonnaise and, for a bit of adventure, a tomato and watercress with a spiced lime and farm cheese spread.

The scones went on the second tier. Usually, she had two types. The first was always her nan's favorite—a light, fluffy plain scone. The second was changeable, according to season and Emma's whims. Today it was lemon and red currant. There was, of course, a small dish of clotted cream, as well as a locally produced raspberry jam and orange marmalade. There was also ginger cake, made with three types of ginger.

The most delicate biscuits and pastries went onto the top tier. In summer, she usually had a Victoria sponge, but as they were heading into autumn, Emma had replaced it with a less traditional almond and orange sponge with a cinnamon cream she was particularly proud of. Two kinds of shortbread—chocolate and vanilla—and Nana Phyllis's famous ginger biscuits completed the offerings.

Once Emma was satisfied that the sandwiches and other items were lined up and ready to be plated, she let Becca start loading up the stands while she went out front to check on Bella and to help greet the first arrivals.

Oliver, naturally, was everywhere at once, alternately supervising, greeting guests, and making sure Emma and Bella hadn't dropped a bit of mackerel or cake.

Emma loved it all. She loved the planning, the baking, the service and talking with the customers. She loved spooning just the right amount of fragrant tea into a pot, adding the hot water and feeling the warm steam against her fingers as she closed the lid. Best of all, she loved her guests' smiles as they relaxed over her food, taking a moment out of busy lives to simply enjoy.

As village natives, Becca and Bella knew most of their regular customers and could be counted on to be friendly and (mostly) cheerful during service. If the sisters had a tendency to get a little too involved in the current gossip, it generally wasn't a major problem.

Today, of course, was different. The speculation about the skeleton in the tunnel was just as lively this afternoon as it had been in the morning. Emma found herself working a little harder than usual to make sure her assistants kept the tea and sandwiches moving.

By the time the last three guests had paid their bills and headed home for the evening, Emma felt about ready to drop.

"A hot bath tonight," she told Oliver. "And a long session of lounging and videos. What do you think?"

"Yes!" agreed Oliver, because of course that meant snuggle time. "And snacks!"

Emma laughed and rubbed his ears. "Yes, there will definitely be snacks. Just let me finish closing up."

"Good!" barked Oliver. "I will go make sure the garden is okay. The fox was back yesterday."

Oliver had an ongoing feud with the local town fox, and

kept up a regular patrol of the B and B's back garden to try to fend him off. He hadn't had much (or any) success at it, but as Oliver frequently reminded her, a noble warrior corgi did not give up.

As Emma began the delicate process of wrapping up the leftover cakes in the takeaway case, the door opened. Raj Patel came in, taking off his cap and tucking it under his arm.

"Raj!" she exclaimed. "I didn't expect to see you today."

"Hullo, Emma." He smiled, but just a little. "Look, I know you're closed, but is there any chance of some of that lemon poppyseed cake? Only I didn't get lunch and I'm not ready to go face the family yet."

"Of course. I haven't even put it away yet. You sit." She pointed to one of the tables. "How about a cuppa to go with?"

"Perfect. Thanks." Raj slumped back in the chair and rubbed his eyes hard.

Emma was not a mother herself, but she was an experienced aunt, and she could tell that Raj needed something more substantial than a slice of cake. She retreated to the kitchen. Becca and Bella had already finished most of the cleanup. She checked in the fridge to see what was available. Fortunately, she still had some of the smoked mackerel salad left. She spread a thick helping on wholemeal bread, and added some fresh tomatoes and cress. Emma contemplated the sandwich. Something was missing, and she knew what it was.

Since she had first opened, Emma had had an arrangement with Genny to sell some of Emma's more portable bakes from her chip shop. Now Genny was returning the favor by providing Emma with a kettle of her traditional Cornish fish soup for the sit-down teas.

Raj's eyes widened as she deposited the tray in front of him.

"Oh, ta, but you didn't—"

Emma cut him off. "I did. Otherwise your mother would be having all kinds of words with me for letting you eat cake without some decent food first. And don't tell me she wouldn't find out," she added.

Raj laughed. "I surrender." He picked up a spoon and tucked in enthusiastically.

Emma went back behind her counter and continued wrapping up cakes.

"Rough day?" she asked.

"Disappointing, is all." Raj took a bite of sandwich.

"What happened?"

Raj shrugged. "Had to ask some awkward questions about, you know." He waved his spoon vaguely toward the floor. "A policeman's lot is not a happy one."

"You can't mean people don't want to talk?" said Emma, genuinely surprised. "Half the village has been in here today, and they've done nothing *but* talk."

"Yeah, well, it's different when it's the local copper disturbing their day with a lot of nonsense, isn't it?" He took another healthy bite of sandwich. "I mean, it was no worse than I expected, but it's still frustrating," he mumbled.

"What about the tunnel?" said Emma. "You must have found something there."

Raj gave her a thoughtful look. "We had a look back as far as we could, twenty meters, maybe. But there was a cave-in at some point and the whole thing's blocked."

"Yeah, Sam talked about that at the party. He said it wasn't stable and that's why his mum wanted the entrance bricked over."

Raj nodded. "It's actually kind of amazing that so much of the tunnel is still standing. But, it's completely blocked now, at least as far as we can tell."

Is it? Emma remembered Oliver saying something about a hole. Did he mean he had found an opening in the cave-in?

"So, are you going to excavate?" Emma asked. "Find out where the tunnel ends up?" After all, there might be another entrance—or more than one, even. There was nothing that said Sonny and the Vincent had to have gotten in there through the Roundhead.

But Raj just looked at her with the patience of the veteran cop for an overenthusiastic civilian.

"Despite what all those BBC shows tell us, it turns out there's a bit of reluctance to put resources into forty-year-old cases. I got myself told in no uncertain terms that once the pathologist finishes their report, I should finish mine."

"Then what?" asked Emma.

"Then nothing." Raj spooned up some more soup. "Report gets filed, the body, or bones, get claimed, or not, but either way, we're done."

Emma felt herself staring. "But it's a dead body! And a stolen motorcycle." A truly valuable motorcycle, according to Brian and Rory.

"Oh, it's a lot more than that," said Raj.

"What do you mean?"

Raj made a face at his soup, maybe regretting how much he'd already said. "You know how it goes in a village. Something out-of-the-way happens and everybody gets to talking about the past. Old hurts and old suspicions get brought out for a really good airing. Makes for the kind of tension between neighbors that nobody really needs." Raj cocked his head at her. "Don't suppose you'd care to tell me what you've heard, you know, round the shop today and all?"

So much for me *cleverly trying to talk* him *'round to telling me what he knows.*

"Just a lot of speculation," she said, and then an idea struck. "I did hear that Reggie Tapp wants to buy the Vincent." Which had the benefit of being true, while staying vague about how she'd found that out.

Raj pulled a face. "He would. It's valuable and impractical. Like catnip to a cat for Reggie."

"What's his story?" asked Emma.

Raj drank the last of his soup straight out of the cup. "Small fish in a small pond who wishes he was a big fish."

"So why isn't he a big fish?"

Raj wrapped both hands around his tea mug. "I don't know him that well, but my da says he just keeps betting on the wrong horse."

Emma nodded. She'd seen plenty of that type while she still worked in finance. "Always on the lookout for the next big thing, but he comes up smelling like tidewater instead of roses?"

"That's it." Raj saluted her with his mug and took a long swallow. "But he does keep looking. You've got to admire an optimist."

"At least his pub does pretty well." Emma had been by the Donkey's Win in the summer and seen the crowds spilling out into the street. "But I reckon he married into that?"

Raj nodded. "And he's got some extra help there. Ma says Marianne—that's his wife—and his business partner do most of the real work."

Emma nodded. She'd seen plenty of that too.

"Thanks for tea, Emma." Raj reached for his wallet.

"Oh, no, on the house," she said. "It was all leftovers anyway."

"Come on, you know I can't. Especially when I'm on duty."

Emma didn't argue. Raj paid and left with a cheery wave. Emma returned to closing up her shop. But her mind wasn't on her work anymore. She kept thinking about Reggie Tapp going round to bother Charles about selling the Vincent, and how Charles said Reggie accused him of murdering Sonny Greenlaw. She thought, for just one second, about ignoring Charles's request for privacy and telling Raj about the argument.

But what would Raj think, hearing something like that?

What do I think? Emma bit her lip. *I think all kinds of things I don't want to think.*

David said *Maybe it'd be best to just let sleeping dogs lie.* Maybe he was right. Except, in Emma's experience, sleeping dogs always woke up.

And that was when the trouble really started.

11

TODAY WAS A GOOD DAY.

Almost all days with Emma were good, but since they'd come to Trevena, they'd gotten even better. In London, Oliver had spent a lot of his time guarding the flat he and Emma shared, and when they went out walking, she was very strict about the Lead.

Now that they were in Trevena, they spent the whole day together. Oliver had made many new friends among the humans in the village, and all their dogs. A lot of times the guests at the B and B brought dogs with them too. It was even better than a park.

But the best part, after getting to spend so much more time with Emma, was that he had all kinds of important work to do.

Take the B and B's garden, for instance. The garden meant a lot to Emma, Angelique and all their friends. They liked to be outside in the sunshine, which was very healthy. Even more importantly, when they were outside, they would sometimes throw sticks and balls, or drop good snacks. It was Oliver's job to make sure that the nuisances, like the squirrels and the magpies, were kept away.

And then there was the fox. Just thinking about the fox made Oliver growl.

He knew they all came back when he was gone. The scents were everywhere. Oliver wished sometimes that he and Emma could just stay here, but then there would be no one to look after the cottage, and the cottage was also important.

So he just had to do the best he could.

Today was very busy. It had been rainy, but now it was just damp, and there were many fresh smells to be investigated and understood, and also many members of the local wildlife to be dealt with. As soon as Oliver had finished chasing a particularly persistent squirrel out from under the roses, he had to deal with a very loud herring gull trying to scavenge scraps from the bins. Oliver did not like gulls. They were big, and mean, and they could sometimes be real trouble. But they were also cowards, and no match for a determined warrior corgi.

Oliver was just giving the retreating bird a last few barks when the breeze freshened. A whole wave of new scents tumbled over him, including one that was extremely familiar.

Oliver whisked around. The Cream Tangerine was sitting on top of the fence.

Oliver trotted over and barked, “What are you doing up there?”

“Why don’t you come up and find out?” She swished her tail cheekily.

“Cats,” muttered Oliver. He turned and started snuffling under the bush. There’d been another squirrel under there. Emma said they were like buses, always traveling in flocks. Or was that sheep? Oliver liked sheep. There were plenty around Trevena. Emma wouldn’t let him organize them though. She said that was a “specialty job,” but she couldn’t quite explain . . .

The cat jumped down and paced beside him.

“Where are you going?” she asked.

“Why don’t you keep up and find out?” Oliver ducked

under the nearest bush. The cat, however, did not take the hint. She just plopped down onto the grass, and for good measure rolled over on her back.

"I'm bored," she announced.

"You're always bored." Oliver stuck his nose out from under the bush and sneezed. The cat sat up and rubbed her whiskers with her forepaw.

"I want to go home," she whined.

Oliver felt a growl rising. "Why don't you?"

"Because my humans are being shouty. *Again.* I hate it when they're shouty."

"That is bad," he agreed. Normally, Oliver did not think much of cats. There were some good ones. All right, there were some that could be mostly reasonable and not too rude. But he did know how hard it was when your human was upset. Before he and Emma came to Trevena, she'd been upset a lot. Sometimes she'd cried late at night. He remembered how sad that had made him. Nobody should be that sad. Even a cat. And her humans really had been shouty this morning. He'd seen it for himself.

Cream Tangerine sat up. "And they haven't fed me in days!"

"That's not true."

"It is." She swished her tail emphatically. *"Days."*

Cats, Oliver knew, could have much different ideas about time than other animals, and most humans as well. Tangerine certainly seemed well groomed, and didn't smell like she was in actual distress. He decided that this was one of those situations.

Oliver scratched his chin. "Why are they so shouty? Are they always shouty?"

"No, not always. Only sometimes. But not like now. Now is different."

"Why?"

The cat stretched out her back, lifting her bum high into the air. "I don't know." She paused, as if thinking it over. "Why don't you tell me? You and your human are always getting into things. My humans say so."

Oliver huffed indignantly. "We do not get into things. We help keep things tidy and organized."

The cat yawned. "Is that what you call it?"

Oliver felt a prickling run along his hackles. He knew the cat was trying to get him upset. He shook himself to settle his instincts back down, but it only partly worked.

"If your humans need help, Emma will help them." It took a lot of effort, but he made himself turn around and trot away. "She always helps her friends."

I need to look for squirrels, he told himself firmly. *They always come back. And there's something new under the hydrangeas . . .*

But the cat was not ready to leave him alone. She bounded up behind him.

"I bet you're just saying that because you can't do it."

"Do what?" Oliver shoved his muzzle under the hydrangeas. *That is definitely new . . .*

"Find out what's wrong," drawled the cat. "You can't and your human can't."

Oliver backed out and faced Tangerine. She blinked at him, and yawned. He felt his neck bristle. The cat started washing her paws, without giving any sign of caring.

"Emma can do anything," Oliver barked.

The cat shrugged, a long ripple that went all the way down her body. "So you say."

"She can!"

The Tangerine stretched her paws forward, spreading out all her toes, and all her claws. "Then let's see her do it. Let's see her find out what's wrong. Then you can tell me. I'll probably even believe you."

Oliver felt his mouth draw back to show his teeth, but he stopped himself. Something was wrong with Tangerine. He could tell. He could almost smell it. He circled the cat, who drew her paws back and started cleaning between her toes.

"You're making it up," he said finally. "You're just bored and you want to make me mad."

Oliver walked away, head and ears high. He should get back inside. Emma might need him.

"No, wait! I mean it!" The cat scampered to catch up. "Something is wrong! Somebody's upset them."

"You're a cat." Oliver lifted his muzzle. "You don't care."

The cat hissed, loud and angry. "Nobody upsets my humans! That's *my* job. They're mine!"

Oliver cringed backwards. He couldn't help it. Tangerine was a big cat, and very fast, he knew. He'd seen her get angry before, but not like this. Maybe she really was worried about her humans.

He scratched his flank. He didn't want to give in too soon. Cats played all kinds of games, and they liked getting others in trouble. He'd seen it plenty of times.

"If something's wrong, then you find out what it is," he said. "They're your humans."

The cat cringed backwards, tail swishing. "I could, if I wanted to."

"Bet you can't," said Oliver.

"I can!"

"Then let's see you."

"Hmmph! Dogs!" The cat leapt onto the chair, the table and the fence, and was gone.

"Cats," growled Oliver.

But now Oliver was restless. Charles-and-David were good humans, even if they did keep a cat. They were friends, and Emma went to play—well, talk and eat—with them a lot. If they were upset enough that the cat could notice, something must be really wrong.

That made Oliver sad.

12

"WHAT'S WRONG, CORGI-ME-LAD?" EMMA ASKED.

She and Oliver were walking home. Twilight had settled in, and the wind off the sea was picking up. Emma was glad she'd worn her duffle coat. There was probably going to be more rain soon (always a safe bet in Cornwall), and it was already getting chilly. After Raj had finished his tea, Emma had washed up and made sure that everything was ready for tomorrow—the buns were shaped and left to prove overnight, the reservations lists were updated and the latest cake selections had been posted to the website. But when she finally whistled Oliver in from the garden, she couldn't help but notice her normally energetic corgi was unusually subdued.

"Nothing's wrong," mumbled Oliver. "Well. Not really. Emma?" He looked up at her with wide, pleading eyes. "Are cats ever right?"

Emma laughed. "Not a question I'm qualified to answer. Did something happen?"

"No. Yes. Not really."

Emma laughed again. "So, something happened with a cat."

"It was being very much of a cat," muttered Oliver.

"Well, you're the one who told me cats start things." Oliver's troubled relationship with Trevena's feline population was second only to his feud with the fox.

"This cat says there's something wrong with her humans."

"Wow. It must be serious."

"She says she hasn't been fed in days."

"I think a lot of cats feel that way." Emma herself was a dog person, obviously, but she had many friends who were cat people, and they regularly complained about their daily pet drama.

"Which cat is this?" she asked.

"The Cream Tangerine."

"David and Charles's cat says there's something wrong?" *Now, that's a sentence I never knew I'd have to say.*

"Yes, she says they're being really shouty with each other."

Emma was quiet for a minute. "Well, she's right. There's something wrong with them. I noticed when we were there this morning. Some of it is the shock of finding Sonny's body with the Vincent, but I think there's something more."

"You'll figure it out, won't you?" Oliver wagged his bum. "The cat says you never will."

I'm being dismissed by a cat. Emma shook her head. *Well, I suppose that's normal.* "Did Tangerine say anything helpful?"

"Cats don't do that," Oliver reminded her seriously.

Emma chuckled. "Well, you tell Tangerine that if she wants to help her humans, she needs to try."

Oliver seemed to consider this for a moment. "That will be hard."

You're probably right. "Don't let the cats get you down, Oliver. We'll figure this all out." She sighed. "At least I hope we will. Now," she added briskly, "we need to get something for our tea."

Oliver's ears and tail instantly perked up. "Tea is always a good idea."

Naturally, Emma agreed with this.

Like a lot of British villages, Trevena had a cooperative store that carried meat and produce from the surrounding farms as well as other locally made goods like clothing, soaps and handicrafts. Emma had a lovely knit cap she'd bought at the Trevena stores, and she had become passionately fond of the bread baked from flour ground at the renovated windmill over in Devon.

Emma pushed open the door. A string of sleigh bells jingled cheerfully.

"Hullo, Emma!" called the plump, white-haired woman behind the counter.

"Hullo, Jean. All right?"

It was a dangerous question, and Emma knew it when she asked. Jean instantly launched into her latest list of triumphs (mostly involving her kids, and their kids), her aches and pains and her complaints about her fellow co-op board members.

Jean had barely drawn breath when Emma heard a familiar voice from over by the dairy case.

"All right, I think that's everything."

It was Pippa Marsh. Oliver barked and bounded over to say hello. Somewhat to Emma's surprise, Pippa wasn't on her own. She was pushing a wheelchair occupied by a wrinkled, mostly bald, old man in a red cardigan. He held the shopping basket on his knees with one hand. The other clutched an aluminum cane.

"Jean, you've got a dog loose in here," growled the man. "Get off!" He waved his cane.

Emma hurried over. "Hullo, Pippa. Come on, Oliver. Let everybody have their space."

"I was just saying hello to Pippa," mumbled Oliver, but he did back away closer to Emma.

"Hullo, Emma," said Pippa. "Have you met my granddad?"

"Not yet." Emma smiled. The old man glowered at her. Despite his dark expression and the years between them, she could see the resemblance to Pippa in the shape of his face and his sharp blue eyes.

"Emma, this is Billy Marsh," said Pippa, speaking up a

little the way people do when they're used to talking to someone hard of hearing. "Granddad, this is Emma. She runs the new tea shop over at the King's Rest."

"Oh, yeah." Billy's eyes narrowed suspiciously. "Can't stand cream teas. All those fussy, frothy little cakes and things. What's wrong with sardines on toast and a jam roly-poly, eh?"

Pippa pulled a face. Billy rolled his eyes. "Oh, what? It's the truth. If I can't tell the truth at my age, when do I get to start?"

"Yeah, yeah," said Pippa. "You just like playing the crotchety old man."

Billy shrugged. "Gotta have some kind of fun. Not like I get to chase the girls anymore, do I?" He tapped his shoe with the tip of his cane.

"Don't mind him, he's hopeless," said Pippa. "Come on, Granddad, we need to get all this stuff home, or we'll be having tea at midnight."

"If you'd learn to cook properly . . ."

"If you'd ever learned to cook properly you wouldn't have to complain about my cooking," said Pippa easily. Obviously they'd had this exchange before. "We're still going to have that talk, right, Emma?"

"Right," Emma agreed. She did very much want to talk to Pippa. She wanted to talk about whatever piece of paper Oliver had seen her take from the tunnel, and whether that "criminal syndicate" she'd alluded to in her article was the same as the smuggling ring that David and Charles had talked about.

"Great, good," said Pippa. "Nice to see you, Emma. We'd better get on, yeah?"

While Pippa and her granddad chatted with Jean and Billy complained about prices, quality and too much fancy stuff, Emma roamed around the various displays. She claimed a loaf of her favorite bread, and some lovely cheddar cheese, and a nice bit of country bacon. She'd just picked the last tomatoes from her garden, and she was thinking thoughts of a toasted sandwich for dinner, maybe accompanied by one (or more) of the leftover cupcakes she hadn't managed to foist off on Genny or Brian. Of course, health was important, as Oliver would remind her, so she added a couple of Bromley apples, which would be fabulous in a green salad.

The shop bells jingled, and everyone automatically looked toward the door, including Oliver. The corgi barked cheerfully as Sam and Liza walked in.

"Well, well," murmured Billy. "Speak of the devil."

"Leave it, Granddad," muttered Pippa. "We weren't speaking of anybody, and you know it."

"What? I'm not doing anything. Hello!" Billy waved his cane. "Sam. Liza. All right?"

Sam flushed a little. Liza had bent over to scratch Oliver behind the ears. Now, she straightened up, and laid a hand on her husband's arm.

"Here, get me over there, Pippa," said Billy. A sly light sparked in his faded blue eyes. "Heard you lot finally found poor old Sonny last night."

"Grandad, come on, we're done here." Pippa didn't make any move to push him closer. "You were the one who said you were starving . . ."

"Just chatting with the neighbors, Pip. Just being friendly." Billy grinned up at Sam. "All friends here, aren't we?"

"Lay off, Billy," said Sam. "It's been a rough couple of days, yeah?"

Billy pursed his lips and nodded sagely. "I'm sure it has. I'm sure it has. How about you, Liza. Bearing up?"

"We'll be fine," said Liza stiffly. "Now, if you'll excuse us. The kids are stopping in for tea tonight and we need to get the shopping—"

"Quite the character, was our Sonny," said Billy. "Very fond of him you were, I believe, Liza."

Liza's mouth snapped shut. Hard.

"Granddad," groaned Pippa.

"Lay off, Billy," said Sam.

Billy did not appear to have heard either of them. "Or at

least, he was very fond of you. And why not? Best-looking girl in Trevena back then, as I'm sure Sam agrees." His grin broadened, and he winked. "Would've had a go myself, if I'd been a younger man."

Liza looked away. Oliver bonked her with his nose, trying to get her attention. But Liza just nudged him back.

"Come on, Oliver." Emma patted her leg. "Good boy."

"Is the wheelie man a friend, Emma?" muttered Oliver. "He's not acting like a friend."

Emma certainly agreed. So, apparently, did Pippa.

"All right, Granddad, that's enough." Pippa collected her full carrier bag off the counter and hung it on the wheelchair handle. "I'm taking you home."

She started pushing the chair towards the exit. Emma got there first and held the door for her. But Billy wasn't done yet. He twisted around. "I reckon you were kind of relieved when Sonny disappeared, eh, Sam? I know your old dad was. After all that work he put in to cover his own tracks—"

"Shut it!" snapped Sam. "Before I forget you're nothing but an old—"

"Old what?" Billy grabbed the chair's wheel to keep Pippa from pushing him out of range. "What am I? Cos I'll tell you, I'm still man enough to give you a good kick in the—"

"Sam, please," said Liza. "Let's just . . . help me sort out what we need for tea." She put a hand over his.

But Sam was still staring at Billy, and Billy was still grinning. It was not a nice expression. The red flush on Sam's neck deepened.

"You know, Sam," said Emma quickly, "I was just looking at my inventory today, and I'm going to need an extra liter of cider this week for the cakes. Is that going to be a problem?"

This was not true, but it did break the stare-down between the two men.

"Uh, no, no problem at all." Sam rubbed the back of his

neck. "Yeah, Liza. Tea. Right. What do you think about a nice bit of lamb?"

"You all go on. Just ignore me." Billy chuckled. "Not going to change a damn thing that happened."

He laughed. He was still laughing as a grim, blushing Pippa pushed him through the door.

"I hope old Mr. Marsh didn't worry you," said Jean as Emma set her loaded basket on the counter. Her eyes flicked toward the chiller where Sam and Liza stood huddled together.

"Oh, no." *Well, actually, yes.* "I just didn't know Pippa had a grandfather in town."

"Oh, the Marshes have been here ages. At least they were. Billy's the last one left, except for Pippa, of course." Jean paused in putting Emma's items in her tote bag. "I know everybody thinks she's a nuisance, but she's really done a good thing, looking after him, especially after his stroke."

"She takes care of him?" Emma remembered Genny saying something about her granddad, but she hadn't made the connection with Pippa being her grandfather's caretaker.

"She does, and all on her own, too," said Jean. "Moved back here, what, all of five years ago now? Dropped out of uni, so I heard, but she's turned herself around since then, what with working for the news and taking care of Billy."

Emma glanced toward the door. Oliver was sniffing around the threshold, looking for new information to help him understand what was happening.

"What about the rest of the family?" said Emma. "Surely they're helping out some?" When Emma's mother got sick, they had cousins coming in from all corners to help with the housekeeping and medical appointments.

"Oh, no." Jean shook her head in a way that managed to be both sad and conspiratorial. "None of them's had anything to do with Billy for years. Leastways not since he got out of prison."

Prison. The word dropped like a stone. Emma found herself staring at Jean. Jean nodded slowly and archly.

"Billy was in prison?" Emma barely remembered to keep her voice down. "For what?"

"Smuggling." Jean leaned in. "And they always did say it was Sam's father who turned him in."

13

THE BACON AND TOMATO SANDWICHES WERE DELICIOUS. Emma turned out all the lights and ate her sandwich by candlelight, watching out the windows as the sheets of rain fell over the green hills and the distant village. Beside her, Oliver happily wolfed down his kibble, plus the extra bacon and tomato.

But as much as she tried, Emma couldn't quite set aside what Jean had told her about Billy Marsh and the Greenlaws. Was she right? Had Sam's father really grassed on Billy Marsh about his smuggling activities? There was certainly some kind of bad blood between them all. If Billy believed Sam's father sent him to prison, that would explain it.

She remembered what Raj had said over the last of his tea.

You know how it goes in a village. Something out-of-the-way happens and everybody gets to talking . . . Old hurts and old suspicions get brought out for a really good airing. Makes for the kind of tension between neighbors that nobody really needs.

It was starting to look like Raj was right.

Idly, Emma found herself wondering if Billy Marsh had

known Reggie Tapp back in the day, and which side Reggie had taken in the Marsh/Greenlaw spat. If he'd sided with Billy, that might explain Liza treating Reggie so coolly when he came to the pub.

Emma sighed. *Probably not going to turn out to be anything that simple.*

Oliver came over and stretch up to put his paws on her knee. Emma smiled and rubbed his ears. She also pulled a crumbled leaf out from under his collar.

And that's another thing.

Emma did have grand plans for continuing her lovely, quiet evening with videos and lounging. However, all that would have to wait until after she'd dealt with the important business of corgi care. After a hard day of squirrel patrol in the damp garden, Oliver's fluffy self needed a good combing, not to mention paw pad inspection and nail trimming. Then, of course, there was the urgent matter of tooth/doggy-breath care.

Fortunately, Oliver loved being groomed. As soon as Emma got out the basket of brushes and clippers and the towels, he immediately started trying to scrabble up onto a chair so he could get onto the table.

What he ended up doing was tipping the chair over with a bang.

"Oops." Oliver hung his head. "Sorry, Emma."

Emma laughed and hoisted him onto the towel-covered table.

Teeth cleaned, ears checked, pads checked, nails checked, all followed by some serious brushing, and Oliver looked like a brand-new corgi.

"Now what, Emma?" Oliver wagged his freshly fluffed bum. "Will there be treats? You did say there would be treats. Well, you should have said it. Maybe you forgot?"

"Yes, I'm sure I did." Emma put him back down on the floor, where he immediately rolled over for a belly rub. "Because there should be treats, for the both of us, and then I've got that new cookbook . . ."

That was when the landline rang.

"Or not." Emma sighed and went to pick up the phone. "Hello?"

"Hullo, Emma?" It was Pippa Marsh.

"Oh, hullo, Pippa. All right?" Oliver heard Pippa's name and scrambled back onto all fours.

"Yeah, thanks. Do you have time for that talk?" Pippa asked. "Granddad's watching telly, so I've finally got a few minutes to myself."

"Yeah, I suppose." Emma pulled out one of the kitchen chairs and sat down. Oliver stretched himself out at full length on the floor and put his chin on his paws, giving her a look that told her he was going to be very, very patient. "I don't really know what I can help you with though. I didn't see anything more than anybody else did." *And I'm not the one who got a chance to go back for a second look.*

"Oh, don't worry. This is all background stuff. Boss wants to do a whole series on 'The Discovery Under The Roundhead.'" Emma could hear the capital letters of the headline. "So I've got to come up with, well, whatever I can."

"I see."

"Emma, ask her about the tunnel!" yipped Oliver. "Tell her I saw her take the paper bit!"

Emma scratched his ears to let him know she heard.

"So." There was a rustling noise on the other end of the line. Emma pictured Pippa leaning forwards and planting her elbows on her knees. "What're you thinking?"

"About what?"

Pippa snorted. "About what? About Sonny Greenlaw's murder!"

"First of all, we don't know it was murder, and second, I'm not thinking anything." *Much.*

"Oh, pull the other one. You've only been plying Raj Patel with tea and cake, not to mention going around talking with everybody involved in the case."

Villages. Emma pinched the bridge of her nose. "I've been checking in with my friends," she said. "Besides, Raj says there isn't likely to be a case." As soon as the words slipped out, Emma bit her tongue.

"Really?" said Pippa. "You're sure?" Emma heard a sound suspiciously like scribbling.

"Well, I mean, he didn't say anything had definitely been decided," she added hastily. "Somebody could still change their mind, but it's a question of resources, or so I've heard," she added, and winced, because it sounded so very limp.

"Right, sure," mumbled Pippa. "And have any of your friends whom you've just been checking in with said anything about Sonny's past? Or had any ideas about how he and the Vincent got into that tunnel?"

Suddenly irritated, Emma decided to turn the tables. "Have you asked your granddad about it? In the stores, he was talking like he knew a few things."

Pippa was quiet for a long time. When she spoke, her tone was low and urgent. "What did Jean tell you about my granddad?"

Emma considered denying it was Jean, but then decided it wouldn't do any good. "That he went to prison for smuggling." She paused, and then added, "Sonny was supposed to be involved with smuggling too."

"Yeah," said Pippa reluctantly. "Yeah, I've heard that."

"And some people think Sam's dad turned Billy in."

"Yeah," agreed Pippa. "And Granddad was always one of them."

Emma felt her eyebrows arch. "Was?"

"Yeah. It seems that Sonny's bones turning up like they did has got Granddad rethinking the old days."

"How so?"

But Pippa didn't answer. At least not directly. "Listen, Emma, I know it sounded bad today. But you've got to understand about Granddad. He's not adjusting real well to his disability. He looks for ways to feel like he's still—I don't know—a force to be reckoned with. Some days the way he does that is to try to get a rise out of people. That's part of why I want to get this cleared up," she added softly. "Before Granddad says or does something he can't take back."

Now it was Emma's turn to be quiet. Her parents, and her grandparents, had always been a source of strength and comfort to her. If Nana Phyllis had been a little outrageous sometimes, she'd always been there for her family when they needed her. Emma couldn't imagine what it was like having to take care of the person who had always taken care of you.

"Is your editor really looking for a series of background articles?" she asked.

"Yes, as a matter of fact he is, and I had to fight to get the job," said Pippa. "We've got maybe three people on the *Coast News,* and this is all anybody wants to talk about. I had to swear up and down I could be objective, and in the end he only gave in because I got the original scoop." Her voice hardened. "But it's obvious what people are going to think, isn't it? And there's no way I was letting anybody dig up Granddad's past without considering any of the other possibilities."

"What kind of possibilities?" asked Emma, although she had the very uncomfortable feeling she knew.

"You're not going to like it."

"Well, now you've got to tell me." Emma tried to make a joke of it, but the words fell flat.

She heard some rustling on the other end of the line. "Well, I called up a friend who works in the Scotland Yard archives. They did some digging for me and found a report of a Vincent Black Lightning that was stolen in Knightsbridge in nineteen seventy-two."

Emma said nothing.

"It was never recovered," Pippa went on. "Now, I'm not saying that David or Charles had anything to do with that theft, but it's a pretty big coincidence, isn't it?"

"So what are you saying?" said Emma, much more curtly than she meant to.

"I'm just letting you know what I've found out, that's

all," said Pippa. "And if I found it out, PC Raj might too, and that's not going to do the Kemps any good."

No, it isn't. Emma felt the back of her neck prickle. And it could explain why the Kemps never reported the Vincent stolen. They couldn't very well report a piece of stolen property when they'd already stolen it first.

And now that possibly stolen property had been found with a dead body.

Emma grit her teeth. She reminded herself that Pippa was frightened. She wanted attention distracted from her granddad's past.

"I have a question for you."

"Okay," answered Pippa warily.

"What did you find in the tunnel under the Roundhead when you were down there?"

Emma expected Pippa to deny that she'd actually gone into the tunnel, or at least to bluster a little. Instead, Pippa just sighed. "I'm not sure. I mean, I know what it is, but I'm not sure what it means."

"You mean you don't want to say."

There was more rustling. Emma imagined Pippa shrugging. "Okay, I don't want to say. Not before I'm sure. It might be absolutely nothing. I've got to do some more research first."

She paused, and when she spoke again, her whole tone had changed. "Look, Emma, we both want to find out what really happened to Sonny Greenlaw. Why can't we work together?"

"The last time I tried to help out a journalist, it didn't go well." In fact, it had ended with an additional death and a friend almost getting framed for the murder.

"Yeah. I heard about that," said Pippa. "But look at it this way—you know me. It's not like I'm some mysterious stranger who arrived on a moonless night." Her voice changed, and Emma pictured her holding the phone closer to her mouth. "Listen," she said softly. "This is important, and not just because it's a story. This could rake up some serious trouble, and it's going to be better for everybody if it can get laid to rest before . . ."

"Before what?"

"Before the past comes back to bite, and not just my granddad."

"No biting," Oliver grumbled sleepily.

Emma didn't know what to say. No one could blame Pippa for wanting to help her family, but how far was she willing to go? And who was she willing to get into trouble to keep Billy out of it?

Emma heard a man's voice shouting in the background. She couldn't understand the words, but the voice sounded like Billy's.

"Yeah, okay, Granddad!" called Pippa. "I've got to go, Emma. Listen, whatever happens, no hard feelings, yeah?" Billy was shouting again. "I'll be right there!" Pippa called, then she said into the phone, "I gotta go. We'll talk later, yeah? Bye."

Emma rang off and stared at the phone for a while.

Whatever happens, no hard feelings, Pippa had said.

Emma found she did not like the sound of that at all.

14

WEDNESDAY MORNING DAWNED, CHILLY AND RAINWASHED. A low mist hung over the hills and crept into Trevena's streets as Emma and Oliver headed down to work. By the time they reached the King's Rest, Oliver was covered in damp, and he shook himself hard, scattering drops everywhere, including all over Emma.

"Oi!"

"Sorry, Emma!" yipped Oliver.

Angelique just laughed at them both and tossed Emma the towel they kept for mornings like this.

Wednesdays were fairly quiet at the shop, even during the summer. Now that it was autumn, Emma had closed down the formal tea service on Wednesdays and Sundays and just kept the takeaway counter open until one o'clock. She also cut back on her daily bakes and gave Becca and Bella the morning off.

But that didn't mean she intended to rest on her laurels. Emma planned to use the extra time to experiment with new ideas. Last month, she'd let it be known among her regulars that she'd be baking some classic rum-soaked fruitcakes for Christmas and New Year's. Now she had a subscription list for the cakes.

Emma was just ducking into the kitchen for the fresh tray of scones she'd left cooling on the counter when the landline rang. Angelique, who was in the pantry working on the daily inventory, made it to the phone first.

"King's Rest," she said, and then listened for a minute. Emma, satisfied the scones were ready, picked up the tray, but Angelique put up her hand. "It's for you." She held out the receiver.

Emma set the scones down, wiped her hands on her apron and took the receiver. "Hello?"

"Hullo, darlin'!" boomed the man's voice on the other end. "This is Reggie Tapp, over at the Donkey's Win. We met at the Roundhead the other night. You remember."

Emma remembered. She also frowned. "Yes, of course. What can I do for you, Mr. Tapp?"

Angelique heard the name, and her brows arched sharply.

"Now, now, none of that. It's Reggie to you." Reggie chuckled. Heartily, of course. "And it's more like what can I do for you." Emma rolled her eyes at the utter predictability of this declaration.

"I've got a proposal I'd like to discuss," Reggie went on. "Say, tonight? What time do you close up shop there?"

"Erm. I'm usually finished around six."

"What's he want?" Angelique mouthed. Emma opened and closed her fingers a few times, making a "chitchat" gesture.

"Super," said Reggie. "Why don't you come by the Win after that? We'll have dinner and I'll lay it all out for you."

What on earth could Reggie Tapp want with me? Emma's curiosity burned, but at the same time warning bells were going off in the back of her mind. She distrusted the kind of flamboyant confidence Reggie exuded. It was usually a cover for something.

Unfortunately, to find out exactly what he was covering up, she had to go talk to him.

"All right," she said. "As long as you don't mind my bringing my dog."

"Why would I mind? See you tonight, then."

Emma agreed he would and hung the phone up.

"What was that about?" asked Angelique.

"Honestly, I have no idea." Emma couldn't seem to stop staring at the phone. "Reggie Tapp wants to talk."

"Does he now?" Angelique's tone was heavy with scorn. "You be careful. That man could talk the fangs off of a snake."

"You know him, then?"

"I've had doings with him, let's say. Fancies himself the big man, although I can't imagine why. Always talks about his deals and his plans. He tried to convince me to sell the King's Rest once."

"He did?"

"Oh yes. Maybe ten years ago. We were just getting started, and, it wasn't going so well just then. Reggie comes around all smiles and offers to 'help me out.'" Angelique made the air quotes. "I hate to admit this, but I almost took the offer."

"What stopped you?" asked Emma.

"Daniel, and the kids. And me-myself. I wanted to build something for myself, and for my family. Not just be working for someone else. I'd had enough of that."

Which led to another question. "Did he ever try to buy the Roundhead?"

Angelique snorted. "Only about a hundred times. You know how it goes in hospitality. There's good years and there's bad years, and whenever things are looking particularly bad, there's Reggie Tapp smiling and laughing and offering to help out."

Emma remembered his hearty congratulations and open smile the night of the Greenlaws' party.

Which reminded her of something else. "I never asked, did you get over to see Sam and Liza yesterday?"

"Just for a minute," said Angelique. "They were quite busy, between fielding calls from the media and trying to work out what to do about—well, Sonny's bones, once they're released."

"How did they seem to you?"

"Overwhelmed," said Angelique. "It's a lot to take in, and what they'd really like is some time and some privacy, which they're not going to get for awhile."

"Yeah, I'd be upset too." She paused. "I don't suppose Reggie's been over to pester them?"

"If he has, they didn't mention it to me. Why?"

"Just wondering," said Emma. "He seems determined to push his way into things. And, well, I ran into Sam and Liza at the stores last night. Billy and Pippa were there too."

"Ah," said Angelique. "I'm sure old Billy had a few things to say."

"Yeah. He did. Did you know he blames Sam's dad for sending him to prison?"

"I think I'd heard that, but I admit I hadn't thought about it much until—well, yesterday, I suppose. But what would that have to do with Reggie?"

"Maybe nothing," said Emma. "Men like Reggie can't resist trying to make themselves the center of attention. If he was going around to pester Charles and David, I thought he might have done the same to Sam and Liza."

"What was he doing bothering those two?"

"He wanted to see if they'd sell him the Vincent, and when Charles said he wouldn't, he apparently accused Charles of having killed Sonny Greenlaw."

"That sounds like Reggie," said Angelique. "It's all smiles and handshakes, until he's not getting what he wants. Then he pulls out the knives."

Emma shuddered. "I don't know when I've ever seen Charles so angry. It was—" Emma didn't let herself finish that, because the truth was, it had been a little frightening. "Disconcerting," she said instead.

Before Angelique could say anything, a familiar voice shouted from the great room.

"Oi! Service!"

Startled, both Emma and Angelique laughed. "Be right there, Genny!" Emma called. She grabbed her tray of scones and pushed through the doors.

Genny stood at the takeaway counter. There was a lot of prep work to be done even in a small chip shop, so she was one of the few people in Trevena who got up even earlier than Emma. Since Reed's Tea & Cakes had opened, she'd gotten in the habit of stopping by to pick up her regular order of biscuits just before opening time. The pickup was usually accompanied by a Chelsea bun and a quick chat.

Oliver zoomed straight up to Genny, barking, wagging and giving her ankles a damp and energetic investigation.

"All right, all right," Genny laughed as she rubbed Oliver's ears. "I'm glad to see you too." She straightened up. "We should get the boys together for a play date." By "the boys," Genny meant Oliver and her Irish setter, Rufus.

"Sounds like a great idea." Emma set down her scone tray. "I've got your order." Emma brought out a paper carrier bag from behind the counter. Inside were two boxes of fresh-baked biscuits—one basic ginger and one jam-and-cream sandwich.

"Ta." Genny set the bag on the table behind her, out of corgi range. Oliver grumbled and flopped down full length to let the world know it had disappointed him severely.

"Cuppa to go?" asked Emma.

"That'd be nice," said Genny. "How have you been?"

Emma shrugged as she pulled down the canister of Genny's favorite oolong tea. "It's been a strange couple of days, hasn't it?"

"Hullo, Genny." Angelique came out from the kitchen carrying a bulky laundry bag. "Come for your biscuits?"

"That, and I'm hiding from Pippa Marsh."

"Is she out and about already?" Angelique set the laundry by the door. "I thought reporters were all night owls."

"She seems determined to defy stereotype," said Genny. "She was on my doorstep at the stroke of nine, and when she left, she was making a beeline for Vintage Style. I hope she doesn't plan to drag the whole village into this."

"Hmm." Emma felt her mouth stretch into a straight, hard line.

Genny narrowed her eyes at Emma. "What?"

"What what?" asked Emma as she fitted the cup's lid in place. "And don't say I'm making that face."

Genny looked at Angelique.

"Was she making that face?"

"She most certainly was," said Angelique. "It's a good thing she doesn't play poker."

Emma threw up her hands. "I give up. Pippa called me last night."

"What did she want?" Before Emma could answer, Genny made a pair of air quotes. "'Background'?"

"That's what she said at first, but then she said she wants to join forces to find out what really happened to Sonny Greenlaw." Emma frowned. "She also said she thinks David and Charles stole the Vincent."

"Why would they steal their own motorcycle?" asked Angelique.

"She thinks they stole it in London, before they came here."

"Oh," said Angelique, deflated.

"Yeah. Oh," agreed Emma.

Genny lifted the lid on her cup and checked the color of the tea inside. "Why was she telling you?"

"She probably thinks that if I'm worried that my friends could be in trouble, I'll be more likely to try to help her find out what really happened to Sonny."

"Well, she's right, isn't she?" said Angelique.

"Yeah." Emma sighed and folded her arms. "That's the problem."

Genny slurped her hot tea carefully. "So's the fact that David and Charles might have stolen that motorcycle." She pressed the lid back down. "I mean, if the police found that out, it wouldn't exactly make them look good, would it?"

"Well, Raj doesn't think we'll have to worry about the police," said Emma. "He thinks they're going to let it all slide."

Genny shook her head. "That'd be a mistake."

"I agree," said Angelique.

"So does Raj," said Emma. "But there's not much he can do about it."

"So what are you doing?" asked Genny. "Or should I say, what are we doing?"

"I don't know." Emma shook her head. "My instincts say stay out of it, but then I was at the shops yesterday and saw Billy Marsh and Sam just about get into a regular old donnybrook. Billy Marsh was implying there used to be something between Liza and Sonny, and he wasn't being very nice about it."

"Billy Marsh hasn't been very nice about anything since he got out of short trousers," muttered Genny.

"And he hinted that Sam's dad was involved in some kind of a cover-up."

"Oh, Sam wouldn't have liked that," said Angelique. "He's very protective of his family, all of them."

"And Jean at the shops said Billy Marsh had been to prison for smuggling, and that Sam's dad was the one who turned him in."

Genny pursed her lips in a silent whistle. "Wow. That could lead to a bit of bad feeling."

It also led to all sorts of questions, none of which Emma was going to have a chance to ask. The door from the car park opened, and Liza Greenlaw walked in.

15

LIZA TURNED IN THE B AND B'S DOORWAY SO SHE COULD shake the rain off her umbrella. Emma felt herself stare, startled. Oliver, on the other hand, yipped and scampered up to her, delighted to see another friend.

"Hullo, Emma." Liza tucked her umbrella into the stand Angelique kept by the door. She also paused to give Oliver a pat. "All right?" she asked as she straightened up.

"Erm, yeah. Good. Right," said Emma smoothly.

Oliver barked. It sounded suspiciously like a laugh.

"Hullo, Liza," said Genny, just a shade too brightly. "Coming down again, is it?"

Liza didn't answer immediately. Instead, she let her sharp gaze travel from Genny to Emma to Angelique.

"Now why do I get the feeling I've just interrupted something?" she asked.

Angelique and Genny both shot accusing glances at Emma.

"Oh, no." Emma put up both hands. "You do not get to blame this on my face."

Liza folded her arms. "Well, come on then, girls. Out with it."

It was Genny who spoke first. "We're nicked," she said.

"We were gossiping, and it was about what happened the other night, and we shouldn't have been and I'm sorry."

Liza was silent for a minute, then waved one broad hand. "It's all right. I can't really blame you, or anybody else, I suppose. I'd be talking too, if it wasn't—well, if it wasn't our cellar."

"Well, now that you're here, you should sit down," said Emma. "Have a cuppa."

Liza smiled. "Usually I'm the one pushing drinks on the public. And I'd love to, but I don't have the time. Sam's back at the pub. We're being allowed to reopen today, and we've got to take stock and all. So give us a couple of the currant buns to go, would you? And two of the Chelsea buns too. And a couple of large teas, yeah?"

"Coming right up." Emma started folding a small white bakery box to hold the buns and a tray with drinks carrier to carry the tea.

"How's Sam's family taking the news?" asked Angelique.

"Well, there's not a lot left who knew Sonny," said Liza. "His parents are long gone, but he's got a sister up in Liverpool. We thought she'd want to know we'd found him." Liza's face tightened.

"And did she?" asked Emma.

"No." Liza's face was grim. "Gave poor Sam an earful, in fact. All about how she wasn't surprised and it was probably Sonny's own fault and he'd broke their mum's heart and . . . well, more of the kind." She shrugged again. "Not that I can blame her, really. Sonny was always in trouble, one way or another, and the family kept having to get him out."

"So it is Sonny?" Emma reached into the takeaway case for the Chelsea buns. "They're sure about that?"

"Sure as can be. Raj told us the dentist who did Sonny's teeth is retired, but his daughter took over his practice and kept her father's old records."

"I'm so sorry," said Genny.

"Yeah," agreed Liza. "It's not good, but it's better to know, isn't it?"

Emma privately thought that Liza sounded like she was trying too hard to convince herself.

"I'm glad they're letting you open in the meantime," said Angelique. "Daniel and I were sure it would be a few more days at least."

"Well, we're still not allowed to use the cellar," Liza told her. "But that's mostly health and safety concerns. We will need to have somebody in to take a good look at the tunnel and the cave-in, but we knew we were going to have to do something like that."

"Liza, I don't mean to be ghoulish—" began Genny.

"I'm sure you don't," replied Liza, her tone deliberately bland. Genny blushed, but she also forged ahead.

"Do they know what happened? I mean, how he died?"

"As a matter of fact, they do. His skull was smashed in—pretty badly, as it happens."

"How awful," murmured Angelique. "I may be naive, but I was hoping for some kind of accident."

"Well, it's not entirely out of the question," said Liza. "Sonny could have been in the tunnel when it collapsed and gotten hit by some falling stones. That's what the pathologist suggested."

"Do you believe that?" asked Genny.

"No," admitted Liza. "I'd like to, but I don't."

"How's Sam doing?" asked Emma as she filled the cups with hot water.

Liza shook her head. "He wants to put a good face on it, but that's mainly for the kids, isn't it? He keeps telling them it'll all blow over and that the police aren't going to waste any time on a forty-year-old case."

"Are the kids worried about that?" asked Emma as she loaded the two currant buns and two Chelsea buns into the bakery box and added a layer of greaseproof paper over top. *Or is Sam?*

Or are you?

"For what it's worth, Raj doesn't think they'll investigate either," said Angelique. "Although it's not for lack of pestering the higher-ups." When she saw they were all looking at her in surprise, she added, "I ran into his mother at Tesco last night. She said he's very disappointed that his governor's dismissing the whole thing. She's worried he's pushing the bosses too hard over it and he might get himself into some hot water."

"But he told me yesterday he doesn't think it's going to just blow over either," put in Emma. "He's really worried there might be trouble."

"Well, Raj." Liza was trying to sound dismissive, but she didn't quite manage it. "This isn't exactly his field of expertise, is it? He's more about traffic tickets and finding lost walkers, and the odd stolen bicycle . . ."

"I don't think you believe that," said Genny gently. "Raj's always been sharp, and he's spent his whole life in Trevena. He knows everybody, and how they all fit together."

"You're right, you're right." Liza watched Emma close the bakery box lid. "And he's right too. Whether there's an official investigation or not, it's not going to just blow over, no matter how many times Sam says it. Especially with Billy Marsh going around shoving his oar in."

"Pippa says he's having a hard time adjusting to his disability, and it's making him angry," said Emma.

Liza snorted, and Angelique nodded in agreement. So did Genny. "Well, that's kind of his granddaughter to say, but I can tell you for a fact Billy never was a nice man. And he was into plenty of dodgy stuff back in the day—everybody knew it."

"I heard he went to prison," said Emma.

"He did, and he deserved it too," said Liza flatly. "And since you heard that much, you probably heard he thinks that Sam's dad was the one who turned him in. Well, he wasn't. Old Walter had no use for Billy, and he blamed Billy for getting Sonny into trouble, but he wouldn't call the revenuers on a neighbor, no matter what he thought personally. Back then, no one would."

"Did Sam tell Raj about that?" Emma asked. "About his father blaming Billy for getting Sonny into trouble?"

"Well, Raj didn't ask, did he?" said Liza. "Hasn't had a chance," she added.

And if there's no investigation, he might not get one. "Is that why Billy was trying to make Sam jealous at the co-op?" she asked. "Because of hard feelings between him and Sam's dad?"

Liza looked from Emma to Genny to Angelique. Emma wasn't sure what she saw, but she clearly steeled herself. "Probably. He wasn't . . . entirely wrong though. Sonny made a play for me, once upon a time." She spoke slowly, as if she was testing out the words. "It didn't mean anything. Sonny made a play for anything in a skirt. Made him feel like a big man."

Even as Liza said this, Emma thought about how she'd talked about Sonny when they'd first found the skeleton. She'd been a little sad, and not just about the fact that the man was dead. There was something else there, Emma was sure of it.

Emma shook open a carrier bag and slid the pastry box inside. "Can I ask you something, Liza?"

Liza glanced at her watch. For a minute, Emma thought she was going to say she had to leave.

"What is it?"

"What was Sonny like?"

The question seemed to startle her. She didn't say anything for a long moment. Oliver, probably sensing her reluctance, stretched up and put his paws on her knee. Liza smiled and rubbed his ears.

"Really, Sonny wasn't too different from the rest of us, back then," she said to Oliver, and to the rest of them. "He was restless. Didn't want to spend his life in a tiny village where everybody knew everything about everybody else. He could be charming." She smiled just a little at some distant memory. "And there were times, a few times anyway, when I got the feeling that if he just had something he really cared about, he'd turn out all right."

"Everybody needs something of their own to work for," said Angelique.

"That's it." Liza shook her head. "Of course, most of the time, I just thought he was a complete wanker."

They all laughed at this.

"Were Sonny and Sam close?" asked Genny.

"No chance to be, really. Sam was all of seventeen when Sonny vanished. Sonny was five or six years older and wasn't really anxious to have a kid hanging about, even if the kid was his cousin, even after old Walter gave him a job and all."

"Sonny worked for Sam's dad?" said Genny. "I didn't know that."

"It didn't last long. Less than a year, I think. Walter hoped it would help settle him down."

"Did it work?" asked Emma, as she pressed the lids down on the cups and loaded them into the drinks tray.

"A bit. He stopped getting into fights quite so much. Kept his head down. Everybody hoped that he was starting to turn around. And then he vanished." The regret in Liza's eyes was soft, but genuine.

Emma found herself wondering if Liza had had more feelings for Sonny than she was ready to admit. She certainly wouldn't be the first teenager to harbor a crush on the local bad boy.

"Anyway, that just proves the point," said Liza. "Walter already had a plan to keep Sonny out of trouble. He didn't turn anybody in, because he didn't have to."

"But someone did," said Emma quietly. "Turn him in. Or at least Billy Marsh thinks they did."

"Well, if someone did, they weren't from around here," said Liza. "You couldn't keep a thing like that secret in a village this size. It would have come out years ago."

"Well," began Genny. "Normally, yes, unless, I mean—"

"What are you on about, Gen?" asked Liza.

"Well, I mean, you have to wonder, since he was involved in the smuggling and all . . . could it have been Sonny?"

16

NO ONE HAD ANY GOOD ANSWER FOR GENNY'S SPECULAtion. But that didn't stop Emma from turning it over in her head for the rest of the day. By the time she closed up the shop, she was almost grateful for her dinner appointment with Reggie Tapp. It would be a welcome distraction.

And if she was careful, she just might be able to find out something that would help her friends.

WHEN EMMA HAD BEEN MAKING UP HER MIND ABOUT whether to open her shop in Trevena, she had decided to scout out the local food and drink scene, however small it might prove to be. The Donkey's Win had been her second stop. It took her all of fifteen minutes to decide that if she did move to the village, she'd be doing her drinking over at the Roundhead.

Not that Emma objected to the modern, or even the trendy. Done with panache and a dash of humor, it could be a lot of fun. What she minded was the tacky, and tacky was what the Donkey's Win had on full display, right inside the door. The taxidermied hindquarters of an actual donkey—hooves, tail and all—hung on the wall next to a framed copy of the lyrics to the faux-folk song "Darcy's Ass," about an improbably drunk donkey who won a major horse race. The donkey's head was over the bar, right between a pair of red deer wearing bowler hats.

It got somewhat better from there, but to Emma, the place gave off an air of trying much too hard. It was wood paneled and was decorated with black-and-white photographs that David and Charles had privately informed her were mostly bought in job lots from local jumble sales. Up by the bar, there were postcard collages that contained the occasional naughty vintage nude. A television played the latest football match, with the sound turned down—not that it could have been heard over the blare of the Europop music. There was an outdoor beer garden as well, with a stage for the occasional live act.

Emma hovered by the unattended hostess stand. Oliver snuffled the floorboards, muttering about what he'd found.

Finally, a mature woman in red and black strode up to them, her face grim. As soon as she saw Emma, however, her expression shifted into a professional smile.

"Can I help you?"

"Um, yes. I'm Emma Reed, I have an appointment with . . ."

"Oh, yes, of course." The woman held out her hand. "How do you do? I'm Marianne Tapp, Reggie's wife."

"Nice to meet you." Emma shook her hand.

Emma thought Marianne Tapp might be about Liza's age, but it was hard to tell. She was a woman who took a lot of care with her appearance. Her hair was dyed a silvery blond, and her pink face was lightly but precisely made up. She wore a cheerful cherry-red tunic top and a heavy gold necklace with matching earrings.

Oliver immediately started investigating around her ankles. Marianne stiffened.

"Soap, polish, tarmac, powder . . ." Oliver sneezed. "She puts on a lot of stuff, Emma."

"How about a table outside?" said Marianne cheerfully. "There's no band tonight."

"That'd be great."

The bar was about half-full. A lot of younger people were eating burgers and chips and drinking cocktails of all kinds and colors. The matching blond bartenders—one young man and one young woman—were both equally pretty, and equally busy.

Marianne took Emma through a pair of French doors into a little back garden set up with metal café tables and chairs. Fairy lights hung in the hedges and tiki torches lined the slatted fence. An ornamental fishpond with an artificial waterfall took up one corner. The tiny stage was dark, and, to Emma's relief, the Europop was much softer out here.

It was a chilly night, and they were the only ones out here. Oliver immediately went into the corgi equivalent of high gear, charging all around the seating area, determined to investigate everything his nose could reach, including the pond.

"There's fish, Emma!" he barked. "Big fish!"

"Here we are." Marianne gestured to one of the little café tables next to the pond. "Can I get you anything?"

"No, I'm fine, thank you." Emma expected her to leave then, but Marianne hesitated. She rubbed one wrist under her gold bracelet, like it itched, or ached. Emma got the distinct feeling she was trying to work up the nerve to ask a question.

"Care to join me, Marianne?" Emma asked.

"Just for a minute," she said, a little too quickly. Emma heard a note of gratitude in her voice, and more than a little tension. She did sit down though, and folded her hands on the table.

Oliver bustled back over to Emma's side and plopped down beside her chair. "Is this going to be one of those long talking times? Will there be snacks? You should come see the fish when you're done. They're a very big, very orange fish."

Emma gave him a quick pat.

"I just wanted to ask how Sam and Liza are doing." Marianne's voice sounded as strained as her manner.

"Well, it's a lot to deal with, isn't it?" Emma answered carefully. "Finding a family member like that."

"Then it's true what everybody's saying. It was Sonny Greenlaw?"

"It certainly seems to be."

Marianne nodded, her face taut. "Do they—do they know what . . . happened?"

"Not really. I understand the skull was broken, so . . ."

"Yes," Marianne murmured. "So."

Marianne stared at her clasped hands. Even in the twinkling fairy lights, Emma could see she'd gone more than a little green.

"I'm sorry," said Emma. "I didn't mean to upset you."

"No, no. It's not your fault. I did ask." Marianne pulled a tissue out of her jacket pocket. She dabbed carefully at her forehead and eyes, so as not to smudge her makeup. "Silly, isn't it? I mean, it barely seems real. It's more like something out of Agatha Christie," Marianne added with a tiny, nervous laugh. "The dead man discovered beside a heap of buried treasure." She paused. "What are they saying about the motorcycle? It was the Vincent, wasn't it? Those . . . David and Charles's Vincent."

"That's the one thing everybody seems sure about."

"They must be delirious to have it back. Reggie seems to think a Black Lightning is worth a lot."

"Brian said the same thing." Emma opened her mouth to ask if Marianne had heard Reggie say he wanted to buy it, but Marianne was already talking again.

"Did they find anything else—with the motorcycle, I mean? Any, well, clues about what Sonny might have been up to?"

"Not much. At least, not that anyone's said yet," Emma added, thinking about Pippa and whatever she'd taken away. "Raj said there was a rucksack with a change of clothes. People said he was talking about leaving town."

Marianne wasn't really listening. She was watching the anemic waterfall trickle down its artificial rocks and between the plastic plants. "I was just wondering if they'd found, I don't know, any photographs or letters or anything like that. I mean, that would really help clear things up, wouldn't it?"

"I imagine it would," Emma agreed. "But if anybody's found anything like that, I haven't heard about it. Raj said they didn't even find a wallet on him." Which sounded very odd when she said it out loud. Emma frowned. Had Sonny been robbed? She hadn't thought about it before, but it was possible. Or maybe someone had taken his ID to try to hide who the body had been. Although in a tiny place like Trevena, that seemed like a forlorn hope.

Marianne shook herself. "Well, whatever happened, it can't really matter to anyone now."

Actually, from the conversations she'd been having over the past couple of days, Emma was coming to the conclusion that Sonny's death, or at least his discovery, did matter, and it mattered to a lot of people.

"Have you lived in Trevena long?" Emma asked.

Marianne smiled. "Oh, I'm a lifer, me. Like Reggie. We met right out of sixth form when he came to work for my dad."

"Your dad ran a pub too?"

"No, Da had a trucking business. Small stuff, strictly local. The pub was Mum's. The Sea and Shell. Just a little place, it was then. Not that there's anything left of it now. Reggie pulled the original down. You see, my parents had neglected the place to the point where it was cheaper just to rebuild rather than to try to repair it."

Emma nodded. She'd heard similar stories from other business owners who found themselves saddled with old, run-down buildings. "Then I imagine your family knew the Greenlaws?"

"Yes, quite well," said Marianne. "Liza and I were friends, you know, at least—well, we were friends." Marianne smiled, but it was that same pleasant, meaningless expression she'd used when she greeted Emma at the hostess station.

"Did you know Sonny?" Emma asked.

"Oh, not really," said Marianne carelessly. "He was a bit older than me, and he . . . well, I'm sure by now you've heard about his reputation."

"Quite the ladies' man, was our Sonny," barked a man's voice.

Reggie Tapp strode up to the table. Oliver scrambled to his feet, ears up and body stiff. Reggie ignored the corgi. He took Marianne's hand and planted a loud kiss on her forehead.

"Oh, Reggie. I didn't see you there." Marianne sounded cheerful, but Emma didn't miss how quickly she pulled her hand out of her husband's.

"No worries, old girl," said Reggie easily. "Look, tell Gwen my guest's here, would you? And maybe get Carla to bring us a couple of drinks?" Reggie smiled down at his wife. Emma felt certain that he meant to appear loving, but from where she sat, he just looked possessive.

A chill ran up Emma's spine. Oliver pressed closer to her. She scratched the back of his head, trying to calm them both. It didn't work.

"What'll you have, Emma?" Reggie asked her.

"Just coffee, thanks." Whatever Reggie had to say, Emma wanted a clear head when she heard it.

"If you insist," said Reggie. "Pint of stout for me, all right?"

Marianne smiled easily at her husband and went off to deliver the orders for food and drinks. Reggie gazed after her, grinning. Emma wondered what was going on in his head. She had a feeling it wasn't very nice.

Slowly, carefully, Oliver tucked his hindquarters so he could sit down. His ears and nose stayed alert, however, and trained towards Reggie.

Emma remembered how Liza had stepped in front of Reggie the other night. She'd been keeping him out of the cellar, but really, she was throwing him out of her pub. She remembered Marianne saying just now that she and Liza had once been friends.

Why had Marianne asked specifically about finding letters with the skeleton? And photographs? Did Marianne know something about Sonny, or about Liza, that she wasn't saying?

Or maybe even about Sam's father, Walter?

A second shiver chased the first up Emma's spine.

Reggie dropped into a chair and leaned back, legs spread. "So, it looks like that turned out to be quite a party I missed the other night."

Emma smiled weakly. If Reggie noticed she didn't answer, it didn't slow him down any.

"It's a shame, really, for a young fella like Sonny to end up that way. But what do you expect? Sonny wasn't one to turn down a drink, or back down from a fight. He was bound to go wrong sooner or later." He shrugged, dismissing the man's life and the fact of his death.

If Emma had had hackles, they would have raised. Oliver looked up at her, worried and protective. She tried to calm herself down, for his sake as much as hers. Once again, it didn't work.

"Everybody says Sonny was involved with some smugglers," she said.

Reggie scratched his chin. "Weeeellll, you might say. Not that it was anything too serious, I mean, not really. There's always somebody out to make a little extra without the Inland Revenue knowing, isn't there? If the lords of creation don't like it, they should change the laws, that's what I say. But, yeah, there were some busted heads and stuff back in the day. Lads being what they are." He touched the side of his nose. "Besides, it's not like he was the only one."

"Really?" Emma leaned forward. Reggie's chest swelled. He was a man who liked to share what he knew. Emma widened her eyes and did her best to look interested—not that it was much of a stretch.

"It was hard times, wasn't it?" Reggie went on. "Fishing

trade was fading fast, the tourism hadn't picked up yet." He paused and a mischievous glint came into his eye. "You really want to know about it, you ask your friends David and Charles."

Emma stiffened. "You're not saying . . ."

Reggie winked. "Now, now, ask me no questions and I'll tell you no lies, eh? But I will say their hands weren't any cleaner than anybody else's back then."

Emma cocked her head toward him. "What about your hands?"

Reggie laughed, loud and hearty. "See, that's what I like! Not afraid to get straight in and mix it up, are you, darlin'? We're going to get on famous, you and me."

Emma decided she didn't need to answer that. Fortunately, Marianne returned just then, carrying a tray with Emma's coffee and Reggie's beer.

"Carla's busy," she said. "And Gwen says she'll have some appetizers out in just a minute."

"That's my old girl." Reggie patted Marianne's rump. Emma looked down into her coffee.

"You knew him, love, didn't you?" said Reggie. "Poor old Sonny?"

"Everybody knew him," said Marianne casually. "To tell the truth, he could be a bit hard to get rid of."

"Lucky for me, you had good taste." He rubbed the small of her back and beamed.

Marianne smiled at him, but there was something dutiful in the look. Emma sympathized. Reggie could not be an easy man to be married to.

Marianne left them, and Reggie turned back to Emma, raised his beer and took a long swallow.

"Ah!" He smacked his lips. "Now then, Emma, I'm not a man who wastes time—not mine, not anybody else's. I said I've got a proposition for you, and so I do."

"I'm very interested to hear what it is."

"'A course you are! Because you're a smart woman." He waggled his finger at her. "Knew it the minute I saw you. So here it is." He spread both hands out wide on the table.

"I want to back your new shop."

Emma deliberately let Reggie's words hang in the air while she drank some more coffee. "I'm not planning a new shop."

"Well, you should be. I told you, I've had my eye on you. You're a sensation. And it's not just during the tourist season, either. You've got the locals lining up. You should be thinking about getting your own place, right now. Well, you need a partner to help you do that, and here he is." Reggie spread his hands.

Again, Emma held back her answer. When she'd first come to Trevena, she had in fact been planning on opening her own shop, but the offer from the Delgados to partner with them at the King's Rest had worked out so well for everybody that she was reluctant to change. Especially since the cost of renovating a commercial kitchen or, worse, building one from scratch, was nothing short of astronomical. There were so many other ways she could be spending her capital—and her energy.

"I know what you're thinking," said Reggie.

Emma raised one eyebrow. Back when she was still working in finance, she'd learned that the secret with dealing with men like Reggie was to simply let them talk. They tended to reveal much more about themselves and their plans than they originally intended.

"You're thinking, 'He's going to want to have a say in the works, isn't he?' Well, you can put your mind at rest there. I'd be your silent partner." His grin broadened to show all his teeth. "So silent you'd swear I wasn't even in the country."

"Reggie!"

The shout cut Reggie off short and turned Emma's head. Oliver jumped to his feet.

A small, bald man in a sports coat and khaki trousers was bearing down on their table, his jowly face thunderous. Marianne strode close behind.

"You rat b—" the man roared. "What the—what are you up to now?"

17

IT WAS NO SURPRISE TO EMMA THAT REGGIE'S RESPONSE to twelve stone of angry middle-aged man bearing down on him was to grin broadly.

"Ben!"

"I'm so sorry, Reggie." Marianne twisted her delicate hands together. "I did tell him you were busy."

"Oh, now, there was no need for that, Marianne. You should know I'm never too busy to see Ben." Reggie waved a broad hand toward Emma. "Ben Leigh, do you know Emma Reed? Emma, this is Ben, my accountant and business partner."

Hollywood central casting could not have produced a more perfect accountant type than Ben Leigh. He was a short, pasty man with a soft middle that hadn't quite yet blossomed into a paunch. His hairline had long ago retreated into oblivion, leaving behind a broad expanse of gleaming scalp. His cheeks sagged and his watery blue eyes bulged behind wire-framed glasses that had a tendency to slip down his long nose. He even carried a leather briefcase.

He was also clearly struggling to swallow his temper. Oliver, of course, started snuffling around his shoes and hems. Emma was just about to call her dog back when Ben set his jaw, reached down and gave Oliver a quick head rub. "Yes, all right, good boy."

Emma patted her knee. "That's enough. Come on, Oliver."

Oliver flopped down beside her chair. "He has cats, Emma. Two. Girl cats."

Ben shoved his glasses up on his nose, and curved his mouth into a smile, clearly determined to be polite. "He's a well-behaved one, isn't he?"

"Mostly," agreed Emma. She held out her hand. "Emma Reed. Pleased to meet you."

Ben shook her hand. "Oh, erm, yes. Ms. Reed. My daughter Gwen says you make a fabulous scone."

"Gwenny ought to know," said Reggie. "She's my chef here."

"Is she?" said Emma, in her best politely interested tone.

"I believe in doing business with people I know," said Reggie. "Character matters. Plus it makes them less likely to sue." Reggie laughed. Ben didn't. He just pulled out a chair and sat, keeping his briefcase on his knees.

"What brings you here tonight?" Ben's question was for Emma, but his eyes slid sideways to Reggie as he asked it.

"We're just having a little chat," said Reggie. "Emma was at the Roundhead when they found old Sonny."

Which had nothing to do with why he'd asked her here. Or so he'd led her to believe. *So why bring it up?* Emma wondered. She also wondered what it was that made Ben hang on to his briefcase like grim death.

"That must have been quite the shock," said Ben politely. He didn't loosen his grip on his case even a little. "They also found the famous Black Lightning, I believe."

"That's right, that's right. Now, that I would have paid good money to see." Reggie grinned and sipped his beer.

"Are you a vintage cycle fan?" Emma asked him.

"Not as such, but a man does appreciate a beautiful machine." He gave Emma a long, meaningful look. Emma felt her skin crawl. Oliver's ears went up, and back, ever so slightly.

"Is that why you wanted to buy it?" Emma inquired innocently.

"*Buy it?*" Ben choked. His knuckles went white. "You want to buy the *Vincent?*"

Reggie rolled his eyes, but a woman's voice cut off whatever he'd been about to say.

"Oh, hullo, Da. I didn't know you were here too."

A young woman in chef's whites came up to the table. She carried a tray with a plate of appetizers that smelled deliciously spicy. Emma decided this must be Gwen, the restaurant's chef. She was a strongly built woman and wore her short dark hair pulled back in a bright blue band. She had her father's pale blue eyes and expressive mouth, but nothing of his nervous attitude. If anything, she gave off the air of someone ready for a fight. This wasn't really surprising. Professional kitchens, Emma knew, were very hierarchical, and tended to be male dominated. A woman who wanted to be a chef had to be able to hold her own.

Oliver of course, had smelled the appetizers and was up on all fours. Emma grabbed his collar, just in case he was planning on charging the chef's ankles. His bum wagged, hard.

"Just had one or two things to say to Reggie," Ben told his daughter. He was trying to speak casually, but the words still sounded slightly strangled.

"Well, you can help with these, then." Gwen set the plate down on the table. "We've got some mini crab cakes with a lime and red pepper sauce." She tucked the tray under her arm and held out her hand. "Emma Reed, isn't it? Nice to meet you."

"Nice to meet you." Like most people who know they have a strong grip, Gwen's handshake was a little careful. "These look fantastic." Emma helped herself to a crab cake, drizzled a bit of the sauce over it and took a bite. It was delicious—warm, spicy and bright with fresh herbs.

Reggie tossed a whole one in his mouth and washed it down with more beer.

"Ah, now, Gwenny, you've done it again!" He raised his glass to her. "She's a genius, she is," he declared. "Did you know there's a pub over Cheshire way got itself two of those Michelin stars? Two!" He held up his fingers in emphasis. "That's what we want here, isn't it, Gwenny? And you're the one to bring it!"

Gwen's face tightened. Clearly, she'd heard all this before.

"Reggie says you two are planning to go in together on a new place," she said to Emma.

"*What?*" choked Ben.

"Ooops." Gwen covered her mouth. "I'm so sorry, Reggie. I didn't realize you hadn't told Dad yet."

But her eyes slid sideways as she said it. Emma felt sure she knew exactly what she was doing. What's more, from the poisonous look he shot towards her, Reggie knew it too.

Emma found herself looking from Gwen to her father and back again. Neither of them was paying any attention to her. Gwen was watching her father with sharp, angry eyes. Ben, on the other hand, was gawping at Reggie.

"Why didn't you tell me, Reg?" Ben demanded. "First I find out you're planning on blowing God knows how much on a ruin of a motorbike and now *this* . . . !"

"Now, Ben, no need to get yourself all wound up. I was just going to sound Emma out for the future, all right? The *future*. That's all. No decisions made, no money changing hands. Just a friendly chat." He paused. "What with everything going so well, and so much new business coming in, there shouldn't be much bother about the money, should there?"

"I just wish you'd talked to me first," said Ben. "But then, I should be used to it by now, shouldn't I?"

"And I know what you would have said." Reggie was grinning again. "You and the wife both. You're too cautious. Always wanting to hold back."

"It's what you hired me for," Ben reminded him.

"So it is. I'd almost forgotten, what with the way things have gone." There was an undercurrent beneath those words. Emma felt it, but couldn't understand it. Reggie was looking steadily at Ben, but Ben's eyes had shifted away.

Reggie leaned back and folded his arms. "Anyway, nothing to worry about, like I say. We were all just talking, right, Emma?"

Now Ben and Gwen both looked at her. In that moment, their family resemblance felt very strong. Emma found herself suddenly wondering how the Leighs had come to be mixed up with Reggie Tapp. Then she found herself remembering what Angelique had said.

. . . *You know how it goes in hospitality. There's good years and there's bad years, and whenever things are looking particularly bad, there's Reggie Tapp smiling and laughing and offering to help out.*

"Yes, just talking," she agreed. "I haven't even heard the full proposal yet," she said.

"There, you see? Nothing to get excited about." Reggie laughed—heartily, of course—and punched Ben in the arm again.

Despite all her curiosity, Emma decided that it was time to get out from between these two. She stood smoothly and flashed them all her best and brightest smile. She also grabbed her bag. "Gwen, the crab cakes are fantastic. Reggie, thanks for the coffee. We'll talk some more once you and Ben have had a chance to sort things out."

Emma and Oliver were already a meter away from the table before Gwen caught up with her.

"Nice exit." The chef fell into step beside her.

"Years of practice. Sorry to miss the rest of your dinner."

"No worries." She paused and looked Emma in the eye. "Care for a tour of the kitchen?"

Emma met Gwen's very pointed gaze.

"Sure," she said. "I'd like that."

Because every instinct Emma possessed told her the chef had something to say. Those same instincts told her she ought to hear it.

18

EVERY PROFESSIONAL KITCHEN EMMA HAD EVER BEEN IN was cramped, crowded, hot and noisy. The kitchen of the Donkey's Win was no different. Orders were shouted in all directions over the sounds of sizzling, not to mention a flood of random thuds and bangs. The smells were enough to make her mouth water. Gwen steered them efficiently through the chaos into a tiny side office and shut the door. Oliver, who was probably already feeling the heat, for once didn't shove his nose into every corner. Instead, he plopped down in front of the office door, panting.

"Emma, listen, there's no good way for me to say this," Gwen began. "But you weren't really going to consider having Reggie invest in your shop, were you?"

Emma gave herself a moment before she answered. Gwen might have a hardened exterior, but she saw genuine concern in the younger woman's eyes. "To tell you the truth, no."

Gwen let out a long sigh. "That's good. Great."

"Glad you agree, but . . ."

"Why do I agree?" Gwen finished for her. "Especially since I work for Reggie, and he happens to be my dad's business partner?"

"Erm. Yeah."

Gwen pressed a hand against the door to make sure it was all the way shut. Oliver, in the meantime, had apparently decided he'd loafed around long enough and was nosing along the sideboards.

"There's something," he mumbled. "There's something."

Gwen folded her arms tight against her. "This stays between us, yeah?" she said to Emma.

Emma nodded.

"There's been some money trouble lately. The pub's doing well, but not great."

"But Reggie just said there was a lot of new business coming in," said Emma.

Gwen looked out the office window at her tiny, noisy kingdom. "Yes, well, Reggie lies. Come by tomorrow and I guarantee you, it'll be dead as a doornail."

"How bad are things?" Emma asked Gwen.

"We're talking about letting staff go."

"Oh."

"Yeah," the chef answered bitterly. "I mean, not that Reggie's said anything about it. That's not his way. Always got to be sunshine and roses with him, doesn't it? But the numbers don't lie. And they're catching up with him, and the rest of us." She nodded towards the half dozen people outside at the cooktops and counters. "I've been trying to get Dad to see it, but . . ." She shook her head. "Anyway, don't let him talk you round. The only person Reggie Tapp is interested in helping is Reggie Tapp, and if he's offering something, it's because you've got something he wants."

Movement in the kitchen caught Gwen's eye, and her mouth tightened. Emma turned to see Ben scooting awkwardly through the kitchen towards the office. Oliver jumped to his feet and darted behind Emma just as the door opened.

"Hey, Da," said Gwen. "What's going on?"

"I'm sorry, I didn't realize you were . . ." He gestured between the two of them. "A little girl talk?" said Ben brightly.

Gwen rolled her eyes. "Try some chef talk, Dad."

"Right, yes, sorry." He smiled stiffly. Emma was suddenly sure he'd not only known that she was down here with his daughter but he very much wanted her gone.

"Just a bit of business," Emma told him cheerfully. "I'm doing a fruitcake subscription for New Year's, and I wanted to talk about putting some ads up in the pub, if you've got a community bulletin board."

Emma couldn't tell whether Ben believed her or not. He just pushed his glasses a little further up on his nose. "Is that so? Well, I'd say yes in a heartbeat. It's been a long time since I've had a proper fruitcake. But obviously we'd need to talk to M . . . Reggie about it."

"Just like everything else," muttered Gwen.

"I'm sure he'll be glad to hear whatever ideas you've got," Ben went on smoothly. "So nice to have met you, Emma. I'm sure we'll be talking more." He stepped back, holding out one arm, very clearly inviting her to leave.

"I'm sure we will," said Emma. "Thanks for the tour, Gwen."

Ben followed Emma and Oliver out through the kitchen. At first Emma thought he also might have something to tell her, but when they reached the kitchen door all he said was "Have a good evening!"

He also pushed the door open to let her out and watched while she walked into the pub's main room.

"He's a herder," said Oliver. "He herded us."

"You are absolutely right, Oliver. The question is why?"

Oliver scratched his chin and shook himself. "You'll find out."

I appreciate the confidence. Because Ben had not only herded them—he was still standing there to make sure she did not turn around and head back into the kitchen.

"Were they nice snacks, Emma?" asked Oliver mournfully. "There were many snacks in the kitchen."

Emma smiled. "The snacks were much better than the company," she murmured and hitched her bag up on her shoulder. "Come on, Oliver. We'll get a proper dinner. Maybe some takeaway?"

"Yes, yes!" Oliver bounced. "Takeaway is always good. Will we see the Patels?"

"Maybe."

Emma had in fact been thinking about it. The Patels ran a popular Indian restaurant. Their naan was crisp and fluffy and the tikka masala was as gloriously spicy as anything she could get in London. Plus, Raj's grandmother made a terrific milky chai that wasn't too sweet.

If Emma was being really, truly honest with herself, however, the main reason for considering dinner from the Patels' was because she might run into Raj's mother, who had a habit of talking about any case her son was currently working on.

But probably she shouldn't do that. Curiosity was one thing. Actively fishing for information from the mother of the local PC was quite another.

Marianne stood at the hostess stand, thumbing her phone. As Emma passed, she looked up abruptly and pulled off her reading glasses.

"Emma," she said, and Emma stopped in front of the stand. "I'm sorry you got caught in that. Reggie never wants to do anything by halves, you see, and Ben's much more cautious, so they can get a little testy with each other." She smiled, but her eyes looked tired.

"Oh, please don't worry about it," said Emma. "Business partnerships can get rocky sometimes."

"Yes. Can't they?" Marianne wasn't looking at her anymore. Her attention had drifted to the barroom, with all the chatter and the blaring music and the guests munching their chips and burgers and Gwen's fancy crab cakes.

"I imagine things were a lot different back in your parents' day," said Emma.

"Wha . . . ?" Marianne blinked, and visibly pulled herself back into the present. "Oh, yes, yes they were. Not that this place was anything special back then. Just a slightly dodgy roadside pub, actually." Memory clouded her eyes for a minute, but she shook it off. "But look at us now!" She smiled toward the busy room. "Reggie did the right thing when he took over. We had to modernize, you see, or we were going under, and my parents just couldn't see that."

But even with all the noise around them, Emma heard a soft undertone of regret in every word Marianne spoke. She clearly missed the old place, even if she wasn't going to admit it.

"Emma?" Marianne said hesitantly. "Maybe you can tell David and Charles I'm sorry about Reggie coming to see them like that. He won't bother them about the Vincent anymore. That was just one of his whims. I'll—" But she broke the sentence off. At the same time, her worried and slightly frustrated expression vanished, replaced by the professional hostess smile that Emma was beginning to think must be second nature. "Well, I'll talk to him. Thank you for stopping in."

"Thanks." Emma smiled, said goodbye, whistled to Oliver and headed out into the much calmer, much quieter Trevena evening.

But she couldn't help wondering if Marianne had just suddenly decided she was sharing too much, or if Marianne, like Emma, had just caught sight of Reggie standing beside the bar.

19

IN THE END, EMMA DECIDED THAT THE BEST CURE FOR HER "meeting" with Reggie Tapp and the rest of the team at the Donkey's Win was a bit of peace and quiet. She and Oliver walked back up to Nancarrow cottage through the fresh, chilly evening while around them Trevena quietly rolled itself up for the night. Her slate-roofed cottage was a welcome sight; so was her refrigerator, with ingredients for a big omelette full of tomato, cheese and fresh herbs, to be shared, judiciously, with Oliver.

"Are you sure that's enough, Emma?" yipped Oliver when he saw the meager size of the portion she put into his bowl. "Eggs are very healthy!"

"So's your kibble, corgi-me-lad," Emma told him.

"But kibble isn't interesting! Your food is always interesting!"

Emma sighed and put a little more omelette in his dish. "When did I become such a pushover?"

Oliver lifted his muzzle and licked his chops. "Is this one of those questions where you really know the answer already?"

Emma laughed. "Yes, I guess it is."

She'd just stretched out on the lounge with a nice cup of

tea, some shortbread, and a new romance novel while Oliver energetically gnawed a fresh rawhide bone under the coffee table, when her mobile rang.

Emma checked the number and hit the accept button.

"Hello, Brian."

"Hello, Emma. Just wanted to make sure you're doing all right."

"Just fine," she said, a little surprised. "Why—?"

"Only someone saw you walking out of dinner with Reggie Tapp."

Villages. "Jealous?"

"If I thought you might consider throwing me over for Reggie, I would be wondering who you were and what you'd done with the real Emma."

Emma smiled. "I also met his business partner and his daughter."

"Ah, Ben and Gwen," he said and paused. "Not too sure giving your daughter a rhyming name is the best idea."

"Just so long as she doesn't have a brother named Ken."

"Sven, actually," said Brian.

"Please tell me you're joking."

"Afraid not. Apparently her mother was Swedish."

"Wow. Do you know them?"

"Nah, not really. They're not local. At least, Ben's not. He comes in when Reggie needs him. Everybody says he got Gwen the chef's job there."

"Hmm."

"Do I hear a touch of skepticism in that 'hmm'?" She could picture Brian raising his eyebrows.

"A touch," Emma admitted. "The way she was talking today was not like someone who was grateful for their job."

"What was it like?"

"Like a worried daughter trying to keep an eye on her old dad, and on me, for that matter." She told Brian how Gwen had warned her against letting Reggie invest in the shop, and how Ben came in to interrupt and hustle her out of there.

She also thought about the look Reggie had given Ben

when he talked about all the new business coming in and everything being just fine, and how Ben had looked away.

"Sounds . . . tense," said Brian.

"It was, and more than a little strange." She remembered Reggie's shark-toothed grin. *I'd be your silent partner. So silent you'd swear I wasn't even in the country.* What was that even about?

"Well, I know you're busy, what with snooping around dodgy businessmen, skeletons in the cellar and fruitcakes on the go, so I thought you might like a nice relaxing day out."

"Hang on, hang on." Emma said. "What makes you think I'm snooping?"

"This is Ms. Emma Reed I'm speaking to, yes?"

Emma sighed and slouched further down on the lounge. "I've gone and made a reputation for myself, haven't I?"

"Would it make it any better if I told you I think it's fascinating?"

"I'll get back to you on that. You were saying something about a day out?"

"I was thinking a drive out to Bodmin Moor Sunday afternoon. We can give the dogs a bit of a run, maybe stop on the way at that pub on the high street. Get dinner on the way back. What do you think?"

Normal people with normal jobs might go out Saturday night, but, as Brian knew, Sunday was Emma's night to kick up her heels, because not only did she close the take-away counter at one, but the shop itself was closed on Mondays.

"I will be free, and I will be expecting you, sir."

They talked a bit more, about Brian's day, about Emma's grand fruitcake schemes, his dad who'd just had cataract surgery and his collie dog, Lucy, who'd gotten into a tangle with a blackberry thicket that ended in a trip to the vet's.

Oliver perked up at the sound of Lucy's name and came out from under the coffee table to put his chin on Emma's shoulder.

"Eagh! I thought we just brushed our teeth."

"I'm sorry?" said Brian.

"No, not you. Just . . . dog breath."

"I get it. Hello, Oliver!"

Oliver barked. "Hello, Brian!"

"He says hello," said Emma.

Brian laughed. At that same time, Emma's phone beeped, letting her know she had another call. She checked the screen.

"Oops, that's Angelique calling. I should take this."

"See you Sunday, then, if not sooner."

They said goodbye. Brian hung up and Emma touched the button to take Angelique's call. "Hullo, Angelique."

"Hullo," she answered. "All right?"

"Hello, Angelique!" barked Oliver.

Angelique laughed. "Hello to you too, Oliver."

"One second, Angelique." Emma balanced the phone carefully on the back of the lounge. Then, she eased her dog back down onto all fours. "All right, you, humans talking now."

Oliver looked at her mournfully and wagged his whole bum. Emma sighed.

"One more second," she called toward the phone. She also kicked her legs off the chaise so she was sitting up straight. Emma boosted Oliver up beside her. Oliver immediately snuggled down and put his chin on her lap.

"Sorry about that." Emma reclaimed the phone. "Corgi readjustment."

"Well, I'm sorry to interrupt your exciting evening in," said Angelique. "I just wanted to hear how it all went with Reggie. Did you find out what he wants?"

"No. Not really." Emma felt her eyes narrow as she remembered the way Reggie had tried to deflect Ben's outburst. Even before she'd talked to Gwen, it had been easy to tell Reggie wasn't anywhere near as open or as honest as he pretended to be. "I mean, he *said* he wants to invest in the shop."

Well, Reggie lies, Gwen had said.

"Does he now?" Emma could picture Angelique arching her brows.

"As a silent partner," added Emma.

"But you don't believe it?"

"Oh, I believe he might want to invest, but I'd believe the world was flat before I'd believe that man could be silent about anything. Besides, if I was thinking of partnering with somebody on a second location, or even a first location, it would not be someone who doesn't bother to tell his partner what he's up to."

"Aha. So I take it you met Ben Leigh as well?"

"And his daughter, Gwen."

"Oh, Gwen. She's quite the girl," Angelique said.

"Do you know her? Brian says they're not local."

"They're not. They're originally from Liverpool, I think, and only moved to Cornwall a couple of years ago . . ."

"Meaning less than ten."

"Village time is different from other time," said Angelique. "You should know that by now. Anyway, he lives over in Treknow, and I'm not sure about Gwen. But she and Pearl did a summer cooking course together a few years back. Pearl says she almost took over the school. Apparently after that she started making a real name for herself in London, but she came down here to help out her father."

"What did Ben need help with?" asked Emma, then, before Angelique could answer, she added, "No, wait, let me guess. Reggie."

Angelique chuckled. "Got it in one. I suspect she's been trying to get Ben to cut ties with Reggie for quite some time now."

"Well, she certainly doesn't trust him. She told me pretty much the same thing you did, that when Reggie does something, he tends to have a few extra motivations tucked in his back pocket."

"Sounds like it was a very interesting meeting."

"That's one word for it," said Emma. "Do you have any idea why Ben stays with Reggie? I mean, he was nearly ready to explode when he heard that Reggie wanted to invest in my shop, not to mention buy the Vincent. Now, I don't know for sure, of course, but I suspect there might be one or two long-standing finance issues there."

"That would be all that long experience in banking shining through," said Angelique. "Reggie has never been known to pay a bill when he could talk his way around it. That attitude tends to give one a remarkably flexible attitude toward business expenses."

"And yet he is still in business," said Emma.

"And yet he is," agreed Angelique. "I've wondered about that more than once myself."

"Do you know anything about his wife?" Emma asked.

"Marianne? Not really, I'm afraid. Only that she was born in Trevena and she married Reggie pretty young, and he took over the pub sometime after that."

"She was asking about the body—well, the skeleton."

"Well, that's not exactly surprising, is it?"

"No, except Marianne wanted to know if anything was found with it, besides the motorcycle. She mentioned letters or photographs."

"That is strange. What do you think she was after?"

"I don't know," admitted Emma. "But she also talked about having been friends with Liza, but something came between them." Emma rubbed Oliver's ears. "I hate to say it, but with Billy Marsh's hints about Liza maybe having been in some kind of relationship with Sonny, I started thinking . . ."

"Always dangerous," quipped Angelique.

"Too right. Anyway, I was wondering if maybe Marianne also had some kind of feelings for Sonny. Maybe they were dating, or something, and maybe Sonny was doing a bit of window shopping, or something," Emma finished, aware she sounded a bit limp.

"That's a bit of a stretch," said Angelique diplomatically.

"I know, except for one thing: so far, Liza's the only one who's had anything nice to say about Sonny, and that includes his family."

Angelique was quiet for a moment. "You think Liza and Marianne had a falling-out over Sonny?"

Oliver rolled over and wriggled. Emma took the hint and rubbed his tummy. "I think we all make a bad decision or three when we're teenagers."

"But we usually don't stay angry for forty years over old boyfriends." Emma heard a clicking noise and realized Angelique was tapping her fingernails on the table. "Have you talked to Pippa about any of this? I should think her grandfather would be able to explain a great deal, if he wanted to."

"It's that last bit that's the key," said Emma. "But even if he wants to explain it, I'm not sure Pippa wants him to."

"I don't understand."

"I think Pippa's trying to protect Billy," Emma told her. "I think she's worried he had something to do with Sonny . . . being in that tunnel. After all, her granddad was involved in the smuggling racket and all, and . . ."

Emma sat up straighter. Her movement caused Oliver to grumble and look up. "Angelique, I've just had an idea. What if Sonny stole something besides the Vincent? Like some money or something?"

"That would make him a very busy young man. I think Genny's idea is more likely—that Sonny was the one who turned in Billy Marsh and his lot."

"Why not both?" said Emma. "I mean, a smuggler is by definition going to have valuable stuff lying about, right? So, Sonny tips off the authorities, steals what he can carry and the getaway vehicle and rides off into the sunset."

"Only something goes wrong," said Angelique.

"Badly wrong," agreed Emma. She fell silent. Oliver looked up from under the table. Emma rubbed his ears distractedly. "It all circles back to Sonny's troubles. So maybe the thing to do is understand just what he had troubles with."

"Or who?" put in Angelique.

"Yes, or who. We know about Billy Marsh, but was Billy operating on his own? I mean, I don't know much about it, but it seems to me that a smuggling ring needs more than one person to make it work. I don't suppose you've heard . . . ?"

"Not a thing," said Angelique. "I mean, people are full of hints and guesses, but nobody names names. I'd say you should ask Pippa, but it doesn't sound like she's the most reliable source right now."

"A journalist who can't be a reliable source," said Emma. "That's probably ironic. But maybe there's another way."

"What are you thinking?"

"I'm just wondering if I'll have time to get over to the library tomorrow."

20

TREVENA'S LIBRARY STOOD ACROSS THE STREET FROM THE sprawling tourist "attraction" known as King Arthur's Castle. Tiny Mrs. Shah, the head librarian, commanded her literary fortress with a firm but loving hand. Her patience with children was infinite, and she was responsible for the little library becoming a social center of Trevena. They hosted book clubs, a knitting club, story times, and movie nights. Emma had even hosted a tea-and-chocolate tasting in the community room.

As far as Emma—or, more accurately, Oliver—was concerned, Mrs. Shah's only fault was that she had a strict No Dogs Allowed policy in her library.

Fortunately, Angelique agreed that Oliver could stay at the B and B while Emma did her research, or tried to. Emma, in turn, swore to Becca and Bella that she'd be back well before for the first seating for tea at one. The Portman sisters had assured Emma they believed her, but the looks they gave each other were filled with meaning and doubt.

Emma had pretended to ignore them. She was determined to get to the bottom of what had happened to Sonny Greenlaw as quickly as possible. If she'd been a little reluctant to fully embrace her inner Miss Marple before, Pippa's newest article on the *Coast News* website had changed all that.

She'd written:

> . . . While the police forensic investigations have centered on the bones found in the mysterious tunnel, the key to Sonny Greenlaw's murder may rest on the rare Vincent Black Lightning motorcycle found with the body . . .

THERE'D BEEN A CAPSULE HISTORY OF THE BLACK LIGHTNING after that. It was pretty potted stuff. Emma had found most of it herself during some early-morning Internet searching. She hadn't even needed to text Brian, although she'd thought about it.

But then Pippa had written:

> . . . while the Vincent's then-owners always alleged the bike was stolen, no report of the theft was ever lodged with the police. According to sources, at the time of the disappearance suspicion swirled through the village due to previous criminal activities rumored to have been perpetrated by the motorcycle's primary owners . . .

Emma's jaw clenched just thinking about it. Pippa Marsh had called Charles a criminal. She'd suggested he'd lied about the Vincent being stolen. Anybody reading that would start asking themselves if the Kemps hadn't reported the Vincent being stolen because they knew exactly where it was.

"HULLO, MRS. SHAH," EMMA SAID SOFTLY AS SHE STEPPED up to the circulation desk.

"Hullo, Emma. How can I help you?" Mrs. Shah wore her snow-white hair in a long braid hanging down her back.

With her warm brown skin, deep black eyes and flowing tunic tops, she looked like a fae queen who had just stepped in from the forest to do some light reading.

"To tell you the truth, I'm not sure you can. I'm just here on sort of the off chance."

"We won't know until we try."

"Well, ever since the . . . stuff was found in the tunnel under the Roundhead—" Emma stopped. "You do know about that?"

Mrs. Shah looked down her nose at Emma, which was a neat trick, as the librarian was one of the few people in Trevena who was actually shorter than she was. "I'm not that deaf yet. I've heard a few things."

"Yeah, well, I heard there was some smuggling going on in Trevena around the time Sonny Greenlaw disappeared, and that he might have had a hand in it. I was wondering who else might have been involved."

Mrs. Shah's dark eyes narrowed. "You were, were you?"

"Pure curiosity," said Emma breezily. "Do you think there might have been something about it in the newspapers from back then?"

The look Mrs. Shah gave her spoke volumes. Specifically, it said, *As a librarian, I am not going to judge why a patron needs their information, I just want you to know you haven't fooled me at all.*

"Well now," she said thoughtfully, "I didn't move here until the nineties myself, so that was all before my time, but there could well be something, either in the newspapers or the court records. Have you asked Pippa Marsh? Her newspaper might have something in their archives."

"Erm. Yeah, well, I did some digging online, but you know, Pippa's still working on the story, and I don't want to risk stepping on her toes."

Fortunately, this was a statement Mrs. Shah seemed ready to accept. "Yes, well, she's always been tenacious. Even as a little girl. If she started on a series, she'd move heaven and earth to track down every single book in it. She used to pester me quite a bit. Not that I minded," she added, smiling at that distant memory of little Pippa burrowing away in her stacks.

"So." Mrs. Shah's tone became brisk. "What year were you thinking of starting with?"

"Around 1972?"

"Right. This way." Mrs. Shah gestured to Emma with two fingers, indicating that she should follow along.

Emma did.

MOST OF THE LOCAL NEWSPAPER ARCHIVE WAS STILL ON microfilm. Mrs. Shah was trying to get a grant to help digitize the collection, but so far had had no luck. She switched on the bulky, noisy machine and showed Emma how to feed in the film reels.

Reading about the small local doings from all those years ago proved to be oddly fascinating. Emma found herself grinning at the announcements of births and arrivals of people she now knew as friends. She wondered about the mystery of who stole the prizewinning cake at the summer fete, or why a bin of fresh, iced mackerel suddenly turned up on the doorstep of the grammar school headmaster.

A charitable drive was organized for coats and toys for disadvantaged children.

The essay that won the secondary school contest was printed, along with a photo of the beaming family and the gap-toothed author in her sprigged dress holding up the certificate.

The jumble sale for the church roof fund was well-attended and, according to the vicar, raised a "gratifying amount."

This year's first prize for roses at the garden fete was Elinore Drake.

In between these little gems was sprinkled more the serious news. Boats were lost at sea. The local fish-packing plant closed and dozens of jobs were lost. A car went over a cliff on a rainy night and was found on the rocks below.

Emma paused to roll her shoulders back and winced at

the crackling noises coming from her protesting joints. She looked at her watch and muttered a curse under her breath. She needed to get back to help serve tea. She'd hoped to stop by Vintage Style on the way, but at this rate, she wasn't going to have the time.

Just one more. She pushed the button and advanced the pages to the next issue.

The front page was filled with an enormous, bold, all-caps headline. Emma read it, and forgot all about the crick between her shoulders.

POLICE UNDERCOVER TREVENA COUNTER-FEITING OPERATION

Counterfeiters? Emma felt her brows arch. *Nobody's said anything about counterfeiters.*

She leaned in close, not wanting to miss a single word. She read:

> Cornwall's reputation for producing smugglers and ne'er-do-wells isn't something that ended with the days of "Poldark." On Tuesday, members of the Devon and Cornwall police disrupted what appears to be a major smuggling and counterfeiting operation based in the sleepy seaside village of Trevena . . .

Emma skimmed the description of seventies Trevena, and how no one could have suspected what was really happening in the cellar of the Sea and Shell public house. . . .

The Sea and Shell. Emma blinked. That was the pub that used to belong to Marianne's family. The one that was torn down to make way for the Donkey's Win.

She leaned in again.

> . . . Three full cases of Irish whiskey were found, alongside many more empty cases and bottles. The real prize, however, was a box of what appeared to be excise stamps, which, when genuine, are affixed to a

bottle of spirits to indicate that all the appropriate import duties have been paid.

"Well, well," breathed Emma. "We are a bunch of busy little bees, aren't we?"

. . . Detective Chief Inspector Edward Tyndall of the Metropolitan police told this reporter that a tip had been received by the Devon and Cornwall police from a "concerned citizen," which led to a call to Scotland Yard as well as the Inland Revenue . . .

So there was *a snitch!* Emma swallowed. *And once the paper came out, everybody would have known it.*

. . . In a plot that could have been dreamed up by Daphne du Maurier, bottles of whiskey and packets of cigarettes were brought into the pub from various clandestine sources. In the cellar, the contraband is alleged to have been fitted out with the authentic-looking tax stickers and then sent onwards to its ultimate destination.

"But who was it?" muttered Emma to the unknown reporter. "You're burying your lede here."

. . . the ring met under the cover of being a social club for local businessmen. The club keeps no records, so no list of dues-paying members could be obtained. However, sources in Trevena suggest that certain persons were frequently seen coming and going from the pub's cellar rooms well after last call.
A photograph on the wall of the main club room taken to commemorate the club's opening shows several prominent local figures, including William Marsh, Colin Roskilly, Paul Pendergast and Walter Greenlaw.

Emma fell back in her chair.

So there it was. There had been a "criminal syndicate" in Trevena, and Billy Marsh had been a part of it.

But so had Sam's father, Walter Greenlaw.

Liza said Walter blamed Sonny's troubles on Billy. She also said Walter didn't have any time for Billy's shortcuts.

If that was true, how had Walter come to be part of this particular "social club"?

Just one more question to add to the pile, Emma thought ruefully. *At this rate, I'll be handing out Christmas cake before we get all the answers.*

But what Emma knew for certain was that if she had found this article, Pippa must have found it as well. So, Pippa knew that Billy really was part of the smuggling racket that Sonny Greenlaw worked for, no matter what her grandfather tried to tell her.

Emma tapped her palm restlessly against the desktop.

"So where are you now, Pippa?" Emma whispered to the screen. "And what are you trying to do?"

As if on cue, her phone vibrated.

"Sugar." Emma tapped the screen. It was a text, from Becca.

Boss? 10 minutes to first seat!

"Sugar, sugar, sugar," Emma muttered as she texted back. On my way.

She stuffed the mobile back in her bag and scribbled down the page and the issue for the article so she could get it printed out.

But the photograph at the bottom of the article caught Emma's eye, and she paused and squinted. It showed four men all with pints in their hands. The two in the front held a wooden sign, neatly painted with the words: PRIVATE CLUB. The one on the right was definitely the young Billy Marsh. He already had that same knowing grin she'd seen when he confronted Sam and Liza at the village stores.

The man on the left had to be Walter Greenlaw. He had Sam's square face and wide-set eyes. He was raising his pint glass and looking directly at the camera. The other two must be Colin Roskilly and Paul Pendergast, whoever they were.

Wait . . . Colin Roskilly. Didn't Pippa say he was over visiting her granddad the other night? Emma bit her lip.

There was a fifth man in the photo too, in the back, on the very edge. In fact, he'd almost been cut out of it. He was younger than the others, and taller. His shoulders were hunched, like he had his hands stuffed in his pockets.

Emma recognized him as well. That was a much younger, much more tentative Reggie Tapp.

21

IN GENERAL, OLIVER LIKED HUMANS. SOME, HOWEVER, were a little bit harder to like than others. Mrs. Shah was one of those. Surely she could tell that he was a well-behaved corgi and would not hurt the books she was guarding. But no. She would not allow any dogs in her library, and so he had to stay at the King's Rest while Emma went out alone.

Oliver liked the B and B, and the garden. He liked Angelique and Daniel and all the guests—well, most of the guests, most of the time—but he was restless today. There was something going on. Emma was worried about their friends, and he wanted to help her. How could he help her if he was stuck in the garden all day?

Oliver stretched out on the patio with his chin on his paws.

"Well?"

Oliver jumped, yelped and spun. The Cream Tangerine stood behind him, swishing her tail impatiently. She'd crept up from downwind, so he hadn't been able to smell her. Oliver was sure she'd done it on purpose.

"Well what?" he grumbled and flopped back down.

"Did you find out? About my humans?" The cat rolled

over onto her back. She looked harmless that way. Oliver was not fooled. "About why they're so shouty?"

Oliver lifted his chin. "Emma's working on it."

The cat rolled over again, coming up on her side. "That means no. Humans always say that when they mean no."

Oliver felt a growl itching in the back of his throat. He got to his feet and nosed at the gravel, trying to find something interesting as a distraction. "Your humans must have stopped shouting by now." In Oliver's experience, humans were shouty in bursts, but then they made it up. Usually this involved food. That might not be all humans, though. With Emma, most things involved food, but she was special.

"You don't even know that much," snarled the cat. "They're still shouting. They're shouting right now."

"And you haven't been fed for days," mumbled Oliver. He started for the poppies, or what was left of them now that the weather had turned colder. There was something there, something new. He almost recognized it, but not quite.

"It's true!" Tangerine bounded up beside him. "I'll show you."

"I can't." Oliver searched at the edge of the bed of leaves and dry stalks. It was here somewhere, he had it—almost, anyway . . .

"Why not?"

Oliver scratched his chin carelessly. "I have to watch for the fox." He was not about to remind the cat that he couldn't hop over the fence like she could.

"Oh, well then." The tip of Tangerine's tail twitched. "That means you've checked the gap."

Gap? What gap? Under the gate? The fox can't get in there. There couldn't be another gap. He'd know about it. He was here every day. He could not have missed it.

Could he?

"Of course I checked," he said. "It's my garden."

"Hmmm . . . maybe I should make sure. You never know." The cat stretched, making herself about twice as long as normal. "After all, foxes are very tricky." With a flick of her long tail, she disappeared under the hydrangeas.

Oliver hesitated. He had, of course, thoroughly investigated under the hydrangeas. He hadn't missed anything. He couldn't have. He was here every day. And what would a cat know about a gap? Cats didn't go through things. They jumped over things. Everybody knew that. And Tangerine was never here. Well, hardly ever. Well, only once every couple of days or so. There was no way she could find something before he did.

But she wasn't coming back.

Cats. Oliver gave an impatient huff. He'd better go make sure she was all right.

Oliver ducked under the hydrangeas, following Tangerine's scent trail. The light was tricky under here, and there were all kinds of new and interesting smells. He would definitely have to come back later.

The left side of the yard was bounded by an old wooden fence. It was so overgrown that you could barely even see it, unless you were under the bushes. Then, the pickets looked like very tidy, very splintery stems sticking up out of the dirt. The fence ran right up to the old brick wall at the back edge of the garden. Oliver knew he had to be careful in here. The remains of an ancient rambler rose still hugged the wall, and the thorns were extremely sharp.

A soft eddy of wind touched his muzzle. Then he saw Tangerine's eyes gleaming on the other side of the wall. She was outlined by a ragged, wedge-shaped gap between the fence and the wall. There were so many little drafts and so many smells coming from so many different directions, he'd missed it until now. The old branch of rosebush slanted across the middle didn't help.

Oliver crept carefully up to the gap, almost on his belly. The dirt smelled very strongly of fox. Oliver growled reflexively. He'd have to tell Emma, and she'd tell Angelique. This was good. This was important.

"Well?" asked Tangerine. "Are you coming?"

Oliver hesitated. He knew he shouldn't. Emma got worried when he left without telling. The one time he'd almost dug his way out from under the gate, she'd gotten very angry, and even told him if he didn't behave, she'd have to leave him at the cottage while she was at work.

Oliver had promised to behave.

But Emma would want to know if David-and-Charles were still being shouty. After all, she was working to find out what had gone wrong for them. They could be shouting something important. Humans did that sometimes when things got loud. Emma said being loud made humans reckless. Oliver believed that. It was the same with dogs sometimes.

Besides, if this was how the fox was getting into the garden, he needed to know all about it. Just like when he'd found the hole under the cottage garden wall. He'd told Emma about it, and she'd been able to block it up immediately. That had been very helpful. She'd said so.

Oliver went all the way down onto his belly. The gap was wider at the bottom. From the other side, the cat watched him without blinking. He pushed forward with his hindquarters, paddling at the dirt and wriggling his whole self. The rose branch brushed the top of his head. The gap squeezed his shoulders. It smelled like fox and mouse and spider and cat and he didn't like it.

And all at once he was through. Oliver scrambled back onto all fours and shook himself, and sneezed. That hadn't been so bad after all. He wasn't even all that muddy. Well, maybe a little muddy. Around the paws. And belly. Not enough to need a bath. Probably.

"Finally," muttered Tangerine. "Let's go." She whisked around, swished her tail, and slipped into the shadows. Oliver followed.

OLIVER WOULD HAVE NEVER ADMITTED IT, ESPECIALLY NOT in front of a cat, but being alone in the streets made him nervous. He knew Trevena very well by now, and the humans were good humans, but without Emma beside him, everything felt very different. There were cars. Even a cat had to be very careful of cars. But what was really hard was that he couldn't run and greet the humans—even the friends he and Emma knew. If they saw him alone, they'd think something must be wrong, and they'd put him inside, or take him back to the B and B, or call Emma, and then she'd think something was wrong. None of that would be any good. He had an important job to finish. So he had to hide behind bins and boxes and under tables where the humans wouldn't see him.

The cat snickered at him, and made a big show of strolling up to humans who said hello and petted her and laughed when she rolled over onto her back and waved her paws at them. Nobody ever wondered about a cat on its own. It wasn't fair. Cats were much less responsible than dogs. Nobody ever asked a cat to herd sheep, for instance, or find missing people, or guard the queen.

From behind the shop's chalkboard, Oliver growled, but only softly.

Finally, they reached David-and-Charles's home. He knew that's where they were, even though he'd never investigated this side of the building before. Their scent was wrapped all around it

Two humans stood outside. Oliver ducked behind a line of big, black wheelie bins. The cat jumped up on top, because she could. Oliver was sure he heard her snicker again.

Oliver ignored her. He stuck his nose out from behind the bin and sniffed, and looked hard.

The humans were definitely not Charles-and-David. But at first, he couldn't tell who they were. Their scent was blocked by the crowd of smells from the bin, and from the fresh clouds of tobacco the one was blowing up into the sky. Then she shook her head, and Oliver almost yipped in surprise. That was Pippa. The other one . . . the other one . . . Oliver pushed forward just a little further. That was Rory, Charles-and-David's Rory.

And he was not happy.

22

PIPPA FINISHED BLOWING HER SMOKE CLOUD. "HE KNOWS something," she said firmly.

Oliver crouched down on the pavement. He knew they wouldn't be able to smell him back here. Human noses were not that good, but their eyes were sharp. He had to hold very still.

He felt the bin shift. Tangerine jumped down onto the cobbles and strolled right up to the humans. She wrapped around Pippa's ankles.

Show-off, Oliver growled, but only on the inside.

"Oh, hello, you," Pippa stuck her cigarette between her lips and petted the cat's long back.

Tangerine went over and butted Rory's shin. "Are you going to feed me?" she meowed. "No one's feeding me!"

"Puss, puss. There's a good puss." Rory scratched her ears.

Tangerine harrumphed and jumped through the cat flap in the door.

"I shouldn't even be talking to you," Rory said to Pippa. "Do you have any idea what that article of yours has done to my uncles?"

"I told you, that was not my idea."

"It's got your name on it," Rory pointed out.

"I know, I know, but it's what my editor wanted, not me. I tried to warn your uncles what was going to happen. I called them. Four times. But they wouldn't listen. Neither would you." She waved the hand holding the cigarette, tracing lines of smelly smoke through the air. "The only thing to do now is to get out a story about what really happened."

"Will you get it through your head? I do not *care* what happened!"

Pippa blew out another cloud. The smell of tobacco filled Oliver's nose and made it itch uncomfortably. Oliver rubbed his nose with one paw, then froze again. But they weren't watching him. They were watching each other.

"I don't get you," Pippa said. "It's your *family*. How can you not want to know?"

"Whatever happened, my uncles will tell me when they're ready," Rory shot back. "Unlike your granddad, they are not bent as a whole box of hairpins!"

"You say that like you don't think I know who Granddad is or what he's done." Pippa waved her cigarette. "Of course he's bent! He was bent back then, and he'd still be going around being bent with all his bent mates if he could get out of that chair."

"Pull the other one. I saw you both walking up the high street just last week."

"Yeah, well, he's fine until he isn't. His side gives out without warning. But none of that means he ever killed anybody."

"Or maybe you just don't want to believe he did." Rory's voice was changing. He sounded sharper, and meaner. Oliver didn't like it. Neither did Pippa. She was holding herself very tall, but she was afraid. Oliver could smell it. "Maybe you should think really hard before you go any further with this crusading journalist act."

That just made Pippa angry. Humans didn't growl, at least not usually, but Pippa came close. "And are you really so sure those uncles of yours are as clean as you think?"

Rory didn't like the way she said that. His whole body went stiff. "What do you mean?"

"Look at it this way: why do you think anybody would hide a stolen motorcycle and a dead body in a cellar?" She jabbed the cigarette toward the street. "I mean, why not push all the evidence off a cliff? Or take the body over to Bodmin Moor and drop it in a bog. Or . . ."

Rory folded his arms tightly and puffed out his chest, trying to make himself even bigger. He was not happy, or comfortable. Oliver could tell, even from here. "Is there even a point to all this?"

"The only reason to put the motorcycle there would be because you were planning to come back for it later. Now, who might want to be coming back for such a rare and valuable motorcycle?" Pippa leaned forward like she was going to say something else—only Rory wouldn't let her.

"Okay, I've got one for you," he said. "Why are you so anxious to try to pin this thing on Uncle Charles?"

"For the hundredth time, I'm *not*. It doesn't have to go that way."

"What do you mean?"

"I mean there's another possibility, and if we play it right, we can get your uncles *and* my granddad out of the line of village gossip."

"So what's your idea?" he asked. His voice sounded softer, and much more like himself. Oliver felt his bum wag in instinctive approval.

Pippa stuck the end of her cigarette in her mouth and reached into her pocket. She pulled something out. It was a bit of paper. Oliver's ears went up. He sniffed, but he couldn't smell anything new.

"It was found with Sonny's body."

"Was found. Very good. What is it?"

"Sonny was working for that smuggling ring way back in the day. I think he not only disappeared, he also ripped them off." Pippa held up the paper. "This is a tax sticker, the kind they put on bottles of booze. Only it's not real, is it? I had it checked. It's a fake."

"And?"

"The smugglers weren't just moving goods along. They were putting counterfeit stickers on the booze so it would look legitimate."

They stared at each other. Slowly, Rory shrank backwards, pulling away, softening his stance.

"What if Sonny had a plan back then?" Pippa went on. "What if he tipped off the Inland Revenue to the smuggling operation, and then, just before they're about to get raided, he steals their money, and their fake stickers, and takes off."

"So what if he did?"

"So, that's going to make a lot of people angry, isn't it? People like, oh, say, Walter Greenlaw."

Rory was watching her closely, like he thought she might jump, or bite. "Greenlaw? Sam's dad? You're saying *he* killed Sonny?"

"I'm saying he could have. He was a member of the smuggling ring, and Sonny was found in his pub." Pippa tucked the paper into her pocket. "In fact, at the time of the raid, Sonny was working in his pub. If we can get those details out there, then *that's* what people will be talking about, not your uncles, or my granddad."

"But you don't know for sure he did it."

"I know he could have, and I know he's dead, so he can't be hurt anymore. The story will just sort of settle in, and everybody will be satisfied, and the village, and you, and me, we can get back to normal. Besides," she added, "the body and the bike were found in his cellar, in a tunnel that everybody says he bricked up himself. I'd say that's pretty suspicious on the face of it."

Rory cocked his head like he was trying to get a better look at Pippa. "So what do you want out of me?"

"I want you to convince your uncles to talk to me. Tell me what they know about Walter Greenlaw. Then I can tell my editors I got my information from a source close to the subject who wishes to remain anonymous."

"What if they don't know anything?"

Pippa ground the cigarette out on the side of the wheelie bin. Oliver wanted to sneeze. Badly. He pressed his paw over his nose. "We'll cross that bridge when we come to it. Come on, Rory, it's a way out for all of us."

Oliver's ears twitched. The door to the shop opened, and the Charles half of Charles-and-David stepped out. He stared at Pippa, and then at Rory. He was not happy. If he'd been a dog, all his hackles would have been raised.

"Rory?" he said. "Rory, what are you doing?"

"Nothing, Uncle Charles." Rory sounded guilty, like he'd been caught digging where he shouldn't.

"What have you been saying to her?"

"Nothing!" Rory spread his hands. "We were just talking."

"You do not just talk to this girl!" shouted Charles. "You read what she's been writing about us! You've seen what it's been doing to David! He's been out of his head all morning! He thinks we're going to be arrested!"

"I wasn't saying anything!"

"He really wasn't, Mr. Kemp!" said Pippa. "I was the one—"

Charles swung around. He stalked right up to Pippa. She cringed backwards, and so did Oliver. "You get yourself out of here, do you understand me!" he bellowed. "And if I catch you hanging around here again, I'll have *you* arrested, for trespassing!"

"Okay, okay!" Pippa backed away. "I just—" She swallowed. "Look, would you just confirm whether you and David did rent a flat in the old Sea and Shell pub when you first came to Trevena?"

"No!" Charles snarled. "No comment! Not now, not tomorrow, not next week." He stalked forward. "And if I catch you talking to anyone in this family again, I don't care if you're young enough to be my granddaughter, I will have your guts for garters!"

23

"HAVE YOU SEEN OLIVER?"

Becca looked up from the delicate cakes on the top tier of the stand. "Not since this morning. I thought he was with you."

Emma's throat tightened. *Not again.* "No, I left him here while I was at the library."

Bella pushed through the door from the great room carrying an empty tray. "You looking for Oliver? He was in the garden last I saw him." She picked up the sandwich stand Becca had just finished loading. "This lot is going to eat us out of house and home!" she sighed and headed back out into the great room.

Emma hurried to the back door. She'd barely made it back to the King's Rest in time to greet Emily Lloyd, her mother and their guests. They were there to celebrate Mrs. Lloyd's seventieth birthday. Since then, Emma had been so busy helping keep the sandwich stands and the teapots filled, she hadn't noticed that Oliver was not scampering in and out like he usually did.

Please do not have run off again. She whistled out the kitchen's back door. *Please, please, please . . .*

"Oliver!" she called, and waited. Her mouth went dry.

Then she heard a rustle, and Oliver shot straight out from under the faded hydrangeas.

"Emma! Emma!" he barked.

"Oliver!" Emma crouched down and he bounded into her arms, a furry bundle of enthusiasm and mud—and a few other things.

"Eeeeagh!" Emma pulled her chin back. "What have you been getting into?"

"Nothing." Oliver dropped back onto all fours, his whole bum wagging. "Well, almost nothing. I found out how the fox is getting into the garden, Emma! There's a gap between the fence and the wall and—"

"Yes. All right." Emma stood up and dusted her hands off. "You can tell me all about it later."

"But that's not all! I heard—"

Emma cut him off and started back for the kitchen. "It's going to have to be later, Oliver. I've got a whole bunch of guests who are waiting on their birthday cake—"

"But I found out about the paper thing, Emma!"

Emma froze in her tracks. "The what?"

"The paper thing!" Oliver barked. "The paper the Pippa lady took out of the tunnel!"

"You . . . How?" Emma stammered.

"She was talking to Rory, and I heard her, and I saw and . . ."

Slowly, the spinning in Emma's head cleared, and one fact became perfectly clear. "Oliver! Did you get out of the garden?

Oliver cringed. "I didn't mean to, Emma."

Emma glanced quickly at the B and B. From here, she could see through both the windows into the kitchen and through the French doors into the great room. In the kitchen, Becca was diligently checking items off a clipboard. In the great room, Bella was setting fresh pots of tea in front of the birthday guests.

Emma crouched down and faced her naughty corgi.

"Oliver! We've talked about this!" she hissed.

"I'm sorry, Emma. But it was important. I mean, not like I thought it was going to be, but it was . . ."

"Emma!" Becca leaned out the kitchen door. "Everything all right?"

"Yes! Coming," she called. Then she put her hand under Oliver's chin to make sure he was looking at her. "We will talk about this later, young man—"

"Young corgi!" yipped Oliver.

"—and in the meantime, you are going to stay. With. Me." She gave him a gentle shake to emphasize the point.

Oliver's ears drooped. "Yes, Emma, I will. I promise." He wagged to let her know he really did mean it.

"Okay." Emma straightened up and pasted on her professional smile. She marched back into the kitchen, with a subdued Oliver right behind.

Thankfully, the rest of the afternoon went off without a hitch. The orange cocoa birthday cake was a big hit. The ladies were delighted when she passed around the fruitcake samples. Everybody was more than ready to tell her about the cakes they had grown up with and their grandmother's special tricks and touches. Emily, who had planned the party, was yawning a bit by the end, but she was happy that her mum was happy. Oliver was right in the thick of it, being as charming as possible, as if to make up for that morning's unauthorized adventure.

Finally Emma was able to shut the door and turn the sign from OPEN to CLOSED. Becca and Bella were clearing the table and stacking dishes into the washer.

"Oliver needs an out," Emma said over her shoulder as she headed into the kitchen and out the back door to the garden. She headed toward the far end, where there were fewer tables and the bushes had started to lose their leaves and she was much less likely to be accidentally overheard talking to her dog.

Oliver plopped himself down on his hindquarters in the grass. "I stayed, Emma."

"Yes, you did." *This time.* "Now. What happened this afternoon? Why did you leave the garden?"

"It was the cat, the Cream Tangerine," he said. "She was here, and she told me that David-and-Charles were still being shouty, and I thought that might be important, so I went to see. Only we didn't get in—well, the cat got in, but I didn't get in, because Rory and Pippa were blocking the door and talking and they talked about the paper and I knew that was important, so I came back to tell you." He finished up, and panted a little. For Oliver, this was a long speech.

"And Pippa said what the paper was?"

"Yes! Yes! It was a sticker!" Oliver barked excitedly.

"A sticker?" Emma exclaimed. The article she'd found this morning had said the smugglers had also been counterfeiting excise stickers.

Oliver scratched, and sneezed. "It was hard to understand. There were a lot of words. They didn't make sense. I tried, Emma!"

"Okay, okay." Being a dog, he was completely comfortable with solid things he had actual experiences or interactions with. But there was a whole world of abstract human concepts that just sailed right over his head, literally and figuratively.

"Were some of the words 'excise' and 'Inland Revenue'?" she asked. "'Fake'? 'Counterfeit'?"

"Yes! Yes!" Oliver bounced excitedly. "That's what they said! Sort of. A lot of those, anyway."

Emma sat back on her heels. Her heart was beating faster. If Pippa had found one of the counterfeit tax stickers with Sonny's body, that backed up her theory that Sonny had robbed the smugglers. What if he'd cleared out with the stickers, thinking he could sell them off later? Or set up in business for himself?

What if he'd gotten caught?

EMMA MULLED OVER THE MEANING OF THE EXCISE STICKER while she finished cleaning up. What she really wanted was to go home to her quiet cottage and curl up on her chaise, but she'd promised herself she'd look in on David and Charles. She was worried that they were still fighting, even if she only had a cat's word for it.

"Then we're driving straight home," she told Oliver. Because of her trip to the library, she'd driven to work this morning instead of walking like she usually did.

"Yes, home is good," he yipped. "You are very tired. Maybe we should get takeaway for dinner. Or fish!" He bounced. "It has been a long time since we got fish!"

"We'll see."

Oliver sniffed. "You mean no."

"I mean we'll see, Mr. Greedy Guts."

Thursday night was not exactly the busiest social night on the village calendar. It was six o'clock and Emma and Oliver pretty much had the high street to themselves. Most of the people who worked in the shops and tiny offices had already gone home.

The light was still on in Vintage Style, however, and this time when Emma pushed on the door handle it opened, ringing the antique brass bell overhead. The smells of dust and citrus potpourri surrounded her. But neither David nor Charles was anywhere to be seen.

Oliver barked and charged for the record display. The Cream Tangerine slid out from behind the shelves and jumped up on the counter, meowing.

"Emma! The cat says . . ."

Emma never found out what the cat said, because the door opened, and David stepped out.

"Good lord!" Emma exclaimed. "What's happened?"

Even from this distance she could see David was so pale it looked like he might faint. Worse, his normally perfect hair was mussed, like he'd been running both hands through it. His shirt collar was crooked, and the front was rumpled.

"Oh, Emma. We weren't expecting you," he said. His voice was hoarse. "I must say, though, now is really not a good time. We were just—"

"Oh, no, let her in," called a hearty voice. Emma's breath caught in her throat.

It was Reggie Tapp.

24

REGGIE STROLLED OUT OF THE OFFICE, RUBBING HIS HANDS together. Unlike David, he appeared perfectly content. In fact, he was grinning like the cat who got into the cream. "Emma! Good to see you, darlin'. We left things at loose ends the other night, but plenty of time to catch up, yeah? I think we're done here, eh, Davey?" He stuck out his hand.

David stared at him. When she had first seen him, Emma had thought he was afraid, but now she realized it wasn't fear that had made David's face go so pale. It was pure, cold rage.

"Yes," David croaked. "We are done. We will discuss the delivery details later. It's being stored with Brian Prowse at the moment."

Reggie's grin spread wider. "Fine. That's fine. Pleasure doing business with you, Davey-boy. Emma? Walk you out?" He gestured broadly toward the door.

Emma itched to know what on earth was happening and how Reggie was planning to explain away Ben Leigh's reaction to their meeting the other night, but she was not going to leave David. Even from where she stood, she could see his long hands trembling from trying to hold his emotions back.

Oliver clearly knew something was wrong. He zoomed back across the shop to stand beside her. Her normally sweet and cheerful corgi was entirely on the alert, ears up, mouth turned down at the corners.

"Sorry," Emma said to Reggie. "It'll have to be later. I'll call you."

"All right, just see that you do, eh?" He waggled a thick finger at her and Emma fought the urge to slap it away. "Clock's ticking on all offers, and you don't want to be crying about missed opportunities later, eh?" He grinned at her, and at David, and sauntered out the door.

"What was that?" demanded Emma. "David? What on earth happened?"

"Nothing." He sounded exhausted. "Just business."

"Business does not leave you looking like you want to put your fist through the wall."

"Emma, I appreciate your concern, but really—"

Emma cut him off. "Where's Charles?"

"He's right here." Charles came out of the office. He didn't look any better than David. In fact, he looked positively sick.

And he wasn't alone. Rory came out right behind him.

"Emma, please," said David. "We'll talk tomorrow. Right now is . . . is . . ."

"Is what?" demanded Rory. "What exactly is going on with you two!"

"Rory, stop," said Charles. "You don't understand what—"

"Bloody right I don't understand!" Rory shouted. "Because you stubborn old gits won't explain it to me!"

"It's really nothing for you to be worried about," said David. He was trying to sound cheerful. Instead, he sounded like he was about to either cry or scream. "It's a private matter between Charles and—"

But Rory wasn't having it. "And you can just stop talking to me like I'm still ten! You're my family!" His voice broke on the last words, and his eyes shone brightly in the shop's dusty light. "I've been defending you! All over the village and to that little b—pest of a reporter! I told them all you had nothing to do with Sonny's death! Now you go and do this!" He stabbed his finger back at the office. "And you tell me not to worry!" He stopped, his expression wavering between anger and confusion. "Maybe she was right. Maybe you are covering something up."

"Enough!" roared Charles.

Rory pivoted toward his uncle. He was gulping air like he'd just run a four-minute mile, and his face was flushed red. His hands flexed, and for one split second, Emma thought Rory might hit him.

David, paper white and shaking, didn't move an inch.

Oliver barked wordlessly. Rory flinched, and then he stormed out the back door.

David winced and looked away. Charles wiped at his mouth, muttering curses into his hand.

Emma stared at them both, then she turned and rushed out after Rory, with Oliver close behind her. By the time she got out the back door, Rory was halfway down the little mews to the high street.

"Rory, wait!" She ran after him. Oliver barked and zipped ahead, skirting around in front of the boy. Then he stopped dead.

"Gah!" Rory exclaimed and pulled up short.

"Got him, Emma!" yapped Oliver proudly.

Rory turned on her. "That dog is a menace!" he shouted.

"You have no idea." Emma patted her thigh. Oliver caught the signal and trotted back to her side, but he was keeping his attention on Rory in case the boy tried to escape. "What just happened in there, Rory?"

He dug both hands into his jacket pockets, visibly trying to rein in a whole host of feelings. When he did speak, the words were high and choked. "They sold Tapp the Vincent."

Emma felt like the whole world had stopped dead. "You can't mean it."

"I mean it. I was out making a delivery, and when I came back . . . the little rat was in the office and—and you saw Uncle David."

"Yeah, I saw," Emma breathed.

"I asked what was going on, and neither of them said anything. It was Reggie who told me. 'Just a spot of business, lad.' You know how he talks. 'Between like-minded gentlemen, eh?' And he got that big sh—sugar-eating grin all over his face." Rory swallowed. "I thought Uncle Charles was going to strangle the rat. I would have done it myself, but that was when you came in."

"But there must be a reason—"

"That's what I'm afraid of," whispered Rory harshly. "Because what kind of reason could they have? What can't they tell me?" He was staring down the mews toward the shop door now. "I've known them my entire life. I spent whole summers in their shop. I thought they *trusted* me—"

"I'm sure they do, Rory."

"Then why won't they let me help? Now, when they really need it?"

Emma had no answer for him. Rory's jaw clenched so tightly she could see a muscle in his temple twitch. Then he turned, ready to stomp off again. Oliver leapt to his feet.

"Rory, wait," said Emma.

"Emma—" he groaned.

She didn't let him get any further. "Do you need somewhere to stay tonight?" she asked quickly. "I can call Angelique and see if you can have a room at the B and B."

She watched him force his shoulders and jaw to relax. "No, thanks," he said. "I've got a mate, he told me I could crash at his place if I need to. I just . . . I want to clear my head, yeah?"

"Yeah." Emma very much understood how he felt. "Be careful, will you?"

His smile was weak, but genuine. "No worries."

Emma watched Rory go until he turned onto the high street. Then she turned and walked back inside Vintage Style. Charles was holding open the office door so David could walk through. David saw her first and stopped. Charles turned more slowly.

Oliver rushed up to Charles, sniffing and barking. For once, Charles didn't stop to pet him.

Tangerine watched them all from the top of a wooden filing cabinet, her tail swishing back and forth like a living metronome.

Emma ignored the animals. Her attention was on the two men. She faced them both, hands on her hips. "All right, you lot." She gave them the same glare she'd given her nieces when they decided to stay out past curfew while spending the week with her. "What just happened here? Why on earth would you sell Reggie Tapp the Vincent? Just the other day you said he couldn't afford it."

"Yes, well, things have changed," murmured David.

"Changed how? Did Reggie win the lottery?"

David drew his shoulders back, or tried to. "Emma," he said, his voice full of wounded dignity. "We do appreciate your concern, but really it's not any of . . ."

Emma slashed her hand through the air, cutting off the protests. "It is my business! You just let your nephew walk out of here thinking you killed a man!"

"Rory doesn't think that," said Charles. He was looking at David. "He knows better."

"I'm sure he will when he calms down," said Emma. "But right now he's hurt and confused, and you two suddenly becoming international men of mystery isn't helping!"

David shuddered. "It's complicated, Emma. I'm sure you and Rory mean well—"

"I'm not," said Charles flatly.

That startled Emma badly. "Look, if I've overstepped, I'm sorry, but you can't keep—"

"Emma," Charles snapped. "Just stop it."

She folded her arms. "No."

"Yes!" he snapped. "This is not something you can butt in and fix. If you care as much about us as you pretend to, you will back off!"

Emma opened her mouth and closed it again.

Charles took a deep, shuddering breath. "And you will leave, right now."

She looked to David. David had shrunk in on himself,

huddling inside his tailored jacket like a frightened child. He looked thoroughly miserable, but he didn't say a word.

"Okay," said Emma. "If that's how it is."

"Yes," whispered David. "That's how it is."

Emma left through the front door. The light snapped out behind her. Reflexively, Emma turned around to look through the window. Inside, she saw David and Charles leaning together, holding each other up in the darkness.

25

"EMMA?" WHINED OLIVER.

Emma didn't answer. She just kept walking. She wasn't even sure quite where she was going. She was too upset by what had happened with David and Charles to be paying attention.

"Emma, Genny's waving at us, Emma." Oliver yipped and scampered into her path. Emma pulled up short.

"Oliver!"

"You should wave back, Emma," he said firmly.

Emma looked around. In her daze, she'd automatically started for home, and now she was standing outside the Towne Fryer, Genny's chip shop. Oliver was right; Genny was standing at the shop window, waving at her.

All right, Emma Reed. It is definitely time to pull yourself together.

She forced herself to smile and wave. Oliver barked, satisfied, but apparently, Genny was not fooled. She came out of her shop, wiping her hands on a side towel.

"Emma! What on earth's happened?"

Emma sighed. She wanted to tell Genny it was nothing, but after admonishing David and Charles for keeping secrets, she couldn't bring herself to do it.

Besides, her dog wouldn't let her. Oliver was already bonking her in the calf with his nose. "You should talk to her, Emma. You always feel better when you talk to Genny."

Out of the mouths of corgis.

"Besides," he added, "we haven't had fish in a long time."

Despite everything, Emma laughed.

"Okay, walking in a daze, chuckling to herself in the high street." Genny put a hand on Emma's forehead. "No sign of fever . . ."

"I'm fine," said Emma. Genny gave her a crooked smile, complete with raised eyebrows, indicating a healthy level of skepticism at this pronouncement. "All right," Emma sighed. "I'm not fine. I just stopped by to see how David and Charles were doing."

"Not good?"

"They just agreed to sell Reggie Tapp the Vincent."

"*What?*" squeaked Genny. Oliver yipped in surprise.

Emma nodded solemnly. Genny grabbed her by the arm, dragged her into the shop and kicked the door shut behind them all. Emma protested feebly, but Genny pulled her into the storage room/office at the back of the shop and planted her in the one chair. She poured a mug of tea from the pot on the desk and put it in Emma's hands. Then she hopped up on the edge of the desk and sat with her legs dangling.

"Start talking," she ordered.

Oliver settled down beside her, and looked up expectantly.

They're all against me. Emma sighed, took a swallow of tea and started talking. She told Genny about Reggie Tapp saying he wanted to invest in her shop as a very silent partner, about how Ben had nearly exploded when he heard the news, about Reggie's cryptic remark about new business and how Gwen had taken her aside specifically to warn her away from partnering up with Reggie. She talked about her morning at the library and how she'd found the article about the counterfeiting/smuggling ring operated by the Trevena Businessmen's Lunch Club out of the basement of the old Sea and Shell Pub. Then she told Genny about going to see David and Charles and how Rory had stormed out on them and how they had turned around and chucked her out on her ear.

"Wow," said Genny when she'd finished.

"Yeah," agreed Emma.

Genny poured herself a mug of tea and drank. "What do you think it means?"

"I think it means David and Charles are in real trouble, or at least, they think they are. I mean, why else would they give in to Reggie Tapp? He must have said something, or done something, to really frighten them."

"But what?" said Genny. "I mean, I know they had some pretty wild times back in the day, but they've never hidden any of it."

"I'm starting to wonder," said Emma. "When we talked last night, Reggie was hinting around that Charles was doing some odd jobs for the smugglers."

"Do you believe him?"

Emma watched the steam rising from her tea. "I think if I arrived in a strange village dead broke and anxious to start a new life, I'd probably be ready to work under the table, and I might not be all that choosy about who it was for."

"But stacking some crates or making some deliveries is still a long way from murder."

"Maybe not far enough," said Emma. "If you've already got a bad reputation, and if you've already stolen something."

"What?"

Emma looked at her tea again. "Pippa Marsh thinks Charles stole the Vincent before they left London."

"You're joking."

Emma shook her head. "She found a police report, or a friend of hers did, from around the right time."

"Well, that couldn't matter to anybody," said Genny. "I mean, if I found out somebody stole my granddad's old car, I wouldn't go fussing over it."

"Your granddad's old car is probably not worth almost a million at auction."

"You got me there," admitted Genny.

"You remember what Brian said—" Emma stopped. "Brian!" She dove her hand into her bag, digging frantically for her mobile.

Genny looked down at Oliver. "Do you know what just happened?"

"Not yet," Oliver barked, not that Genny understood him.

"Just give me a minute." Emma touched Brian's number and pressed the phone to her ear.

"Emma!" Brian picked up on the first ring. "I was just going to call you. I meant to earlier, but I had to make a run out to—"

"That's all right," Emma said hurriedly. "Did I hear right, that you've got the Black Lightning there at the shop?"

"That's what I wanted to tell you. Charles and David asked me to hold it for them. I picked it up this afternoon. I thought you might like a closer look."

He knew her so well. But it wasn't just curiosity. There might be a clue left behind by Sonny, or by whoever had moved the Vincent into the tunnel. Of course, Raj would have already looked, but he might have missed something.

"Not an offer I'm going to say no to. I'll be there in a few." She rang off and looked at Genny. "Any chance of some fish and chips to go?"

DESPITE ITS SIZE, BRIAN'S GARAGE AND SHOWROOM COULD be easy to miss. The former farm was tucked behind a winding line of bulky Cornish hedges. Emma eased her vintage Mini Cooper up the long dirt drive and parked in front of the brick cottage that now served as the sales office.

She had just set the parking brake when Brian came out of the office with his shaggy collie dog trotting happily beside him.

"Lucy!" Oliver bounced up and down on the passenger seat. "Hello, Lucy! We've got fish!"

Lucy barked back with enthusiasm.

"I don't know what he just said." Brian opened the door so Emma could climb out. "But I think Lucy approves."

"Maybe she smells the fish." Emma pulled out the carrier bag. "Genny's finest."

"Brilliant!" Brian took the bag, and her hand. "I'm starving. This way, madame."

There was a small patio behind the office where Brian and his family had set up a picnic table so that on nice days there was a place to eat lunch besides the office or the garage. It might be a little chilly, but Emma was glad to be out in the fresh air and autumn twilight. Brian had no candles, but he set a large torch on end and they sat beside it to eat curried fish and salty chips with plenty of malt vinegar, all washed down with thick white mugs full of strong tea. Emma felt her shoulders and mind relaxing. While the humans ate, the dogs alternated between begging for scraps and chasing each other around the yard.

"So how did the Vincent get here?" asked Emma.

"Charles called me," said Brian. "He said that the police didn't need to, or didn't want to, hold it, but he and David didn't want to try to keep it at the shop, so I picked it up for them."

"Has anybody else called you about it?" she asked, thinking about Pippa and her report that the Vincent had been stolen. Evidently PC Raj hadn't thought to ask about how the Kemps had gotten the Vincent in the first place, and Pippa hadn't thought to tell him.

Brian bit into another vinegary chip. "Not today. Pippa Marsh did call yesterday. Wanted a bit for her article. Why?"

"Because the Kemps have agreed to sell the Vincent to Reggie Tapp."

"Never." Oliver, who had come up to the table to see if anything interesting had happened yet, wagged optimistically.

"I stopped by there after work today, and Reggie was

just leaving." Emma tossed Oliver a chip, which he caught neatly. This brought Lucy over to stretch out on her side next to him, thumping her fringed tail.

"But why?" Brian fed a chip to Lucy. Thankfully, there was no judgment here about table scraps. "Charles has no use at all for Reggie."

"Yeah, well, there's the problem," said Emma. "Pippa told me she found a police report from the seventies about a Black Lightning stolen in Knightsbridge."

Brian's mouth pursed in a silent whistle. Emma broke another piece of fish in two. Oliver sat up. So did Lucy. Emma looked sorrowfully at her fish, and then glanced at Brian. No help there. He was already chuckling.

"Maybe, but if they, or he, did steal it, it would help explain why Reggie Tapp was able to pressure them into selling it." Emma held out the fish halves. Both dogs surged forward and gobbled them up right off her palms.

Brian handed her some extra napkins.

"Would there be any way to positively identify this Black Lightning?" Emma asked when she was done cleaning up.

"Easy as can be. They're all individually numbered."

"Right. So if Reggie knows about the police report, he could also have found the original owners, or their family, and someone could still file charges. Charles could go to jail." Other countries might have time limits on when criminal charges could be brought, but the UK did not. If someone wanted to make a complaint, it would not matter that the theft—if it happened—had happened half a lifetime ago. "And if Reggie thought he could convince David and Charles to give him the bike at a discount, or get a loan, or something, he could turn around and sell it for closer to its real worth, and use the difference to pay off his debts." She was missing something. She felt sure of it. It was in the back of her head, but she couldn't remember what it was.

Brian folded his arms and leaned his elbows on the table. "But why would they agree? If the Vincent really was stolen—I mean before it was stolen from David and

Charles—it would take the police all of five minutes to identify it. Giving it to Reggie wouldn't accomplish a thing."

"That assumes the police are investigating, which Raj says they aren't."

Brian swirled the last bit of tea in his mug. "Do you think Reggie only threatened to turn them in for grand theft?"

"Either that or—" Emma hesitated. "Rory was there, and he seems really afraid they might have had something to do with Sonny's death."

"But you're not?"

"I don't know," Emma breathed. "I wish I did, but I don't. I mean, they're my friends." She spread her hands helplessly. "But they might have been working for the smuggling ring. What if they knew something? Or saw something . . ." *Or worse.*

"Yeah," said Brian, agreeing with what she said, and what she hadn't. "I've known them both my whole life, and the Greenlaws too."

"I don't see how the Greenlaws could possibly have anything to do with this mess. If they knew there was a body down there, would they open up the tunnel?"

"I don't mean Sam and Liza," Brian said to the last few chips in his takeaway box. Emma watched concern flicker across his features. "I mean Walter, Sam's dad. He's the one who bricked over the tunnel. You'd think he would have noticed there was a body in there."

Emma frowned. "Unless the body wasn't there when he sealed the entrance. I mean, a tunnel's got to have two ends, doesn't it? What if Sonny and the Vincent were brought in from another entrance?"

"It's possible. If it happened before the cave-in blocked the tunnel."

"But Emma!" barked Oliver. "There's a hole! I know there is!"

"There's something else," she told him. "Actually, there's several somethings."

"Somehow I'm not surprised." Brian refilled Emma's

mug. Emma took a swallow of fresh tea. She was going to be up all night at this rate.

Oliver and Lucy had both settled down onto their bellies, but neither one was ready to give an inch when it came to watching the humans for possible additional scraps.

"You remember when we caught Pippa down in the Roundhead's tunnel?" Emma asked Brian. "She found something down there she didn't bother to tell Raj about."

"She did? What was it?"

"A tax sticker, like the ones they put on liquor bottles. A fake one." If Brian asked how she knew about this, she'd figure out something to tell him. Later.

"That's . . . unexpected."

"Not really, as it turns out. I was at the library today, and I found this." Emma pulled the printed-out article from her bag and handed it to him. "It says that those smugglers were using counterfeit tax stickers too, and that Sam's father was one of the people arrested."

Brian's brow furrowed as he read. "I never heard anything about that. They must have let him go."

"The only thing is, Liza said the other day that Walter Greenlaw didn't want anything to do with Billy Marsh and his lot. Except there he is." Emma pointed at Walter's smiling but blurry face in the photo.

"Well, maybe Walter covered it up for the kids," said Brian. "It's not the sort of thing you'd want to discuss over the dinner table." *Especially if he'd been involved in a murder.* But neither of them said that out loud.

"It doesn't look good, does it?" said Emma. "And it goes with something Billy Marsh said the other day. About how it was Sam who should be worried, because it was his dad who closed up the tunnel." She felt her throat tighten. Brian reached across the table and took her hand.

"Hey," he said. "No need to worry yet. We don't have anything like all the facts."

"I know, I know." She wiped at the corner of one eye. Oliver whined and put his chin on her knee. Emma patted him, not certain who was reassuring whom. "I just . . ."

"Want to get this away from our friends?" he asked.

"Just like you do," she answered.

"Guilty as charged." Brian held up his hand.

Emma felt a small, unhappy smile form. "Guess I can't complain about Pippa anymore."

"What do you mean?" asked Brian.

Emma's mouth puckered into a tight smile. "I might have accused her of trying to cover up for her grandfather."

"Well, if I was going to nominate anybody as being up to no good back in the day, Billy'd be top of the list." Brian touched the picture of Billy on the printout.

"What about the other two, Roskilly and Pendergast?"

"Sounds like a firm of solicitors." Brian squinted closer. "But I don't know them, at least, not right off. I mean, they don't necessarily have to have been from the village, do they?"

Brian closed his empty takeaway box. Lucy whined pitifully, and Oliver yipped. "There's another angle here."

"I'm all ears."

"Your ears are not that big," grumbled Oliver.

Brian wiped his mouth on his napkin. "Come with me."

26

BRIAN WAS A GENERAL MECHANIC, AS WELL AS THE OWNER-operator of Trevena's only taxi service. However, his specialty, and his true love, was vintage cars.

They strolled over to the converted (and massive) cow barn that he used as a showroom. Brian hauled open the sliding door and threw the big knife switch on the wall to bring up the lights.

Emma had never thought much about cars before she and Brian started dating, but even she had to admit the rows of carefully preserved and restored automobiles were an impressive sight, especially the 1937 Rolls Royce Phantom that he hired out for special occasions like wedding parties and major anniversaries.

Oliver and Lucy, had, of course, followed Emma and Brian into the showroom. The two dogs immediately galloped off to take care of the important business of investigating tires and corners.

"What is it about vintage cars?" asked Emma. Brian had sold her her 1966 Mini Cooper and now she wouldn't part with the car any more than she'd part with Oliver.

"What do you mean?"

"What's the fascination?" She gestured toward a cherry-red Mustang convertible.

Brian shrugged. "What's the fascination with a good cake?"

Emma shrugged back. "It's pure pleasure, obviously. Everybody's happy to see you when you're bringing cake. It's the connection to family and friends. And it's a skill, isn't it? When the sponge and the cream come out just right, you know you've really done something. It's a small something, but it's real."

"This is skill too." Brian stopped to contemplate a low, sleek Jaguar that would have looked at home in a James Bond film, back when James Bond was still Sean Connery. "Skill to design, to build, to drive. It's connection too. These machines get passed down through families. Stories get built up around them. Plus, a love of vintage cars means you're part of a community. A small, pretty daft community," he added. "But it's ours."

The Vincent waited on a tarp in the back corner. It looked a bit of a wallflower back here away from the bigger, more brightly colored automobiles.

"Aren't you worried about someone breaking in and driving off with it?" asked Emma. "I mean, if it's worth as much as you say it is?"

Brian laughed. "If anybody tried to drive that now, they wouldn't get very far. It's been in a hole for forty years, remember. The tires are rotted out and the sparks are all corroded. I drained the petrol before it could gunk up the tank any more, but the oil's a congealed mess."

"Oh," said Emma, a bit deflated. "Shows you what I know."

"Don't be so hard on yourself." Brian tucked his arm through hers. "Just take a good look at her. What do you see?"

"I see a motorcycle with flat tires," said Emma. "And a sidecar."

Brian gave her arm a little shake. "Try again. Put yourself in Sonny's place. Think about it from his perspective."

Emma frowned at the machine, but she did try to do as

Brian suggested and really look. She had to admit, even just sitting there all battered and dusty, there was a kind of drama about the machine. She pictured herself in the sidecar with a scarf around her hair and a pair of sunglasses on, while Brian was in the driver's seat in a black leather jacket and . . .

And she had to stop before she started blushing like a schoolgirl.

Focus, Emma.

"All right," she said out loud. "Here I am. I'm a village punk from back in the day, but I'm not completely stupid. I'm already running all kinds of risks just doing what I do."

"Also, it's very possible I've just robbed a bunch of dangerous men, and maybe grassed on them too," put in Brian.

"So, why do I add stealing the most recognizable vehicle in town to my worries?"

Brian nodded. "I need to get out of town, fast. I could hit the road and try to get a ride from a passing lorry, have them drop me over in Bodmin maybe, where I can catch the bus. Or just hitch all the way to London."

"So why do I do it? A bike is better than a car on the back roads, and uses less petrol, so there's that. But there are other bikes around. Why do I need this one?"

"Because I know where it is, and because I know the person who owns it is out on a late job, so I've got a chance," said Emma, thinking of David and Charles running errands for the smugglers. She stared at the bike, willing herself to see all its details. Then, all at once, she got it.

"And it's got a sidecar. He wasn't going alone. He was taking someone with him." She pressed her hand over her mouth. "The Trevena Casanova was going to run off with a girl."

"Only something happened on the way," said Brian.

"Like her boyfriend found out," suggested Emma. "Billy Marsh has been hinting around that Liza had something going on with Sonny."

"I heard that too," said Brian. "I know she denies it, but if it was true, it would be a motive for Sam—"

"Or Liza herself," said Emma. "Or Marianne Tapp."

"*What?*" exclaimed Brian. "How'd she get into this?"

"She was asking me if anything was found with the Vincent, like letters or photographs."

"Good lord." Brian stared at the Vincent in disbelief. "Was anybody living the quiet village life back then?"

"Starting to look like not, isn't it?"

Emma moved forward, gingerly, like the Vincent was a marble statue in a museum. This close, she could see the old black leather of the sidecar seat. She tried to imagine squeezing herself into the little egg-shaped compartment. She reached down, meaning to run her hand under the seat.

"Wait." Brian stopped her. He pulled a pair of work gloves out of his back pocket and handed them to her.

The gloves were too big, but Emma pulled them on anyway. Oliver put his paws up on the edge of the sidecar and wagged.

"What are we looking for? I could help, if you boosted me."

Emma chuckled and ran her hands into the nooks under the seat. When she saw the amount of grime that came up on the canvas gloves, she was really glad she'd put them on.

"Emma! Emma!" barked Oliver. "There's a thing! A thing!"

A second later Brian said, "What's that?" and brought the torch down lower.

Now Emma saw it. Something glistened faintly under the torchlight. She must have pushed it out when she was digging around under the seat. She stripped off one glove and picked it up in two fingers.

Brian whistled. Oliver barked.

It was a ring—a thin, plain gold band with a tiny diamond chip.

"We were right," said Emma. "There was a girl. And Sonny wanted to marry her."

27

FRIDAY MORNINGS WERE GENERALLY BUSY AT THE SHOP. Even in a quiet village, at the end of the week, people seemed to need that extra lift that came from a perfect scone or currant bun and a cup of really good tea.

As far as Emma was concerned, that made Friday the perfect time to start pushing fruitcake.

The wider world might make fun of fruitcake, but for many families, it was still an important part of holiday and New Year celebrations. Personally, Emma had always loved it, but that was because she'd grown up on her Nana Phyllis's homemade cake, rather than the claggy stuff from the tin. The trick was that the cakes had to be started two months ahead of time so they could be properly "fed"—that is, thoroughly soaked with rum.

Her plan was to put samples of fresh cake out on the takeaway counter, brushed with a rum simple syrup, and gauge customer interest in the various flavors.

Maybe I can even put some out at the village stores. I'll talk to Jean about that, Emma mused as she slid the three different tins into the oven. She was confident in the basic sponge. It was Nan's recipe, after all, which meant it was practically perfect. It was the fruits and nuts that wanted adjusting. She loved her Nan, but her recipes could come off as a bit old-fashioned. Emma wanted to make sure she had a fruitcake that was in tune with the modern sensibility.

She'd even been able to keep a straight face while she told Angelique that. Just not for long.

There was another reason for Emma to be keeping herself busy, of course. If she was mixing her sponges, and slicing crystalized fruits, and wondering how she was going to handle things today because Bella called to say Becca had come down with the stomach flu, then she wasn't thinking about David and Charles, or Sam and Liza, or Reggie and Marianne, or how any of them could have been involved in a forty-year-old murder. She'd much rather be considering the merits of glacé cherries, candied orange peel and stem ginger.

"Pearl sugar or no pearl sugar?" she muttered to her printed-out recipe. "Try it both ways? Why can't I make up my mind?" She pressed her hand against her forehead.

"You need a walk, Emma," said Oliver. "You are very tense."

Oliver was right. The truth was there weren't enough cherries and orange peel in the world to keep Emma from replaying her fight with David and Charles, and the way they'd simply let Rory leave without patching things up. She'd hoped that talking things over with Brian last night would make her feel better, but it hadn't. At least, not for long.

Of course, they could be wrong. She could be wrong. It could be that the Kemps had worked out how much it would cost to refurbish the Vincent and had simply decided it would be easier to sell it. But if that was true, why did they look so devastated? And why fight with Rory, and her, about it?

Reggie must have said or done something to change their minds. But what was it? Had he really found some proof of theft?

Or murder?

"No," she muttered to the oven. "I don't believe it. Whatever happened, it wasn't that."

"What happened to who?" asked Angelique. There were only two rooms reserved for the weekend, and she was working on her own lists and her plans for the maintenance that the B and B needed during the off season.

"David and Charles," Emma answered. She'd told Angelique about how the couple was going to sell the Vincent to Reggie, and about the old article she'd found about the smuggling ring, and about how Sonny had wanted the Vincent because he wasn't so much vanishing as eloping. She'd left the ring with Brian, because he could lock it in the shop's safe. He had promised to phone Raj first thing and let her know what he heard. She'd only checked her phone for texts a dozen times, never mind that it wasn't even eight in the morning yet.

"Emma, you need to step back," said Angelique seriously. "David and Charles are grown men. Rory is too. Sometimes people have to work their troubles out for themselves, especially when it comes to family."

"Their troubles involve an insanely valuable motorcycle and a basement full of bones," Emma pointed out.

"And you were the one who used to fret that if you got too involved with a mystery, you might accidentally muck up the evidence or something."

"The evidence has already been mucked up." Emma told Angelique about Pippa's article and her subsequent conversation with Genny. She glossed over the fake tax sticker Pippa had found, because she still didn't know how to explain how she'd heard about that without dragging Oliver, and questions about her sanity, into it.

"Pippa." Angelique sighed sharply. "That girl's got a good heart, but her head is not always in the right place."

"I do understand how she feels," said Emma. "If it was my grandfather, I'd want to protect him too."

"Well, it seems to me that if you're serious about finding out what happened to Sonny, then Billy Marsh is the one you want to talk to."

"I thought about that," Emma admitted. "I just haven't worked out how to get him to talk to me yet."

"You'll never know until you try," said Angelique sagely. "And I should up your shop rent for making me resort to clichés this early in the morning."

"You probably should, but you are a saint."

"I am that," she agreed easily.

"The person I really want to talk to is Marianne," said Emma. "Her family was smack in the middle of . . . whatever it was that happened. She must have known something about it." And she might have been in love with Sonny. And she might not have been the only one.

"Then talk to her," said Angelique. "She's probably at the Donkey's Win by now. Friday is their busy night and she always gets in early. You have another two hours before the counter opens."

"You see?" Oliver poked her calf. "You need a walk."

"But my bakes . . ." began Emma.

"I'll pull them out for you."

"You sure you don't mind?"

"Frankly, I'd rather have you doing something other than wandering about the kitchen muttering to yourself. I can't concentrate."

"I was not—"

"You were," barked Oliver helpfully. "A lot."

"I'm sorry," said Emma sheepishly to them both. "And thanks." She took off her apron and collected her bag and coat. "I'll be right back, I promise."

It was a chilly morning, but at least it wasn't raining. Emma hurried down the high street. The Donkey's Win was out at the edge of the village, but that still put it no more than fifteen minutes away. Emma walked briskly, trying to think about how she was going to approach Marianne.

I wanted to ask about your parents . . . I found this article . . . ?

Did you ever maybe hear . . . ?

Was your dad smuggling bootleg whiskey? Did your mum help?

Emma sighed, and her breath puffed out in a white cloud. "This was a bad idea."

"Walks are never a bad idea," said Oliver.

"I don't mean the walk. I mean . . . oh, darn it." She stopped and dug her hands further into her pockets. "What am I even doing, Oliver?"

"Standing still," said Oliver. "And talking to yourself."

"My very literal corgi." Emma rubbed his ears. An idea struck her. Emma pulled out her mobile, then hesitated, but only for a minute. She touched Pippa's number. Emma was still angry with the journalist about what she'd written about David and Charles, but Pippa had access to sources of information that might help sort out what had happened all those years ago, including her grandfather.

The phone rang, and rang again. Emma glanced at her watch. She hoped Pippa really was the early riser she was rumored to be. It was barely gone eight o'clock.

On the third ring, she answered. "Pippa Marsh."

"Pippa, it's Emma Reed," she began.

"Emma! What's going on?"

"I wanted to talk to you about Reggie Tapp."

"You've heard, then?"

Emma's brow furrowed. "Heard what?"

"Oh. Wow. Well. I'm at the Donkey's Win right now."

Emma felt her heart thud heavily against her ribs. Oliver picked up on her change of mood and pressed closer. "Has something happened?"

"Too right it has. Reggie Tapp's dead."

28

"DEAD?" REPEATED EMMA. "BUT . . . I JUST TALKED TO HIM the other day. He seemed fine."

"What did you talk about?"

"I . . ." *I was watching him gloat about having driven two friends of mine into a corner.* "He had a business proposal. He wanted to invest in Reed's Tea and Cakes."

"I see." There was a scribbling noise. Emma imagined Pippa taking notes.

"What happened? I mean, how did he die?"

"They don't know. Or at least, they're not saying—yet."

"Oh, erm. I think . . . I've got to go, Pippa."

"So do I. I expect I'll see you soon."

She rang off before Emma could answer. Emma stuffed her mobile back in her bag. She knew what she should do. She should turn around and go back to the King's Rest, or back home. Anywhere but the Donkey's Win. But she wasn't turning around. She wasn't even slowing down. In fact, she was almost running, and Oliver was trotting to keep up.

"Emma! Is it bad, Emma?"

"Yes," she panted. "It's really bad."

* * *

BY THE TIME EMMA GOT THERE, THE DONKEY'S WIN WAS IN the process of being cordoned off. She came up on the same side as the pub's car park. Two constables she didn't know were stringing yellow caution tape along the beer garden's fence. Through the slats, Emma could see PCs and EMTs moving around the beer garden, measuring things, snapping photos, talking to the knots of staff and taking notes.

Out front, a crowd of neighbors and curious onlookers spilled across the sidewalk and partly into the street. Gwen Leigh stood by the fence with a huddle of kitchen staff. Her white coat stood out sharply among their jeans, black T-shirts, and billed caps.

It was all too much for Oliver. He barked urgently and dove for the wicket gate and the walk to the pub's front door.

"Oliver, no!" shouted Emma.

To Oliver's credit, he tried to put on the brakes, but he skidded on the brick path and tumbled under the caution tape, through the unlatched gate and straight in the path of the woman striding out of the pub.

"Who let this d—dog in here!" she bellowed. Oliver scrambled to his feet, and sneezed, and ducked his head. The woman stared at him. "Oh. It's you."

"Sorry!" Emma hurried forward, digging frantically in her bag for Oliver's lead.

"Hullo, Emma," said Detective Inspector Constance Brent. "I suppose I shouldn't be surprised."

"Erm." Emma clipped the lead onto Oliver's collar. As she did she got a glimpse of a man sprawled facedown across the ledge of the fountain. Even from this angle, he was very obviously dead.

Reggie. Emma swallowed hard.

Constance stepped right into her field of view. Emma blinked in surprise, and found her voice.

"Hullo, Constance."

DCI Constance Brent of the Devon and Cornwall police was a tall woman with a sturdy build, a no-nonsense air and a dry sense of humor that was sometimes hard to appreciate. She kept her hair cut short enough that it stood up in spikes on her head. Every time Emma had seen her, she'd been wearing slacks and a jacket. Today's ensemble was olive green over a black shell, and she'd knotted a blue silk scarf around her neck. As usual, she had an enormous handbag slung over her shoulder.

Emma had met the inspector a couple of times since she'd moved to Trevena. Both times, there had been a dead body involved. They had formed a sort of friendship, and Emma (and Oliver) had been able to help her answer some difficult questions. This still surprised Emma. It surprised Constance too, and while she was glad of the help, she was also clearly torn about having a civilian so involved in what she (rightfully) regarded as police matters.

Constance folded her arms. "I suppose you're about to tell me you know something about this?"

"Erm. Actually, no. I mean, I was just on my way over, but . . ."

"Why?"

"I wanted to talk to Marianne, about, well—" Constance was glaring at her. Emma closed her mouth. Constance was not really mad at her, Emma knew. She just did not like murders happening in her territory. Emma couldn't blame her for that.

"I sense this is going to be a long story." Constance sighed. "Come on." She looked down at Oliver. "Both of you."

EMMA THOUGHT CONSTANCE WOULD TAKE THEM INTO THE pub. Instead, she led them back around to the car park and opened the door on her battered Range Rover. "In."

Emma boosted Oliver onto the back seat and climbed in after. Constance shut the door behind them, went round to the other side and climbed in herself. She dropped her bag into the footwell. Oliver promptly stuck his nose in. Constance rolled her eyes and moved the bag to the front seat.

Oliver looked affronted, but Emma scratched him between the ears. Since there was really no place for him to go, she also unclipped his lead. Grumbling wordlessly, he settled down in the footwell. He scratched himself vigorously under the collar and proceeded to make himself comfortable on top of Emma's feet.

"All right," Constance said. "What were you coming to talk to Marianne Tapp about?"

"Erm . . ." began Emma.

Constance's eyes narrowed. "What's the matter?"

"Nothing. I'm just trying to work out where to start."

"So it is a long story?"

"Yes."

"Score one for me, then." Constance pulled her little notebook out of her pocket, and a mechanical pencil. She clicked the button on top. "Start wherever you want."

"Um, okay. You've heard about the skeleton that was found in the Roundhead?"

Constance nodded. "PC Patel has been making sure everyone's heard about it. A Wilson Greenlaw, wasn't it? Said to have been some kind of a local ne'er-do-well?"

"That's right. Well, people have been saying that Sonny—that's what he was called—was connected to a local group of smugglers, and I thought there might be some old newspaper report about them somewhere, so I went to the library to look and I, well, we, me and Mrs. Shah—she's the head librarian—we found this." She pulled the copy of the article out of her bag and handed it to Constance.

Constance took her time, reading the article carefully.

"Very interesting," she said. "But what part of all this were you going to talk to the Tapps about?"

"Well, erm, that pub the 'social club' met in belonged to Marianne's family before she married Reggie. They pulled it down to put up the Donkey's Win. And if you look, that's

Reggie there, right at the edge of the photo." Emma pointed to the figure at the edge of the little crowd.

Constance did look, and she made a few notes.

"So, this social club was a blind for the smuggling ring," said Constance. "And you think Marianne might know something about it?"

"Or Reggie might. Might have." Emma hesitated.

"Appears to have drowned in the fishpond," said Constance.

Emma blinked. "I'm sorry?"

"You were about to ask how he died, even though you know you shouldn't," Constance told her. "He was found facedown in the ornamental fishpond out back of the pub. Initial indications are that he drowned. Alcohol may have been a factor."

"Oh," said Emma. "Gosh."

"As you say. So, why were you coming to talk to the Tapps? Why not the Greenlaws? Or the Kemps?" she added. "I'm told they were the last owners of that motorcycle that was found with the skeleton."

"Well, I'd been talking with Reggie just the other day—"

"Ah. Now, see, you'd left out that bit. What were you and Reggie talking about?"

"He said he wanted to invest in my tea shop. I told him no."

"That's a long way from the subject of the skeleton in the basement."

"Yes, well, while I was waiting for Reggie, Marianne was asking me about the skeleton. I was there when they found it . . ."

"Of course you were," said Constance, patiently, as if Emma had been trying to explain that Oliver ate her homework.

"It wasn't my fault," Emma protested.

"I didn't say it was, but go on."

"All right. So, when I was meeting Reggie for dinner, Marianne asked me if anything had been found with the motorcycle, I mean, aside from the skeleton. She specifically mentioned letters or photographs. I thought at first she might have been worried about love letters or something."

Constance raised one inquiring eyebrow.

"Sonny was supposed to have been a ladies' man," Emma told her. "But when I found the article about the smuggling ring being caught operating out of her parents' pub . . ."

"You thought she might be afraid that there was something with the body that would rake all this old news back up again."

"Yes. I mean, you know, I thought she might not want her family, or her husband, to be implicated in what might be an old murder. Although if it was love letters, that could still happen. And we did find a ring."

"A ring?"

"Oh, gosh, yes. In the sidecar of the Vincent. Brian Prowse and I. He's got the Vincent stored in his garage, and we had a look—" Constance was eyeing her with much less patience than before. "It wasn't evidence yet!"

"No one said it was. You found a ring?"

"Yes. An engagement ring. We thought maybe Sonny was planning on eloping with somebody. Not that that necessarily was the reason he died, but it would help explain why he stole the Vincent, so he could elope in style."

"Maybe. Maybe not." Constance stared at the article again, her face hard. "May I keep this?"

"Um, yeah, sure."

"Thank you." She folded the article up and tucked it into her notebook. "What else have you got?"

"Sorry?"

"Emma," said Constance sternly. "A body was found in a cellar. Friends of yours are connected with the death. You cannot expect me to believe that the only thing you've done for the past couple of days is stick to your knitting."

"I don't knit?" Emma tried.

"Cupcakes, then. Come on." Constance gestured with two fingers. "You've been looking around. What have you found out?"

"I'm not sure . . ."

"For instance," said Constance, "we've heard that Reggie had been drinking more than usual lately, but not why."

"Oh. Well, Gwen and, well, other people all said Reggie had money trouble, but I don't know what kind."

"There." Constance beamed. "This is exactly what I'm talking about."

Emma felt her cheeks heat up. Oliver squirmed, and a low rumbling filtered up from the footwell. She and Constance both looked down. Oliver had fallen asleep and rolled over onto his back.

"It's been a hard morning," said Emma.

"I can sympathize," murmured Constance. "Now, when you say Gwen, I'm assuming you mean Gwendolyn Leigh, who is"—she flipped back through her book a couple of pages—"the chef at the Donkey's Win and also the daughter of Benjamin Leigh, who was Reggie Tapp's business partner and accountant?"

"Yeah," said Emma. "Right after I met with Reggie, Gwen pulled me aside to warn me off investing with him. She said there were some real money problems, and that the pub wasn't doing as well as people thought." Emma paused. "Did you want to know that when I was talking with Reggie, Ben Leigh showed up and he was clearly angry, and he got angrier when he found out that Reggie not only wanted to invest in my business, but that he had talked to Charles Kemp about possibly buying the Vincent? But Reggie went and said something about how there was a lot of new business coming in so they were all just fine?"

"Yes. I did want to know that. Thank you." Constance scribbled down some more notes. "Anything else?"

"Erm. No. I don't think so."

"For instance, you didn't hear anything about David and Charles Kemp also being involved with this smuggling ring back in the day?"

"Erm . . ." Emma hesitated. "Well, now that you mention it, I guess I did hear that. Yes."

"So, one more time. Anything else?"

Emma looked down at her snoring corgi. He looked very peaceful. She wished she could curl up with him.

"Emma?" Constance's stern voice cut through her thoughts. "If you're trying to figure out a way to cover for some friends of yours, don't, all right?"

"Oh, sugar," Emma muttered. "It was my face, wasn't it?"

"Afraid so. Now come on, out with it."

Emma took a deep breath. "Reggie might have been threatening Charles Kemp."

"Might have?" echoed Constance

"I didn't actually hear what happened," she said quickly. "All I know is that when Reggie went round to Vintage Style to talk about maybe buying the Vincent, he also said something about Charles and David needing all the friends they could get now that Sonny had been found. But he came back a second time and . . . and that time they agreed to sell. I don't know anything more than that," she added quickly.

"Cross your heart?" muttered Constance as she scribbled down another note.

"Sorry?"

Constance sighed and closed her notebook. "I appreciate that you want to protect your friends, Emma. It's natural. But you know how much it hurts us if we don't have all the facts right up front. Not only does precious time get wasted, but the wrong people get accused, and I know you don't want that."

"Yes, I do know, and no, I don't."

"Right, so we're on the same page here. If you hear anything that might help us out, on either case, you call me and I'll put it down to a tip from a concerned citizen, yeah?"

"So you're going to investigate Sonny's death as well?"

Constance looked down at her notebook, clearly irritated. "At this point I don't see as we have any choice. Maybe these two incidents have nothing at all to do with each other. Maybe it's just a bad accident with bad timing."

"But you don't think so?"

"No, I don't. I think PC Patel was right from the beginning. When that tunnel got opened, a lot more got uncovered than some bones and an old motorcycle."

Emma considered this. "Naturally, I'm not going to ask why you think some bad feeling from forty years ago has led to the death of an obnoxious and probably drunk pub owner."

Constance looked her right in the eye. "And naturally I'm not going to tell you that Reggie has a bruise we can't account for."

"No, of course you couldn't tell me about that," replied Emma.

Constance nodded. "Because you see, if I told you that, you might conclude he'd been strangled, because you couldn't know that the bruise is on the back of his neck, right under his collar, and perfectly round, about ten centimeters across."

"If I did know that though, I might wonder if he'd been pushed up against something before he died," said Emma. "Maybe knocked unconscious."

"Or if something had been used to hold him down in the water while he drowned," replied Constance. "Yes. In your place, I would be wondering the same thing."

29

WHEN EMMA AND CONSTANCE CLIMBED OUT OF THE RANGE Rover, Pippa Marsh was right there waiting for them.

"Hello, Chief Inspector!" Pippa sang out. "Is it true Reggie Tapp's been found dead?"

"Ah, the media arrives," said Constance. "Hello, Pippa. How's your granddad?"

"He's doing very well, thanks. Is it true Reggie was found in the fishpond? Is foul play suspected?"

Constance's gaze slid to Emma. "No comment," she said, and Emma got the distinct feeling it was both a reply to Pippa and an order for her.

Just then, a slender woman PC strode up. Oliver of course tried to lunge forward to find out where her shoe tops had been. Emma caught him by the collar just in time. "Hey, guv!" She held up a plastic baggie. "We found these in one of the drawers. PC Patel thought you should know."

Constance took the baggie and squinted at the capsules inside. "Right. Get those tagged and sent to the lab right away, yeah? And make sure the pathologist knows we need a solid tox screen, just in case there's something besides alcohol in our man's bloodstream."

"So, alcohol may have been a factor?" said Pippa brightly.

"No comment," said Constance, again looking hard at Emma. "There will be a formal statement for the press *later*."

Constance marched back toward the pub, and Pippa turned to Emma.

"So, what happened?" asked Pippa.

"I'm surprised you don't already know," said Emma. She also winced inside, because that was very close to what Constance had said to her.

Emma's gaze slid involuntarily toward the garden fence, and the police milling around the other side. Oliver was on his feet, watching her closely. Emma wondered if he knew how much she wished she could let him in there.

"I'm good, but I'm not that good," said the journalist. "What did she tell you?"

Emma shrugged. "What would she tell me?"

"She told you a lot, Emma," Oliver yipped. "Weren't you listening? You should have been listening."

"Okay, Oliver." Emma bent down and gave his head a quick rub. Oliver subsided and started casting about on the gravel for interesting new smells. She found herself looking at the garden again.

"But if Brent's here, they can't think Reggie's death is an accident," Pippa was saying.

Emma forced her attention back to the reporter. "I really don't know."

"Somehow, I don't believe you. Did she say anything about Reggie's after-hours meeting?"

"Sorry, what?"

Pippa grinned. "So she didn't. I talked with a couple of the staff." She nodded toward the cluster of kitchen workers. "And they said Reggie was still sitting out in the garden at closing. They thought he was waiting for someone, but they couldn't say who."

"Oh. No. Constance didn't say anything about that."

"Any guesses?"

Emma's gaze shifted toward the garden again. At her

side, Oliver's ears perked up, signaling he was also paying close attention to what was happening. *Stop it, Emma. You'll give yourself ideas.*

"No guesses, no bets, no idea," said Emma firmly. She set her back to the garden. *No peeking.*

Pippa cocked her head, as if trying to decide what she was actually hearing. "Why are you mad at me?"

"I'm not mad at you," Emma insisted. Oliver harrumphed. *Great, I'm being contradicted by the corgi.* "You've got a job to do," she said to Pippa. "If I were you, I'd be right here too."

"As it happens, you're not me, but you showed up anyway. Why's that?"

Time to change the subject.

"How about I ask you one?" said Emma. "Have you told DCI Brent about the tax sticker you found down in the Roundhead's cellar?"

Now it was Pippa's turn to stare. "I'm going to kill that Rory," she muttered.

"It wasn't Rory," Emma told her.

"Then who was it?"

"Must have been my dog."

"I almost believe you're serious," breathed Pippa.

"What's important here is that you have to tell the police what you found," said Emma. "They're trying to work out if the discovery of Sonny's body is connected to Reggie's death. They need to know about that sticker."

Pippa's mouth stretched out into a tight line, and she glanced toward the pub. Her face shifted uneasily. "So, you didn't tell her just now?"

"No. I wanted to give you the chance," Emma said. "If you volunteer the information, Constance will overlook a lot. It might help later, if she really starts wondering about your granddad. You said it yourself—when you were there before, it wasn't an official crime scene, so you didn't really do anything wrong."

Pippa looked away, and rubbed the corner of her eye. "I've got to get going," she muttered. "I'm on the job."

"Yeah, me too," said Emma. "I've got a set of experimental fruitcakes waiting for me back at the shop."

"You're going to have to catch your dog first."

IF THERE WAS ONE THING OLIVER KNEW ABOUT HUMANS, IT was that you had to watch them carefully. Even Emma. It wasn't just that she sometimes worked too hard and forgot about important things like walks. It was that what she said with her voice and what she said with her body could sometimes be two different things.

Right now she was talking to the Pippa lady, but her attention was on the garden, where all of Raj and Constance's friends were looking around. Everything about Emma told him she wanted to be looking around there with them. Which made Oliver want to look too.

But he knew he shouldn't. He should stay with Emma. He should sit-and-stay. He really should.

Except Emma needed to know who had been in the garden. That was important too. She kept looking over there. He knew her well. He almost knew what she was thinking. She wanted to be in there. She wanted to be looking and doing, not just talking.

But she couldn't.

That meant it was up to him.

Emma turned around, putting her back to the garden. Oliver wagged his bum and put his nose down and wandered away, following the blurry scents on the car park tarmac.

Which all just happened to lead toward the garden, and the fence. Well, it was sort of a fence. Not much of a fence, just a lot of wooden slats meant to keep out big slow things, like humans, not clever and observant warrior corgis.

The only problem was, that garden was full of police humans, and they might not understand how important it was that Emma find out everything she could about what had happened. Even from here he could smell the bad scents that made him want to cringe and bark. But he would not give up. No.

But he would have to be quick. Oliver crouched low. Very quick.

EMMA STARED AROUND FRANTICALLY, JUST IN TIME TO SEE Oliver darting through the beer garden fence.

"Oliver!" she shrieked. "Oh, sugar!" She sprinted after him.

The fence around the Donkey's Win's beer garden was barely a fence. The slats were widely spaced and clearly intended to keep out mildly inquisitive humans, not determined corgis who could not read the word "CAUTION" no matter how large it was printed on bright yellow tape. Oliver was through the fence and up on the other side before you could shout "What on earth are you doing, you naughty dog, get back here!"

Emma ran up to the gate without thinking. The tape caught her attention and she pulled up short just before she broke through, windmilling her arms in a less than dignified fashion.

A blue-coated constable she didn't recognize materialized right in her path, his arms stretched out on either side.

"I'm sorry, miss, I need you to step back now," he said.

"Yes, I know, I'm sorry, but . . . that's my dog," she finished.

Over the PC's shoulder, she saw Oliver zipping back and forth all around the beer garden, nose to the ground, trying to be everywhere at once.

At least he didn't head straight for the body.

Reggie Tapp now lay on his back beside the tacky fishpond in an open body bag. He was pale and waterlogged. He wore the tweed jacket he'd had on when Emma first met him. Someone in a white clean suit knelt beside him, taking pictures.

"You need to move back now, miss," said the PC firmly.

"Yes, I know, but . . ."

Oliver zoomed over to the fountain, and the body. The person in the clean suit yelped and toppled backwards.

Of course it was just as Constance walked back into the garden.

"Get that damn dog out of here!" she snarled.

"Sorry!" Emma called, standing on tiptoe to be seen over the PC's shoulder. "I, um, Oliver! Oliver, heel! Now!"

Thankfully, Oliver heard that she was serious. He stopped sniffing beside the body and slunk back over to her. "Sorry, Emma!"

"It's all right." She gave his ears a quick scratch. "But we can't be here right now."

"Why not? The cat is."

"The cat . . . ?" Then Emma saw what he was talking about. The window at the back of the bar was open, and the Cream Tangerine was sitting on the windowsill.

"Yes, well, the cat's on the windowsill, not in the garden. We need to give Constance room to do her work. Come on." She started away from the gate. Oliver followed, reluctantly.

"But we should help," he grumbled. "I can help. You wanted to know who was there. I know!"

Emma sighed. She could try to say she did not want to know, but she'd be lying, and Oliver would know it. Having a talking dog could sometimes be a double-edged sword.

Emma looked around carefully, but no one seemed to be paying attention. They all stood in their own little groups, talking to each other or looking at their phones. Emma knelt down and lifted up Oliver's front paws so he was looking right at her.

"Oliver, listen. This is serious. Do you really know who was in the beer garden with Reggie?"

"Of course!" Oliver huffed. "A noble warrior corgi always knows!"

Or at least, he thought he did. Oliver frequently tried to convince her that his sense of smell was infallible. He also tried to convince her that baths were an unnecessary waste of time.

"Did you have time to recognize them? The scents, I mean?"

"Of course!" yapped Oliver. "Well, most of them. A few of them."

Emma reminded herself to be patient. "So, who was there?"

"Lots of people! The lady you talked to—the sad, nervous lady with all the fake flower and powder smell . . ."

Emma took a deep breath. Being a dog, Oliver paid much more attention to what a person smelled like than he did to what their name was.

"Do you mean Marianne?" Emma asked. Of course she would be there.

"Yes! Yes!" barked Oliver. "And the snacks lady, and the sad man . . ."

The snacks lady had to be Gwen. Since she worked there, that was hardly surprising—her trail would be all over the garden. "The sad man" was trickier. "The sad man we talked to the other night? Ben Leigh? The one with the bald head and the glasses?"

"Yes!" Oliver wagged his whole bum.

"He was here recently? Last night?"

Oliver's wag got a little less certain. "Not long ago. Since the last time it rained. He was clear." To Oliver, the smell and the person sometimes seemed like the same thing. "Almost as clear as the David part of Charles-and-David, and Rory. He was here. I can show you where."

"Oh." Emma swallowed. *Oh no, no, no.*

Oliver wagged hopefully, for once missing Emma's change of tone. "And the grumpy man."

"The grumpy man?"

"In the chair with the wheels. He was in the garden." He paused again. "So was the Pippa lady."

30

EMMA CLIPPED THE LEAD BACK ONTO OLIVER'S COLLAR and dutifully retreated a bit further into the car park. Pippa was nowhere in sight. Emma let out a small sigh of relief.

She tried to tell herself the fact that both David and Rory had been at the Donkey's Win recently didn't mean anything. It was a pub. Half the village could be coming and going on any given night.

Except that since both David and Rory were furious with the pub's owner, there was no reason for them to stop by for a quick drink.

And what about Billy Marsh? Pippa I can understand. She was probably quizzing Reggie about Sonny and the Vincent. But what on earth was Billy doing there?

On the other hand, Billy had been in the "social club" back in the day, and so had Reggie.

The only good thing about Oliver's list was that he hadn't mentioned either of the Greenlaws. Not that Emma could really relax about that. Oliver hadn't had a whole lot of time. He might have missed something.

She rubbed her eyes, suddenly extremely tired.

"Emma?" Someone touched her shoulder.

It was Gwen. Despite everything, she looked crisp and fresh in her white chef's coat.

"You all right?" Gwen asked her.

Emma shook herself and managed a smile. "Yeah, yeah, fine. It's just . . . it's a shock."

"Tell me about it." Gwen shivered.

"You didn't . . . find him, did you?" The kitchen staff were generally the first ones into a restaurant in the mornings.

"No, it wasn't me. Thank goodness. But . . . I don't know, maybe it should have been." Her gaze strayed toward the garden fence. From this corner of the car park, they could just see the cops moving back and forth. "I mean, I parked right there." She nodded toward a small green Volkswagen. "I could have seen something through the fence, if I'd looked. But I didn't." She wrapped her arms tight around herself. "I just went right in through the front and got to work. Just like any other day."

"Then who did . . . ?"

"Marianne. Poor woman," Gwen added softly. "I mean, I had no use for either of them, but well, you wouldn't wish that on anybody, would you? I heard the scream and when I came out of the kitchen, she was running towards me. I couldn't understand what she was saying, something about Reggie. So I sat her down and went to look." She paused, and Emma saw memory flicker behind her eyes. "She'd pulled him out of the fountain and—well, anyway, I had James call the cops."

"Where's Marianne now? Has anybody called her people?" Emma paused. "Does she even have any family?"

Gwen shook her head. "Wouldn't know. Dad might. I think I heard him say her folks died a while back, and I know she and Reggie never had kids. But that's really it. We weren't exactly close."

"What about Reggie's family?"

Gwen's face hardened. "Don't know, and honestly, I don't care. As far as I'm concerned, the world's better off." She saw Emma's surprise but she just shrugged. "I'm not going to pretend. The man was worthless. Treated his people like they were replacement parts. I couldn't keep any decent staff for more than a couple of months."

"But your dad worked for him." *And so did you.*

"Yeah, well, we do what we have to, don't we?" she said grimly. "And believe me, the only reason I stayed on is—"

She didn't get to finish. A battered silver Honda roared into the car park and screeched to a halt. The door flew open and Ben Leigh all but fell out of the driver's side.

"Gwen!" Ben hurried over and wrapped his daughter in a huge hug. Oliver tried to go over to give Ben his usual thorough sniffing, but Emma pulled him back.

"Emma!" he yipped. "Emma, the Lead's too short, Emma!"

This one time, though, Emma did not give in.

"What are you doing here, Dad?" Gwen pushed herself back just far enough to see his face.

"Marianne called me. Are you all right?" Ben gripped her forearms and looked anxiously into her eyes.

"Yes, yes, I'm fine," Gwen assured him firmly. "Why did Marianne call you?"

Emma was wondering the same thing. But Ben wasn't listening. "Have you talked to the police yet? What do they say? Do they know anything about—"

"Dad." Gwen cut him off. "You've got to calm down, yeah?" She nodded toward Emma.

"Oh. Yes, right. Sorry." He coughed. "It's just when I heard what had happened, and I knew you'd already gone into work, I got frightened. Not thinking straight." He rubbed at his forehead. "You're right. I should have called you first, but Marianne asked me to come right down."

"It's all right, Dad. Look, if Marianne wants to talk to you, you should probably go find her, right now." It seemed to Emma that Gwen spoke those last words with extra urgency, and she found herself wondering about that. "I'm going to see if the cops need anything else from me or my staff. If they want to talk to you—"

"I'll be fine, Gwen," her father said. "This isn't the first time . . . well, it isn't the first time."

Gwen nodded. "As soon as we're both done, I'll meet you back home, okay?"

"Yes, yes, all right." Ben squeezed his daughter's hand once more and hurried away, presumably to try to find Marianne Tapp.

"You all right now?" Gwen asked Emma. "I should be with my staff."

"Yes, yes, I'm fine," Emma told her. "Go on."

Gwen nodded and went back to stand with her people.

It struck Emma how quickly Gwen had taken charge of her father. She hadn't exactly talked down to him, but she'd been very calm and very firm, like she was used to being the one who had to stay steady in a difficult situation.

"Emma?" said Oliver. "You can unclip the Lead now. I'll stay right here."

Emma ignored this. Probably Oliver meant it, but there was too much excitement to be sure, and the possibility of picking up extra bits of information wasn't worth testing Constance's patience any further.

Somewhere in the depths of her bag, Emma's mobile pinged.

"Sugar," she muttered as she dug for it and tapped the screen.

It was a text from Angelique. You all right? Just heard about Reggie.

Because nothing is faster than the village grapevine. I'm fine, she texted back. Had to talk to DCI Brent. Back soon.

She'd just touched send when the phone pinged again. This time the text was from Genny.

WHERE ARE YOU? REGGIE TAPP IS DEAD!

At the Donkey's Win and I know.

Why am I not surprised? There was a pause, presumably while Angelique typed some more. What happened?

Movement caught Emma's eye. She looked up to see Marianne Tapp coming out of the pub, with Ben Leigh right beside her. Her eyes automatically darted over to where Gwen stood with the staff. All the chef's attention was riveted on her father. Emma was too far away to make her expression out clearly, but she could see how stiffly Gwen held herself.

Whatever Gwen saw as she watched her father and Marianne together, she did not like it.

Emma's phone pinged. It was Genny again—three question marks and an exclamation point.

Right. Yes. What happened to Reggie. Drowned in the fountain, Emma typed. Maybe drunk accident.

There was a longer pause this time. You believe that?

Emma bit her lip. I want to.

You coming here or am I going there?

Meet you at King's Rest. She hit send, and also set the phone to vibrate and stuffed it back into her bag.

"Come on, Oliver," she murmured.

Oliver yelped wordlessly and bounded along beside Emma as she made her way over to where Marianne and Ben were standing.

Marianne saw her before Ben did. "Oh, hullo, Emma," she said. "I didn't realize you were here."

Emma didn't bother offering an explanation for her presence. After all, there really wasn't one. *Not a good one, anyway.*

"I'm so sorry about what happened," she told Marianne instead. "Is there someone that should be called?"

"Yes. That's what we should do now, isn't it?" Marianne looked toward the pub. "Call people. Make arrangements. Start cleaning up."

"You don't have to do anything," said Ben. "I'll take care of it."

"That's very thoughtful of you, Ben." Marianne gave him a kind, tired smile. "But really, you're going to have enough to do without looking after me."

"But you shouldn't be alone," said Emma.

"Actually, I want to be alone. Very much. I haven't been alone in . . . years." Marianne turned her face toward Emma, and Emma couldn't help noticing her eyes were completely dry.

Marianne saw the way Emma was watching her. She touched her face, as if to confirm the fact that no tears had been shed.

"Oh, no. Don't worry about me, Emma. I'm all right, really. It's just . . . well, I'm sure you've guessed Reggie wasn't the easiest man to live with."

"I . . ." Emma searched for something kind to say. Nothing came, so she settled for honesty. "Yeah, I thought that's how it might be."

"I did my best," she said. "For better or worse, in sickness and in health. I never took any of it back, and he did love me. In his way. It's just that he loved so many other things more."

The color drained slowly from Ben's ruddy cheeks.

Marianne laughed a little and patted his hand. "Oh, no. Not like that. He never cheated on me, not that I know of. But he loved money and bragging rights and fixing problems. Sometimes, I think he deliberately created problems just so he could take the credit for fixing them."

"Come on, now, Marianne," said Ben. "You know you don't mean that."

Marianne looked at him steadily. She clearly did mean it, but she wasn't going to contradict him in front of a relative stranger.

"I'll tell you what," Ben went on. "If they're done with you, how about I take you home? You shouldn't drive, you know, not when you're still in shock and such."

"Yes, I'm sure you're right. You go talk to the detective inspector. I'll wait here."

Ben looked uncertainly at Emma but evidently couldn't think of a polite way to ask her to leave Marianne alone.

Emma couldn't help remembering how Ben had come into the kitchen while she was talking to Gwen and herded her and Oliver out the door.

It was really starting to seem like Ben did not like people talking about Reggie. Or at least, he didn't like Emma talking about Reggie.

"I'll be right back." Ben bustled away.

"He's frightened, Emma," said Oliver. "Did Constance scare him?"

She scares me sometimes. Emma rubbed his ears. But somehow she didn't think it was fear of Constance that put all that uncertainty in Ben's eyes.

"Don't mind Ben," Marianne was saying. "He's appointed himself my guardian angel." She smiled tiredly. "Emma, can I ask you something?"

"Of course."

"Who do you think could have killed Reggie?"

Emma opened her mouth, and closed it again. "Oh, I have no idea, Marianne . . ."

"But you're going to try to find out, aren't you?"

"No, really, the police are on this. You can trust Detective Brent. She's really good . . ."

"I'm sure she is. But you're still going to try, aren't you?" She sounded lost, and exhausted. Emma felt a twinge of guilt. She couldn't imagine what Marianne was going through right now. Whatever she did, or did not, feel for Reggie, she'd been married to him for decades. Of course she wanted to know what had happened.

"I . . ." Emma swallowed. "Maybe I'll hear something."

The smile on Marianne's face was one of quiet disappointment. "Well, if you do 'hear anything'"—she paused for the air quotes—"will you tell me?"

"I'll help however I can," Emma said, and hoped it was answer enough. Especially considering what she had to say next. She'd been planning on asking Marianne about her family's connection to the old smuggling racket, but Reggie's death had changed the whole picture. "Marianne, can I ask you something?"

"Well, I suppose turnabout is fair play," she said with a weak smile. "What is it?"

"Did you know Reggie was trying to buy the Vincent from the Kemps?"

Now Marianne looked genuinely surprised. "Trying? He told me he had bought it. Or at least, that they had promised to sell it."

"Do you know why he wanted it?"

"Well, it will come as no surprise to you that we had money trouble. Reggie's reach always did exceed his grasp. Always," she repeated softly. "So he thought if he could buy the Vincent, he'd be able to sell it at a profit and pay off our debts." She twisted her hands. "As far as Reggie's ideas went, this one was almost practical."

So, it was a moneymaking scheme, Emma thought. At the same time, something nagged at the back of her mind. She was forgetting something. Something Reggie had done, or said. *Something about money?*

"Do you know why he thought David and Charles would sell to him?" Emma asked. "I mean, even in the shape it's in, I gather it's quite valuable. The Kemps could make a lot of money themselves, especially if they got it fixed up and sent it to auction."

Marianne was staring down the road. Her expression was distant. Emma had no way to tell what she was thinking.

"Yes," Marianne said. "And I said something similar when I first heard the idea. But Reggie was sure he could persuade them. To tell you the truth, I didn't think much of it. Reggie was always sure he could persuade people to do what he wanted. Sometimes he was even right." Then she blinked up at Emma. "I'd heard you and the Kemps are friends, Emma. Why aren't you asking them about this?"

"We are friends, I just . . . well, when we talked last, they weren't very happy with me."

"Well, Charles always did have a temper, and he never liked people mucking about in his life, or his business."

Of course Marianne would have known David and Charles back in the day. Emma itched to ask if she was thinking about any particular incident, but her time was up. Ben was on his way back.

"We are all set, Marianne," he said as soon as he reached her side. "DCI Brent says we can go, and I've told Gwen I'm taking you home."

"Oh, wonderful," said Marianne, but the word rang hollow. "I'll just get my things. Thank you, Emma," she added. "You've been a great help."

She seemed to mean it, but for the life of her, Emma couldn't understand how she'd helped Marianne. Marianne wasn't going to give her any hint, though. She just straightened her shoulders, put a hand up to smooth her hair and strode across the street without looking back.

Ben hurried along beside her. He did look back, and right at Emma.

It was not at all a nice look.

31

STILL REPLAYING THE INTERACTION WITH MARIANNE AND Ben over in her mind, Emma retreated to the sidewalk. Oliver trotted along, looking up at her eagerly.

"What are we doing now, Emma?"

"Good question." She glanced at her watch. "Sugar!" Emma dug her mobile out of her bag and punched the number for the King's Rest.

"Angelique?" she said as soon as the owner picked up.

"Emma, where are you?" asked Angelique urgently. "You all right? Genny's here, and she says you're over at the Donkey's Win."

"Yes, I am, and I'm fine, I just . . . I want to check on the Kemps, and maybe the Greenlaws. I need—"

"—to ask a huge favor but can I help Becca and Bella with the takeaway counter if they need it?" Angelique finished for her.

"You are a saint a thousand times over. I swear I'll be back in time for tea."

"You better be," called Genny from the background. "And you need to promote Becca!"

"Did you hear that all right?" inquired Angelique.

"I did. You can tell Genny she's right, and I will. Today, as soon as I get back."

Angelique laughed. "Go, go. We've got it covered here."

Emma thanked her profusely and rang off.

But before Emma could take another step, the phone rang again. Mouthing a few choice words, she yanked her mobile back out of her bag and checked the screen.

And immediately hit the accept button.

"I'm fine, Brian," she said.

"Oh, good," he answered. "Because everyone is saying Reggie Tapp's been found dead."

"He has, and I'm at the pub, and I had to talk to DCI Brent, but I'm all right. Really."

"I knew you would be." She could hear both the smile and the sincerity in his voice. "I just wanted to see if you needed backup. Or a ride. Or a shoulder to cry on."

"You are a darling," she told him, and she meant it. "Not yet, on any of those. Although that may change. I'm just on my way to check in on Charles and David. Oh, and you're probably going to get a call from the police about the ring we found."

"Reckoned I would as soon as I heard about Reggie. You'll ring me back when you can? Let me know how things are going?"

"Yes, absolutely. And Brian—"

"Yeah?"

"Thanks."

"No worries," he answered softly, and the warmth in those two words made Emma's heart roll over like Oliver when he needed a belly rub.

They said goodbye and hung up.

"Right." Emma shoved her mobile back into her bag. "Vintage Style, Oliver, quick as we can."

"Hurray!" he yipped. "Running!"

THEIR PACE WAS NOT QUITE A RUN, BUT AT TIMES IT DID reach a fast jog. Much to Oliver's annoyance, Emma kept a firm grip on the lead. Village traffic was slower and more cautious than the traffic in London, but Oliver was excited and she was not about to give him the chance to zip across the street without looking both ways.

They were both out of breath by the time they reached Vintage Style. Emma was just about to put her hand on the door latch when she heard her name being called from overhead.

"Emma!" David was leaning out of the upstairs window and waving.

"Right." She sucked in a deep breath and started up the stairs.

"Emma," panted Oliver, as he scrambled up beside her. "You were going to talk to them, Emma."

"Climb now, talk later," mumbled Emma.

"But, Emma—"

Above them, David pulled the door open to let Emma and Oliver inside. "Thank goodness you're here!"

"What is it?" Emma hurried inside. "Is something wrong?" She flinched as soon as she said it. Of course something was wrong. Reggie Tapp was dead.

Charles stood in the kitchen, the landline's receiver pressed to his ear.

"We don't know, that's the problem," said David. "Have you heard from Rory, by any chance?"

"No, nothing," said Emma.

Charles slammed down the receiver, and cursed for a long time. Oliver's ears pricked up, and Emma hoped he wouldn't be asking her what some of those words meant.

"The police are looking for him," said David quietly. "About . . ."

"Yeah," Emma said before he had to finish.

"The little idiot was heard threatening Reggie Tapp last night!" roared Charles toward the phone.

"Oh, no." It seemed Oliver and his nose were right again. Rory had been at the Donkey's Win. *But threatening him?* "I can't believe it," she said out loud. "Rory wouldn't have been so stupid as to go and do something like that," she added, trying to muster at least a little optimism.

"Well, we don't know that, do we?" Charles glared at the phone as if it was the machine's fault. "Because we don't know where he is! I swear I'm going to throttle the little git. First he gets after us to talk to Pippa Marsh, and then he up and vanishes . . ."

"Emma?" Oliver bonked her with his nose. "Emma? The Lead?"

Emma bent down and unclipped the lead. Oliver immediately headed over to the windowsill where Tangerine was folded up in full breadloaf pose. The cat looked out the window and swished her tail slowly. Oliver plopped himself down underneath the window.

"Rory was after you to talk to Pippa?" Emma asked David and Charles.

"Yes," said David. "He seemed to think we should be telling our side of the story, or something."

"I don't suppose—" she began.

"No," said Charles flatly.

"We argued about that," David admitted. "And then . . . well, you saw what happened later that afternoon. Rory didn't come home last night, and he isn't answering his phone."

"Oh, lord." Emma bit her lip. "He told me he has a mate he was thinking of crashing with. Do you have any idea who that could be?"

"Lyle Draper." Charles was still glaring at the phone. "That was him I was on the phone with just now. He said Rory was gone when he woke up this morning."

Emma's jumbled thoughts turned over yet again, and much to her surprise, an idea surfaced.

"Hang on." Emma pulled her mobile back out, touched a number on the recent calls list and waited while it rang.

"Who are you calling?" Charles came out of the kitchen to stand beside David.

"Long shot," said Emma, just as the ringing cut off. "Pippa?"

"Emma," the reporter answered. "What's going on?"

"Have you seen Rory Kemp? This morning maybe?"

David's eyebrows arched. Charles looked at his husband and mouthed Pippa's name, clearly questioning.

"I was a little busy this morning, as you may recall," Pippa was saying. "Why?"

"Because his uncles are worried sick, and the police are looking for him."

There was another pause, a longer one, accompanied by some uneasy rustling in the background. "Yeah, okay," said Pippa. "If I see him, I'll tell him he should call."

"Or you could just hand him the phone."

"What makes you think—"

Emma didn't let her get any further. "Please, Pippa."

There was more shuffling. "Emma?" It was Rory.

Charles snatched the phone out of her hand. "Rory? Are you all right?"

"Yes, fine, Uncle Charles. I'm sorry. I should have come back last night, but . . ."

"Where are you? I'm coming to get you."

"I told you, I'm fine. I'll be back . . ." Emma heard Pippa's voice in the background, and then she heard Rory curse. "I'm on my way, right now."

"Good. Thank you." Charles rang off and handed Emma back her phone. "Thank you."

"How did you know where he'd be, Emma?" asked David.

"He was talking to Pippa the other day. She was probably trying to get him to help her with her 'background'"—she made the air quotes—"for her article about Sonny. She showed him a tax sticker she found in the tunnel when she was down there the night we found Sonny and the Vincent. I had an idea she might have wanted to know if Rory told anybody she'd been poking around in the tunnel . . ."

They were both staring at her like she'd grown an extra head. "I said it was a long shot," she finished.

"Well, what matters is he's on his way home," said David.

"What matters is the cops are after him," said Charles.

"I'm *sure* it's just some sort of mix-up," said David. "Rory will set it all straight."

But Charles folded his arms and didn't answer him.

"Do you want me to stay?" asked Emma.

"No, you'd better go," said David. "Somebody in this village should be minding their store today."

"All right, but if you need anything . . ."

"We'll call. I promise," said David.

"Um, that is, I don't suppose you've heard, well, something new? About Sonny?"

"David," said Charles. "We are trying very unsubtly to chuck her out of here."

"Yes, well, I was just wondering, and"—he frowned seriously at Emma—"don't you bother trying to say you weren't asking around."

"Well, as it happens—" Emma reached into her bag. "Oh, sugar. Constance has it."

"Has what?" asked Charles.

Emma's answer was cut off by the sound of footsteps clomping up the outer stairs.

"Rory," said David and Charles together. Charles raced for the door and threw it open.

Rory stood on the landing, rumpled and unshaven. He'd clearly slept in his clothes, and if his mate Lyle had offered to loan him a comb, he hadn't accepted.

Charles yanked him inside.

"Unc—" But the rest of what he was going to say was cut off as Charles enfolded him in a strong hug.

32

"WHERE HAVE YOU BEEN?" EXCLAIMED CHARLES, WITHOUT letting go of his nephew. "What if your mum had called, eh? What would I have said?"

"She did call." Rory pulled back, but gently. "This morning. She saw the news."

"Oh." David closed the flat door. "I imagine she was less than pleased."

Rory gave a one-shouldered shrug. "She just wants to make sure you're okay. Offered to pay for the lawyer."

Charles threw up his hands. "Well, isn't that just like her? Nothing's happened yet, and my sister's already sure we need a solicitor."

"Nothing's happened?" Rory gaped at him. "Which part of 'nothing' involves the dead guy everyone knows you were on the outs with?"

"Never mind all that for now," said David hastily. "Tell us where you were. There's . . . there's an unfortunate rumor going around."

"Some dafty says they saw you yelling at Reggie Tapp before he copped it," translated Charles. "That true?"

Rory looked towards Emma. "Don't worry about

Emma," said Charles. "The village is going to hear all about it anyway. They might as well hear the truth."

Emma looked away. *I suppose I should get over being surprised when people say things like that.*

"You will tell us the truth, won't you, Rory?" said David.

Rory's answer was to collapse onto the couch.

"Oh, dear." David sat down beside him. "Emma, be a darling . . ."

"I'll make some tea," said Emma before he got any further. "I know where everything is."

She plugged in the kettle and found the tea, the pot and the cups. A quick peek into the fridge revealed eggs, bread and butter, along with some mushrooms and half an onion in the drawer.

Perfect.

Oliver, of course, came to supervise. Emma patted his head and laid her ingredients out on the counter.

"Now, let's have it," Charles was saying in the living room. "The whole thing."

"On one condition," said Rory.

"Rory," said his uncle sternly. "Now's not the time to be playing about."

But Rory evidently wasn't in the mood to be persuaded. "I wouldn't be in this mess if you'd been straight with me yesterday, so, yeah, I think I get to lay down some conditions here too."

"All right, all right," said David quickly. "We understand, don't we, Charles?"

"So, no more mucking about, all right?" said Rory. "When I ask a question, you answer it."

"Yeah, yeah, okay," growled Charles. "Now, what happened?"

David kept a well-organized, and small, kitchen. It was easy to find the bowls and the frying pan. Emma deftly sliced the onions and mushrooms and got the butter melting in the pan. None of the Kemps was paying her any attention, except for Tangerine, who jumped down from her tree and slid around the corner of the kitchen to see what was happening.

"Yeah, well, when I left here, I didn't know what to do, did I?" Rory ran a hand through his hair and scrubbed at the back of his scalp. "I sort of wandered down by the cliffs, trying to get my head together, you know? I was really angry."

"We know," said David.

Rory shot him a grateful glance, and then turned to Charles. "Look, Uncle Charles, if you, if *either* of you, had anything to do with what happened to Sonny back then, will you just tell me? Please?"

David and Charles looked at each other. David looked away first.

"Uncle David?" said Rory.

Emma slid onions and mushrooms into the hot pan, trying not to make any noise. Tangerine evidently decided her cooking was not interesting enough and paced back to the living room, where she jumped up on David's lap.

"Whatever was going on with Sonny, he took the truth with him when he vanished." David somehow managed to sound completely serious even while the large, orange cat was making herself comfortable on his lap. "I swear it. I don't know what he had going on and I don't know how he died."

He spoke firmly and without any hesitation. Emma believed him, and yet she couldn't help feeling that there was still something else under there.

Emma cracked the eggs right over the vegetables.

"Emma," yipped Oliver.

"One minute, Oliver," Emma murmured as she stirred her concoction. It wouldn't be anything as elegant as an omelette; just a quick fry-up.

"But Emma—"

"Not now, Oliver." She sprinkled some shreds of cheddar cheese over top of the egg mixture.

"Emma!" Oliver bonked her hard on the ankle. "Your bag is buzzing, Emma!"

"Oh. Oops." Emma abandoned the pan and dove for her bag on the kitchen pass.

It was Genny.

"Oh, sugar, sugar, sugar." Emma hit the accept button.

"WHERE ARE YOU?!!!" shouted Genny before Emma had a chance to draw breath.

"I'm so sorry," she gasped. "I'm with David and Charles."

She was stage-whispering into the phone, but not softly enough. Both men heard their names and finally looked up to see that she'd taken over the kitchen.

"Oh, come on, Emma! Really?" exclaimed Charles.

"Oh, good lord. Is everything okay?" Genny was asking in her other ear.

Emma lifted her chin. "You all need to eat," she said to Charles. Then she added to Genny, "Yes, it's fine. I'll be there soon, I promise. Bye." She rang off before Genny could protest.

"Emma!" barked Oliver. "Emma, it's burning!"

Emma dashed back to the stove, lifted up the pan with one hand and shut off the cooktop with the other.

"A smoke alarm corgi. How very useful." David looked down at the cat curled up in his lap. "Why can't you do that, Tangerine?"

"Cats aren't useful," said Oliver.

Tangerine opened one eye and closed it again in an attitude of unmistakable feline contempt.

"She's incorrigible, that's what she is," announced Charles to the world at large.

"Emma or the cat?" quipped David.

"Irrelevant," announced Emma as she set the pan back on the stove. "It's done, and I can't eat this all myself." Although the truth was that she was hungrier than she'd thought a minute ago.

"I'll help, Emma!" barked Oliver. Tangerine meowed. "The cat says she'll help too," he translated. "I don't think mushrooms are good for cats. I think I heard a human say that."

"Well, I'm sure it wasn't a cat saying it."

"I'm sorry, what was that?" asked David.

"Erm. Nothing. Can somebody get some plates?"

Soon, they were all sitting around the table with plates of mushroom scramble and mugs of tea.

"This doesn't get you off the hook, you know," David said to Rory as he pushed a full mug of tea at the boy. "You still haven't told us where you went after you were walking on the cliffs."

Rory drank his tea and took up a forkful of scramble.

"I went to the Roundhead. I wanted a drink."

"Yeah?" mumbled Charles around his mouthful.

Oliver watched Emma cut into her portion of scramble and whined, very gently. For the sake of peace and quiet, Emma slipped him a bit of eggy mushroom. She did not miss the smug look Oliver gave the cat before he munched up the morsel.

"Yeah." Rory sighed. "And I had a drink, or two, maybe. And then Liza told me I should go home, and I told her I was fine, and she told me she didn't care actually, and threatened to toss me out of there."

Charles didn't actually chuckle, but a light sparked in his eye. "I hope you took her seriously. I've seen her in action."

"Yeah, well, you'll be glad to know that I did," Rory told him. "Anyway, it was getting late and it was cold, and I was still angry and . . . well, I wanted to do *something*. Anything seemed better than just wandering around."

Charles's jaw clenched. Emma got the feeling he wanted to interrupt, but had just caught himself in time. David probably had a similar feeling, because he laid his hand on Charles's wrist.

"So what I thought was that I'd go over to the Donkey's Win and tell Reggie to lay off."

"You shouldn't have," said Charles. "I told you, we had it handled."

"Yeah, right. You had it handled so well you weren't even going to tell me what happened. Not yesterday afternoon and not from forty years ago," Rory added, and popped a mushroom into his mouth.

"We'll get there," said Emma. "You said that's what you wanted to do. What did you really do?"

Rory sighed. "I did go over the Win, but it was pretty crowded. I mean it was Friday night and everything, wasn't it? So instead of shoving through the bar, I thought I'd go round the side, you know where there's that gate from the car park, so the bands can bring their gear through and stuff?"

They all nodded.

"Yeah, well, when I looked over the fence, I saw old Billy Marsh in the back garden. He and Reggie were having a drink." Rory took another swallow of tea. "And I thought, well, great, I can get both the old geezers at once, can't I? Only then, Billy starts shouting and waving his cane, and Reggie, he's on his feet and backing off like he thinks Billy's gone mad, and everybody else is on their feet. I couldn't see much after that, but I did see Pippa."

"Wasn't she with them before?"

Rory frowned. "You know, now that you mention it, I didn't see her right off. Maybe I just wasn't paying attention." He shrugged. "But I saw her then, and she got hold of her granddad's cane and started yelling at him, and at Reggie, and he's shouting back at them both, and next thing I know she's grabbed her granddad's chair and shoved him out the gate. I don't even think they saw me."

"What was Reggie saying?" asked Emma.

A muscle in Rory's cheek twitched. "Mostly 'get out and stay out.'"

"Oh, right."

Emma found herself admiring Pippa's nerve. The young woman had stayed on the job, even knowing the police would eventually find out about her part in an argument between Billy and Reggie.

Or maybe that was why she stayed on the job—so she could keep trying to dig herself, and her grandfather, out of his hole.

But why would she go to the Donkey's Win in the first place? What did either of them hope to get out of Reggie? Her thoughts stopped in her tracks. Rory said he hadn't noticed Pippa at first. *What if it wasn't Reggie she was there to talk to? What if she was trying to get to someone else?*

But who?

"And this was all before closing?" she asked.

"Yeah, would have been at least an hour to go," said Rory. "Why?"

"Something Pippa told me this morning, actually," said Emma. "She was talking to the kitchen staff, and someone told her that Reggie was still at the Win at closing, like he was waiting for someone."

"Well, it wasn't me," said Rory. "By the time Pippa and Billy got chucked out, I'd decided maybe bawling out Reggie hadn't been such a good idea after all, and I went to Lyles's and we drank too much of his beer, and I crashed on his couch, and woke up when Pippa called and said she needed to talk." He paused. "She has this theory about how it was Walter Greenlaw who killed Sonny."

"Walter?" exclaimed Charles. "Why does she think it was him?"

Rory shifted his weight uncomfortably. "I'm not sure she does. Not really. But he could have done it. I mean, he was a smuggler, wasn't he? And he knew about the tunnel, and Sonny was found in his pub and all, *and* he's the one who bricked the tunnel up." He stopped, but then added softly, "Besides, he's dead, and nobody can send him to prison."

"Is that why you were after us to talk to her?" asked Charles. "To try to build some kind of case against Walter?"

"Yeah, actually," said Rory. "She thought—we thought—if we could put the story around that it was old Walter, people would stop talking about you two and her granddad so much. But now Reggie's gone and gotten killed, and that idea's been chucked in the bin." Rory pushed his plate away and folded his arms. "All right. That's my bit. Your turn."

Charles and David exchanged one of their long glances. Emma thought they must be trying to decide who was going to go first.

The sound of footsteps on the stairs outside dropped into their silence. Everybody jumped. Oliver dashed over to the door and snuffled along the threshold.

Somebody knocked. David's frown wrinkled his whole face as he got up to answer. He glanced through the door window, and Emma saw his shoulders slump.

"Who is it?" asked Charles.

David didn't answer. He just opened the door. PC Raj stepped in, with DCI Brent right behind him.

"Oh, good," Constance said, "you're all here. I'm afraid we've got some questions."

33

NORMALLY, EMMA WAS GLAD FOR A CHANCE TO FALL INTO her work. Tea and cakes, and time with guests and friends, made for a busy, cheerful day, no matter what might be going on outside the shop.

Today, though, she simply couldn't concentrate.

Her mind would not stop trying to sort out everything that had happened this morning. She also couldn't stop wondering what Constance had asked the Kemps, and what they'd said in return. Constance had been very polite, but very firm, when she shooed Emma and Oliver out of the flat.

Nothing was made easier by the fact that all anybody could talk about was Reggie's (possible? Probable?) murder. Everyone in Trevena seemed positive his death was connected to the discovery of Sonny's bones. It was just a question of how.

"Too clever for his own good, was Reggie," said Matt Walsh when he stopped in for his rock cake and English breakfast tea. "Always trying to get his fingers into things. Wouldn't be surprised to hear that some of his old friends came round for a visit."

"Good thing he was such a fast talker," remarked Amelia Little. "Ever since he was a boy, he had plenty to talk himself out of. Sonny could have used a little of that at the end, I'll bet."

"They do say Sonny got in a bit deeper than he should," remarked old Dan Pryce, as he took the ginger scone he bought for his wife every day. "But I'd bet my last shilling it was Reggie who sold him out in the end. Somebody may have decided Reggie shouldn't get a chance to tell his side."

"I'm sure old Billy Marsh knows a thing or three about it," added Maggie Herman. "I wonder if the police have talked to him yet?"

As soon as Maggie said that, all the guests had looked to Emma.

Emma smiled weakly. "Sorry," she mumbled. "Have to check on the scones." She beat a hasty retreat to the kitchen with Oliver at her heels.

Of course, it didn't stop there. Everybody who came in wanted to hear what Emma thought, and what she'd seen over at the Donkey's Win. Everybody was sure that DCI Brent must have told her something in confidence. Emma was so busy fending off probing questions, she could barely keep the incoming orders straight. The day turned into a true group effort. It took Becca's insouciant efficiency, and Genny and Angelique's experienced assistance, bolstered by Oliver's herding instincts, to help Emma keep the shop running.

When they finally shut and locked the door promptly at five, Emma sank into the nearest chair with a grateful sigh.

"You look all in," said Genny as she scooped leaves into the Brown Betty pot to make tea. As she was adding the hot water, Angelique came out of the kitchen carrying plates of fresh bread spread with soft farm cheese. Oliver trailed hopefully behind.

"Here, eat." Angelique deposited the plate in front of Emma.

Emma stared at the food. "I'm the one who feeds people."

"And we're the ones who feed you." Genny set down the

cup of tea next to the plate. She also handed one to Angelique.

"But the kitchen . . ." she began.

"Becca's got it." Genny opened the bin of kibble that Angelique kept for her guests' dogs and filled a bowl for Oliver. Oliver looked at it, his eyes filled with gentle disappointment.

"Cheese is better," he muttered. He also tucked in.

"You are promoting Becca, yeah?" Angelique asked Emma.

"We're talking about it tomorrow," Emma told her. She'd even found a minute to put a reminder on her calendar. "And there will be a raise involved, I promise."

"Good," said Genny. "She's earned it. Now." She picked up her cup in both hands and planted both elbows firmly on the table. "Spill."

Emma sighed and picked up a slice of bread and cheese. Oliver immediately abandoned his kibble and sat up on his haunches, looking pitiful.

"Might as well get it over with," said Angelique.

"Thank goodness for long walks along the cliffs." Emma put down one of the smaller plates and a bit of bread and cheese.

"Yes!" mumbled Oliver. "Walks are very healthy. You need a walk today, Emma. You will feel better."

Emma smiled. It was a little odd getting used to others, including her dog, looking out for her, but she found she really couldn't complain all that much.

"Now, you were saying . . ." prompted Genny. "About what actually happened to Reggie?"

Emma hesitated. These two women might be her best friends, but Constance had been talking to her privately. She had to be careful about how much she shared. "Honestly, I didn't see much," she said. "But it looks like Reggie drowned in the garden fountain at the Donkey's Win. He might have been drunk."

Angelique frowned. "I'm not a great admirer of Reggie

Tapp, but I never knew him to get drunk. At least, not that drunk."

"Me neither," said Genny.

"Maybe he got some bad news," said Emma. "Or he was upset. Rory says he'd had an argument with Billy Marsh earlier." She paused and sipped the tea. "What really worries me is that somebody told the police that they saw Rory arguing with him too."

Genny leaned both elbows on the table. "What does Rory say?"

"That's the real problem," said Emma. "Rory admits he went over to the pub to have it out with Reggie. He wanted Reggie to stop pestering his uncles, and he'd had a bit to drink himself."

"That's definitely not good," said Angelique.

"But he says it wasn't him Reggie argued with. He says he saw him shouting at Billy Marsh, and that Pippa was there with him."

"Did he say what that was about?" asked Angelique.

"He didn't get close enough to hear," Emma told her. "Rory says he left without even talking to Reggie, and one of the kitchen workers says Reggie was alive and well at closing time."

"So who said they saw the pair of them arguing?" asked Angelique.

"I've no idea," said Emma.

Genny frowned. "Do you suppose there's somebody who wants to get Rory in trouble?"

"Not necessarily," said Emma. "Memory's not always a reliable thing. Somebody may have gotten mixed up about what happened."

"Alcohol may have been a factor," intoned Angelique solemnly. "It was Friday night in a pub, after all."

"After all," agreed Emma.

"Well, at least Rory had a good reason to want to go yell at Reggie," said Genny. "If Reggie was putting pressure on my family, I'd yell too." Emma and Angelique both grimaced in sympathy. "But what could Billy have wanted from Reggie? They've never had much use for each other."

Angelique poured herself a bit more tea while they all considered this. "Emma, didn't you say Reggie was part of that supposed social club with Billy Marsh back in the day?"

"Oh, right, you told me about this," said Genny. "Reggie was in the photo with the others, yeah?"

"Yeah," agreed Emma, then she stopped.

"What is it?" asked Genny.

"Somebody grassed on the smugglers," said Emma. "It said in the article that there was an anonymous tip from a 'concerned citizen.'" She made the air quotes with one hand. "Pippa says Billy said it was Walter Greenlaw. But what if he changed his mind after Sonny's body was found?"

"What do you mean?" asked Angelique

"Well, we'd been wondering if Sonny could have been the grass. But what if Billy decided it was Reggie?"

"There's a thought," said Genny slowly. "Reggie was in that picture of the club, wasn't he? But he wasn't arrested with the rest of the smugglers."

"If he had been arrested, everybody would know," said Angelique. "And I never heard anything of the kind, did you, Genny?"

Genny shook her head. "Maybe they let him off because he was so young at the time, or maybe he wasn't there when the raid happened." Genny paused and took another swallow of tea. "Which would be an interesting coincidence on its own."

Emma took another bite of bread and cheese. Oliver had curled up beside his empty kibble bowl. His eyes were drooping. "Could Sonny and Reggie have been friends? They were both young men at the time, both skirting the edge of serious trouble, and neither one of them was caught up in the raid. And—" Two puzzle pieces suddenly clicked together in Emma's brain. She sat up a little straighter.

"And?" prompted Angelique.

"And Sonny might have robbed the smugglers. What if he and Reggie were in it together? Reggie calls down the cops while Sonny steals the cash and the fake excise stickers."

"With the idea that they'll split the take?" Angelique shook her head. "They would have to have planned it all well in advance. A raid takes time to set into motion."

"Maybe they did," said Emma. "They certainly could have."

"So how does Sonny end up dead while Reggie ends up a semi-prosperous if unpopular pub owner?" asked Genny.

"Maybe somebody found out about Sonny's part in the plot, but not about Reggie's," said Angelique.

"Or maybe Sonny decided to leave town without giving Reggie his share," said Emma.

"Are you saying Reggie killed Sonny?" asked Genny.

Emma looked down at Oliver, who had fallen into full evening snooze. "It's a possibility, isn't it? If they were working together, Reggie would be expecting something from the robbery. Or maybe he caught Sonny committing the robbery and they fought. If Reggie knew about the tunnel under the Roundhead—" She stopped again.

"Now what?" asked Genny.

"Does anybody know if there was a tunnel under the Sea and Shell?" asked Emma. "I don't remember if the article said anything about it."

"There could have been," said Angelique. "There was supposed to have been a whole network of them, once upon a time."

"Now you're wondering if it was not just *a* tunnel," said Genny, "but the same tunnel."

"It would make sense, wouldn't it?" said Emma. "If Sonny got killed by Reggie, or any one of the smugglers? They could have hid him in the tunnel, and maybe even deliberately caused the collapse behind him."

"Assuming anybody let them back in there after the raid and all," said Angelique.

"Yeah, but if—"

"You're piling up a lot of ifs," said Genny.

"I know, I know," admitted Emma. "But it is possible. Reggie could have killed Sonny and hid the body and the motorcycle down the tunnel, and who'd be the wiser? Everybody knew Sonny was planning to leave town, so nobody wonders when he doesn't show up to work."

Genny clinked her fingernails against her tea mug. "You might be overcomplicating this. Sonny was working at the Roundhead for Walter Greenlaw, remember. It really could have been Walter who killed him, and put him in the tunnel in the Roundhead's cellar."

Which certainly would be the simpler answer. "But the tunnel was bricked up by then," said Emma. "Sam says his mother insisted when they were kids."

"Maybe he's misremembering," suggested Angelique. "Or maybe it wasn't as solidly closed up as people were led to believe."

Because Walter was part of the smuggling ring. Emma nodded. Maybe Walter had left a secret entrance to the tunnel, just in case it was needed.

"Sonny could have hid his loot in there," Genny went on. "And got killed when he went in to get it."

"But none of this answers the question about why Billy would be foolish enough to go yelling at Reggie in the middle of a Friday night crowd," Angelique pointed out.

"Unless he was covering for Pippa," said Emma.

"Okay, you're going to have to explain that one," said Genny.

"Well, Rory said he saw Billy and Reggie sitting together, but he didn't see Pippa until things started to get really heated. What if it wasn't Billy who wanted to come to the Win that night? What if it was Pippa?"

"Why?" began Genny.

"Because she was looking for something," said Angelique. "Evidence of crimes, new or old."

"Maybe even evidence of the tunnel entrance," added Emma.

"But that was before closing," Genny pointed out. "And

you said Reggie was seen alive afterwards. Would Billy have come back and killed Reggie? Could he even? He can't drive, and he can't walk very far, and I can't believe Pippa would be willing to help her grandfather commit murder."

"Pippa wouldn't have to," said Emma. "Billy could have called a friend from the old days to help."

"Like Colin Roskilly," suggested Genny. "He was over at their house the night Sonny was found."

"And he was arrested in the raid," Emma pointed out. "I remember his name from the article."

They were all silent for a moment, letting that particular fact settle in.

"I hate to say this," said Genny. "But could it have been Pippa who went back? Maybe Reggie threatened her granddad and she decided she had to do something about it?"

Which was another idea that required some time to settle. Especially since Pippa had been so anxious to talk to Rory this morning. Maybe she had noticed him watching the argument outside the Win. Maybe she had been trying to find out what he knew, so she'd be able to get her story straight.

Emma took another swallow of tea. It didn't help.

"So the question becomes, how could anyone possibly prove any of this?" asked Angelique.

"If it was me, I'd start by talking to Billy," said Genny.

"And how do you convince Billy to talk to you?" replied Angelique. "Especially about something that could land him back in jail? Or, even worse, get his granddaughter into real trouble?"

Emma put her mug down. "Well then, we'll just have to come up with an idea, won't we?"

Because whatever it was Pippa had been doing at the Win that night, they needed to find it out.

34

"WHERE ARE WE GOING NOW, EMMA?" ASKED OLIVER.

"Home," Emma told him as she shifted her grip on the covered pan of chicken and spicy rice that Angelique had given her. "We need to get the car. There's shopping to be done." An idea had come to her shortly after Angelique had asked if they could run a dish over to the Roundhead. In her mind's eye, she was seeing a recipe card from the very back of the box she had inherited from her nan, and lists were starting to create themselves in her imagination.

"Hurray! Can we put the top down?" Oliver loved riding in their vintage convertible.

"You won't get cold?"

"Viking warrior corgis are never cold!" he declared. "You might need a hat."

Emma chuckled. "We'll see. First, we're going to the Roundhead." She would have delivered Angelique's dinner for the Greenlaws in any case. But, she reasoned, if she really was going to try to talk to Billy Marsh, she wanted to make sure she had the Greenlaws' side of the story first. Billy, after all, liked to make trouble, and Emma felt sure he wasn't above telling a few little white lies.

"This is good," mumbled Oliver. "Walks and rides. This

is very healthy." He sneezed. "Will they have the biscuits there? There has been a lot of upset. Maybe they forgot about biscuits?"

Emma laughed. "I don't think Sam and Liza would forget something that important."

But when they got to the Roundhead, the little courtyard was empty, and the sign on the door had been turned to CLOSED. There was a light on inside, though. Emma peered through the window and saw Liza moving about behind the bar. There was no sign of Sam.

Emma rested the pot against her hip and knocked on the door. Liza turned to look, and then came to let them in.

"Hullo, Emma."

"Hullo, I've been sent as a representative from the King's Rest." She held up the pot. "Angelique wanted me to bring this over."

Liza lifted the lid. "Looks lovely," she said politely. "Care to come in?"

"Erm, is it okay?" Liza was not sounding like her usual energetic self. In fact, there were dark circles under her blue eyes.

"Oh, yeah." Liza stood back so Emma and Oliver could step inside. "It's only the cellar that's off-limits. Again."

"Where's Sam?"

"Over at the brewery with Ned and Martha. They wanted to talk with the staff about what's happening." Martha was the Greenlaws' daughter. She handled the marketing efforts for their ale and cider. Thanks to her, the Roundhead's products were making their way into pubs and stores around the UK. Liza said she was eyeing the US and Canadian markets as well. "This thing with Reggie has . . . well, it's a disaster, isn't it?" She put the pot down on the bar. Oliver came over beside her and sat up on his haunches, ears up and nose in the air. Despite all her worries, Liza smiled and rubbed his ears.

"He's gently hinting for a biscuit," said Emma.

"There's a surprise." Liza pulled one out of the jar beside the register and let Oliver take it from her fingers to munch.

"Have you seen the Kemps?" Liza asked as she straightened up. "I keep meaning to get over there, but—" She gestured vaguely toward the cellar stairs. "Someone was saying their nephew might be in some trouble over this."

"That's a long way from certain," said Emma, and she hoped that was the truth. "Someone says he was arguing with Reggie, but he says he didn't even talk with him that night. On the other hand, he says he saw him and Billy Marsh having a set-to over . . . something."

"Yeah, well, that's easy to do with Billy," said Liza ruefully. "Something to drink?" she asked.

"Ginger beer, maybe?"

"Coming right up." Liza brought two bottles up from under the counter and opened them. She sat down at the nearest table, and gestured for Emma to join her. Oliver, having nosed about the floor and decided he'd gotten every single biscuit crumb, came to stretch out on his belly under Emma's chair.

"I don't like speaking ill of my own neighbors," Liza said. "But Billy's been carrying a grudge ever since he got out, and that makes for thirty years of keeping a chip on his shoulder."

"Did you know him, back in the day?"

"Couldn't miss him. He was always in and out of the old Sea and Shell with his mates. Me and Marianne were tripping over one of them nearly every day."

Emma took a sip of her spicy drink and felt the warmth going down to her toes. "Marianne mentioned you two were friends back then," she said carefully.

"Oh, yeah. We stuck together. She was raised in a pub, and I worked in one. We both got some hassling for that, and it was easier when there were two of us, you know?" Emma did. "So, what happened?"

Liza stiffened. "What did she tell you?"

"Nothing," said Emma. "I think maybe she would have, but Reggie was listening."

"Oh, yeah, well, that would explain it." Liza relaxed a bit. "Can't imagine what it must have been like living with that man. But as to me and her—I've never been really sure what happened. One day she just stopped talking to me. Passed me right by in the street without a word to say. I didn't understand it. She hung up whenever I called. I even wrote her a letter, but she sent it back, 'Return to Sender, Address Unknown,' like in the Elvis song." She cocked an eye towards Emma, and Emma nodded. She had in fact heard the song. "Gave our postman a bit of a laugh, that did."

"And she never told you why?"

"Never. For a while, I assumed it was her parents' doing, because I was going out with Sam at the time, and the Greenlaws and the Hartfords had had a falling-out. But even after they passed, she never had a word to say to me."

Emma took another drink of ginger beer. The silence was abruptly broken by the unmistakable rumble of corgi snores. The women smiled at each other. Emma rolled her eyes.

"Look, Liza," she said, "I know you and Sam don't really want to talk about it, but, well, there's an old article about the raid on that smuggling ring operating out of the Sea and Shell. It lists Walter Greenlaw with the people who got arrested. He's in the picture with the members of the social club too."

Liza was silent for a long moment. "I didn't know about the photo."

"The police do."

"Yeah. Your DCI Brent's been here about it." Her voice hardened. "And I'll tell you the same as we told her. Walter was part of the gang. It was good money, wasn't it? And nobody thought much about putting one over on the revenuers. But when Sonny got in on it too, Melinda put her foot down. She'd never liked Walter being involved, and she wasn't having their nephew mixed up with it. Actually threatened to walk out if Walter didn't quit."

"So he quit?"

"He quit, and he tried to get Sonny to quit too. Gave him the job here, promised to take him into partnership and all." She took another long swallow of ginger beer. "After that, Sonny said he was done with them, and we all believed him."

"Why?"

Liza glared at her. "Oh, come on, Emma."

"I know, I know, it's really not my business, but do you know that Sonny really quit? Could he have just said he broke off with the smugglers, but then kept right on anyway? I mean, as you say, it was good money."

"I might have wondered the same thing," said Liza, "if I hadn't been there when Colin Roskilly came round and threatened to give Sonny the beating of his life if he went and said one word about what he'd seen or done."

"Colin Roskilly."

Liza nodded. "He was the one we were really frightened of, back then. The rest were all right, in their way, but Colin was . . . well, he was mean."

Emma nodded, and wondered about Billy, and Colin, and what Colin thought about Sonny's bones being found.

Which led to another question. "Liza? Do you know if Reggie and Sonny were friends back then?"

Liza considered this. "Friends? I suppose they were. They drank together, and got into fights together." She paused. "You know, it's funny. Everybody thought it was Reggie who would leave the village. Go to Liverpool, maybe Manchester, and be the big man, but that's not how it turned out."

"Instead he married the boss's daughter."

"Funny old thing, love, isn't it? Never would have bet on it lasting either, but here we all are." Liza shrugged. "Still, there's people that said Sam and I would never make it. Too young when we got married, they said, and the families were definitely not in favor, but we knew." She smiled fondly.

"So, that bit with Billy saying you had something going with Sonny back in the day . . ."

"Oi." Liza set her bottle down with a thump. "I swear, with the way Billy goes around stirring up trouble, I'm surprised it was Reggie who went and got himself killed." Emma opened her mouth. Liza glowered at her. Emma closed her mouth. "And the answer is no. There was never anything between me and Sonny, but yes, I did go out with him. *Once*. And it didn't go like I expected, did it?"

"What happened?" asked Emma.

"I'd had a row with Sam. A bad one. I was seventeen and an idiot—"

"Every seventeen-year-old is an idiot," said Emma.

Liza rolled her eyes. "Too right. Well, I got this idea in my head that I should try to make Sam jealous, and that I could use Sonny to do it. So, when there came the Friday night dance over at the Miner's hall, I asked Sonny to take me.

"He said yes, but he didn't take me to the dance. He took me out walking instead. I remember being scared. I'd had to deal with a few punters on the job, and I knew what was what. But it wasn't like that. He . . . he told me he knew why I wanted to go to the dance with him, and he said he wasn't going to let me mess things up with Sam like that. Said I should give Sam another chance."

"I thought Sonny was this notorious ladies' man."

"We all did," said Liza. "I couldn't believe what I was hearing. I burst into tears and all. I mean, I didn't really *want* him to make a try for me, but I wanted him to want to, if that makes any sense at all."

"For a seventeen-year-old who just had a big fight with her boyfriend, yes."

"Anyway, when I got over that, he took me home. He kissed me on the forehead like I was his baby cousin. I went to bed and stayed awake all night, absolutely mortified. I couldn't believe what I'd done. Anyway, in the morning, Sam came round and apologized. I asked him why he'd changed his mind about what he'd said and all, and . . . he told me Sonny had dragged him out of the dance and told him to stop being such a . . . well, such an idiot and that whatever it was he'd said to me, he should take it all back. We made up, and . . ." She shrugged again. "When Sonny disappeared, I was actually sorry. Everybody was slagging on him, including his own family. I wanted to tell them what he'd done for me and Sam, but I was too embarrassed. So I never did."

"Why do you suppose—" began Emma. "I mean, with his reputation and all . . ."

"Why didn't he kiss me? Because he had a girl," said Liza. "He told me. Oh, not who it was. But he said he was getting some money together to take them both away. So I guessed she must have been married or at least engaged. I thought it was all terribly romantic."

"Sounds it," said Emma, thinking of the Vincent and the sidecar. "So I guess when he vanished, you weren't surprised."

"Not at first. I was a little surprised when no one said any of the local girls were gone too. But then I just thought his girl must have been over in Bodmin or Treknow or some such. Either that or he'd just been giving me a line so I wouldn't feel so bad."

"No," said Emma. "I don't think he was. We . . . that is, they . . . well, a ring was found in the Vincent's sidecar. An engagement ring."

Liza's face went utterly blank. Then slowly, sadly she shook her head. "Well, poor her," she whispered. "And poor him."

Before Emma could say anything else, they both heard the sound of the side door opening. Liza turned around in time to see Sam coming through the pub's TV room.

Under Emma's chair, Oliver awoke with a snort.

"Who? What? Where!" he barked.

"Easy does it, Oliver." Emma laughed and gave him a pat.

"We're still here," he grumbled.

"Sorry," Sam said. "Didn't mean to startle anybody." He bent down to kiss his wife. "Thought you'd be gone home already, Liza."

"Just chatting with Emma here, and Angelique sent over some of her rice stew for tea." She nodded toward the pot on the bar.

"Oh, well, tell her ta muchly," said Sam. "That'll be grand."

"Emma was asking about the old days."

"Is she?" He gave her a scowl that Emma was fairly sure was meant to be humorous. "Do I have to consider banning you and Oliver?"

"No, no," said Liza quickly. "It's all right, really. I don't mind."

"All right, then." Sam took his wife's hand. "Sorry, Emma, but answering more questions about Sonny, or Reggie, isn't exactly how either of us want to spend the evening. You understand."

"Of course." Emma got to her feet. "Good to see you both. I hope . . ." She hesitated, searching for the right words. "I hope this all clears up soon."

"It will," said Sam firmly. "At least, our part will. My dad worked hard all his life. He adored my mum, never raised a hand to any of us kids, any friend of his needed him, he was there. We always had somebody sleeping in the spare room, or Da would find them a little extra work if they needed it. Once we got married, he pitched in here, helped keep the whole thing going until he could turn it over to us. He had nothing to hide. Ever. And neither do we."

Which to Emma signaled the end of the conversation. She smiled and they all said goodbye and wished each other a pleasant evening. Sam held the door for her and Oliver.

Emma glanced over her shoulder as they left. She hadn't been able to help noticing that when Sam made his firm declaration about Walter having nothing to hide, Liza looked away.

And now she looked seriously worried.

35

"WHAT IS THAT SMELL?" ANGELIQUE'S ENTIRE FACE WRINkled up as she walked into the B and B kitchen.

"Suet." Emma leaned over and peered at the recipe card. *Nan, why couldn't you have had tidier handwriting?*

"Suet?" Angelique came over to peer at the bowl of shredded, creamy-white fat. "You'll have the local vegetarians up in arms."

"No help for it." Emma bent back to grating more shreds off the cold, greasy brick.

After she and Oliver had left the Greenlaws last night, they had driven out to the Tesco to pick up a few specialty items for the pudding she planned. Fortunately, she had a brilliant raspberry jam she could use for the filling, and the B and B's kitchen equipment included a steaming basket.

"So, what are you making?" asked Angelique as she tied on her apron.

"Dead man's arm."

Angelique swung around. *"What?"*

"Sorry. It's jam roly-poly. Used to be called 'shirt-sleeve pudding' or 'dead man's arm.'"

"Well, could be worse. Could be spotted dick."

"I love spotted dick," said Emma, putting a bowl on the

scale so she could weigh flour and sugar. "It was one of Nan's specialties."

"Your nan who had four husbands?" Angelique looked at her owlishly. "No comment whatsoever."

"Be nice about my nan," replied Emma loftily. "She's the reason we were booked solid for cream teas all this summer."

"I am eternally grateful to Nana Phyllis and light candles to her memory," replied Angelique placidly. "But what's the pudding for?" she asked as she headed for the refrigerator. "Not for tea today?"

"Not our tea. This is a bribe for a bent old man."

Angelique pulled up short. "You don't mean Billy Marsh?"

"Yes, I do."

"Emma, are you sure you want to go taking a poke at him?" asked Angelique seriously. "Just yesterday you were suggesting he might have killed Reggie Tapp."

"Nobody's going after you when you've brought their favorite pudding."

"All right." Her friend sighed. "I just hope you know what you're doing."

I hope so too, thought Emma. *Believe me.*

THE MARSHES LIVED ON THE NORTHERN EDGE OF TREVENA, where the village stretched up into the hills. Theirs was one of a ring of semidetached houses between the old village and the outlying farms. It was a newer house by Trevena standards, meaning it had been built in the last half of the twentieth century. It sat in the middle of a row of identical houses, with identically sized front gardens and identical doors behind low brick walls.

Both Emma's hands were occupied with the covered dish she carried, so she twisted around and rang the bell with her elbow.

"Now, remember, Oliver," she said as she straightened back up and wriggled her shoulder to try to resettle her carrier bag, "Billy doesn't seem to be overly fond of dogs, so you need to be on your best behavior."

"A noble corgi is always—" began Oliver.

"I know," she said. "But extra special best today?"

"Okay, Emma." Oliver sat up proudly.

After a bit, they heard some shuffling inside. But the man who opened the door wasn't Billy Marsh.

"Who're you, then?" He squinted up at her. He was bald as an egg, and his pale skin was speckled by age. He had a permanent hunch and leaned hard on an old-fashioned wooden cane. But the slate blue eyes that peered at her were clear and keen, and openly suspicious.

Oliver barked once and wagged his bum, trying to smooth the way. The man glanced down at him, and his mouth puckered up. Oliver plopped back on his hindquarters.

"Erm. Hullo. I'm Emma . . .

"Who's that, Col?" Billy shouted from inside the house.

Col? Emma felt her eyes widen in surprise. This was Colin Roskilly?

"Some bird," the man called back over his shoulder. "Says her name's Emma. Got a dog with her."

Oliver barked again in friendly greeting. Carefully the man, Colin, bent down and rubbed his ears. Emma was fully aware that even bad people could like dogs, but there was always something encouraging about seeing Oliver get a warm welcome.

"What's she want?" called Billy.

"Dunno," shouted Colin back. Then he squinted up at Emma. "What do you want?"

"I've brought tea." Emma held up her covered dish.

"She's brought tea," Colin shouted.

There was a shuffling and a thump, and Billy appeared, making his slow way up the hallway.

"What's that?" He waved his cane at the dish.

"Jam roly-poly," said Emma.

Colin's eyebrows shot up. "It never is."

"Straight from my nan's recipe box," said Emma. Oliver barked in agreement.

"Well," said Billy. "You'd better come in, then, hadn't you?"

"Do you mind my dog?"

Billy looked down at Oliver. Oliver wagged and laughed up at him. "Nah. He's all right." Billy backed up carefully. "Never understood small dogs myself. Bit useless, aren't they?"

Thankfully, Oliver decided that best behavior meant ignoring the old man's grumbles. He stayed right at Emma's side as Colin led them past the stiff, gold and brown front room and tiny dining room and into the kitchen.

"Mind you," Billy was saying, "I knew a fellow had one of them sausage dogs, whatchamacallems—"

"Dachshunds?" suggested Emma.

"That's it. Amazing ratter that dog was. So I suppose you've got your uses too, eh?" He looked down at Oliver.

"You'd be surprised," said Emma.

"Wouldn't be the first time," Colin said. "I'll put the kettle on, shall I, Bill?" He shuffled to the stove.

"Do that."

"Pippa's not home?" Emma set the dish of pudding down on the oilcloth-covered table.

"Nope," said Billy. "Out on the job. Probably best her keeping out of the way. Now then—" Right in the middle of the sentence, Billy stopped, and staggered, catching himself with his walking stick. Emma was about to ask if he was all right, but he waved her away. "I'm fine," he gasped. "Fine."

He might have been fine, but he also gripped the edge of the table and eased himself into the chair. Oliver scampered over to sniff at his shoe tops, and Billy didn't even grouse about it. Emma saw a thin sheen of sweat on his forehead and how his left arm lay limp and motionless across his lap.

"So, tea," she said cheerfully.

"Cups up there." Billy waved towards a cabinet with his right hand. "Plates next to it."

"Right."

While Colin managed the intricacies of kettle, teapot and three heaping spoonfuls of English breakfast tea, Emma pulled down the plates. Oliver made his circuit of the kitchen, investigating all the nooks and corners before going to settle down in front of the sliding glass door that looked out on the tiny bit of garden. Outside, there were a couple of plastic chairs, turned over to keep their seats from getting damp in the rain. No flowers lined the chipped fence, and the grass was growing long.

The entire place, in fact, had a feeling of slight neglect about it. Everything in it had seen some hard use, including both Billy and Colin. But it was all clean and recently tidied.

Emma set the short stack of plates down on the table and then unwrapped the jam roll. It was still warm; so was the thermos of custard she pulled from the tote bag. Emma cut a thick slice of pudding, poured a lavish helping of custard over top and set the plate down in front of Billy.

Billy stared at it. "You'll have my heart doctor after me for this."

"Should I take it back?"

"You'll lose your hand you try, girly," he said menacingly. Colin laughed, a hoarse, wheezing sound that ended in a cough and an expletive about cigarettes.

Emma served both men and cut her own slice. She actually liked a suet pudding, at least every now and again. There was a rich texture to the sponge that nothing else could quite match, and the combination of custard and jam tasted like her childhood.

Colin poured out the tea, which was pitch-black and strong.

Billy took a healthy swig and raised his mug in appreciation.

"Ah! Now, that's proper tea, that is. Stuff Pippa tries to give me, weak as water." He forked up a big mouthful of jam roll. "This is good too."

"Haven't had a pudding like this since I was a boy,"

added Colin. "Where were you when I was in me twenties, eh?" He leered.

"In nappies." Emma topped off his cup.

He laughed. "Your nan, then."

"Happily married to her third husband." Nana Phyllis's charm, and her baking skills, had ensured she only lived alone as long as she wanted to.

"Ah, well." He shrugged and stuck back into his jam roll.

Emma ate, and let the two old friends eat. Finally, Billy finished, wiped his face and pushed the plate away. "Another slice?" Emma inquired.

Billy narrowed his eyes at her. "Now, then, sweetheart, I know when I'm being bribed. What do you want?"

Emma decided that now was not the time to dance around the subject. "I want to ask you about Sonny, and about the smugglers, back in the seventies."

Billy took another swallow of tea, but his eyes never left her face. "Sounds like one of them old bands, doesn't it, Colin?" he said.

Colin chuckled. "Sonny and the Smugglers. Would've made the hit parade. Not that you'd know what that is," he added to Emma.

"I'm not as young as I look."

"Well, maybe." Billy looked her up and down, slowly and deliberately. Emma just kept looking steadily at him. Finally, Billy shrugged.

"What could you want to know? Man's been dead for donkey's years. Why not just leave it alone?"

"Because Reggie Tapp hasn't been dead for donkey's years."

"Oh, well, him." This time Colin shrugged, dismissing Reggie as coolly as Reggie had dismissed Sonny back when Emma sat down with him at the Donkey's Win. "Whatever it was, I'm sure that was his own fault."

"Reg was always a big one for bringing trouble down on his own head," added Billy.

"Was there anything recent?" asked Emma.

Billy put down his fork and eyed her. "Look, sweetheart, I appreciate the pudding and all, but what's your game?"

"I want to find out what's going on." She looked him dead in the eye. "The cops will only muck it up, won't they?" *I'll apologize to Constance later for that one.* "And friends of mine might get hurt when they do."

Billy took a swallow of tea, then he heaved himself to his feet and shuffled over to the sideboard. He opened the drawer. Emma saw he'd regained use of his left arm. He pulled out a bottle of whiskey. He returned to his chair, poured a generous slosh into his cup. He passed the bottle to Colin, who filled his own cup. Both men drank deeply.

When Billy set the cup down, he looked at her, long and searchingly. Emma turned her best bland office face toward the pair of them. Despite what all her friends thought, she actually could hide what she was thinking. She just needed the right circumstances.

Billy pursed his mouth, and let it go with a loud popping sound. "If Reggie was up to anything new, I couldn't tell you about it," he said. "That one was too clever for his own good, and he never got over the fact that he never got anywhere with it. What was he really?" He waved his good arm. "Man with a tacky pub in a seaside village, not even any kids, and his wife's the brains of the outfit. Reggie kept trying to find a way round it all. Overcompensation, that's what they call that. Oh-ver-comp-en-sa-tion." He dragged the word out.

"I'm familiar with the concept," said Emma blandly.

"I'll just bet you are." Colin snickered.

Emma ignored this. "You said Marianne was the brains of the outfit?"

"Sure she was—was, probably still is," said Billy. "Who do you think kept that accountant fellow in line, even after his girl, Gwen, showed up looking to get her dad out of . . . whatever it is he's gotten into. You seen the arms on that one?" He held up both arms like an angry wrestler. "She could've folded Reggie up and stuffed him down the bleedin' drain anytime she wanted to." He paused.

Colin eyed his friend over the rim of his cup. "Maybe she did."

The look the two men exchanged was so sharp Emma felt her skin crawl. Oliver's ears shot up like he had heard a stray noise, and he trotted instantly to Emma's side. She scratched his ears, mostly to cover the fact she felt so suddenly disconcerted.

They're just joking, she told herself. *You can't take a stray remark from an old reprobate seriously.*

"I'd gotten the idea that Marianne's parents were involved with the social club, back in the day," she said.

"Well, that's not exactly a secret, is it?" said Billy. "Old man Hartford was in transportation, and of course, his missus ran the pub."

"Knew the value of what they had too." Colin rubbed his fingertips together. "Charged us a very pretty penny to use that basement, they did."

"So why weren't they arrested during the raid? Where were they?"

"That has remained a great mystery," he said sagely. "They must've gotten word from someone, because when the day came, there was not a Hartford to be found."

Oliver evidently decided the situation was calm enough that he could do some important investigations of his own. The corgi began nosing about under the table and chairs, looking for crumbs.

"Could the Hartfords have tipped off the cops?" asked Emma.

"Nah. Not them," said Colin. "They was making money hand over fist as it was. From the rent, of course," he added. "Why would they deliberately muck up a good thing?"

"Did Marianne know what was going on?" asked Emma.

"'A course she did," said Billy. "Girl was sharp as a tack. Nothing got by her."

"So why'd someone like that marry Reggie?"

"That is another one of life's mysteries," Billy admitted. "I heard he did stick by her after the raid. Her parents might not have been arrested, but they didn't exactly get off scot-free either. The revenuers were all over them for years afterwards. Trucking business collapsed. So did the pub."

"Seems like nobody was interested in going near the place for a while there." Colin's eyes gleamed as he said it. Emma found herself wondering how much he had to do with the desertion.

"Bloody mess, that's what it was," said Billy. "Was Reggie had the idea to tear the old place down and start over from scratch. Just about the only good idea the man ever had." Colin nodded in solemn agreement.

Emma petted Oliver's ears, thinking furiously. "So just what was Sonny's connection to the social club?"

Colin shrugged and took another swig of whiskey-laced tea. "Well, you need someone to do the odd jobs, don't you? Fix things up, run errands here and there. He seemed right for it. Problem was, Sonny was not real good with what they call boundaries."

"Boundaries?"

Billy nodded. "Had him some of what they called comm-un-istic sympathies, did our Sonny."

"I'm sorry?"

"Not a lot of respect for the concept of personal property," explained Colin helpfully.

Finally, Emma was able to connect the dots. "Was he stealing from your lot? On the regular?"

Billy nodded slowly. "Spare bits of cash here and there, but it was starting to add up."

"Once the lads figured it out, and we had a little talk with him. Told him he was out of a job as far as we were concerned."

Emma looked from one man to the other. She tried to picture them as they'd been as tough young men, ready to defend what they saw as theirs. "So you threw him out. He didn't quit?"

"That's right," said Colin. "He didn't even put up that much of a fuss. Knew we had him dead to rights. The Greenlaws had been after him to get out anyway."

Emma thought about this. She thought about a young,

proud man being given the push by his . . . colleagues and employers? She thought about Sonny and his friend Reggie getting together for a few drinks afterwards to grouse about the whole thing, and maybe coming up with a plan to get a bit of their own back.

"Know what you're thinking," said Billy abruptly.

"What's that?" asked Emma.

"You're thinking maybe Sonny tried to get a bit of his own back." Emma arched her brows. In fact, that was awfully close. "Well, he did. Wasn't too long after that we opened up the club room one morning, and what do we find? Cash box cleared out and Sonny vanished."

"How much did he, or whoever it was, get?"

"Couple thousand quid it was."

Our local smugglers were more successful than I'd thought. Back in the seventies, that would have been a serious amount of money. In fact, it would have been more than enough to make a group of criminals very angry.

Emma sipped her tea. So far nobody'd said anything about a large amount of cash being found with Sonny's body. What had happened to it? Had the murderer taken it back?

If the murderer was one of the smugglers, certainly. One of the smugglers, or Reggie, or even Walter Greenlaw.

Because none of this took Walter out of the picture. Sonny was one of his family and working in his pub. He could have found out about the plan to rob the smugglers any of a dozen ways.

He could have been in on it.

"But it wasn't just cash Sonny took, was it?" she said. "He took the counterfeit excise seals."

Billy didn't so much as bat an eye. "Now, we wouldn't know anything about that, would we?"

"That kind of thing would be highly illegal," put in Colin.

"Of course," Emma agreed. "And you didn't see Sonny the night the club got robbed?"

"Neither hide nor hair," said Billy firmly.

"And not afterwards?"

"Nope," said Colin. "And if you talk to your friend the detective inspector, she'll tell you we said the same to her. Whatever happened to poor old Sonny, it wasn't anything to do with us. Not that we didn't think about it, mind you." He scratched his chin, hard. "That was a good bit of dosh he had off us."

Emma was still considering this when Oliver leapt to his feet all at once and zoomed to the front door, knocking over Billy's walking stick as he raced past.

"Oi! Watch it, ya daft dog!" he bellowed.

Emma leaned down to pick the cane up, and that was when she heard the door open and Oliver barking.

"Oliver?" Pippa's voice drifted down the hallway. "What are you doing here. What . . ."

Pippa came into the kitchen with Oliver bounding beside her. She saw Emma sitting with Billy and Colin, and her whole face tightened up.

"Well, well." Pippa folded her arms. "What's all this, then?"

36

"HELLO, EMMA," SAID PIPPA WARILY. SHE STEPPED OVER TO her grandfather's side, moving carefully to avoid stepping on Oliver, who was busy trying to get a good sniff at her shoes and trouser hems while wagging his bum the entire time. "What's going on?" She kissed her granddad on the forehead.

"Just having a bit of pudding and a nice chat, Pippa." Billy patted his granddaughter on the small of her back.

"Made for a nice change from biscuits out of the packet," added Colin. "Nothing for anybody to worry about."

"Yeah, sure," said Pippa, looking right at Emma.

Billy reached up and took hold of Pippa's arm. She turned toward him.

"Colin's right. There's nothing to worry about," he said firmly. "Come on, sit down. Emma, how about some of that jam roly-poly for my girl here, eh?"

"Sure thing." Emma picked up the knife, ready to cut a fresh slice. Oliver immediately abandoned his inspection of Pippa's ankles and came to Emma's side, in case of crumbs.

"No thanks," said Pippa flatly. "I just ate."

"Oh." Emma put the knife down again. "Well, if you're sure?"

"I'm sure."

Oliver plopped down on his hindquarters, defeated.

Pippa took her camera bag off from around her shoulders and set it on the table. "So what were you three having your nice little chat about, then?"

"Oh, Emma here's very interested in the old days," Billy said. "And the old gang." He raised his mug to Colin, who raised his in answer.

"Now, why am I not surprised?" Pippa picked up the whiskey bottle and carried it back over to the sideboard.

"Don't mind her, Emma," said Billy. "She's just had a long day. You go on. You were going to ask me another question."

"Granddad—" Pippa groaned as she deposited the whiskey back in its drawer.

Emma's gaze shifted from Pippa to Billy.

"I told you never mind her," said Billy. "You go on. Ask me anything."

Emma made up her mind. If Billy was in the mood to talk, she wasn't going to waste it. "Did you never think it might have been Sonny who grassed on your lot?"

Billy grinned, at her and at his granddaughter. "I thought about it," he admitted.

"But then Walter gave himself away," said Colin.

Emma sat up straighter. Her sudden motion made Oliver scramble back up on all fours. "How was that?"

"We suspected for years," said Billy. "But it was Pippa got it all confirmed, wasn't it, Pip?" He beamed proudly at her.

To her credit, Pippa remained remarkably calm. But Oliver clearly sensed something. He slipped over to her and stretched himself up until his paws were on her knee. When Pippa reached out to scratch his head, Emma saw her hand tremble.

Her voice, however, remained perfectly steady. "Yes, that's right."

"How?" asked Emma. "Especially after all this time?"

"Sorry," said Pippa. "Have to protect my source."

Emma leaned forward to protest at the same time as Oliver dropped back down onto all fours. But Pippa held up her hand. "Look, Emma, I know you're trying to help your friends, but what you know today, half the village will know tomorrow. I just can't risk it. Everything else will be in the news tomorrow, I promise."

"See, as it turns out, it was Walter put Sonny up to it," said Billy, clearly enormously pleased with himself, and his granddaughter.

Emma blinked. Oliver, registering her confusion, put his paws up on her chair. Emma scooped him up and laid him across her lap.

"I'm sorry," she said. "What did Walter put Sonny up to?"

"The robbery, convincing Sonny to skip town, the lot." Billy drank off the last of the tea. "That was all Walter."

"Oh, he looked like butter wouldn't melt in his mouth," said Colin. "But he was a nasty customer, was our Mr. Greenlaw."

"Takes one to know one," said Billy.

"Shut it, you," said Colin, but without any real heat. "Walter's problem was he didn't like to get his hands dirty. He believed in letting others take the risks."

"'Plausible deniability' they call that now." Billy chuckled. "Plausible deniability could have been Walter's middle name."

"But how do you know it was Walter? I mean, it seems like it could have been any number of people." Emma scratched Oliver's neck, hoping the gesture would help keep her own thoughts calm. She'd been thinking this exact thing, just a few minutes ago—how Sonny was working in Walter's pub, how they would have shared a grudge against the smugglers. They also would have shared a need for money.

And blood's thicker, isn't it?

"Because as it happens, before everything went pear-shaped for us, Walter had lost a great deal of money at the dog track, and his missus was threatening to leave him," said Colin.

"Needed to get that money back, didn't he?" Billy gave Pippa a sideways glance. "And the next thing you know, there we are being ripped off and sold out."

Pippa nodded in serious agreement.

"But . . ." Emma rubbed Oliver's head, trying to gather her thoughts. "I'd heard Melinda Greenlaw was angry because Walter was in so deep with the smugglers."

"Pah!" Billy barked. "I'll bet that was Sam talking. Blind as a fecking bat, isn't he? Won't hear a word against dear old dad."

"Well, Walter was family," Emma tried.

"Fooling yourself isn't real family," Colin sneered. "Real family is when you know who they are and what they've done and you still hang together."

"You take me and Pippa, now." Billy gestured back and forth between the two of them. "She's not perfect, and neither am I, but we're straight with each other. We *know*. She doesn't go around pretending I'm any kind of hero, and I don't act like she's all sweetness and light. Doesn't matter—we stick together."

"Sam, though, puts his fingers in his ears and sings la-la-la," Colin said, his voice going high and squeaky. "Swears his dad was the only Simon Pure among all British pub owners. Wouldn't even take an extra bottle of good stuff at Christmas." Colin rapped his knuckles on the table. "Gets right up my nose, that does."

"But Walter did get out of the trade?" Emma pushed.

"He pretended to," said Pippa.

"See, that's the key there." Billy grinned. "He *pretended* to. But it was just to get himself out of the way while he sent Sonny in." Billy leaned forward. Oliver tilted his ears toward the old man, as if that would help him understand. Maybe it would. "Sonny wasn't really a bad kid. Pinched a fiver here and there, mostly to buy his records. Kid stuff. We woulda taken him back, given time, but we didn't have it, did we? Never should have left him to Walter's tender mercies," he said, and Emma heard the genuine anger in his voice.

"It was Walter talked him into it, and Walter grassed on them all when it was done," said Pippa.

"Wouldn't surprise me at all if it was Walter put poor Sonny into that tunnel," added Colin.

Emma looked to Pippa. "And I imagine that will be in the news tomorrow as well."

Pippa shrugged. "Let's say the public is going to be able to draw its own conclusions."

Emma wrapped her arms around Oliver, who obligingly snuggled closer.

"So, is this what you were arguing with Reggie about the night he died?" Emma asked Billy. "Whether Walter was responsible for grassing on the smuggling ring?"

"All right, that's enough," snapped Pippa. "I've got work to do. You can read all about it, like a normal person—"

"Now, Pippa no need to knot yourself up," said Billy calmly. "It's a natural enough question under the circumstances." There was a gleam in his eye. Emma got the sudden feeling that Billy was enjoying himself. A glance at Colin's puckered smile confirmed it.

Billy Marsh was not a nice man, and he liked to make trouble, and he was making it now.

"As it happens, that is what we were arguing about," he said, his tone smooth and confident and not at all worried. "I had Pippa take me over there. We really wanted to talk to Marianne, find out if her old dad had told her anything about Walter that could help back up Pippa's article." He touched the side of his nose. "Only Reggie got in the way, didn't he? Said we had no business sneaking about bothering his wife, and we could just shove off. Well, I may have said a few angry words in the heat of the moment." He shrugged. "But could you blame me?"

Emma felt her brow furrow. This version of events didn't sit with what Rory had told her. Unless, of course, she'd just been making too much of him not seeing Pippa. After all, she could have left the two men alone for some completely mundane reason, like a trip to the ladies' or something.

"How much of this did you tell DCI Brent?" Emma asked.

"Now, that part is none of your lookout," said Colin flatly.

"Would you—" she tried, but Billy cut her off.

"Look here, Miss Emma Reed. I'm grateful for the pudding and a chance to reminisce, as it were, but what I do or do not decide to tell the cops is my very own business. I don't care how chummy you might be with them. Oh, yes, I know about that. Pippa"—he jerked his chin toward his granddaughter—"says you and that lady inspector are thick as thieves. You should excuse the expression," he added.

"Well." Emma put Oliver back down on the floor. It was clearly time to go. Whatever game Billy and Colin were playing with her, it was coming to a close, and she didn't think anyone here would take kindly to her overstaying her welcome.

"Thank you for the tea and the chat," she said. "I should probably be going. You're welcome to the rest of the pudding." She stood up and reclaimed her bag. "Can I ask just one more thing?"

Billy shrugged. "Ask whatever you want."

Emma didn't miss the dark look Pippa shot him.

"Doesn't mean you'll get an answer, does it?" Colin added and wagged a knowing gray eyebrow at his friend.

"The tunnel under the Roundhead. By any chance, did the other end open into the cellar at the Sea and Shell?"

Billy regarded her steadily. "I'm sure Pippa will come round with your baking tin in the next day or two," he said.

"Absolutely." Pippa also stood up. "I'll walk you out."

Emma thought about saying there was no need, but one look at Pippa's grim expression and she decided not to bother. The other woman clearly had something she was going to say, whether Emma wanted to hear it or not.

She was right. Pippa followed Emma and Oliver out onto the stoop and closed the door behind them.

"Now, you listen to me." Her voice was low, but every word was perfectly clear. "I catch you bothering my granddad again, I will make your life in this village so miserable, you and your little dog will be running straight back to London." Pippa poked her in the chest.

"Hey!" barked Oliver. "Hey, you can't do that!"

But Emma just drew herself up to her full height, which admittedly was not very impressive, but it was the thought that counted.

"Was it Rory?" she asked.

Pippa drew back. "What?"

"Your source," said Emma. "Did you talk Rory into backing up your story to take suspicion off him and his uncles?"

But Pippa just shook her head slowly. "Nice try, but I am not going to reveal my source. Now, you have a nice evening, and you remember what I said." She stepped back into the house and slammed the door.

Emma and Oliver both winced, hard.

Emma turned on her heel and marched back to the drive and her Mini Cooper. Oliver trailed protectively behind, either making sure they weren't followed or making sure she kept going in the right direction.

Emma opened the door on the passenger side and boosted Oliver up into the seat.

"Oliver," she said as she fastened his car harness around him, "when Pippa came in, did you get a good sniff at her?"

"Of course," yipped Oliver. "Gravel and petrol and tarmac and tobacco and beer." He shook himself. "The beer was new. She doesn't usually smell like beer."

"Could you tell where she'd been?" Emma asked. It was another long shot, and she'd never be able to explain it to anybody, but—

"A corgi can always tell!" declared Oliver. Emma waited. Oliver sneezed and shook himself and scratched under his chin. He mumbled under his breath and his ears drooped. Emma felt her spirits sink along with them.

All at once, Oliver's ears shot back up. "Dead otters!" he yelped.

"What?"

"Powder and dead otters! And beer! On her shoes! Pippa was with the sad lady! At the noisy beer place!" He sneezed again.

"The Donkey's Win?"

"Yes! Yes! There! With the snacks lady and the sad lady!"

"Well, well." Emma climbed in behind the wheel, but for a moment she did nothing but sit there and stare out the windscreen. "And well again."

Because if Oliver was right, Pippa's confidential source might very well be Marianne Tapp. It would make sense. She could have talked to Marianne while Billy was distracting Reggie.

There was another possibility.

Billy knew Emma talked to the police. Billy had waited years to get back at the man he believed had done him wrong.

An article in the paper would help scratch that itch. But an announcement from the police accusing Walter Greenlaw of that long-ago murder would be even better.

The problem was, Walter's involvement would explain so much, including Sam's defensiveness. He really could be in denial about his father's activities.

It would also explain how Sonny had come to be in a tunnel that was supposed to have been bricked over.

But there was still the question of Sonny's mysterious girlfriend. Could that really have been Liza? Could she have been lying about what happened between her and Sonny?

There was something else as well. The three people around that kitchen table all believed she was a careless gossip. Pippa had just said as much. They all believed she'd start talking indiscriminately about what she'd heard in this kitchen.

It was entirely possible they were making sure she was told the story they wanted the rest of Trevena to hear.

37

AS FAR AS EMMA WAS CONCERNED, THERE WAS ONLY ONE way to cure the turmoil her conversation with the Marshes and Colin had left inside her.

"Yes, takeaway!" Oliver barked as they pulled up to the curb in front of Patel's Royal Indian. "This is an excellent idea!"

The Patels' restaurant was a small place—just a handful of tables in a cozy room decorated with silk hangings and photos of lush Indian landscapes. Today, Mrs. Rishi, PC Raj's tiny, round grandmother, was at the register, and she was chatting with Gwen Leigh.

"Hello, Emma!" Mrs. Rishi greeted Emma warmly. Oliver barked and laughed up at her. "And hello to you too, Oliver. How can we help you both today? Tikka masala?"

"Please, Mrs. Rishi," said Emma.

"Me as well," Gwen said. "Proper hot, all right?"

"One hot and one mild." Mrs. Rishi made a note on her pad. "It won't be a minute." She bustled toward the back to put the order in.

Gwen turned to Emma. The air of firm resolution she'd worn this morning had faded. In fact, she looked thoroughly deflated. Her spiked hair was limp and her shoulders hunched, like she was waiting for something unpleasant to come creeping up behind.

"I didn't expect to see you here," Emma said.

"Well, it's been a long day, hasn't it?" Gwen ran one strong hand through her hair. "And it's the best Indian for miles."

"How's your father?"

"Barely seen him." A spasm of anger tightened Gwen's face, and it took an effort for her to smooth it away.

"I imagine Marianne and your Dad have been left a lot to sort out."

"You could say, yeah," agreed Gwen, her voice both tired and bitter.

"Are they going to open the Win again?"

"As it happens, they are." Gwen looked out through the glass door to the street. "Be good for the staff."

"And you?" asked Emma. "What are you going to do?"

"Well, I guess I'm going back too," she said. "Gotta do something, don't I?"

There was a lot underneath that blunt statement. Emma just wished she knew what it was.

Oliver jumped to his feet and gave a tiny whine. A second later, Emma smelled the mouthwatering scent of spices and fresh bread. Mrs. Rishi came bustling out through the swinging door, a carrier bag in each hand.

"There now!" She handed Emma one bag. "Mild for you and Oliver." She handed the other to Gwen. "And proper hot for you, and on your own head be it."

Gwen's smile was weak. "I accept full responsibility."

They both paid and walked out into the deepening twilight.

"You headed back to the B and B?" Gwen asked Emma.

"No, home." She gestured up the hill. "I'm at Nancarrow cottage."

"Would you like a ride? I go right past there."

Emma wasn't sure if she believed Gwen or not, but she was certain the other woman wanted to talk. "Thanks, but I've got my car."

"Oh, right," she said, but her disappointment was clear. They strolled down the street a few steps. A whole flock of thoughts swirled through Emma's mind. Including Colin's offhand speculation that Gwen might have had something to do with Reggie's death.

Emma didn't believe that for a second, of course. At the same time, there was a lot about the Leighs' connection to the Tapps that she simply didn't understand.

Except that the second she thought that, she remembered the way Marianne's hand had touched Ben's.

Emma stopped beside her car and waited for whatever Gwen had to say next. She was certain there must be something.

"Emma?" Oliver bonked her calf. "The food smells very good, Emma. Should we go home now?"

But at the same time, Gwen met her gaze.

"Everybody says you're the local Miss Marple. Is that true?"

"Erm." Emma glanced toward the restaurant. "A bit, yeah."

"And you worked in a bank, or something like that? Before you came here?"

"Something like that. But I don't—"

But Gwen cut her off. "I think Reggie was cooking the books."

Emma blew out a long, silent whistle. At the same time, she couldn't exactly say she was surprised. Reggie, with his love of expensive toys and his flexible attitude toward bill paying, might also have had some creative notions when it came to accounting practices.

"What makes you say so?" Emma asked Gwen.

"There've been nights when I'd catch my dad sitting up late, staring at his computer screen, typing slow, trying to make things add up. I just—I had the feeling that something wasn't right. I asked him about it, and he tried to make out like it was nothing. But he was lying, and I knew it."

Emma nodded. There were a lot of ways a business

could be used to shuffle money around. And if any one part of this mess was clear, it was that Reggie had always believed himself to be just a bit cleverer than the rest of the world. That sort of person tended to believe they could get away with all sorts of things.

Oliver stretched out on the pavement beside her, depressed and clearly worried about the eventual fate of the dinner in Emma's bag.

"Do you have any proof?" Emma asked.

"Some," said Gwen. "I managed to get a couple of screen shots off Dad's laptop and compared them to my copies of the invoices. They didn't match. And there were records of invoices I'd never seen."

Emma nodded. This was an old game. "Have you told the police?"

"I want to," said Gwen. "But how do I do it without getting Dad in trouble?"

"I'm sure you can work something out," said Emma. "Especially if whatever he has to tell them can help clear up Reggie's murder."

"Maybe."

"You've got to try," said Emma. "I know it's hard, but this could be a chance to turn himself around."

To her surprise, Gwen laughed. It was a harsh and bitter sound. "Turn himself around," she echoed, her voice full of irony. "Dad's been trying to turn himself around for years, hasn't he?"

"I don't understand," said Emma.

Gwen bit her lip and looked over her shoulder to make sure they were still on their own. "You cannot tell anybody else this. Anybody."

"All right."

"Dad has a gambling problem," she said. "And he's always telling me how he's trying to 'turn himself around,' but he never does." Her voice went hoarse, and Emma saw her eyes glittering in the twilight. "I've tried to get him into a program, but it never seems to take, you know? Anyway, he . . ." She swallowed. "A few years ago, he borrowed some money from a client. He said he planned on paying it back."

"Oh, Gwen." Emma touched her shoulder, but Gwen just shook her off.

"Yeah. Well, Reggie found out. I don't know how, but he did, and Reggie paid back the money for Dad." She looked down the street toward the sea. Emma wondered what she was remembering. "And Dad never did get caught, except that, of course, now he owed Reggie." Her voice dropped to a near-whisper. "That's why he started working here. It was because Reggie needed someone to doctor his accounts who wouldn't talk."

Because, of course, if Ben turned Reggie in, Reggie would turn right around and turn Ben in.

"I know this is hard, Gwen, but the cops are going to get into Reggie's finances." *If they haven't already.* "And if"—*when*—"they find out that Ben's been helping doctor the books, he's going to be in trouble anyway."

"You think I haven't tried to tell him that?" Gwen snapped. "He won't budge. He says he's got it covered and that I shouldn't worry. He says—" She bit her lip. "He says it's all going to be okay."

"Did he say why he thinks that?"

She shook her head. "I can't even tell if he really believes it, or if he's just trying to make me feel better."

"What can I do to help?"

She hung her head. "I have to find some way to convince him that it's not okay, and it will not be okay. Something I can actually show him that he can't just brush all this off."

Anger simmered in her voice, but more than that, Emma heard her fear and simple frustration.

"Have you tried to talk to Marianne?"

"Not yet. I figured she had enough going on."

"I understand that."

"Could you, I don't know, do whatever it is you do? Get that detective to listen to you?"

Emma sighed. "She'd listen to you. I promise."

"I know I should, but I can't. Not with Dad . . . with things like they are."

Oliver was nosing restlessly at the pavement. Emma knew him well enough to tell he was trying to find something to distract himself with. She understood how he felt.

"Gwen," she said slowly. "Do you know if your dad and Marianne are, well, friends?"

Gwen's brow furrowed. "Yeah, they're friends."

Emma wanted to ask if they were more than friends, but the look on Gwen's face spoke volumes. She suspected they were in a relationship, and she wasn't happy about it. Emma swallowed.

She also wondered if Reggie had known there was something going on with Ben and his wife.

"If I wanted to talk to your dad, do you think he'd talk to me?" she asked.

"He will," Gwen said. "If I have to tie him to the chair."

"All right, then," said Emma. "Can I give you a call?"

"Yeah." They exchanged numbers, and Gwen wished her and Oliver good night.

Emma buckled Oliver into the Mini's back seat and set the takeaway bag on the front seat.

"Don't you trust me?" whined Oliver.

"Always." She kissed his head. "Except when you're very hungry."

Oliver drooped, but he didn't argue.

Emma climbed into the driver's seat and slammed the door shut. She rested both hands on the steering wheel and watched while Gwen climbed into her battered green Volkswagen Golf and pulled away from the curb.

"Oliver, how did we get here?"

"We drove, Emma," he reminded her, patiently. "We're in the car now."

My literal corgi. "I mean in the middle of this mess with Reggie? Everybody says they want us to help figure it out, except everybody's trying to protect somebody." David and Charles were trying to protect each other. Rory was trying to protect them both. Pippa wanted to protect her grandfather. Sam was trying to protect his father's reputation, and Gwen was just trying to protect her father.

But in Gwen's case at least, those efforts had backfired. Because if Ben Leigh was being blackmailed by Reggie *and* having some kind of affair with Marianne Tapp, he had not just one motive for murder, but two.

So did Gwen.

Come to that, so did Marianne.

38

THE TAKEAWAY REQUIRED A BIT OF GENTLE WARMING IN the cooker, but afterwards it tasted magnificent. Emma and Oliver shared the rich tikka masala and naan, and a salad with greens and apples. They sat in their own garden, and Emma left her phone inside. She needed time to clear her head, and there was a growing feeling inside her that she might not have too much longer before things went well and truly pear-shaped.

Five a.m. came very early, and with it came Pippa's latest article in the *Cornwall Coast News.*

DID A PUB FEUD KILL SONNY GREENLAW?

Two public houses squared off against each other over the slice of the smuggling trade that ran through Trevena village in the early 1970s . . .

Emma set her toast and marmalade down and read, barely remembering to blink.

. . . records show that Walter Greenlaw, owner of the Roundhead, and Tommy and Mildred Hartford, the

> husband-and-wife owners of the Sea and Shell, were both involved with the smuggling/counterfeiting ring . . .

A fresh description of the smuggling ring and its activities followed, most of which Emma had read before.

> . . . but sources who were privy to the facts at the time reveal that Greenlaw and Hartford had had a falling-out over division of the profits . . .

"Yeah, yeah, 'sources,'" she muttered. "What sources?"
"What's a source?" asked Oliver.
"An imaginary friend," she answered irritably.

> . . . the result was that Greenlaw left the gang with, sources report, a considerable grudge against his former compatriots . . .

Oh, no, Pippa! What are you doing*?*
But Emma knew, of course. It was the same thing Pippa'd been doing all along—protecting her family with everything she had.

> . . . the death of Reginald Tapp adds fresh urgency to the question. Could the same old grudges that killed Sonny Greenlaw have come roaring back to take another life?

Emma closed her laptop and pressed her hands against the lid.
"Emma?" Oliver looked up at her anxiously. "Emma, is it time to go?"
"Yes." She made herself get to her feet. "I think it is."

THE WALK DOWN TO THE B AND B HAD SELDOM FELT SO dark and cold. Emma huddled inside her duffle coat and tugged her knit cap over her ears. Soon she'd have to get out

Oliver's winter coats, which would add at least ten minutes to getting ready each morning. Oliver regarded being bundled into wool plaid as beneath the dignity of a brave and noble corgi.

She also veered off to stop by the Roundhead, but the pub was shut up tight.

It's Sunday, she reminded herself. *They're probably just sleeping in, like sensible people.*

It was, in fact, entirely possible. But that didn't make her feel any better. She couldn't stop thinking about Sam, and how he'd feel when he read Pippa's accusations. She remembered Colin and Billy in that faded kitchen, carefully setting up their story, and drawing Pippa in to confirm the important details.

All so Emma would repeat the right things when she talked to her friends, doing her bit to keep the village grapevine primed with the proper story.

She also thought about how both men carried canes, and about the round bruise Constance had found on Reggie's back. Could that have come from the foot of a walking stick pressed against a man's back? Billy might not have had the strength to do it, but Colin might, especially if Reggie was drunk.

She could almost see him, grim and silent, using his cane to hold Reggie facedown in the fishpond. She could certainly imagine both old men sitting at that kitchen table, passing the bottle back and forth, and deciding what story to spread around afterwards.

Which got Emma wondering if Pippa's source was none other than her granddad.

But would Billy use Pippa like that? Emma considered this. He might. She almost hoped so, because the other possibility was that Pippa already knew what had happened and was helping her grandfather by helping with the cover-up.

Which was far more possible than Emma was comfortable with.

"Do you want to talk about it?" Angelique asked as Emma walked into the warm kitchen. Of course, she paused to give Oliver a good head rub.

Emma did not bother to deny there was something she wanted to talk about. She was quite sure it was written all over her face.

"Did you read the article from the *Coast News* this morning?" she asked.

"First thing," said Angelique.

"Emma?" barked Oliver. "Emma, Angelique will take care of you, Emma. I should go see the garden."

"Sorry, corgi needs an out." Emma took a side towel and jammed it under the kitchen back door to prop it open. Oliver zoomed out into the damp morning. Emma watched him for a moment, thinking about muddy paws and the fact that bath night was overdue.

Which was easier than thinking about the question Angelique asked next.

"Do you think any of it's true?"

Emma opened her mouth, and closed it again. "I don't know," she admitted, turning back toward her friend and the well-lit kitchen that was practically her second home. "It could be."

Angelique raised both eyebrows. Emma swapped out her knitted cap for her kitchen hat. "Colin was visiting Billy when I got there yesterday. The pair of them were more than willing to talk about the old days, maybe in a bit of a roundabout way." She tied her apron around her waist. "They both said that it was Walter Greenlaw who turned the smugglers in, and they both stuck to that story, even though they admitted that they didn't know why Marianne's parents weren't arrested when the raid finally happened." She took the mug of strong tea Angelique handed her. "And Pippa did say she had a source to back it up, but she wouldn't say who it was. And Billy admitted he and Pippa had originally gone to the Win to talk to Marianne, not Reggie. So maybe Marianne told them some of the story."

"Huh." Angelique leaned both her elbows on the counter. "Have you thought that Pippa's source could be her granddad?"

"Oh yeah," Emma said. "But I don't know. It could as

easily have been Marianne, or even Reggie himself. I'll tell you what though, it didn't need to be an old grudge that killed Reggie. It could have been a brand-new one."

"Oh-ho?" said Angelique. "What have you found out?"

Emma told Angelique about her conversation with Gwen outside the Patels' restaurant. Angelique's eyebrows arched until they practically touched her hairline.

"Do you think Gwen realized she was giving you a motive for her father to have murdered Reggie?" Angelique asked.

"I don't think so," she said. "She's like Pippa. She's all wrapped up in trying to protect her family."

"It sounds to me like they're both frightened." Angelique shook her head in sympathy. "And of the same thing—that someone they love has done something very stupid."

"I know," said Emma. "I can't help feeling that no matter what the answer is, someone's family is going to get broken up by this."

"Hey, now." Angelique touched her shoulder. "This is not your fault. You know that, right?"

"Except it is," said Emma. "If I hadn't let my curiosity run away with me, I wouldn't have people trying to get me on their side to sort out two separate murders!"

"You were helping your friends," said Angelique.

"And look what I've done," said Emma gloomily. "It's just what I've always been afraid of. I've made things worse."

"That's not true—"

But Angelique didn't get any further. The back door slammed open, making them both jump. Emma whirled around, ready to scold Oliver about charging around in the kitchen, but it wasn't Oliver behind her.

It was Sam Greenlaw. He'd clearly left home in a hurry—his hair was tousled and he hadn't shaved. His corduroy shirt was buttoned wrong.

"Was it you?" he demanded.

"What?" Emma blinked hard.

"The source! Pippa's source! Was it you?" he roared.

"Sam," said Angelique. "You need to calm down."

The door banged open again. This time it was Oliver,

who charged in, diving low to get himself right between Emma and Sam.

"Back!" he barked. "Back! Back!"

Sam, startled, did pull back. Oliver backed up too, until he was all but sitting on Emma's toes.

"Quiet, Oliver!" Emma admonished him.

Oliver stopped barking, but he didn't move out of the way. All his attention remained focused on Sam.

"All right, everyone," said Angelique firmly. "That's enough. Sam, what are you talking about?"

"Emma was over at Billy Marsh's yesterday," he said. "Were you feeding him and Pippa that . . . that trash about my da?"

Emma's jaw dropped. She'd been caught up in the idea that Billy and Colin were using her to do their gossiping for them. She hadn't even stopped to consider that someone might think she was providing Pippa with the anonymous tidbits that had been laced so liberally through her article.

"Of course not!" she sputtered. "I would never!"

"Oh, wouldn't you?" Sam sneered.

"Why don't we—" began Angelique at the same time as Emma said,

"Sam, listen—"

But he just pulled back. "Do you know what? I don't think I will." He turned on his heel and strode out the door.

Oliver scampered to the door behind him. "He's gone," he barked. "Emma, are you okay?" He rushed back to her and immediately stretched up to put his paws on her knee. "Are you okay, Emma?"

"Yes, yes." She rubbed his head. "It's all right now."

Except it wasn't, and all three of them knew it.

THE REST OF THE DAY, EMMA TRIED TO KEEP HER HEAD down. She baked. She freshened up the arrangement of the cakes and buns in the takeaway case. She set out her fruitcake samples and sign-up sheets. She smiled at her guests, cleaned her counters and did her best to avoid talking about Pippa's juicy little article.

The rest of the village, however, was not so ready to be done with that news.

"Don't see why anybody's surprised," said Matt Walsh. "Old Walter Greenlaw always was a cagey one. Knew more than he told, and that's for sure."

"Everyone knew he'd fallen out with that whole Hartford clan," added Amelia Little.

"Greenlaw was awfully quiet after Sonny went and vanished," said Dan Pryce archly. "You'd think there'd've been a bit more fuss, him being family and all."

Emma smiled, and wrapped up people's Sunday buns, and handed over their tea, and tried to keep her mind where it belonged.

It didn't work.

It was a little after noon. The shop had cleared out for a moment, and Emma was leaning against the counter and taking a big swallow of lukewarm tea. All at once, Oliver's ears went up and he dashed to the door. Brian walked in, ducking under the low doorway.

Emma set her mug down.

"You're early," she said, trying to sound cheerful, and normal.

"I got a call from Angelique." He folded his arms and leaned against the display case. "She said you're pushing yourself too hard."

"I'm not," said Emma.

Brian looked at her. She couldn't have said exactly how he did it, but when he gave her this particular look, she always knew right away that he didn't believe her, and he forgave her for it, but she should try again, all right? It was a lot to pack into a look, but Brian managed it handily.

"At least, I don't mean to be. It's just . . . things kept happening."

"Here, now." He reached over the counter and found her hand. She may have reached up to him. "You look all in."

"I am," she admitted. "I didn't sleep very well last night."

Brian raised up their hands and circled the case, until he was standing on the same side as she was. He took her other hand as well and leaned close. "Let me take you away from all this," he murmured.

Emma looked up at his beautiful smile and deep blue eyes, and her heart quite literally skipped a beat. Or maybe that was just Oliver bonking her in the calf.

"I can't," she said miserably. "I've got too much to do." If she really was taking Becca on as an apprentice, she needed to make a plan, and more lists, and then she needed—

Oliver bonked her calf again. "Go on, Emma," he said firmly. "You have not been getting out enough. It's not healthy, Emma." He bonked her a third time for good measure.

"You're ganging up on me," she said plaintively.

"Absolutely." Brian took her gently by both shoulders and turned her so she faced the door. The dratted man also picked up her bag. "Come on, Oliver, we're getting out of here. Right now."

"But . . ."

"I've already called Genny, and she called Becca. They'll be here—"

"They're here now." The door opened again, and Genny strode in. "At least this half is. Is she going?"

"She's going," said Brian.

"*She* is standing right here," Emma reminded them.

"Not for long." He hooked his arm through hers. Genny held the door. Oliver followed close behind.

"Come on, come on, walkies!" he yipped.

Emma resigned herself to fate and let them both steer her out into the sunshine. Maybe fate wouldn't be so bad, at that.

39

BODMIN WAS A SMALL VILLAGE, LIKE TREVENA, BUT WHERE Trevena stood open to the sea and sky, Bodmin village was tucked deep in the hills at the edge of the moor from which it took its name.

They drove slowly, just enjoying each other's company and the crisp feel of the autumn day. Brian had brought his collie dog, Lucy, and she and Oliver snuggled up happily together in the back seat. They stopped at the pub and the two of them (well, the four of them), shared a ploughman's lunch, with a half pint of shandy for Emma and a half of stout for Brian. Then they drove out to Bodmin Moor. Bodmin wasn't as famous as its bigger cousin, Dartmoor, but that was a bonus as far as Emma was concerned, because it meant it was also much more empty. Right now, the peace and quiet were exactly what she needed.

From the tiny car park, they climbed the long, sloping hill. They wandered through the remains of the Bronze Age settlement.

Oliver and Lucy chased each other through the short, wet grass. Oliver even managed to track down one of the wild ponies that lived on the moor, and of course, he had to bark at it. The pony was unimpressed. It snorted and put its head down.

"What a terribly rude pony," laughed Emma as Oliver retreated back to her side.

"Yes, he is," he barked. "And he's new. He shouldn't be on his own. He should be with his family. I told him, but he wouldn't listen."

Emma laughed and rubbed his head.

At last they reached the hilltop and looked over onto the broad, flat spread of the moor itself. The wind was brisk enough to sting Emma's cheeks, but the sun was fresh and warm. The dogs, both as out of breath as their humans, flopped down onto the grass, panting.

Brian tucked his arm through Emma's.

"Feeling better?" he asked.

"Much. Thank you."

"My pleasure," he said easily. "So, what's happened that you don't want to talk about so much?"

Emma sighed. "I'm not even sure. It's just—this business with Sonny, and now Reggie. It seems to be hitting awfully close to home. Everyone seems caught up in it one way and another, and—" She shook her head. "It's what Raj Patel said at the beginning. All these old rumors and secrets are getting set to tear people apart."

She told him about her visit with Billy and Colin, and how Pippa came and found them together, and how they'd all told her the same story that Pippa had written for the *Coast News*.

"Do you really think Bill could have killed Reggie?" Brian asked.

"I don't know," she said. "If you'd asked me yesterday night, I would have said no."

"Why?"

"Because I'd just talked to Gwen Leigh, and she told me that Reggie was cooking the books at the Win. She'd seen her father working with what looked to her like fake invoices and"—she paused and watched Oliver and Lucy chasing each other around one of the boulders that dotted the moor—"and she said that Reggie had blackmailed her father to work for him, and . . . well, okay, I haven't got any proof of this next bit."

"Go on." Brian tucked both hands in his pockets.

"Keep it to yourself, but I think Ben and Marianne might be having an affair."

Brian pursed his lips and whistled softly. "Whew!"

"I am certain there's an attraction there. So all that got me thinking that maybe Constance was right. Maybe Reggie's death had nothing to do with finding Sonny's skeleton."

"You think it might have been one of the Leighs?" he asked.

"It could be," she said. "And I admit, it was Colin Roskilly who put the idea in my head. He made a remark about Gwen, about how she was strong enough to have done it."

"And if she was telling you the truth, she had a motive."

"She came down here to look out for her father," said Emma. "She said she'd been trying to get him away from Reggie for some time, but he just wouldn't go. Maybe she decided to force the issue."

"But you've changed your mind since then?" said Brian.

The wind shoved Emma's wild curls across her face. She shoved them back, and then had to shove them back again.

"Maybe. I don't know. Something's missing. Anyway." She dug her hands into her duffle coat pockets. "I'm giving it up."

Brian didn't say anything.

"I'm just making things worse," said Emma. "I'm going around unearthing old gossip and trying to build puzzles when I don't have all the pieces, and the whole village knows I'm nothing but a nosey old gossip and—" She looked up at him. "And you can stop looking at me like that."

"Like what?"

"Like I'm adorable. I'm serious."

Brian sighed and put an arm around her shoulders. She resisted the urge to snuggle up to his side, but only for about a second and a half. How was it he was just the right size for her to fit against so comfortably? It was annoying. He shouldn't be this perfect. She was too old for this kind of perfect.

"You're serious," agreed Brian. "And you're worried about your friends, and you're also not wrong," he added. "What happened to Sonny, and now Reggie, has got people on edge. Just yesterday, I had to get in the middle of a shouting match between Kyle Westerly and Jacob Simms. They were taking sides over whether old Greenlaw had anything to do with Sonny, and how maybe it was Liza who could say more than she did."

"Oh, lord."

"Yeah," Brian agreed. "So it's no wonder you feel like this could get bad. It already has."

She leaned her head against his shoulder. "So what do we do?"

He kissed the top of her head lightly. "Same as always. Try to sort it out."

Emma straightened. "Speaking of . . . where have those dogs gotten to?"

Brian looked around. "Over by the logan stone. There."

"Come on, we'd better get over there before somebody defaces an ancient monument . . ." Emma paused, and squinted. "Wait a minute—" she began.

"Isn't that David?" Brian finished.

40

....

THE LOGAN STONE WAS ACTUALLY FOUR BIG, ROUNDED stones, stacked in perfect balance to form a tower that was at least three meters tall. David stood beside it, dressed in vintage tweed and a pair of green wellies. He even had a wooden staff with a leather thong at the end. As Brian and Emma reached him, he was in that odd posture that came from bending over to pet both Oliver and Lucy, while looking up and around to try to find their owners.

"Well, my goodness." David straightened up as they reached him and adjusted the paisley scarf he'd tied around his neck. "I certainly didn't expect to see you two here. You four, I suppose I should say." He rubbed Lucy's ears. Oliver barked in affirmation, or maybe to remind him that he wanted a head rub too. "Will they be all right off the lead?" David asked. "I understand there's still quicksand around here."

"Not up here there isn't," Emma assured him. "The worst that could happen is somebody gets into an argument with one of the ponies." She looked down at Oliver as she said it. Oliver hung his head, but he also wagged his bum.

"What brings you out, David?" asked Brian.

"Fresh air." David drew a deep breath. "And the scenery." He waved his stick down over the rust and green expanse of the moor that stretched all the way to the horizon. "Remarkable how something so empty can be so beautiful, isn't it?"

"Yes, it is." Emma had always loved the solitude and drama of the moor when she was a girl. The fact that it reminded her of her favorite Daphne du Maurier and Sherlock Holmes stories also helped.

"Charles not with you?" Brian asked David casually. Emma felt a small rush of gratitude, because she'd been wondering the same thing.

"No," said David softly. "No he's not."

I'm done, she reminded herself. *I'm not going to dig anymore. I'm not going to make anything worse. I'm not . . .*

Brian looked down at her, like he knew what she was thinking. She set her jaw. He raised one eyebrow.

"Why isn't Charles here?" yipped Oliver. "They are David-and-Charles. Charles should be here. Should I look for him, Emma? Is Charles lost?" Oliver immediately put his nose down and started casting around the ground, looking for a scent. Lucy barked once and joined him.

Emma gave up.

"So, David," she said. "What's wrong with you and Charles?"

"Nothing's wrong," he said.

"Try the other one," she told him. "Even your cat can tell something's off."

"What are you talking about?"

Emma ignored this. "You two have been on edge ever since they found the Vincent with Sonny's body." *And you were at the Donkey's Win the night Reggie died.*

"Well, yes, of course," said David. "Who wouldn't be? Finding a valuable possession with a skeleton and then having a murder happen on top of it, and police questioning people and . . . well, everything. I mean, it would put any reasonable person off, wouldn't it?" The edge on David's words implied ever so slightly that Emma herself was not an entirely normal person.

Can't exactly argue with that, she thought ruefully.

"It's more than that, David, and you know it," Brian said firmly.

"So does the rest of the village," put in Emma. "And if Detective Brent doesn't know it already, she's going to soon."

Slowly, carefully, David bent his knees and settled down onto the ground. He laid his stick across his legs and stared out toward the horizon. Brian sat down as well. Emma, ignoring the popping in her knees, settled beside him. After a minute, both dogs came and piled on top of their humans. Emma snuggled Oliver close, grateful for his wriggly warmth.

"Back when all this started, you said Sam and Liza didn't need to hear any more rumors about their family," she said to David. "I thought you were talking about Sonny then. But you were talking about Walter, weren't you?"

"You have to understand," said David. "When the smuggling ring fell apart, when everybody knew there'd been a grass—well, the gossip was that vicious. Walter came in for a lot of it, and by extension, so did his family. It left Sam badly bruised, and I'm not just speaking metaphorically," he added. "There were a couple of nights Charles and I helped clean up the worst so his mum wouldn't worry too much."

"But that's not what's been bothering you," said Emma. "Or at least, not all of it."

"We're all friends, David," added Brian. "Whatever it is, we just want to help you, and Charles."

"It was so long ago," he murmured. "I never thought it could matter. Not anymore."

Emma waited. Oliver wriggled out of her lap. He slipped over to David and poked him in the side. David looked down. Oliver stretched up and nuzzled him under the chin.

David sighed again, and rubbed Oliver's back.

"Charles and I left London more or less on impulse. We had just what we could fit in a couple of rucksacks. It felt such a marvelous adventure." He smiled. "Running away does when you're that age, doesn't it? But eventually, you need to eat, and you need a place to stay, and it wasn't like we were going to find a squat in Trevena. Back then, there wasn't even a hostel.

"I was able to get a job at a tailor shop, and Charles worked as a driver part-time for Old Man Hartford."

"Marianne's dad?" asked Brian.

"The same," said David. "But we soon found out that by working for Hartford, Charles was also working for the smugglers. Nothing so very bad. A delivery here and there. Moving the merchandise around to keep it ahead of the revenuers. But it worried me. He was starting to stay out late again. Then someone got beat up and . . ." He swallowed. "I was afraid he was falling back into old habits, and this time we were out of places to go. So, when Sonny started saying he was going to leave town, I made him an offer, and he accepted."

"What was the offer?" Emma asked.

David ruffled Oliver's ears absently. "The Vincent. I said we'd sell it to him. The only thing was, I didn't tell Charles."

"Oh," Emma said.

"Yes. Exactly. So, on a night when I knew Charles was going out on a job and wouldn't be back until morning, I took the Vincent and met Sonny. Sonny paid me and rode off, and I never saw either one of them again, until Sam opened the tunnel."

"And you never told Charles."

David bowed his head. "I was afraid of how angry he'd be if he found out. He loved that bike. It was so beautiful. Like a work of art. I know that sounds mad, but there it was."

Emma smiled up at Brian. "I know it happens. You'd think it was a perfectly made chocolate sponge or something."

David smiled too, but the expression was brief. "So, when he got home and found the bike gone, and he assumed it had been stolen, I let him go right on assuming. It was just easier that way."

"What did you tell him about the money?" asked Brian.

"That it had come from an uncle of mine who I'd written

to a couple of weeks ago. It was enough for us to put down the first month's rent on a little space for our record shop, and, well, the rest is history."

David paused, and when he spoke again, his voice was soft and harsh. "But you see, it's all gone wrong."

"How?" asked Emma.

David moistened his lips. "We were seen."

"Who? You and Charles?"

"Me and Sonny."

Emma opened her mouth, but before she could say anything, a whole new set of thoughts dropped into place. "It was Reggie, wasn't it?"

David's head drooped. Oliver whined and licked his chin. But this time, David failed to smile.

"Reggie wasn't accusing Charles of Sonny's murder, was he?" said Emma softly. "Charles lied about that. Reggie was accusing you."

41

DAVID TWISTED HIS STICK IN HIS HANDS. "CHARLES LIED TO cover the real accusation up. Everyone already believed he was capable of murder, so the gossip was, well, expected, I suppose. He didn't want . . . well, I'm the nice boy, aren't I? Reputation is important. It's all a bit ironic, don't you think?" he added with a touch of grim humor in his voice.

"Oh my lord, David," said Emma. "You have to tell Charles what really happened."

"Tell him I've been lying to him for decades?" David shot back. "That should go over well."

"It's better than having him think you might have killed Sonny," said Emma. "Or Reggie."

"I'm sure Charles doesn't really—" began Brian. But David turned toward them again, and the anguished look on his face robbed Brian of whatever he'd been about to say. "Ouch," he said instead. "Sorry, mate."

"I could have killed Reggie, you know," said David. "I should have done it. But I was a coward . . ." He swallowed, and wrapped one arm around Oliver. Fortunately, Oliver was patient as well as nosey, and always seemed to know when a friend needed comfort. "Instead—I went to the Donkey's Win." His voice dropped to a whisper. Emma could barely hear him over the sound of the wind rushing over the stones. "The night that Reggie died. I snuck out after Charles was asleep. The place was closing up, but Reggie was still there. He was fairly drunk already. I told him that I didn't care what he said about me meeting Sonny before he died. He could even go to the police if he wanted. In fact, I was going to tell them myself." He paused, and straightened his shoulder, as if remembering that bit of defiance.

"I thought I'd take the pressure off Charles. I thought, I felt, I was sure, I could even go carry my threat through, if I had to." He looked down at his hands. "Charles was right. I used to be a much better liar. He told me to clear out. And I did." He shrugged. "Not exactly the heroic act of defiance, in the end."

"David," said Emma gently. "You need to tell them the truth—the police and Charles."

"I know." He sucked in a deep breath. "I had hoped I could keep putting it off, but I can't. It's already gone much too far. That's why I came out here. To think what to do. It's not easy to decide how to break someone's heart."

"Charles's heart is made of sterner stuff, mate," said Brian. "You have to trust him."

"Brian's right," said Emma. "Unless of course, the problem is you're just really embarrassed by being chased away by a drunk Reggie Tapp, and don't want to admit it."

David barked out a laugh loud enough that Oliver tumbled over onto his side. "Oh, my lord, Emma! I believe you may be right."

"Come on, then." Brian climbed to his feet. He held out a hand to pull Emma up and then turned to David. David accepted his hand and, with the help of his stick, levered himself awkwardly to his feet. "No time like the present."

"And at my age, that's about all the time there is." David pulled out a handkerchief, brushed down his trousers and wiped his hands. "Thank you both. All of you," he added to Oliver. "It's good to be reminded one has friends."

"Anytime," said Emma. "But, David, can I ask—"

"What is it, Emma?"

"What did Reggie say to you? When you confronted him?"

David's mouth twisted up in regret, and anger. "He laughed in my face. Called me a few names, and then he said—" He squinted, looking for a memory. "Well, it's odd. He said that the Vincent was his ticket out and he was taking it. It was his turn, he said. I remember his face. It was like I was seeing the real him for the first time.

"'I'm done with this damn cage,' he said. 'I'm out of here, and you are not stopping me.'" He paused. "There may have been a few other words in there."

Memory dropped heavily into Emma's mind.

"Oh, sugar!" she exclaimed. "That's it!"

"What?" said Brian and David together. Well, Brian, David and Oliver.

"I've had the feeling I was forgetting something for the longest time. It was something Reggie said to me while he was talking about investing in my shop. He said he would be a silent partner, *so silent you'd swear I wasn't even in the country*." She stared at them both. "He was already planning to run away by then. He'd started planning right after they found Sonny and the Vincent."

They stood in silence for a long moment. Lucy, bored with all the humans just standing about, barked to Oliver and loped down the hill towards the muddy little car park. Oliver zoomed after her, and then stopped as if remembering something, and then zoomed back to Emma.

"It just keeps happening, doesn't it?" Brian remarked thoughtfully.

"I'm sorry?" said Emma, distracted by Oliver's antics and Lucy's energetic barking.

"The Vincent," said Brian. "Everybody keeps seeing it as a way out. You and Charles." He nodded towards David. "Then Sonny, then Reggie."

David blinked. "I hadn't looked at it that way, but I suppose you're right."

"Well, what I don't get," said Brian, "is that if Reggie didn't leave Trevena back then, why would he suddenly want to go now? Trevena is, was, his home. He's the one who built that pub back up after everything fell apart. He was a big man here."

"Except he wasn't really, was he?" said Emma.

"He always acted like it," Brian pointed out.

"But what if it was just that?" Emma's whole body stiffened. "An act? To fool other people. What if it was—overcompensation?"

Oliver bounded up to her and jumped up on his hind legs. "You got it, Emma! I know you got it!"

She rubbed his ears with both hands. Maybe she did. *Just maybe.*

"I don't understand," said David.

"It's been bothering me, that," Emma told them. "Why did Reggie stay in Trevena? Why did he let his ambitions be limited to one pub and a line of talk?"

"Incompetence?" said Brian flatly. "He was all talk and no do. I hate to say it, but it's what everybody knew."

"It's certainly what we all assumed," said David.

"But what if it was more than that?" said Emma. "What if Reggie didn't leave because he couldn't? Because something was holding him here?"

"Something or someone?" asked Brian. "I suppose it's possible, but how would you find it out? You can't exactly ask Reggie."

"There's Marianne," said Emma.

"You could try, certainly," said David. "I don't know her very well, but I can tell you she's been keeping herself to herself for the best part of her life. I'm not sure she'd be ready to open up over a nice cup of tea and a slice of cake."

He was probably right. Emma remembered what Liza had said about how Marianne broke off their friendship without so much as a backwards glance. "Well, then we'll have to do the other thing."

"Which other thing?"

Emma smiled down at Oliver, who was casting around in the grass. "Follow the money."

42

THEY ALL WALKED DOWN THE HILL TOGETHER, WITH THE dogs leading the way. It was a fairly easy ramble, except for the part where Oliver got too excited and tumbled tail over teacup for a good four or five meters.

"Are you going to be all right?" Brian asked David when they got back to the cars.

"I think so," said David. "And I do promise faithfully that as soon as I've told Charles and Rory what happened, we will all be going to DCI Brent."

"I didn't actually say—" began Emma.

David smiled, and this time it reached his keen eyes. "But you were about to, dear." He pointed at her. "Don't try to fool me."

Emma held up both hands. "I never would. But if you want, I can call Constance, let her know to expect you."

"Yes, thank you," he said. "That will help keep me honest." He twisted his hands around the walking stick. "I think it will be a relief, in the end, to have it all out in the open." He chuckled. "Something a person like me should know, eh? Well, I'm off." He straightened up. "Thank you, Emma, and you, Brian." He bent stiffly and patted Oliver. "And you, old chum."

Brian and Emma watched while David climbed into his surprisingly practical Volvo and drove off.

Emma looked up at Brian.

"You're doing the right thing," he said.

"I wasn't going to ask—"

"Yes you were," said Oliver. "I could tell. And you are. You're helping. You should always help."

"See?" Brian bent down and rubbed the corgi's chin. "Oliver agrees with me."

Emma grinned. "I reckon he does."

AS SOON AS BRIAN DROPPED HER AND OLIVER OFF AT Nancarrow cottage, Emma pulled out her mobile and hit Constance's number. The detective chief inspector picked it up on the second ring.

"Hullo, Emma. Anything interesting for me?"

Oliver was scratching at the garden door and whining urgently. Emma went to open it for him.

"Well, it's really just a heads-up." She dropped onto her chaise and rested an elbow on her knee.

"Oh?"

"Yes, David Kemp has something to tell you about the Vincent and Sonny Greenlaw. He should be calling soon."

"David Kemp?" Constance echoed. "Of Charles-and-David fame?"

"Yes." Emma paused. "You sound surprised."

"I am, rather," Constance admitted. "But never mind that. Can I ask what it's about? Or are you sworn to secrecy?"

"Not exactly, but as it turns out, the Vincent wasn't actually stolen, at least, not from Charles and David."

"I see. That . . . is interesting." Emma heard a clicking sound, and pictured Constance compulsively pressing the button on her mechanical pencil.

"In a good way, or a bad way?" asked Emma.

"Both and neither," said Constance. "There've been some competing theories of the crime, or crimes, circulating. This might just put some weight on the scale. I'll be honest with you, Emma, this one is a right mess."

"Yeah." Emma watched through the door as Oliver circled the garden, very clearly on patrol. "I've noticed. Have you had a chance to look at Reggie's finances yet?"

There was a pause and some rustling, and Emma pictured Constance leaning forward. "What makes you ask that?"

"Well, he was so careless about money, and his accountant was so horrified about his plans before he died, I thought maybe there might have been some trouble."

"All kinds, actually, according to what we've heard so far," said Constance. "But nothing criminal that we've been able to find. Just a lot of bad ideas."

"Oh," said Emma, disappointed.

"Yeah, my feeling exactly," added Constance. "It would have been much easier if he and that money man of his had simply been fudging the accounts."

But if Ben and Reggie weren't up to something dodgy, what were those invoices Gwen found? Emma frowned.

Oliver came trotting back in. He shook the evening mist off his coat and plopped down on the mat at the foot of the chaise. "Snacks?" he asked.

"In a minute."

"Sorry?" said Constance.

"Oh, nothing," said Emma. "Just talking to my dog."

"Ah. Yes. Well, either my cop senses are completely playing up on me, or you have someone else you're thinking of talking to."

"Erm, maybe?"

"Like the accountant Ben Leigh, who knows better than to say a blasted thing to the cops about his former-and-current employers' finances, some of which may not be in the records he's handed over."

"Oh, well," said Emma casually, "I don't really know him."

"Neither do I," Constance admitted. "But I'd like to. Rather a lot, actually. Because right now, if I had to hazard a guess, I'd say Reggie's death is most likely to be the result of his own idiocy right here in the present, and I'm not just talking about his business habits."

"What are you talking about?"

"We could have cleared all this up in fifteen minutes if the man hadn't been such a cheapskate."

It might have surprised some people to hear that a man who could waste thousands of pounds on get-rich-quick schemes could also be a cheapskate, but Emma knew it happened. Her father had constantly shaken his head over clients who were penny-wise, but pound-foolish.

"What did he do?" Emma asked Constance.

"You might have noticed there's CCTV cameras bolted to pretty much every inch of the Win, inside and out."

"Erm, no, to tell you the truth, I hadn't."

"Well, we did, and of course, we asked for the video. Thought we'd be finished in ten seconds flat. That was before Mrs. Tapp confessed to us that they were all fakes. Her husband put them up because it was cheaper than hiring an actual service. Swore to her they'd save hundreds a year on insurance as well."

And doesn't that sound just like Reggie. Emma rubbed her forehead. It also explained why Constance had been in such a bad mood that day at the Win.

Emma thought again about the Win, about Gwen, and Ben, and about Marianne. She thought about how Marianne was described as the brains of the outfit by an old smuggler who ought to know. She thought again about Colin and Billy, sitting in the kitchen with their whiskey-laced tea.

She thought about Liza and her story of how Sonny had tried to play fair with her and Sam.

She thought about how Reggie started getting ready to leave town the day after the Vincent was found.

She also thought about the Leighs, and how nine times out of ten when somebody did something really foolish, there was money at the bottom of it.

"Can I ask you one thing?" she said.

"If it is just one thing," said Constance.

"Was Reggie poisoned? You found those capsules . . ."

"Oh, those." There was some more shuffling in the background. Emma pictured Constance opening a fresh folder. "Roofies. Marianne Tapp says they took them off some kids last summer, dropped them in the drawer, and forgot about them. We're writing her up for not reporting the incident, but no, Reggie had nothing in his bloodstream beyond an injudicious amount of alcohol. Cause of death is very clearly and unambiguously drowning, and yes, in the fountain where he was found. Anything else?"

"Would you answer me if I said yes?" asked Emma.

Constance paused. "Probably not right now, no," she said. "And I've got a call coming through. Have to ring off. Good luck."

Emma rang off on her end. "You too," she said to her silent phone.

Oliver got to his feet and stretched up to put his front paws on the edge of the chaise. Emma smiled and boosted him into her lap.

"What now, Emma?" he asked.

She didn't answer right away. Instead, she petted his long back thoughtfully. She felt sure that one way or another, Reggie's death was connected to finding Sonny and the Vincent. The problem was, she couldn't tell whether that connection was because of something that had happened in the past or something that was happening now.

But Sonny had been planning on leaving town, and he'd died.

Now, forty years later, Reggie had been planning on leaving town, and he died.

Was that really just a coincidence?

"What else could it be?" she asked herself, and Oliver. "What's the other similarity between the two of them?"

Oliver scratched his chin. "Between who?"

"Reggie and Sonny. They were both leaving town, they both wanted the Vincent to do it. They both died. They both . . ." She stopped.

Sonny had robbed the wrong people to get the cash to run away with his girl.

Reggie had some cash he wanted to park in a safe, incongruous investment, like a little local tea shop. Which was a great way to hide money.

Or to launder it.

43

ON A NORMAL MONDAY, EMMA WOULD HAVE BEEN IN AT the B and B around eight o'clock. Just because the shop was closed did not mean the shopkeeping actually stopped. As she'd told Marianne, Monday was her day for sitting down with invoices and her sales records so she could plan her bakes for the coming week. Today, she also had to sit down with Becca and Bella and talk about the future.

It turned out, the sisters already had firm plans. They wanted to go into business together—specifically, to set up a lunchroom specializing in traditional Cornish treats. "Going beyond pasties and all, yeah?" Becca said. In lieu of a raise, or a promotion, what they wanted was lessons in how to manage a business.

Emma thought it was a terrific idea and said she'd be happy to help the sisters learn more of the behind-the-scenes work of running a restaurant.

They were shaking hands all around, with Oliver looking up at them to make sure no crumbs were going to drop, when the door opened again and, to Emma's surprise, Mrs. Patel walked in.

"Oh, I'm so sorry," she said. "I didn't mean to interrupt."

"Not at all; we were just finishing up here." Emma nodded to her two newly minted apprentices. Becca elbowed her sister, who elbowed her back, and the two gathered up their things, said goodbye to Mrs. Patel and headed out into the foggy morning.

"Can I get you a cup of tea?" Emma asked.

"Oh, no, please don't trouble. I had forgotten you were closed today. I'll come back another time."

"It's no trouble, really." Emma couldn't believe Mrs. Patel had simply forgotten that Emma was closed on Monday, considering half of Trevena was closed today.

Emma got up and went behind the takeaway counter to pull down a fresh mug.

"Oh, well." Mrs. Patel unwrapped the scarf from around her head and resettled it onto her shoulders. She sat down, but didn't take her coat off. Oliver sat down beside her.

"Is there anything I can help you with?" Emma asked as she set down a fresh cup of tea.

"Well." Mrs. Patel took a sip of tea. "I feel so embarrassed. We are having a breakfast meeting with the restaurant staff today and I was hoping to get some of your marvelous Chelsea buns."

It wasn't like Mrs. Patel to leave something like that until the last minute. *Something is definitely going on.*

"I'm afraid I don't have any buns," said Emma. "But how about some apple cake? That's always nice in the morning."

"Oh, that would be marvelous," said Mrs. Patel brightly. "If you're sure it's no trouble?"

"None at all." Emma got up and went to her display case. She pulled out the loaf cake she'd baked on Sunday, still wrapped up and untouched. "Will this do?" She held it up for Mrs. Patel to see.

"That would be perfect. I don't know where my head is this morning. I'm sure it's this awful business with Reggie Tapp. It has Raj very worried, you know. Very worried," she repeated with a shake of her head.

The mention of Raj sent a jolt right through Emma.

"Well, I hope his people are listening to him now," she

said, hoping her voice sounded casual. "I know he was trying to tell them that things might get difficult."

"Yes, yes, and he is feeling it very much. He thinks he should have tried harder to get a proper investigation started as soon as they first found poor Sonny."

Emma pulled out a cardboard flat and began folding it into a bakery box. "I'm sure he did his best."

"I try to tell him it is not his fault, but you know how young men can be. He takes everything to heart. Has your detective friend said anything to you? About what they are thinking?"

"No, not really. Not yet. I mean, she has to be careful, doesn't she? If it gets out she's oversharing with a civilian, she could get into real trouble." Emma placed the cake in the box and folded the lid down.

"Yes, of course," said Mrs. Patel as Emma came back over to the table. "Raj says the same thing. He told me just this morning, 'Ma, you can't go talking to everybody about this. Especially, well, just anybody.'"

Emma felt her mouth quirk up. "He told you not to talk to me, didn't he?"

"Well, you know, Emma, you have a bit of a reputation."

"I know, and I don't blame him at all. Erm." She paused while curiosity wrestled briefly with her conscience. "I don't suppose he said exactly what you shouldn't talk to me about?"

Mrs. Patel cocked her head. "You know, he did, as it happens. He was very clear. He said that I should not tell you that they are thinking of actually arresting Sam Greenlaw."

"Sam?" Emma said as calmly as possible. "Really?"

"Yes. Can you imagine! But it seems they have some new little bit of information or the other . . ." She shook her head.

What information? Emma wanted to scream. *What's happened?*

"Gosh," said Emma. "And here I was worried about

Rory. There was a rumor going around that somebody said they saw him arguing with Reggie the night he died."

"I had heard something about that," Mrs. Patel said. "But you know, he wasn't really in danger, not for long."

"Oh?" Emma arched her brows.

"Yes. As soon as they found out the time of death, they were able to take him out of the picture. It seems Reggie died around one o'clock, you see, and Rory's friend Lyle was able to say that Rory was still in the flat at that time. He remembered because they microwaved a pizza around then." She shuddered delicately. Emma sympathized with her feelings, but at the same time, she'd never felt so glad for the existence of bad frozen food.

"Not that there was ever much suspicion," Mrs. Patel went on. "Everyone knows Rory's a good boy. Raj didn't believe it when Mr. Leigh told him what he'd seen, even when Mrs. Tapp said it was true as well."

Mr. Leigh? It was Ben who lied about what he saw? And Marianne backed him up?

"Gosh," breathed Emma. "Well, I don't believe Sam had anything to do with Reggie's death, any more than Rory did. Maybe it's just another rumor?"

Mrs. Patel shrugged eloquently. "I'm sure I don't know. All I can say is that Raj was very clear that he did not want you to know this, because he was worried you might go around asking all sorts of questions that no one had thought of yet, and coming up with alternate theories and I'm sure I don't know what else, and I told him that I didn't care what other people said, that you are a bright woman and you'd never go around interfering just for the sake of it. But if you knew that someone was making a mistake, well of course you would do your best to help, like anyone would."

"Of course," said Emma, her thoughts whirling. "Well. You can tell Raj not to worry. It's not like I know anything the police don't, and if I did find something out, I'd tell them right away."

"And I'm sure he'll realize that once he's thinking

straight. He's just very worried right now." Mrs. Patel got to her feet and picked up the box. "Thank you for the lovely cake. I'm sure it will be just the thing. You have a good day now." She smiled warmly and turned to go.

"Mrs. Patel?"

"Yes?" She looked at Emma over her shoulder.

"Isn't it horrible that someone's accusing Sam? I didn't even know he was there the night Reggie died."

"Well, Raj says the person who made the accusations was there and saw him." Mrs. Patel leaned in. "And Sam is refusing to talk with the police. Liza is very worried," she added sadly. "I only hope Raj will be able to sort it out soon."

"I'm sure he will. You have a nice day, Mrs. Patel." Emma smiled and kept on smiling until Mrs. Patel had left and the door had swung shut behind her. Then she collapsed into the nearest chair.

"Emma?" Oliver wagged at her. "Emma, what's wrong?"

"Tell you in a second, corgi-me-lad." Emma dug her mobile out of her pocket and hit Genny's number.

"Genny?" she said as soon as her friend picked up. "Can you come to the King's Rest? Mrs. Patel's been here, and we've definitely got a problem."

44

"*SAM?*" EXCLAIMED GENNY. "THEY'RE SERIOUSLY CONSIDERing arresting *Sam*?"

Emma, Genny and Angelique were all sitting in front of the fireplace in the B and B's private parlor. Not only was it cozier, with its overstuffed chairs and vintage tea table, but it was less likely that someone would walk in on them. To make extra sure of their privacy, Emma set Oliver to keep watch on the front door.

"Yes!" he had barked immediately. "No one will get in! A corgi is vigilant!"

Emma had smiled and rubbed his ears.

"I can't believe it." Angelique poured herself a fresh cup of tea. It was of course impossible for such an important discussion to happen without tea. "Well, I believe it. It makes sense, but—"

Genny stared at her. "What part of arresting Sam can possibly make sense?"

"The part where Sam might have killed Sonny because Sonny was going to run off with Liza," said Emma miserably.

"And then Sam killed Reggie because Reggie figured out that he'd killed Sonny and tried to blackmail him," finished Angelique. "Unfortunately, it makes for two birds with one very sad stone."

"But why would Reggie blackmail Sam?" said Genny. "I mean, to get some money obviously, but what did he need the money for?"

Genny looked from one of them to the other, like they both might start skipping about the room and singing about fairies in the garden. "You cannot really believe that Sam killed Reggie, or Sonny."

"No, I don't," said Emma. "But I can see how somebody might." Especially if Sam had gotten stubborn and decided not to talk with the police, with or without a solicitor.

"And here I thought it was Rory and Charles who were in trouble," said Angelique. "I wonder what changed?"

"The Kemps went to the police," said Emma.

"Did they?" Genny arched her brows. "I hadn't heard this bit."

"It just happened yesterday," Emma told her. "That may have made the difference, especially since they'd be able to say that Reggie was pressuring Charles to get him to hand over the Vincent before he scarpered."

"Do we know Reggie was going to scarper?" asked Angelique.

"Would you stay here after you'd threatened and blackmailed half the village?" replied Genny.

"Excellent point." Angelique nodded.

"Plus Reggie more or less told me that was his plan," said Emma. *So silent you'd swear I wasn't even in the country.* "Only I didn't realize it at the time."

"And with everybody keeping so many secrets, no one was sure what really did happen back then," added Emma. "It left them all vulnerable to Reggie's threats."

"Reggie certainly wouldn't have been above using that sort of uncertainty against someone," said Angelique.

"And here I thought I already had plenty of reasons not to like Reggie Tapp," muttered Genny.

"Too right," said Emma. "He must have felt so clever, using everybody's secrets against them."

"But hang on." Genny set down her mug. "If I was the cops and Reggie came to me with a story like that, I'd want some proof. What kind of proof could he have had after all these years?"

"Well, Reggie did have a witness, if he ever needed one," said Emma.

"A witness?" said Genny. "You don't mean Marianne?"

Angelique looked into the depths of her teacup, as if trying to read the future, or maybe the past. "Would Marianne have lied for Reggie? If she knew it would send someone else to prison?"

"She might not have lied for Reggie, but she might lie for herself," said Emma. "That pub and her marriage were all she had. If Reggie could convince her that the pub was in danger from this investigation, she might lie to save it. That's what this whole thing has been about," Emma added. "Everybody involved has been trying to protect what's theirs."

"Why would the pub be in danger?" asked Genny.

"Because there's still an active smuggling operation going on in the basement."

"Never," announced Genny. "Reggie couldn't possibly be running a thing like that."

"He wasn't," said Emma. "But Marianne is."

Angelique and Genny exchanged a long, meaningful look.

"Emma," began Angelique, "you know I have the greatest respect for you—"

"But this time, you really have lost your mind," Genny finished for her.

"I know how it sounds," Emma admitted. "But I think Marianne is still running a smuggling racket. I think Ben is helping her, and I think Reggie was a smoke screen."

"But why wouldn't it have been Reggie running the racket?" asked Angelique. "He and Ben already worked hand in glove."

"Two reasons," said Emma. "First, because it was successful, and Reggie couldn't manage his way out of a wet paper bag."

"What's the second reason?" asked Genny.

"The Vincent."

"Sorry," said Angelique, "you've lost me."

"I think he was going to sell the Vincent to get some money of his own so he could finally get out from under Marianne and Ben."

"Now I know you've lost your mind," said Genny.

"Hear me out," said Emma. "It was Billy Marsh who hit on it. Reggie was all about overcompensation. He was a failure. He wasn't even in charge of his own illegal operations. If he got hold of the Vincent, he could convert it into enough cash to run away with." Emma shook her head. "After all, that's what that bike is for, isn't it? Running away? Reggie even said as much to David."

"So, what happened?" Genny's brow wrinkled. "Marianne killed Reggie to stop him from running away?"

"It's possible. He'd know all her secrets, or most of them, anyway. He'd been going around making threats, which she had to have heard about. Maybe she didn't want to risk him coming back to threaten her."

"I just don't believe it. Not Marianne," said Genny. "She couldn't. She's completely under Reggie's thumb. Everybody knew it. You've seen her."

"Maybe Reggie wasn't the only one putting on a good show," said Emma. "Maybe Marianne used the assumptions everybody heaped on her as a disguise." She would have been used to assumptions too. Liza had said as much when she talked about the two of them joining forces against unkind ideas about girls who worked in public houses.

They all fell silent, sipping their tea and trying to organize their thoughts. That was when Oliver started barking out in the great room.

"Here! Here!" he barked. "She's here! She's here!"

Emma jumped to her feet, pushed open the parlor door and found herself face-to-face with Pippa Marsh.

45

"PIPPA!" ANGELIQUE ALSO STOOD UP. "YOU'RE WHITE AS A sheet, girl. Sit down." She took Pippa's arm and guided her to one of the plush chairs. Emma hurried out to the take-away counter.

"Was that right, Emma?" Oliver bounded behind her. "Was the Pippa lady who you were waiting for?"

"Close enough," said Emma. "Thanks, corgi-me-lad." She rubbed his ears and then reached down a clean mug. "Now she needs tea." Emma might be mad at Pippa for her insinuating articles, but there was no denying she looked awful.

When Emma got back with the mug, Genny took it and poured out the tea.

Pippa gulped the brew gratefully. Slowly, the color began to return to her cheeks, but her hands were still shaking as she set the mug down on the tea table.

"Is it true?" she asked them all. "Are the police really going to arrest Sam Greenlaw?"

Emma, Genny and Angelique all exchanged a look over the reporter's head.

"Nothing's happened yet," said Emma.

"'Yet.' Oh, my lord." Pippa groaned. "This is all my fault!"

"Your fault?" Angelique sank down into her chair so she could face Pippa directly. "How could it be your fault?"

"Is this something to do with that article you wrote?" Genny asked. "About Walter Greenlaw?"

"I just thought I was helping Granddad," Pippa said miserably. "I thought it wouldn't matter if a dead man got accused of something! I never thought Sam . . ."

"Pippa," said Emma gently. "What's happened?"

"Granddad went to the cops," she croaked. "He went to the cops and he flat-out lied. Of all the things I never, ever thought he'd do."

Emma remembered Billy sitting in his kitchen talking about real family. *She doesn't go around pretending I'm any kind of hero, and I don't act like she's all sweetness and light. Doesn't matter—we stick together.*

It now seemed that Billy was taking that idea further than Pippa had been ready for.

"What did Billy tell them?" Genny asked Pippa.

"He said that Sam was afraid that people would realize his dad had killed Sonny, and that Sam had threatened Reggie and Granddad both if they said anything."

"Oh, Pippa," murmured Angelique.

"I thought . . . I thought I knew him. I thought I knew how far he'd go. I never . . . I didn't . . ." Tears trickled down her cheeks.

Emma ran for the box of tissues she kept on the takeaway counter. Angelique covered Pippa's hand with her own.

"You have to go to the police," said Angelique. "Let them know that your grandfather lied."

"Yeah, and why should they believe me, after what I printed?" Pippa wiped her sleeve across her eyes. "And if I say I made it up, I get fired." She sniffed. "I should get fired. I knew I had gone too far and I did it anyway. I—" She choked back a sob.

Emma handed her another tissue and Pippa blew her nose. "There's still a way out," she said. "But you have to be straight with us. You and your granddad were at the Win the night Reggie died. What were you doing there?"

"Noth—" she began, but she stopped and swallowed again. "I was trying to get to Gwen Leigh." Pippa's cheeks flushed. "I saw her talking to you. I figured something must be up."

"Pippa!" Genny exclaimed. "Were you following Emma?"

"Maybe a little." For the first time since she'd come in, she showed some of her normal defiance. "But after you tried to sweet-talk my granddad, can you blame me?"

"I suppose not," said Emma, albeit a little grudgingly. "Did you see her? Gwen?"

"Yes, but not for very long. I never should have tried while she was still on shift, but I guess I wasn't thinking straight."

"What did you two talk about?" Emma asked.

"Money, mostly. How the pub was barely making ends meet, but no one seemed to be worried about it, even her dad. I was disappointed, actually." She took another gulp of tea.

"Listen, Pippa," she said. "We've got—well, I've got—a theory, but it's going to take all of us to prove it. Are you willing to help?"

"Sure." Pippa dragged her tissue across her damp cheeks. "I mean, if I can, yeah."

"I need you to talk to your Scotland Yard contacts," said Emma. "Find out if there's been any smuggling activity around Trevena recently."

Pippa frowned. "Like how recently?"

"Say, in the last five years?" said Emma. "It'd be booze and cigarettes, just like in the old days."

"Okay." Pippa glanced at the clock, dug her mobile out of her purse, touched a number and held the phone to her ear. "Yeah, Barney, it's me . . . Yeah, I know . . . I know . . . Yes, I do know." She rolled her eyes and wiped at her face. "But I need just one more favor . . . No, this time I mean it, really. This is *it.* All I need to know is if anybody's been looking at smuggling out of Cornwall in the past, say, five years. Yeah. Right. When I say Cornwall, I mean Trevena. Yeah. I'll wait." She paused. Her eyes flickered restlessly back and forth as she listened.

"But DCI Brent must have checked into this," whispered Angelique.

"Why?" Genny whispered back. "There were already plenty of reasons right up front for Reggie to be dead. Why would she go poking about for new ones?"

"Yeah, I'm still here," Pippa was saying into her phone. "Okay, thanks, Barney. I owe you." She rang off and stuffed her mobile back in the bag. "Barney's with the Inland Revenue," she said. "And he says they've been tracking possible smuggling going on out of Trevena for a bit now, but they haven't been able to build a case."

Which could be because the person doing the smuggling has a lot of experience, thought Emma. *Generations of it, in fact.*

"Pippa," said Genny, "do you think your granddad could be involved?"

"Yesterday I would have said there was no way. Now—" She shook her head. "I just don't know."

Emma took a deep breath. A plan was forming. A somewhat desperate and possibly entirely daft plan, but they were running out of time.

"We need to stay calm," said Emma. "It's possible we can clear all this up in the next day or two. Maybe," she added.

"Why maybe?" asked Angelique.

"Because everything depends on whether or not I can actually sneak into the Donkey's Win."

46

"DO YOU UNDERSTAND THE PLAN, OLIVER?" ASKED EMMA.

"Of course I do!" he yipped.

It was ten o'clock at night. Emma's blood was fizzing from adrenaline and the particular mix of excitement and dread that came from being an adult staying up past bedtime. She and Oliver were in the car park of the Donkey's Win, right next to the fence. They had walked here from the B and B, however, because if everything went well, it was going to be a long night, and Emma didn't want anyone wondering about why her car was still there after closing.

Emma had knelt down and was pretending to fuss with Oliver's collar. She'd also unclipped his lead.

"This is really important, corgi-me-lad." Emma took Oliver's face in both hands so she could look into his eyes. "We've only got one chance."

"We can do it!" Oliver wagged his entire hindquarters. "I remember everything. A noble warrior corgi is thorough, and careful, and stealthy." He crouched down so his belly was on the pavement. "Stealthy is important, right, Emma?"

"Stealthy is very important," she agreed. "For both of us."

She stood up and looked around. On the other side, the

beer garden was about half full. A lot of people had congregated around the fishpond, no doubt discussing Reggie's drowning. No one was paying any attention to them.

Emma made a shooing motion with her right hand. Oliver slunk across to the fence and disappeared under the scraggly bushes. Emma tucked the lead into the tote bag she'd brought. It already held a set of black clothes, a torch, and the portable tool kit her friend Rose had given her as a housewarming present. Because experience showed that you never knew when a screwdriver might come in handy.

Then Emma pasted a hopefully sunny smile on her face and headed for the Win's main entrance.

THERE'D BEEN A HEALTHY DEBATE BACK AT THE KING'S REST over whether Emma should make her break-in attempt before or after the Win opened back up. In the end, Emma decided on after, because, honestly, what was easier than walking in through an open door?

But when Emma saw Marianne on duty at the hostess stand, she almost turned around right there. Unfortunately, Marianne saw her first.

"Well, hullo, Emma," Marianne said, her voice betraying nothing but bland, professional cheerfulness. "I wasn't expecting to see you tonight."

"Yeah, well, we were really run off our feet, and then there was an extra catering order, and I just couldn't face another sandwich at home." Emma hoped the implied exhaustion would cover any wobbles in her voice. "Have you got room for one more?"

"I'm sure we do. Outside?" she asked, her tone just a touch too casual.

"Inside, if you don't mind. Bit cold for me tonight."

Marianne's smile said she understood. "Come on. We've got a quiet corner."

"I admit, I'm a little surprised to see you here as well," said Emma as Marianne led her to the corner booth and laid the menu on the table.

"Yes, well, to tell you the truth, I'm a little surprised too." Marianne put the menu down on the table. "But the house was so empty . . . I felt like I had to do something."

"You are going to keep the place going, then?"

Marianne looked around, and Emma saw a flicker of bitter emotion cross her features. "For now, anyway. Ben thought it would be a good idea, to help keep me busy, and, well, it's been in the family, one way and another, for so long." She dipped her gaze to where her fingertips rested on the table. "And the truth is, I'm not sure what else to do with myself."

"It's hard to make a change when you've worked all your life."

"And yet you did it," said Marianne. Emma wondered if she imagined the hint of envy underneath those words.

"Yes, but I didn't stop working. I just changed careers."

Emma smiled, and Marianne smiled, and Emma hoped she couldn't hear how loud Emma's heart was beating.

Walk away, she begged silently. *You're busy, and you should go take care of your guests.*

But Marianne didn't walk away. Instead, she leaned across the table.

"Emma, can I ask you a favor?" she asked earnestly. "This is for your sake as much as it is for mine."

"Erm, yes, sure." Emma felt perspiration prickle along her scalp.

"Stop trying to help." Marianne touched her hand. "Ben told me you'd been around to see him, and I suspect you've been talking to Gwen as well?"

"Well, you see . . ." began Emma.

"On top of whatever ideas you've been putting in DCI Brent's head—"

Emma's mouth had gone very dry. She thought about attempting a laugh, but quickly realized that would be a nonstarter. "If you knew Constance, you'd know nobody puts ideas into her head except Constance."

"Nonetheless. I'm sure your heart's in the right place, but you'd do better looking after your shop and your friends." Her face had gone dead serious, perhaps even a little frightened. "I'm sure they're all going to need your help a great deal very soon."

Wasn't that what Reggie had said to David and Charles back in the beginning? Emma's thudding heart squeezed uncomfortably. "I'm not sure what you mean."

But Marianne didn't answer. She just straightened up. "I'll send Cory right over. Enjoy your meal." She gave Emma her hostess's smile and strode away.

And that is not in the least bit menacing. This may have been a bad idea after all, Emma-me-lass.

NORMALLY WHEN EMMA WAS DINING ALONE, SHE BROUGHT something to read with her. Tonight, though, as she ate her roast beef sandwich and drank her coffee, Emma watched the kitchen staff going up and down the side stairs. Judging from the way they kept bringing down armloads of towels and paper products, the storerooms must be on the floor above.

All the while, Emma kept turning Marianne's words over in her head. Had they been meant as a threat? Or a warning? Emma had come to believe that Marianne was using Reggie and Ben for her own ends, but what if she was wrong? What if Marianne was just what it said on the tin—a meek woman who had been, for better or worse, dependent on her charming ne'er-do-well husband? And what if that dependency had just been transferred over to the desperate little accountant?

She did say it was Ben who wanted the pub to stay open, and he would have a reason to, wouldn't he? If he still has a gambling problem, he's going to need the money.

Emma told herself it didn't matter. They'd sort that bit out later. The important thing tonight was to stick to the plan, and not to overthink things.

Easier said than done.

Emma lingered until the bell rang for last call. Then she

paid her bill, picked up her bag and her tote, headed into the loo and locked herself into a stall.

Between them, Emma, Genny and Pippa had assembled an all-black outfit that was a reasonable approximation of what the kitchen staff at the Win wore. Angelique had contributed a black, billed cap that was a relic of one of her son's summer jobs.

Once she'd finished the awkward business of changing clothes in a loo stall, Emma stowed her bag and street clothes inside the tote and pulled out the pencil and clipboard she'd brought. It was a universal truth that nobody ever questioned the person with the clipboard. That person was counting something. Stock and inventory were ongoing chores in a kitchen. Somebody was always counting.

Emma slung her tote over her shoulder and, clipboard in hand, trotted up the stairs.

Nobody so much as gave her a second glance.

THE WIN'S UPPER FLOOR HAD A NARROW HALLWAY DOWN its center, lined on both sides with matching doors. The first one was labeled STORAGE. Emma glanced behind her, dug into her tote and pulled out a pair of food service gloves. She pulled them on. Then, heart in her throat, she tried the handle.

Her luck was in. Not only was the room open, it was full of wire shelves that were stacked with boxes of paper goods—napkins and loo roll, and cardboard trays for takeaway.

Emma closed the door.

There was a stack of big paper towel boxes on the floor. Emma shifted the pile toward the door and then ducked into the space behind it. She stuffed her tote under the shelves and settled down behind the stack.

She double-checked that she had her phone on mute. She pulled her knees up to her chest and wrapped her arms around her knees.

Now there was nothing to do but wait.

* * *

IT WAS A LONG WAIT. EMMA NODDED OFF A COUPLE OF times. The last time, she woke up with a crick in her neck and the panicky realization that she couldn't feel her right hand. It was completely dark, but her phone told her it was one a.m.

The same time Reggie died. Emma tried very hard not to let that thought linger. She failed.

Slowly, stiffly and with a lot of bad language, Emma hoisted herself to her feet. She fumbled around until she found her tote, and then the torch. She held her breath, switched it on, and froze in place, listening. But there was nothing.

Emma slid out from her hiding place and tiptoed to the door. She stopped again, and listened again.

Still nothing.

Emma opened the door. The hallway outside was dark and silent. So was the stairway. Her ears started to ring from her straining, but everything was quiet. She couldn't even hear a car passing or the rush of the autumn wind off the sea.

Right. Emma sucked in a deep breath. *First things first.*

She had to get Oliver in from the garden. Of course, he had paid attention to the plan. It wasn't as if his part right now was very complicated. All he had to do was wait for her whistle. He knew it would be a long wait, but Oliver could be very patient when he wanted to.

He would not have wandered off. Not this time. He would not have gotten distracted by a fox. Or by the Cream Tangerine, or any other cat. Not this time.

Emma swallowed hard and tried to hurry down the stairs while keeping quiet at the same time. She tried to tell herself it didn't matter if she made a little noise. The place was closed up for the night. There were no close neighbors. The security cameras were fakes. No one could hear her. No one would see her.

That didn't stop her heart from trying to beat its way out of her rib cage as she turned the lock on the door to the garden. No alarm went off. No motion-sensitive light flashed on. Emma switched off her torch and dragged the door open.

Out in the beer garden, nothing moved.

Emma licked her lips and tried to whistle, but all that came out was a silent rush of air. She licked them again. Still nothing.

Frustration and fear collided hard inside her. She stuck two fingers in her mouth, blew hard, and reeled backwards from the shock of the sharp, high note.

Then . . . nothing.

Emma's heart plummeted.

All at once, a bush rustled, and Oliver shot out like a furry arrow, zooming straight inside. He skittered to a halt and shook himself, scattering damp everywhere.

"Oi!" Emma cried, but she couldn't help laughing from relief.

"Sorry, Emma." Oliver scratched his nose hard and sneezed.

"It's okay. Now, remember, we've got to be quick—"

"I think it's too late for that."

Emma decided to ignore that. "—and stealthy."

"Yes! Stealthy!" Oliver slunk low on his belly and paddled forwards.

Right. Like that. Emma followed.

There was just enough light from the EXIT sign for Emma to find her way down the stairs. Once there, she switched the torch back on. She kept it pointed towards the floor and waited for her eyes to adjust.

Oliver, of course, didn't bother to wait. He was already zigzagging around the room, nose to the tiles.

The Donkey's Win used the cellar as a staff room. There were lockers and tables and chairs arranged to form a mini break/meeting space, complete with whiteboards with the tasks for the next day's (today's, really) opening written up in colored markers. There was a time clock and hampers for used aprons and other linens.

"Anything?" Emma couldn't make herself speak above a stage whisper.

"Lots of people," mumbled Oliver. "And cardboard and plastic and mud and . . ."

Emma grit her teeth and forced herself to be patient. She started zigzagging herself, looking for breaks in the tile, or suspicious cracks in the wall, or anything else that might indicate a secret entrance.

Maybe this was a mistake. I mean, why would they leave the tunnel open? It's not as if—

"Emma?" barked Oliver. "Emma, there's something here. Emma!"

Her corgi was scrabbling at a patch of tile right beside the wall. "It's here, right here! There's a breeze. It smells like dirt, and mice, and spiders."

"Oh, thanks for that." Emma knelt next to him. Carefully, she ran her gloved fingers along the seam of the tile. *Nothing. Nothing . . .*

Then she felt it, a little niche, so narrow it might have been mistaken for a flaw in the grout. She could get her fingers in there, but just barely.

Right.

Emma pulled out her tool kit, extracted the flat-head screwdriver and slipped the blade into the niche between the tiles. There was some wriggling and some swearing before she found the trick of it and levered up an entire square section of tile.

"Yes! Yes!" Oliver backed away, while also wagging his bum like he meant to shake it off. "I told you there was something!"

That "something" was a wooden trapdoor, complete with an iron ring for a handle and a sliding bolt to hold it shut.

Emma's inner twelve-year-old—the one who had spent her summers looking for secret passages and nefarious doings—turned cartwheels in the back of her mind.

Emma leaned in close to examine the latch. The metal of the bolt was clean. In fact, it was gleaming. Someone had taken care of this. Which meant someone had recently used it.

"Look out, Oliver." Emma adjusted her gloves and slid the bolt back.

The trapdoor was heavy, and her angle was awkward. Emma grit her teeth and pulled. The door lifted back silently. Somebody had been oiling the hinges as well.

With the trapdoor open, Emma could see a steep wood ramp. She shone her torch down. The ramp ended at an earthen floor, and although it was hard to tell from this angle, it looked like there was a tunnel leading off to the left.

"Is this it?" Oliver stuck his head into the hole.

"Some of it."

"We're going down there?" Oliver sounded at least as excited as twelve-year-old Emma. "We can go down there, can't we?"

Emma knew if she was smart, she'd close the trapdoor right now. She'd hurry back to the King's Rest, call Constance from there and hope that the detective didn't ask too many awkward questions about how Emma had found all this.

But there was no way twelve-year-old Emma was going to let forty-five-year-old Emma leave without at least taking a look down this mysterious hidden stairway.

At the same time, the plots of a dozen haunted house movies flashed through her mind. All of them involved the heroine suddenly being locked in a small room away from help and friends.

"Right, then." Emma applied the screwdriver to the screws holding the bolt and latch on the trap door. It took some more work, and some more swearing, but she got the hasp off. She dropped it and the screws into her bag.

She picked the torch back up. "Okay, Oliver, let's go."

Carefully, Emma started down the sharply sloped ramp. Behind her, Oliver put first one paw on the splintered wood, then another. He scooted forward—

And yipped frantically as he lost all control and slid down into the dark, scrabbling madly until he landed in a heap at the bottom.

"Oliver!" Emma forgot all about stealth and bolted the rest of the way. But Oliver was already back on his feet. He sneezed, and wagged.

"That was brilliant! Can we do that again? Can we?"

Emma clapped her hand over her mouth to smother the laugh. "Maybe later," she breathed. At the same time, she wondered to herself, *Why a ramp? Why not stairs?*

A moment later, though, she answered herself. *Because if you're moving big loads up and down, it's easier to shift them.*

She also shone her torchlight up the ramp. She couldn't help noticing it was at least half a meter broader than the trap door overhead. She directed the beam toward the roof. She was certainly no expert, but it looked to her like the wood around the trap door was mismatched, like maybe the entrance had once been bigger.

Maybe even a lot bigger.

"Emma?" Oliver bonked her calf. "Emma, what are we doing now?"

Emma didn't answer. She just took another deep breath and shone her torch into the dark tunnel. She started forward, with Oliver right beside her.

47

THE TUNNEL WAS LOW AND SMELLED OF DIRT AND DAMP. The stabilizing timbers overhead were shoved straight into the packed earth. Short as she was, Emma had to resist the urge to duck. The place felt old, and cold. Emma shivered.

Oliver sneezed, and scuttled ahead, nose to the floor.

"Back! Back!" he barked, and Emma squeaked, and slapped her hand over her mouth.

"Sorry, Emma! There were spiders."

"Oh. Thanks." Emma said weakly.

"Also mice, and . . ."

"Okay. Let's just keep going."

"Right." Oliver bustled forward, obviously deciding it was his job to clear the way. Emma followed, not entirely sorry.

At first Emma tried to keep count of her footsteps, but she soon gave that up as a lost cause. The tunnel went on further than she'd thought. *Have we passed the edge of the garden? The car park?* she wondered. *Are we under the high street yet? We must be . . .*

The one thing she did know was that, except for herself and Oliver and some anonymous vermin, the tunnel was empty. There certainly wasn't any sign of smuggled goods. Emma looked for traces of recent footsteps in the dust, but there was nothing.

"Oliver?" she breathed.

"People," said Oliver without lifting his nose. "People, and petrol and dirt, and mice and . . ."

And still no sign of any goods, or boxes or anything else. Emma bit her lip. Maybe the place had been cleared out after Reggie died? In case the cops, or anyone else, got lucky and found the tunnel?

Up ahead, the tunnel took a ninety-degree bend. "Okay, Oliver," she said. "If we haven't found anything by the time we get there we . . ."

But Oliver was already at the bend. "Emma! I found something, Emma!"

Emma shone her torch round the corner. "Yes," she breathed. "You sure did."

This section of the tunnel was lined, floor to ceiling, with stacks of crates and cardboard boxes.

"Wow!" Emma let her torch beam travel along the stacks. "How long has this lot been here?"

Oliver snuffled the nearest crate. "Not long."

Emma stared at him. "Oliver, this is important. Can you really tell?"

"A corgi can always tell!" announced Oliver. "They smell fresh, not like the dirt, like in the other tunnel. These are all petrol and outdoors and people. All kinds of people."

"Any people you know?"

Oliver's ears drooped. "Um . . . the smells are all mixed up and maybe they've been down here kind of a little while, but not too long, some days, and . . ."

"That's okay, never mind," murmured Emma as she rubbed his ears. She checked her gloves to make sure she hadn't torn them on anything and folded back the flaps of one of the boxes. Inside were rows of glass bottles with newspaper, rags and straw stuffed between them. She pulled a bottle out. It was whiskey, some brand she'd never heard of.

"And what's missing?" She checked the top. It was a screw top, and no excise sticker to be found.

"Voilà," she murmured. "Somebody has in fact been

keeping up the family business." She put the bottle back and closed the box.

"Should we keep going, Emma?" Oliver wagged at her. "There's lots more tunnel—"

There was, but Emma felt like they'd already pushed their luck far enough tonight. Her inner twelve-year-old was pouting, but Emma frowned at her sternly.

"We can come back after we've told Constance what we've found," she told herself, and her corgi. "We should get back."

A trickle of dirt drifted down the wall. Emma shivered and tried not to think about how long those roof beams had been there. "Definitely getting back now."

She turned and started back the way they came. Behind her, Oliver huffed and grumbled, but eventually at least, he fell into step and they both hurried back towards the stairs.

We did it. Emma felt herself grinning. *We found the secret smuggler's tunnel. We—*

"Emma!" barked Oliver suddenly. "Emma! Somebody's there!"

Emma whirled around, but Oliver had already dashed off ahead. Emma raced after him, trying to follow her bouncing torch beam and praying she wouldn't trip and fall flat on her face.

Emma was out of breath by the time she and Oliver reached the ramp. Oliver was panting hard, but he didn't pause. He tried sprinting up the ramp, but he just yipped and slid backwards onto his rump.

"Oliver!" hissed Emma

"But Emma, it's bad! It's bad!" he whined. "It's closed."

Closed?

Emma tilted her torch up and saw Oliver was right. The trapdoor was closed.

Emma scrambled up the creaking ramp until she was crouched right under the tunnel roof. She set the torch down. She put both palms against the splintery wooden trapdoor and pushed.

The door didn't budge.

48

"OKAY," BREATHED EMMA. "OKAY, WE'RE NOT GOING TO panic." She pressed both hands against the trapdoor and tried again. It still didn't budge. She got her shoulder up against it and heaved, or at least she tried to, but it was impossible to get any real purchase against the ramp. Then she turned and used her fists, hammering hard against the rattling wood. "We. Are. Not. Going. To. Panic!"

The door still didn't move.

"Emma." Oliver put his forefeet on the ramp and wagged. "If we're not going to panic, what are we going to do?"

"Yeah." Emma slumped down onto the ramp. "That's a good question."

Because right now there didn't seem to be a whole lot of other options.

"Okay. Phone." She yanked her mobile out of her pocket and lit up the screen.

And got the NO SERVICE message.

"Sugar," she muttered. "Sugar, sugar, sugar!" She pressed her phone right up against the trapdoor. The screen flickered. Emma bit her lip.

NO SERVICE.

Emma took a deep breath.

"Okay, okay. This isn't really that bad." She made her way carefully down the ramp, and just as carefully sat on the tunnel floor beside Oliver. "When we don't check in, Angelique and Genny will call the police."

That was the plan in case things went wrong. If Emma did not turn up at the King's Rest by eight in the morning, her friends were to call Constance directly and let her know where Emma had gone.

It was also the only reason her friends had agreed to go along with Emma's scheme.

"It'll all be okay." Emma patted Oliver's side. "All we have to do is wait. They'll find us."

Under the hidden trapdoor, in the cellar, which Emma had only found because she had Oliver. The trapdoor which right now might just have something very heavy sitting on top of it. Put there by somebody who knew that the secret tunnel had been broken into, and who might just know Emma, or somebody like Emma, was down here.

I will not think about Sonny's bones. I will not think about Sonny's bones . . .

"Genny and Angelique will tell the cops what we were doing," she said, to cover up the way in which she was most definitely not thinking about Sonny's bones. "Constance and Raj are really smart. All we have to do is wait." She rubbed Oliver's back.

But Oliver wasn't ready to settle for this. "We could go down the tunnel some more," he suggested. "We could find the Roundhead. You said you wanted to find the Roundhead."

Emma bit her lip and stared away into the darkness. It was one thing to explore a strange tunnel when there was an open door at her back. It was another to be trapped, and to wander off into the dark. Visions of all those horror-show heroines turned up to stand next to Sonny's skeleton.

"We should wait here for someone to find us," she said.

Oliver sneezed. "But what if it's the bad person who shut the door?"

Emma closed her eyes. She really wished he hadn't said that.

"Okay." She got to her feet and slung her tote bag over her shoulder. "Let's go."

They did go. They went around the bend, and past the crates of smuggled goods, and kept on going from there. The dark was disorienting, and the dry earth walls seemed to press in on her.

She wondered how long her torch batteries would last.

She wondered if this was even possibly a good idea.

A fresh trickle of dirt slithered down the wall. Emma screamed and dropped the torch. Oliver barked, bounced, and fell over on his side.

"Okay, okay." Emma pressed her hand against her chest. She also picked up the torch. "We're just going to pretend that never happened and . . ."

But Oliver's nose went up. He gave a wordless yip and dashed off into the tunnel.

"Oliver!" hissed Emma, and then she remembered that she didn't have to be quiet anymore. "Oliver!" she shouted.

"Here! Here!" barked Oliver, losing his words like he did sometimes when he was really excited. She saw him vanish around the bend in the tunnel. "She's here!"

She? Fear gave Emma a fresh burst of speed as she ran after him.

Oliver had come to a dead stop in front of what looked to Emma like a lump of solid shadow. But as she got closer, she saw it was a huge pile of dirt and stones and broken timbers.

Cave-in. Despite everything, her curiosity pricked up and reminded her that she had come here with more than one errand. Yes, she had wanted to find out if the tunnel was still used for smuggling, but Oliver was right. She had also wanted to find out if the tunnel under the Win was the same one that opened out into the Roundhead.

Oliver was at the base of the cave-in, barking up the side of the dirt pile.

To Emma's shock, the dirt pile answered.

"Marouw."

Marouw? Emma shone the torch up toward the ceiling. There, at the top of the cave-in, sat a very fat, very familiar marmalade cat.

"Tangerine?" Emma exclaimed. "How . . . ?"

"She wants to know what we're doing here," Oliver reported. "She thought all the humans had gone home."

"What are we doing here?" choked Emma. "Never mind that! What's she doing here! Has she been here the whole time?"

"Of course not," huffed Oliver. "I would have found her."

The cat meowed again, and Oliver barked back, "I would! I would!"

This was evidently enough for Tangerine. The cat turned neatly around and vanished into the dirt pile.

"What the . . . ?"

Oliver put two paws up on the pile, stretching his body out to its fullest length. "There's a hole!" he barked. "There's a hole and the cat is through."

"Call her back!" cried Emma. "Ask her what's on the other side."

"I'll try, Emma!" Oliver started barking, high and sharp. "Come back! Come back!"

Nothing happened. Oliver dropped back down. Emma pressed her hand against her mouth to keep back a whole set of curse words.

Suddenly, Oliver jumped to his feet. "We've got treats!" he barked. "Treats!"

It was the magic word. Slowly, delicately, the cat emerged from the cave-in, shaking each paw as she picked her way down the side of the dirt pile.

"Right. Now we bribe the cat," muttered Emma. She dropped her tote and dug out her bag. Inside, she pulled out a packet of Bacony-Bites. The packet proudly proclaimed them *Every puppy's favorite!*, but evidently they worked on cats as well. Tangerine ate three.

Emma fed Oliver another three.

"Now, Oliver." Emma wiped her fingers on her slacks. "Ask her what's on the other side of the cave-in."

Oliver approached the cat carefully, making a series of soft whuffs and grumbles. The cat shrugged in a long ripple of fur and meowed with what sounded to Emma like total indifference.

"She says it's a cellar," Oliver reported. "She says it belongs to a grey-haired lady human and a big man human and they're always chasing her out of there, but they keep forgetting to close the window at the back and . . ."

"It's the Roundhead." Emma stared at the cave-in. "So, this is the same tunnel, and the same cave-in." Which meant that Sonny, and the Vincent, could have been brought in from the old Sea and Shell. Despite everything, Emma felt a thrill of hope. This meant that Walter Greenlaw was not the only reasonable suspect for Sonny's murder.

Which right now does not help us at all. Emma shone her torch up toward the top of the pile. This time she saw the gap the cat was using. Or at least she thought she did. "There's no way I'm going to be able to get through there."

"But I could, Emma," said Oliver.

"No," said Emma flatly.

"But, Emma—"

"No."

"But the cat—"

"No, Oliver!" Emma's voice shook. "That pile could come down on your head and I'd never be able to get you out! I'm not going to risk losing you!"

Oliver whined and cringed, and Emma got on her knees and hugged him, hard.

Tangerine, showing her contempt for all things human and canine, bounded up the dirt pile. Oliver barked, whether encouraging or scolding, Emma couldn't tell.

"Come on," she said. "We'll go back to where the boxes are, and wait there." That way if the "bad person" came down the tunnel, they'd be at least a little hidden.

Fortunately, Oliver didn't argue. They made their way back up the tunnel. Emma found herself missing the cat. There was reassurance in all that feline insouciance. If the cat wasn't worried, how bad could things be? She checked her phone. Still no service. It was two thirty. Hours left to go.

Oliver's ears twitched. "Emma—"

But Emma had already caught it—a low scraping noise that dragged at the very edge of her hearing. Reflexively, Emma ducked back against the wall. Then she remembered to switch off the torch.

"Hullo?" a voice called. Distance and dirt walls distorted it past recognition. "Is someone . . . is someone there?"

Oliver whined and backed up against Emma's shins.

"Hullo?" called the voice again. "Please! Is someone there?"

Now Emma did recognize it.

It was Marianne.

49

"WHAT DO WE DO, EMMA?" WHINED OLIVER.

Emma took a deep breath, and made a decision.

"Yes!" She switched the torch back on and stepped around the corner. "Yes, we're here!"

"Here! Here!" Oliver barked for good measure.

"*Emma?*" exclaimed Marianne. "Good lord, Emma, is that you?"

"Yes, it's me!" Emma shouted back. Oliver barked. "I mean us!"

Oliver, abandoning all caution, raced up the tunnel. Emma followed, a little more slowly. When she reached the ramp, she saw Marianne leaning over the open trapdoor, silhouetted by the cellar's fluorescent lights.

Emma scooped Oliver up and slogged up the ramp.

"Emma, what on earth is all this?" Marianne pulled back as Emma boosted Oliver and then herself out of the hole. She blinked in the bright light. She also saw that one of the metal storage shelves was standing crooked. She guessed that was what had been holding the trapdoor down.

"I saw Gwen leaving," Marianne said. "She almost ran into me and I—"

"Gwen?" Emma gasped. "Are you sure it was Gwen?"

Marianne drew back, affronted. "Of course I'm sure."

Emma stared at her, bewildered. She'd been so sure it was Marianne and Ben who were working together. Could she have been that wrong? Could it have been Ben and Reggie all along, and Gwen had gotten desperate trying to protect her father?

I could have been spotted while I was trying to hide, Emma thought. *Gwen could have known we were there the entire time and wedged the trapdoor shut behind us.* She closed her eyes and swallowed. *And here I thought I was being so clever.*

"Emma?" Oliver whimpered and wriggled. "Emma, you're holding me too tight."

Emma put her corgi down and patted his back. She couldn't seem to make her thoughts move properly.

"What in heaven's name is going on here?" demanded Marianne.

Emma took a deep breath. "Erm, I'm sorry, Marianne, but we need to call the police."

"What for? Because you found the old tunnel?" Marianne stopped. "*How* did you find the old tunnel?"

"A corgi can find anything!" Oliver barked proudly.

Marianne looked down at the corgi with an expression that reminded Emma abruptly of Tangerine's contempt.

Which raised another question.

"Marianne? It's two thirty in the morning. What are you doing here?"

"I could ask you the same thing," said Marianne, her voice studiously bland.

"Erm, yes, well," said Emma. "I was trying to find out if someone was still using the tunnel for smuggling."

Marianne stared down at the trapdoor, her eyes wide. "You can't be serious," she breathed.

"I'm sorry," said Emma. "But there's a whole load of whiskey crates down there. Maybe cigarettes as well. They're brand-new," she added.

Marianne's hand strayed to the collar of her blouse. "Ben," she squeaked. "We should call Ben."

"I'm not sure that would be a good idea, Marianne," said Emma as gently as she could. "I'm sorry, but if it was Gwen who trapped me and Oliver down there, she and Ben might be working together."

"I can't believe it," said Marianne. But she also couldn't seem to tear her gaze away from the floor. "How could they even know, what would have—" She stopped again. "Reggie," she groaned.

"Maybe we should go upstairs," suggested Emma.

"Yes, yes," agreed Marianne. "I, we, yes. I'll make tea."

"And I'll call the police."

"No!" Marianne held up both hands. "No, please. Just, just let me get some tea first. Or a drink. Yes. Just, I need to calm down, and then we'll call the police. I can't, I don't—" She pressed both hands to her cheeks. "I don't want them to see me like this."

"Yes, all right," said Emma slowly. "Let's just get upstairs, yeah?"

"Yes." Marianne scurried toward the break room door, and Emma and Oliver followed.

EMMA WAS NOT HAPPY. OLIVER COULD TELL. IT WASN'T anything she said, because she wasn't saying anything. But she was holding herself too stiffly, and she was watching the sad, nervous lady too carefully.

Emma thought something was wrong. But what could be wrong? They were out of the tunnel. They were upstairs in the pub room full of excellent smells.

"I'll just . . . I'll just go plug the kettle in." Marianne darted behind the big wooden bar.

Emma sat down at one of the tables. She put her tote bag down and pulled out her shoulder bag, and her mobile.

"Keep an eye on her, Oliver," she murmured.

"Yes, Emma," Oliver yipped. He trotted over to the bar, but then a gust of wind ruffled the fur on the back of his neck. Reflexively he whirled around.

"How on earth did you . . . !" Sad Lady Marianne pressed her hand against her chest. "Dratted cat."

She was right. It was a cat. *The* cat, specifically. Somebody had left the doors to the beer garden open. Tangerine slid across the threshold and jumped up on a chair and then up onto the table.

"You shouldn't be here!" Oliver barked at the cat.

"Neither should you." The cat yawned. "But I guess since you were too afraid to follow me into the other cellar . . ."

"A corgi is never afraid!" Oliver barked.

"Shut up, shut up, you stupid dog," muttered Marianne.

Oliver plumped down on his haunches. "That's rude!" he grumbled.

"I have to agree with you." The cat rubbed a paw over her ears. "Rude, and she likes sugar."

"Sugar?" Oliver grumbled. "What sugar?"

"The sugar she just dumped into the pot-thing." Tangerine craned her neck and swished her tail. "Lots of it. I hope your human likes sugar."

"No, that's not good," grumbled Oliver. "Emma likes sugar, but not in her tea."

"Oh, well." The cat rubbed her whiskers. "She's not going to like that tea, then."

Oliver trotted over to the bar. Marianne was dropping some tea bags into the pot and lifting up the electric teakettle to pour the water in.

That was strange. Oliver scratched his ear. He had watched lots of humans make tea and drink tea. They never put the sugar in the pot. He wondered if the cat had made a mistake. Cats made mistakes.

But maybe he should tell Emma anyway.

EMMA WAS JUST TUCKING HER MOBILE BACK INTO HER BAG when Oliver came scampering across the room. "Emma! Don't drink the tea, Emma!"

"What!" she exclaimed reflexively. "Why?"

"I'm sorry?" called Marianne. "Did you say something?"

"I did!" barked Oliver

Emma stared at him, and then at her. An entire peal of warning bells rang in the back of her mind.

"No. Sorry." She made herself smile at Marianne. She pulled the packet of treats out of her bag and bent down to feed the last one to Oliver.

"There, what is it, good boy?" she murmured.

"She made the tea wrong, Emma," he grumbled. "She put the sugar in first."

Emma stared at him. "How . . . ?"

"The cat said," Oliver told her. "Cats make things up, but not like this. You don't like sugar in your tea, Emma," he added, as if she might have forgotten.

Emma straightened up slowly. She stared across to Marianne, who was moving around behind the bar, getting down mugs and setting them on a tray, along with a teapot. And a sugar bowl.

Memories assembled themselves inside her. The warning bells pealed again, and Emma's throat closed. She swallowed, and swallowed again.

"Oliver," she breathed. "I can't believe I'm about to say this, but I need your help, and the cat's."

50

OLIVER TROTTED BACK OVER TO TANGERINE, WHO WAS still sitting on the table washing herself. She stopped licking her paw and looked down at him.

"Well?" Her tail switched.

"Sorry about that," Emma was saying to Marianne. "Corgis get really restless."

"I've heard that. They're herding dogs, aren't they?" Marianne carried the tray over to Emma's table and sat down with her.

"Cattle. Yes."

Oliver flopped down on his side and tried to think. He did not understand cats. He had a feeling he never would. But Emma had given him a job, and it was important. He needed an idea.

What would Emma do? He scratched his nose and shook his ears and wagged his bum. And he knew.

He jumped up.

"There," said Marianne. "I hope it's not too strong. I got in the habit of making it the way Reggie likes it."

"Are you bored?" Oliver asked the cat.

Tangerine rubbed her ears with her paw. "What do you think?"

"I'm sure it's fine," Emma said. "I don't mean to be a pest, but is there any milk?"

"I can help," Oliver said.

"No, I'm sorry," Marianne was saying. "Maybe in the kitchen . . . ?"

"How can you help?" Tangerine yawned.

"Want to play tag?" Oliver wagged hopefully.

"Not really, no."

"Oh," said Emma. "Well, don't bother. I'll just take sugar."

"You know I can catch you," Oliver told Tangerine.

The cat swished her tail impatiently. "You can't catch me."

"Yes I can," Oliver yipped.

"Should we separate them?" asked Marianne anxiously.

"Oh, no worries there," said Emma. "They're old friends, really."

"You can't catch me," Tangerine said lazily.

Oliver lunged.

EMMA THOUGHT HER FACE WOULD CRACK FROM THE STRAIN of trying to keep her smile steady. She reached for the sugar bowl and put a heaping spoonful into her brimming cup. And stirred. And stirred. And tapped the spoon on the rim of the mug. And set her spoon down.

Marianne picked up her mug. Emma picked up hers.

The cat's indignant screech knifed through the air. Emma jerked around in time to see the Cream Tangerine streak across the floor with Oliver zooming after her. The cat tried to veer, but Oliver dove down low, like he meant to slide straight between her legs. Outraged, the cat yowled again and leapt up onto the table, right in the middle of the tea things.

Mugs, pot and sugar bowl flew every which way. Tea poured out across the table and the floor.

"You stupid, stupid cat!" Marianne screamed. Then she looked up at Emma, her face flushed. "Oh, I'm so sorry.

I . . . I'll just clean up and . . ." She grabbed up the overturned pot.

"It's okay, I've got this." Emma snatched up a napkin and dropped it into the spilled tea.

"Oh, no, I'll get it." Marianne reached for the napkin, but Emma caught her wrist. They stared at each other.

"Emma!" shouted a new voice.

It was Genny, and Angelique, with Brian right behind.

"We're okay!" Emma called to her friends, but she kept her attention on Marianne. "It really was you," she said. "You killed Reggie."

Emma let her go, slowly. Marianne collapsed backwards into her chair, just as slowly.

"It was only fair," Marianne whispered. "You see, Reggie killed Sonny."

51

"REGGIE KILLED SONNY?" EXCLAIMED GENNY. "I THOUGHT she did." She gestured toward Marianne.

Emma twisted around and stared at her friends. "What are you even doing here? I told you to call 999!"

"We did," said Angelique.

"I hope you didn't think we'd just sit around afterwards," said Brian.

"No, I guess not." Emma took his hand and squeezed. Marianne turned her face away.

"Emma?" Oliver bonked her in the ankle. "Emma, you shouldn't drink that tea. That tea smells really bad, Emma."

Yes. I'm sure it does.

She turned to Marianne. "The police didn't find all the roofies when they searched the place, did they?" she said. "You held some back, just in case you needed them later."

Marianne's sigh was short and sharp. "Well, if you hadn't decided to make a full-time career out of being a nosey parker, it wouldn't have been necessary, would it? I didn't mean to at first, but I wasn't sure I could make that story about Gwen stick, you see. So I had to do something."

"So it was you?" said Angelique to Marianne. "You killed Sonny and Reggie?"

"I did not kill Sonny!" The force of Marianne's shout lifted her right out of her chair. "How could I? I loved him!"

"Oh," breathed Genny.

Brian shifted his stance just a little, just so he was slightly in front of Emma. At her side, Oliver was on all fours, his ears up and alert.

If Marianne noticed any of this, Emma couldn't tell. She just collapsed back onto her chair.

"I loved him," she repeated. "We were going to run away together."

"You were Sonny's mystery girl?" said Emma. "Not Liza?"

"Her?" Marianne laughed bitterly. "She was just a chance for him to feel all chivalrous. He liked having a role. It didn't matter what he got to do, Robin Hood or Lancelot, just as long as he got to play it to the hilt." She set one of the toppled mugs upright, then the other.

"I was engaged to Reggie at the time," she went on. "It was really my parents' idea. They were charmed by him. Thought he'd be an asset to the businesses." She righted the sugar bowl, and put the lid back on. "I was willing to go along with it, but then I started spending more time with Sonny—" She pressed her hand against her brow. "Do you know what the irony of that is? That part was Reggie's idea."

"You spending time with Sonny?" said Emma.

Marianne nodded. She picked up the spoon and laid it parallel to the sugar bowl. "He told me he thought Sonny was up to something, because of Walter, you see. The Greenlaws were already fighting with my parents, and Reggie said he was sure they were all planning to double-cross us somehow."

"But really, Reggie was planning to double-cross Sonny," said Emma.

Emma pulled the empty puppy snacks packet out of her bag. She took up the tea-soaked napkin and tucked it inside. Constance might need it for analysis later. She hoped the spare Bacony-Bite crumbs wouldn't get in the way of that.

Marianne watched her every move, but did not try to stop her.

"Reggie found out about me and Sonny, and he knew if he lost me, he lost the pub and the trucking business, and my parents, and all his little dreams of building up some kind of empire." She gestured vaguely around the pub. "So he turned on the charm. He swore to Sonny he wasn't angry, and that he'd help him and wished us both very happy and . . ." She swallowed. "And then came the night we were actually supposed to leave, and there I was, waiting with my bag all packed, only Sonny never showed up." Her voice dropped to a harsh whisper.

"The next day I went round to find Reggie. He swore he hadn't seen Sonny, that he must have run out on me, and, and Reggie swore he'd kill him when he caught him and—" Marianne's voice faltered. "And I believed him. I *believed* him." She spat the words out. "I let him have me on the rebound. I kept up the trade on the side. I—" She looked up abruptly. "How did you know it was me? Everybody else thought it was Reggie who ran the show."

"Not everybody," said Emma. "Billy Marsh said you were always the brains of the outfit."

"Did he?" Marianne arched one eyebrow. "I must remember to thank him."

"But what actually *happened?*" asked Genny. "To Sonny, I mean?"

Emma looked at Marianne. Marianne waved her hand again. "Oh, do go on. I'm sure you know at least as much as I do."

Emma hesitated, but then she said, "Reggie and Sonny decided to rob the smuggling ring. They called Scotland Yard and tipped them off to where the operations were and started cooperating with the revenuers. That way, they knew they'd be warned when the raid was going to happen. When word came down, Sonny stole the money and counterfeit stickers. For what it's worth," she said to Marianne, "we found an engagement ring inside the Vincent's sidecar. I think he really was planning to come get you when Reggie caught up with him." *And smashed in his skull.* "He must have hidden the body and the Vincent until after the raid, and then, when he knew the tunnel would be empty, he moved them down there."

"Yes," said Marianne listlessly. "I asked him about it, when Sonny was found. He asked me what did I expect? That he was going to let some wanker cheat him out of what he'd been working for? Then he told me he'd put up with my bossing around long enough and he was clearing out." She laughed softly. "He said he was tired of me holding him back. Me!" She laughed. "As if I wasn't the one who'd been keeping us afloat for all those years, with him throwing away every penny I brought in. But the really funny part is, he said it was Ben who'd talked him into leaving."

"Ben!" exclaimed Angelique.

"I know, I couldn't believe it either," said Marianne. "Ben was playing on his ego, feeding him the money and a line about what a genius he was and how he should be free to really stretch his wings." Marianne smiled distantly. "Ben really does love me, you know. He thought if he just hung on long enough, I'd just let Reggie go, and take up with him instead."

"Would you?" asked Brian.

"Maybe. Ben was really much easier to manage. But they found Sonny first." Marianne folded her hands neatly in her lap. "You see, that was when I knew what must have happened. I suppose I should have suspected, but honestly, I never thought Reggie had the nerve to do anything so . . . dangerous."

"And when you realized Reggie had killed Sonny, you killed him," said Emma.

Marianne nodded. "He'd done half the job for me. He was so very drunk. We argued, and, well, he always did talk too much when he drank. And I shoved him. And he teetered and fell into the fishpond, and while he was trying to get up, I grabbed one of those horrible, tacky tiki torches and shoved him back down." She frowned. "It didn't take long at all. Then I just went home and waited for opening time."

They all stood silent for a long moment. Brian put his hand on Emma's shoulder, and Oliver pressed close. Emma found herself deeply grateful for them both.

For them all, she corrected herself, looking at Genny and Angelique.

"But why kill him?" asked Genny. "You could have just called the police."

"Called the police?" Marianne's brows arched. "Me? While sitting on a tunnel full of illegal whiskey and cigarettes and a hard drive full of phony invoices?"

"Well, well," said a woman's brisk voice.

They all turned. Constance Brent and PC Raj stepped into the great room. Constance's sharp gaze swept across the gathering. "What's all this, then?"

52

AS IT TURNED OUT, THERE WASN'T MUCH TO DO AFTER THAT. Constance and Raj took Marianne back to their headquarters, where she made a full confession, including how she'd attempted to frame Gwen.

"It's important to have a backup plan," she said.

Pippa moved out of her grandfather's house and in with Charles and David. She and Rory Kemp were seen together a lot, in the cafés and on the cliffs. Eventually, there were rumors of shouting matches between Pippa and Billy, and Pippa and Colin, and Pippa and Rory.

But at Marianne's trial, Pippa pushed her grandfather's wheelchair into the courtroom so Billy could take the stand as a witness for the Crown, with Colin Roskilly backing up every word he said.

After that, Pippa moved back in with her granddad, and rumors of shouting matches stopped. As she predicted, she lost her job, but she started working with Martha Greenlaw on her marketing plan for the family's ale and cider. Soon rumors started that they might be starting their own publicity firm.

Also, Pippa and Rory were still seen walking together a

lot. Despite their recent differences with Pippa and her family, Charles and David were rumored to be quietly pleased.

Sam and Liza had a long talk with their children and decided the tunnel should be sealed back up and the money for the renovations put into expanding the brewery instead.

Which left only one more thing to be done.

IT WAS A FROSTY SATURDAY IN NOVEMBER. EMMA, BRIAN, Oliver and Lucy all stood outside the showroom of Prowse's Vintage Cars along with Charles and David. Together, they watched the thoroughly practical sub-compact Toyota ease up the dirt drive and park. The woman who climbed out was plump and aging with mild blue eyes and very pink skin. Her silver hair had been carefully teased and she smiled nervously at all of them.

David bustled forward immediately.

"Mrs. Holland? David Kemp. What a pleasure to finally meet you." David shook her hand gently and gave her his finest smile. Emma could see her unease melt away.

"Mr. Kemp—" Mrs. Holland began.

"Oh, dear, no, no, no. David." He laid his hand on his breast.

"Sharon," Mrs. Holland told him.

David drew her over to where Charles stood. "My husband, Charles."

"How do you do?" Charles shook her hand.

"I'm well, thank you."

"And our friends, Emma Reed and Brian Prowse." David turned her to them. "Brian has been taking care of your father's motorcycle while we found you."

"Oh, hello," Sharon said, a little distractedly. But that was understandable, because both Oliver and Lucy had lost patience and surged over to snuffle and bark. Fortunately, Mrs. Holland just laughed at this attention. "Oh what good dogs!" She grinned as she rubbed ears and patted backs. "I really wasn't expecting such a lovely welcoming committee!" She beamed. "And you . . . you really have Dad's Vincent here?"

"If you'll just step out this way?" David gestured toward the showroom door, which Brian dragged open with extra flourish.

Mrs. Holland, followed by the rest of their crowd, stepped inside. Charles threw the switch on the lights, while David moved to stand beside the object hidden underneath blue tarpaulin.

"Are we ready?" asked David. Ever the showman, he grabbed the tarp with both hands and hauled. "Voilà!"

There stood the Vincent, cleaned and polished from handlebar to tailpipe, gleaming in the autumn sunlight.

"Oh . . . my." Sharon touched the handlebar lightly. "It really is a beautiful thing, isn't it?"

"I've always thought so." Charles looked over to David. "It's time it went home."

"My old da loved it. He never did stop talking about it. Here." Sharon reached into her bag and brought out a little photo album of a kind Emma hadn't seen in years. She opened it carefully. "That's him," she said as she handed the album to David. "And the Vincent."

Of course they all crowded round to see. Sharon's father was a lean, long-necked man. In the black-and-white photo, he wore a pair of pleated pants and a leather jacket, and carried a helmet tucked under one arm. Next to him stood the Vincent. A pretty, dark-haired woman sat in the sidecar, smiling and waving at the camera.

"That's Mum," said Sharon. "They were just off on their honeymoon trip. Going up to Scotland." She smiled fondly at the photo. "Mum always told me Dad swept her away on this motorcycle. We all thought it was so romantic." She tucked the album back into her bag. "But how did you ever find it?"

"Ah. Yes." David glanced at Charles, who rolled his eyes as if to say, *This is your show.* "I'm afraid that's a rather long story. Perhaps you'd care to come into the office? Emma's brought us some of her marvelous fruitcake."

"Oh, that sounds wonderful!" said Sharon. "I haven't had a proper fruitcake in years."

"Hurray!" barked Oliver. "Teatime!"

ACKNOWLEDGMENTS

To everybody who helped keep me sane and pointed in the right direction while finishing this book, especially my husband, Tim; my son, Alex; and all the members of the Untitled Writer's Group. Once again, guys, I couldn't have done it without you. I'd also like to thank my very patient editor, Jess, and my fabulous agent, Lucienne.

Finally, I'd like to thank Craig Beresford, who introduced me to Richard Thompson and the "1952 Vincent Black Lightning."

Said James, "In my opinion, there's nothing in this world

Beats a '52 Vincent and a Redheaded girl."